SHERLOCK HOLMES

in Little London

1896 The Missing Year

Books by John Wesley Anderson

A to Z Colorado's Nearly Forgotten History, 1776-1876

Sherlock Holmes in Little London, 1896 The Missing Year

ZacBox and the Pearls of Pleiades

R.S. Kelly, A Man of the Territory

Native American Prayer Trees of Colorado

Rankin Scott Kelly, First Sheriff, El Paso County, Colorado Territory

Ute Indian Prayer Trees of the Pikes Peak Region

SHERLOCK HOLMES

in Little London

1896 The Missing Year

By

John Wesley Anderson

CIRCLE STAR PUBLISHING
COLORADO SPRINGS, COLORADO

Published in the United States of America

CIRCLE STAR PUBLISHING
P.O. Box 60144
Colorado Springs, Colorado 80960

Anderson, John Wesley
Sherlock Holmes in Little London, The Missing Year / John Wesley Anderson
First Edition: October 2020

Library of Congress Control Number: 2020948402

ISBN 978-1-943829-17-0

Publisher's Cataloging-in-Publication Data

Names: Anderson, John Wesley, 1954-, author.

Title: Sherlock Holmes in Little London: 1896, the missing year / John Wesley Anderson.

Description: Colorado Springs, CO: Circle Star Publishing, an imprint of Rhyolite Press LLC, 2020.

Identifiers: LCCN: 2020948402 | ISBN: 9781943829170

Subjects: LCSH Holmes, Sherlock--Fiction. | Doyle, Arthur Conan, 1859-1930--Characters--Sherlock Holmes. | Private investigators--United States--Fiction. | United States--Description and travel--Fiction. | Detective and mystery stories. | Historical fiction. | BISAC FICTION / Mystery & Detective / International Crime & Mystery

Classification: LCC PS3601.N5442 S54 2020 | DDC 813.6--dc23

PRINTED IN THE UNITED STATES OF AMERICA

Circle Star Publishing is an imprint of Rhyolite Press LLC

Cover/Book design/layout by Donald R. Kallaus

To the greatest detective who never lived, Sherlock Holmes, and his intrepid companion, Doctor John H. Watson and to the author who brought them to life and gave them to the world—Sir Arthur Conan Doyle.

Chapter 1

January 20, 1896 2:30pm

221 B Baker Street, London, England

UPON RETURNING TO MY WARM FLAT at 221 B Baker Street, which I lease in London with my unique friend Sherlock Holmes, I was greeted on the stairwell landing by our landlady, Mrs. Hudson, carrying a silver serving tray and wearing a frown upon her face.

"See what it is he has done now, Dr. Watson," Mrs. Hudson said in frustration.

"What is it this time madam?"

"Your flat-mate up there has ruined my best tea service."

"Whatever did he do?" asked I, peering over the tea service to take a closer look.

"Well, just look at these two china tea cups here, they're smeared with black charcoal dust and my beautiful little saucer here has a purple stain all over it."

"I believe the purple might be iodine, hopefully these will wash off alright. If not do let me know and I'll speak to him about paying to replace them, Mrs. Hudson."

"Oh, it's not about money, your Sherlock Holmes has paid me more than enough money to pay for this entire house twice over; it's about tidiness and well, common courtesy, traits your inquisitive friend seems to care nothing about," Mrs. Hudson concluded as she headed down the remaining stairs to the first floor.

"I will speak with him Mrs. Hudson," I replied as I removed my topcoat and gloves.

"Won't do any good," she replied as she stopped at the bottom of the stairs and turned to look back up at me, "the only person who seems to have any influences whatsoever over Mr. Sherlock Holmes is his brother Mycroft."

"Sherlock Holmes does seem to regard his older brother as his intellectual equal, if not his better, on rare occasions," I concluded as I continued on up the stairs.

"Will you be staying in for supper this evening, Dr. Watson?" Mrs. Hudson asked as she glanced back up to the top of the stairs toward where I was standing.

"I don't have any plans to be out and would very much appreciate an opportunity to dine in with Sherlock Holmes this evening, thank you," replied I.

"Well, I'm not so certain Mr. Holmes appreciates it, he has simply come to expect that I should serve him dinner regularly, along with any number of his cohorts who might happen by unannounced. Yesterday it was Scotland Yard's Inspector Tobias Gregson, now there's a gentleman for you; he stopped by for a long discussion with Mr. Holmes. The day before it was Billy, Mr. Holmes' young page from those Baker Street Irregulars, along with two of his dingy little friends. Between the three of 'em those boys ate five beef sandwiches and devoured an entire cherry pie which I had just pulled from me oven. Acted as if they hadn't eaten in days; which I suspect they hadn't, which is the only reason your friend, Mr. Holmes, is in the least bit tolerable; otherwise I have no doubt he would qualify as the worst tenant in all of London."

I listened as Mrs. Hudson's voice trailed off from the bottom of the stairs and then I slowly opened the door leading into our airy sitting room to find Sherlock Holmes on his knees bent over our umbrella stand constructed out of the lower leg of an African elephant. Sherlock Holmes was intently studying the handle of my umbrella with a round magnifying glass and appeared not to even notice I had entered the room. I walked up behind him and bent forward directly behind him as he was staring at a bluish-purple stain on the ornate handle of my best umbrella when he finally looked up and saw me.

"Ha! There you are my good man!" he said as he jumped up, grasped me by the arm and dragged me over to our dining table. "Sit here," he commanded, as he spread a thin layer of black India ink across a small rectangular shaped glass plate. For a man who doesn't exercise regularly, I am continually amazed at his physical strength and doubt I could have resisted his grip even if I were a mind to; truth be told, I am always intrigued by the depth of his rather narrow interests.

"Now, simply relax your hand," he instructed as he shook out my hand aggressively from the wrist, as if to loosen it. Then he grasped each of my fingers, one by one and began rolling them across a thick ink film until the surface of each of my fingertips and thumb were covered with black ink. As I watched I noticed how the tips of each of his fingers on both of his hands were also stained with black ink. Then, looking up at his face I was somewhat amused to see two black ink smears on his chin and a bluish-purple stain around his nose and mouth.

"How are your experiments with the iodine fuming progressing?" I asked, trying to suppress a laugh at his being completely oblivious to the ink stains upon his face.

"I am somewhat pleased with my progress thus far; however, I must make note to paying closer attention when using the iodine fuming apparatus. This morning I hastily constructed the apparatus using a stem from one of my old clay pipes."

"Why, whatever happened?" I asked, studying the bluish-purple stain encircling his nose and mouth.

"Well, as I was intently consumed counting the ridges of my own inked fingerprints, I absentmindedly picked up the iodine fuming device and in feeling the familiarity of the clay stem in my hand, inadvertently placed it in my mouth and inhaled deeply. As you may well imagine, my mistake became readily apparent; it felt as if a bolt of white lightning had instantly flashed through my brain followed by a never-ending series of firework explosions going off inside my head!"

"Whatever did you do?" asked I.

"Well man, I howled and danced around the room, then dropped to the floor and rolled into a ball over there in the corner by the fireplace, clasping my head in my hands."

"Whatever happened next?"

"Mrs. Hudson, upon hearing all the commotion above her head, ran up the stairs and burst into our sitting room to see whatever was the matter. I felt as if an intense rush of cocaine had come and gone in an instant. I opened my eyes to find Mrs. Hudson staring at me while I was sitting on the floor by our umbrella stand. Once I recovered she began looking about the room muttering something about her best tea service being ruined. That's when I'd spotted the handle of your umbrella standing upright here in the umbrella stand.

"I see," said I, thankful I hadn't arrived two minutes earlier to have been a witness to such an unsettling spectacle.

"Here," said Sherlock, as he slid a clean sheet of foolscap paper in front of me on the table and began to carefully roll my inked fingertips across the thick tan colored paper. When he finished he whipped out his round magnifying glass from his inside suit coat pocket and began a most concentrated study of my inked fingerprints which had been deposited upon the paper.

"Will this wash off?" I asked, as I tried to clean the black ink stain from my fingertips with my white handkerchief. He pretended not to hear the question; I pretended not to already know the answer. "In due time, perhaps," was the best possible outcome I could imagine.

"There," he said contently, laying his thick magnifying glass on our sturdy dining table and leaning back in his chair, announced resolutely, "That is your umbrella."

"Yes, I know that," I said, adding wistfully, "I could have told you that had you asked."

"That is not the point," he said, placing the stem of his clay pipe in his mouth and then striking a match, which he held steadily above the tobacco bowl and looked down cross-eyed to ensure he hadn't accidently placed the stem of his fingerprint fuming device between his lips again. "You may have been mistaken, or intentionally trying to deceive me about that being your umbrella, but I can prove the fingerprints upon its handle are a perfect match to your fingerprints." I watched as he inhaled deeply from the stem of his clay pipe and then blew out the match with a puff of grayish blue smoke.

"I can see where that ability could prove rather useful to someone in your line of work."

"Indeed," he said, "criminal cases continually hang in the balance of trying to prove the identity of a known criminal or establishing the innocence of a man falsely accused. While fingerprints, palmprints and even footprints from a crime scene have been in use as evidence since the Qin Dynasty, what has been lacking is a systematic method of cataloguing fingerprints for identification purposes."

"I see," said I as I gave up on my failed attempt to clean the black ink off my fingertips and tucked my now ink stained handkerchief back into my suit coat pocket.

"Furthermore, I maintain that we must exploit every resource known to modern chemistry to advance our methods of developing latent finger or palm prints on various surfaces for collection and identification purposes."

"Yes, I can well imagine having a wide array of chemical powders might prove very beneficial," I said as I withdrew my handkerchief once again and turned my attention to attempting to remove the blueish purple ink stain from the handle of my nearly new umbrella.

Sherlock Holmes tapped the stem of his pipe on a letter lying face up on the table before him, "I have been in correspondence with a young college student in France; one Edmond Locard, who is presently engaged in writing his doctoral thesis on what he refers to as his Exchange Principle. Young Locard confirms what I have said all along, that when a suspect commits a crime, he always takes something from the crime scene and leaves something behind, such as his latent fingerprints which can be proven to match the unique fingerprints on his hands. When I finish documenting my findings this afternoon I intend to mail my full report to young Edmond Locard, along with your inked fingerprints. He, in turn, will supplement my report and forward both to Sir Edward Henry, the appointed Inspector General of the Bengal Police."

"Why involve Sir Henry?" I inquired.

"Sir Henry has been requiring the police in Bengal to fingerprint criminals as a means of identification since his appointment to Inspector General of Police in 1891. Sir Henry has agreed to conduct a doctorial evaluation of young Locard's thesis. Sir Henry, along with the assistance of two of his able bodied sub-inspectors, has also been working diligently with Francis

Galton and Alphonse Bertillon to develop a fingerprint classification system, but again, what we must not lose sight of is the refinement of better fingerprint collection methods, chemicals and techniques."

"Indeed," said I in agreement.

"People can say what they will about the French or the Canadians, but when it comes to the forensic sciences I appreciate that they seem to have an infinite capacity for taking pains. It's a very bad definition, but it does apply to detective work. I believe a hundred years from now the names Locard, Henry, Galton and Bertillon will stand as giants in our rapidly evolving field of forensic science."

"Do you not want the name Sherlock Holmes to be remembered among them?" I asked of my friend.

"Heavens no," he replied with a laugh, "In the year 1996 no one on earth will possibly know the name Sherlock Holmes. That is unimportant, what is important is to know if you were successful on your errand this morning to secure the back issue of the Strand Magazine I requested?"

"Indeed I was," I replied handing him a back copy of the Strand magazine dated December 2, 1895.

"Excellent, my dear Watson," he said as he turned quickly to the top of page three, above the fold. "Ah, here it is, an amusing little article on alchemy."

"Alchemy?" I asked, somewhat incredulous in having spent the better part of my morning at the Strand searching through the archives for an out-of-date article only to amuse my peculiar friend. "Are you referring to the speculative chemical process of turning baser metals into gold practiced during the Renaissance Period of the Middle Ages?"

"Precisely," Sherlock replied and without looking up from the magazine article, handed me a telegram. "This telegram arrived by special courier at 10:15 this morning, shortly after you had departed on your errand. What do you make of it?"

I read the telegram aloud, "To Mr. Sherlock Holmes, 221 B Baker Street, London (Stop). The Emperor of India advises he will no longer be in need of your services (Stop). You may stop by the southside of the River Thames at 10:30am tomorrow morning to collect your final payment and discharge instructions (Stop). 2Dec1896 Burleigh P3 Ag CYM (Stop). Why, this is nonsensical," I protested, "Everyone knows there has not been an Emperor of India for centuries and whatever for are you being sacked and who pray tell is CYM?"

"It's all very straightforward really," Sherlock Holmes replied, as he relit his pipe, walked over and plopped down in his overstuffed easy chair, closed his eyes, and then explained, "CYM is my brother, Mycroft. This is a little game we devised as boys when we were growing up so only we would know what the other was saying. The first three letters of his name are reversed, clearly indicating that the intent of the letter should also be reversed. Now, with that nuance in mind, please read the telegram again.

"To Mr. Sherlock Holmes, 221 B Baker Street, London (Stop)," I read aloud then made the reversal to the rest of the message in my head and read the next sentence aloud, "The Empress, rather than Emperor, of India advises she, rather than he, is in need of your services, my word man! Could this telegram possibly suggest Her Majesty Queen Victoria herself is in need of your investigative services?" I asked in astonishment.

"It would appear so," my friend replied seemingly unphased at the prospect of having received a telegram a few hours previous requesting a meeting with the Queen of England.

"Please do go on," Sherlock Holmes requested, his eyes remaining closed as he blew smoke slowly from the corner of his mouth.

I reread the words on the telegram, "You may stop by along the southside of the River Thames at 10:30am tomorrow morning to collect your final payment and discharge instructions (Stop)," I again reversed the cryptic message and continued to read aloud, "You may stop by the southside of the River Thames, I assume that means the north side?"

"You assume incorrectly, southside is referring to Southwalk, of the Tower Bridge which as you know opened for public transit two years ago. While the bridge deck is freely accessible by pedestrians or carriages, the bridge's twin towers, engine rooms and high-level walkways are accessible afterhours by admission only; therefore, South Tower is a perfectly controlled setting for a clandestine meeting such as ours. Please continue."

"Then I suppose 10:30am must be intended to mean 10:30pm, which is thirty minutes after the South Tower is closed, suggesting the person requesting this meeting is a person of some high stature in having access to this grand landmark after having been closed to daily traffic."

"A reasonably good deduction," Sherlock Holmes replied, handing out one of his rare compliments on my continual attempts to learn something of his methods.

"The date 2Dec1895 and the rest of the encoded message Burleigh P3 Ag CYM (Stop)?" I asked completely perplexed as to the meaning.

"The date is correct, Burleigh is obviously the street where the Strand Magazine is located, P3 clearly is in reference to the article here on page three and Ag is the symbol for silver on the list of chemical elements, the reverse of which is, as you know, Au for gold," Sherlock Holmes concluded as if explaining something of a trivial nature to a young child.

"Why not simply say silver, meaning gold?" I asked?

"Elemental my Dear Watson; Mycroft used the symbol for

silver Ag, which translates to the symbol for gold Au, to intentionally draw my attention to Antoine Lavoisier, who created the initial list of 33 chemical elements in the year 1789. Lavoisier, as you may not know, was executed by guillotine."

"How ghastly," I commented trying to erase from my mind what a horrific scene that must have entailed.

"No doubt there is something dark and sinister about all of this," Sherlock Holmes concluded.

"Evidently," I whispered in agreement.

"Which is why I ask that you accompany me tomorrow night."

"Me?" I asked in astonishment, "The telegram says nothing about inviting me to this secretive rendezvous to meet with Her Majesty on the Tower Bridge tomorrow night?"

"Nonsense, I would be lost without my Boswell," Sherlock Holmes uttered as he stood from his chair, walked to the fireplace, and retrieved his violin from the mantel, signaling the end to our conversation. "Mycroft well knows that I am more likely to be successful in our little adventure with you at my side; besides, the reference to payment and receiving my instructions suggests the benefit of having someone, such as yourself, on hand to chronical our progress and keep track of any financial transactions as they may occur. I have no doubt you will once again be an invaluable asset on this case which will no doubt prove to be of high importance."

"Very well," said I, adding, "it certainly sounds as if this inquiry may prove worthy of careful documentation. I shall begin immediately to record every detail in my personal journal." I withdrew the small black leather-bound pocket journal from my inside coat pocket. In having chronicled dozens of Sherlock Holmes previous cases, I had found it to be most beneficial for me to carry a new journal at the beginning of each calendar year. As the New Year 1896 was less than three weeks old, my journal had only two pages of personal notes and an old grocery list for Mrs. Hudson, which I tore out and discarded. I began documenting this case at the top of a fresh page, which I numbered Page 1, and dated this first journal entry as January 20, 1896; a year I suspected would prove most interesting before it concluded.

"One more small request Dr. Watson," Sherlock Holmes said as he drew the violin bow gently across the strings of his Stradivarius, playing the opening notes of Mendelssohn's *Lieder*, which he knew to be among my favourites.

"Yes, of course, what is it?" I asked as he glanced over the top of his violin at me.

"Would you be so kind as to bring your service revolver with you tomorrow night?"

Chapter 2

January 21st, 1896 10:15pm

Tower Bridge, London, England

A COLD MIST HUNG CLOSELY OVER THE RIVER Thames, like a wet blanket, while the dark gray clouds over London's cityscape blotted out the light of a three-quarter moon. I watched out the window of our hansom cab and reminisced how it had been but two short years since Sherlock Holmes and I attended the grand opening of the Tower Bridge which was suspended gracefully over the River Thames. It is not an exaggeration that I may have set my eyes upon this engineering marvel a hundred times over; yet its majestic silhouette never fails to capture and hold my admiration for the civil engineers, architects and the five major contractors who built this magnificent structure.

Erected downstream of the London Bridge, the design of the Tower Bridge was selected from more than 50 designs which had initially been submitted. Constructed in the traditional Gothic style, the bridge spans over 800 feet in length, with a clearance above the high watermark of 139 feet to accommodate the spring high tide. When the two drawbridges are fully opened they allowed for the passing of the tallest of masted sailing vessels. The Tower Bridge has since become recognized the world over as an iconic symbol of London.

As we grew nearer our destination, my excitement continued to rise to the point I could not contain it any longer and turned to Sherlock Holmes sitting beside me in the cab, who hadn't uttered a single word since we had departed from our flat on Baker Street. I asked, "What do you make of this case?"

"I make nothing of this case," Sherlock Holmes replied as he continued to observe every building and person we passed on the darkened street.

"But don't you have any provisional theories?"

"None whatsoever," he replied and then added, "As I have stated previously, I find it is a capital mistake to theorize before one has data. Insensibly one begins to twist the facts to suit the theories, instead of theories to suit the facts."

My friend grew quiet again as I looked out my window and tried to still my excitement. The rhythmic clomp clomp of the horse's shod hooves striking against the cobblestones soon slowed from a trot to a walk, announcing our pending arrival. Sherlock Holmes rapped his sturdy walking stick on the inside roof of the carriage to gain the attention of our driver.

"We shall walk from here," Sherlock Holmes announced to the driver as he pushed the carriage door open into the dark night.

As I emerged from the hansom I noticed we were still a hundred yards or more from the gas lights burning on each side of the South Tower entrance. From having accompanied my inquisitive friend on countless other adventures I had learned it was his habit to approach his destination on foot affording him an opportunity to take in his surroundings. As we strolled toward the entrance I noticed the darkened street was nearly deserted, save for a nondescript older two-horse carriage parked nearby. We passed two dockworkers sharing a pint as they watched a small boat, pulling a cargo laden barge, struggling to make headway upstream.

"Not much to see here," I commented innocently, adding almost as an afterthought, "one might expect a little more security given the position of the person we are about to meet."

"On the contrary my good Doctor," Sherlock Holmes replied. He paused in front of the driver attending to the two horses harnessed to the well-used black carriage parked before the entrance of the South Tower. "Excuse me my good man; do you happen to have the time?"

"Sir," the driver replied, coming naturally to attention as he withdrew his pocket watch from his vest pocket. He held his timepiece up to the dim light cast by the carriage lantern and said, "I read the time to be 10:19."

"Thank you," Sherlock Holmes replied as he tipped his deerstalker hat respectfully, adding, "We have an important meeting and wouldn't want to be tardy."

"No sir, that wouldn't do," the driver said as he slipped his pocket watch back in his vest pocket, slid the small tin door on the carriage lantern shut and turned his attention back to adjusting the well-worn carriage harnesses.

Once we had walked beyond hearing range of the carriage Sherlock Holmes said to me in a low voice, barely above a whisper, "This is precisely the heightened level of security I would have expected, given the nature of our meeting. Surely you noticed the thin trail of gray smoke being emitted from the smokestack on the boat pulling the barge, suggesting the engine was not working at anywhere near full power and I suspect the cargo aboard that barge is not one anyone would care to try to take by force. The two dock workers sharing the pint were undeniably military men and heavily armed, as indicated by their military postures and protruding bulges beneath their matching gray overcoats. I surmise there were two more heavily armed men inside the carriage, given the flattened condition of the springs beneath the carriage, suggesting the hansom was not entirely empty. Then of course there was the military bearing of the driver, his answering my question as to the time in precise terms; 10:19, and the crest on the silver ring on his right ring finger confirmed he is with the 1st Battalion of the Coldstream Guards at Windsor Castle; enlisted, no doubt, officers prefer gold rings, which as you know are more costly. When the driver closed the small door to the carriage lantern, he signaled those watching across the street that we were who they were expecting and are to be allowed inside unmolested."

"I hadn't noticed any of those things," I admitted, once again astonished at how much my companion observes which goes unnoticed by the rest of human kind.

As Sherlock Holmes opened and held the heavy metal door leading inside the Tower, he nodded his head directing me toward the stairwell, "I apologize in advance for us having to take the stairs, it is the only way for us to reach the upper level; however, I have allowed five minutes for us to take frequent breaks along the way."

I very much appreciated how my friend, without drawing attention to my war wound, was aware of my weakened physical condition from being shot in the leg by a jezail bullet during the Second Afghan War. I took full advantage of the few extra minutes Sherlock Holmes had planned into our schedule as we ascended the multiple levels of wide stairs. Our arrival on the upper level of the Southwalk Tower was precisely on time, as expected; 10:30pm.

As she stepped forward I observed how at 77-years-of-age, and standing barely five foot in height, Queen Victoria still projected a grand image as she approached Sherlock Holmes with her right hand extended in greeting. "Ah, Mr. Holmes, so good of you to come, I have heard so much about you."

I watched as Sherlock Holmes bowed his head respectfully

before the Queen of England and shook the tiny hand she held out before him. "I am honored to meet you, My Majesty, and look forward to hearing how I might be of service to my Queen and my country."

Then turning her attention toward me, Queen Victoria extended her right hand and said, "And you are no doubt the intrepid Doctor John H. Watson, British Army medical doctor formerly with the 5th Northumberland Fusiliers and then of the 66th Berkshire Regiment of Foot." Looking me in the eye in a kind grandmotherly way she continued, "Not that you were in any shape to remember, but I visited your troopship, the HMS Orontes, once, as you were being transported home after being wounded at the Battle of Maiwand in 1880."

I stepped forward and leaned against my cane as I bowed to accept her hand, "I am honored to meet you and regret I don't remember much about my time aboard the HMS Orontes returning home here to England. However, I am fully aware that I am not alone when I express my sincere appreciation for your ever vigilant concern over the welfare of your troops serving in the British military; thank you."

Queen Victoria nodded at my reliance on a cane to steady myself as I bowed and said, "I sincerely appreciate your compulsory military service and personal sacrifice, Dr. Watson." The Queen released her grip on my hand and smiled as she said, "I have very much enjoyed reading the many stories you have published in the Strand documenting the investigative prowess Mr. Holmes has demonstrated during the fascinating investigations you have chronicled over the years and I am delighted to see you standing alongside your friend here this evening."

"Mr. Holmes," Queen Victoria said as she turned her full attention back to my friend, the man who she had summoned to meet her at a clandestine location under the cover of darkness.

"Madam?" Sherlock replied.

"As you can well imagine, what I am about to tell you may cause grave consequences for the Crown were it to become widely known; therefore I must ask that this inquiry remain strictly confidential. And while I encourage Dr. Watson to chronical every detail, I request the report of this investigation not be disclosed publically until at least one year after my death."

"Agreed," Sherlock Holmes replied and then turned to look at me.

"I as well," I said and added sincerely, "long live the Queen."

The Queen smiled at me, nodded her head, and then continued. "Very well," the Queen said as she directed us to a small round table with three chairs, illuminated by a red candle burning brightly in the center of the wooden table. "Shall we sit?"

As we took our seats the Queen slid a small burgundy colored velvet pouch across the table to Sherlock Holmes and said, "Your retainer and your assignment, should you choose to accept it."

The Queen and I watched as Sherlock Holmes carefully emptied the contents of the pouch, a handful of large gold coins, into the palm of his hand and glanced up with a questioning look upon his face.

"I would ask you to please inspect these coins carefully and tell me what, if anything, you might detect," the Queen said.

I watched as Sherlock Holmes spread the burgundy velvet bag flat upon the table in front of him and examined both sides of each gold coin briefly by candlelight, placing them one at a time on top of the velvet pouch. He then stacked the heavy coins on top of one another and picked up the entire stack with his right hand. Then, with the practiced skill of a faro dealer at Monte Carlo, held the stack upright in his right hand and dropped them one at a time into the palm of his left, as he listened to the metallic clicking sound of each coin as they dropped upon the stack.

He then spread the ten gold coins out across the velvet pouch in an arc and with his long slender index finger pushed one of the coins toward the Queen—his inspection I would not have imagined had taken him any more than thirty seconds.

"Other than detecting this one coin to be a rather good counterfeit, judging from its lesser weight and absence of a golden luster, I can detect nothing at all from these coins," Sherlock Holmes replied as he slid the velvet bag with the gold coins laying on top over to me.

I picked up the coin he proclaimed to be a counterfeit in my left hand and then picked up one of the other nine coins in my right hand and compared them closely by the light of the candle. The two coins, as well as the eight resting face up on the velvet bag in front of me appeared identical; 1893 Queen Victoria-Jubilee Head Two Pound Gold Double Sovereign coins. In hefting the weight of the coin in my left hand, while doing the same with the coin in my right hand, the one in my left hand did feel slightly lighter, and perhaps lacked some of the gold luster the other coins displayed; however, had Sherlock Holmes not mentioned those two distinctions aloud after his inspection I doubt I would have noticed any differences at all.

"Therein lies the problem, Mr. Holmes," the Queen replied as she shook her head solemnly from side to side. "That is all the authorities at the Royal Mint or Scotland Yard have been able to detect after a month long investigation into this mystery. This issue arose during a routine end-of-year audit at the Royal Mint revealing that one out of every ten of our Two Pounds 1893 Jubilee Gold Double Sovereign gold coins in the mint vault are counterfeit."

"How many coins are we talking about," I inquired of the Queen as I placed the ten coins back into the velvet pouch.

"At a minimum 6,000 coins. These gold coins were part of our gold reserve, similar to the American's gold reserve at their Fort Knox. What is more distressing than the financial loss is the loss of confidence in the British monetary system and potential adverse effect on the world's economy. The price of gold has remained stable since Sir Isaac Newton served as master of the U.K. Mint in 1717. The only exception was 1797 to 1821 during the Napoleonic Wars."

"Have any of these counterfeit gold coins been found in circulation?" Sherlock Holmes inquired.

"Not a one," the Queen replied, "which adds to the mystery. This does not appear to be a common case of embezzlement."

"What, may I ask, does the Royal Mint do with the coin dies at the end of each calendar year?" Sherlock Holmes asked.

"Provided they are in good condition, the reverse dies are reused the following year; however, the obverse dies, depicting the year the coins were struck, are all destroyed under the watchful eye of the Director of the Mint or his assistants. Throughout the year each of the coin dies, as you can imagine, are carefully inventoried and stored in a vault separate from the coins."

"How many mint employees would have access to both vaults?" Sherlock Holmes asked.

"While there might be as many as 8–10 employees who have the combination of one of the vaults or the other; however, there are no more than 2–3 employees who would have access to both vaults; the Director of the Mint and his top one or two deputy directors."

"I will require a complete list of all ten mint employees' names and home addresses for those who had access to either vault for the calendar years 1893, 1894 and 95," Sherlock Holmes requested.

"Consider it done," replied the Queen.

"Why not simply focus on the 2 or 3 employees who had

access to both vaults?" I asked.

"While that is a reasonable start point to begin an inquiry, I suspect the more experienced detectives at Scotland Yard, including Inspectors Gregson and Lestrade, have already eliminated the upper tier Mint employees as obvious suspects," Sherlock Holmes replied as he turned from me to the Queen.

"That is true," the Queen said, "Scotland Yard's finest have thoroughly investigated this case, beginning with the handful of Mint administrators who had access to both vaults and methodically eliminated them as possible suspects. The investigation thus far has confirmed the three senior administrators at the Royal Mint are all highly trusted long-term employees with impeccable records."

"As I would have expected," Sherlock Holmes said, then turning to me explained his thinking in terms I could understand, "Since none of the counterfeit coins have surfaced on the street, I suspect a more organized criminal enterprise is at play, one with a clever mastermind behind this intriguing caper. A conspiracy involving two or more mint employees who would have a combined access to both vaults is certainly not out of the question. Furthermore, these culprits must have an intimate understanding of the minting process—specifically the coin dies —and access to the raw materials and other minting equipment, not to mention the patience to wait for the proper opportunity to present itself. Also they had to have the ability to replace the genuine coins with the fake coins and then remove the 6,000 genuine gold coins from the mint undetected."

"This does become rather complex, doesn't it?" I commented aloud thinking through each of the steps as Sherlock Holmes had explained them.

Turning to the Queen again Sherlock Holmes said, "If you can have the list of employee names and home addresses delivered to my home at 221 B Baker Street tomorrow morning I shall begin immediately; however, since we are meeting tonight in this clandestine location I suspect there is far more to this assignment than what we have discussed thus far?"

"You are most perceptive," Queen Victoria replied, "As I have been told by your brother Mycroft and others who have previously benefited from your unique investigative skills. This particular investigation may require some extended international travel, discretion and someone with an advanced understanding of chemistry."

"Do go on," Sherlock Holmes said, "I am most intrigued by the facts thus far and willing to travel abroad if necessary."

"In addition to the retainer of these nine proper Two Pound Double Sovereigns you will have an unlimited line of credit to be drawn upon at the Royal Bank of England or any other international bank when traveling abroad. The only other government official who knows of your assignment is Prime Minister Salisbury and tomorrow morning he will open a joint bank account in both your names. Whenever you are in need of funds, or simply wish to inform the PM or myself of your whereabouts, simply make a withdraw; even number amounts suggest all is progressing as expected, withdraws of any odd amounts suggests you have encountered some difficulty and may be in need of assistance."

"Understood," Sherlock Holmes replied.

"This case must be maintained on a strict 'need to know' basis and therefore will be identified by a code word, to be written not spoken," the Queen instructed as she wrote seven letters upon a small piece of yellowed paper with a pencil and held it up for us to read privately.

Printed across the small paper in neat handwriting was one word—NORBURY. After assuring that each of us had read the word she had written on the small piece of paper, the Queen held the parchment against the open flame of the candle and "poof" the paper disappeared in a flash.

"Flash paper," Sherlock Holmes said knowingly, adding, "a wise precaution."

The word was easy enough for me to memorize as it was the name of a small town in England which served as the location for one of the short stories I had written, *The Adventure of the Yellow Face.* The details of this case had been widely published, along with illustrations from Sidney Paget, in the Strand Magazine in 1893. The story concluded by Sherlock Holmes making this special request, "Watson, if it should ever strike you that I am getting a little overconfident in my powers, or giving less pains to a case than it deserves, kindly whisper 'Norbury' in my ear, and I shall be infinitely obliged to you." I was impressed the Queen had not only read this short story I had written, but was conveying the message this case was deserving of our best efforts.

"Further," the Queen said, "you, Mr. Holmes, while in the secret service of Her Majesty, will be known secretly by the number 003."

"Very well," he said.

"May I ask why this case was not assigned to 001 or 002?" I inquired.

"That is a reasonable request," the Queen said, "While I have no doubt 001, Sir Sean Conley, would rise to any request from his Queen, he is getting on in years and the physical demands of this assignment may prove most arduous. As to 002 he has not been heard from since boarding a White Star passenger liner, the RMS Republic, in Liverpool headed across the pond to the United States. Regrettably, he failed to get off the ship when they docked in New York harbor over two weeks ago. This inquiry, you see, does carry an element of serious danger."

"I expected as much, given the level of security prearranged for our meeting this evening."

"We shall take every precaution," I acknowledged as I patted my service revolver tucked snugly into the pocket of my overcoat.

"Please understand, Mr. Holmes, my need for secrecy extends beyond your reasonable expectation of safety; regrettably, the PM and I may both be required politically to maintain some element of plausible deniability. Should you accept this assignment, there are certain international trade restrictions at play and therefore it cannot be made public that you are acting under the authority of the British government."

"Understood and agreed," Sherlock Holmes stated, answering for the both of us.

"And now this is where things become a bit convoluted," the Queen said.

"Please continue, I suspected there was still more to the story," Sherlock Holmes replied.

"You see rumors have surfaced among mint employees suggesting that these gold coins were not stolen from the mint at all, they were simply turned from gold into a baser metal."

"Who would want to do such a thing?" I asked in astonishment.

"Someone who wants to undermine the British government by eroding the public's confidence in the Crown's production of gold coins and therefore disrupt the world's economy," Sherlock Holmes answered as the Queen nodded her head in quiet agreement.

"But how on earth could anyone possibly turn gold coins into a lesser metal?" I asked.

The Queen explained, "As you both know alchemy, the process of turning baser metals, such as lead, into noble metals, such as gold, has been practiced throughout Europe, Africa and Egypt for centuries."

"Ah, alchemy," I thought to myself, as I glanced out of the

corner of my eye at Sherlock Holmes sitting beside me who had just yesterday sent me out on an errand scouring the back issues of the Strand for a short article written about this very subject.

The Queen went on, "While I don't give much credence to there being actual alchemists, once thought to be practiced among the black arts, there are a handful of mint employees who have started rumors suggesting the process of alchemy might be reversible through electrical means. We are just now on the brink of a scientific discovery concerning the effects of electricity upon various metals, or so I am told by my science advisors who believe the experiments being undertaken by the Americans in making use of alternating current verses direct current may yield unprecedented scientific results."

"What a fascinating case," Sherlock Holmes said.

"I do hope this investigation proves worthy of your talents Mr. Holmes," the Queen said as she stood to leave.

"I wouldn't have missed this investigation for all the world," Sherlock Holmes said as he stood, shook her hand and bowed his head respectfully.

"And my good Doctor Watson," the Queen said as she turned to bid me farewell, "I hope this matter doesn't take you too far away from your patients and other duties."

"I have a medical colleague here in London who I trust to look after the few patients I have at present," I replied as I shook the hand of the Queen again and bowed my head as she turned to leave.

Sherlock Holmes extended his right elbow to escort the Queen the short distance to the top of the stairs where a pair of plainclothes security escorts appeared out of the darkness.

I heard Sherlock Holmes say quietly to one of the guards, "We shall wait thirty minutes before we take our leave and then depart by the North Tower so as not to be followed."

When Sherlock Holmes returned to the small table he sat down and withdrew his clay pipe from the pocket of his Inverness cape, "Won't you join me for a smoke my good man? I suspect this case may be a two-pipe problem."

I took a seat at the table next to my friend, retrieved a cigar from my own coat pocket and snipped off the end with my small pocket knife. Sherlock Holmes struck a sulphur match on the underside of the table and offered me a light.

"Thank you," said I, and then looking at the face of my friend in the light of the match asked, "How could you possibly have known the Queen was going to bring up the subject of alchemy?"

"I didn't know," Sherlock Holmes said as he held the lit match above the clay bowl of his pipe, "but when Inspectors Gregson and Lestrade separately asked my opinion on the subject, on two different occasions, I inquired of my brother Mycroft his thoughts on the matter. As you well know Mycroft is associated with several somewhat secret societies across the British Empire and the subject of alchemy seems to have been of high interest to the Masons and the Templar Knights dating back to antiquity. There are subjects my brother is not at liberty to disclose, not even to his own biological brother; however, in his telegram he was kind enough to direct my attention to the recent article published in the Strand Magazine."

"I wish I had paid more attention to what had been written," I confessed. "I only glanced at it briefly; but seem to recall the article mentioning something about two Americans conducting electrical experiments abroad that has caused a bit of a dust-up of some kind or another."

"Yes, the two notable Americans are Thomas Edison and Nikola Tesla, both are presently residing in New York City," Holmes replied as he puffed on his pipe and then added, "There has been some speculation, as the Queen mentioned, how alchemy might be achieved through some process applying electricity."

"Americans do seem to be the inventive type don't they?"

"Indeed they do and when it comes to the emerging field of electricity Thomas Edison has been credited for having invented many devices in the field of electrical power generation, as well as in sound recording and mass communication capabilities. The Austrian born Nikola Tesla, who migrated to the Colonies a few years ago, has since become an American citizen and worked for Thomas Edison a short time before striking out on his own. At issue is this contention over direct electrical current verses alternating currents, the outcome of which is certain to have a global impact upon the power industry for years to come."

"I recall Tesla having made quite a splash three years ago at the 1893 Chicago World's Columbian Exposition, when he demonstrated a better way to generate electricity using an alternating current," said I, then asked, "You don't give any credence to this notion of reverse alchemy do you?"

"Heavens no, nor does the Queen I suspect," Sherlock Holmes replied, and then continued, "However, this theory coming to the forefront now may suggest someone has cleverly embedded a tantalizing cover story to hide their criminal misdeeds at the Royal Mint."

"That would suggest whoever is behind all of this is very clever indeed," said I.

"Clever and deadly, possibly even the Napoleon of Crime," Sherlock Holmes replied, his tone reminding me of the British agent who disappeared at sea during his recent trip to the States. I watched as my friend slowly tamped fresh tobacco into the bowl of his clay pipe. "There is an intriguing common denominator to all of this," he said as he struck another match to light his second pipe.

"What might that be?" I asked.

"Not what, but who," he replied, handing me the velvet bag containing the gold coins. "Would you be so kind as to keep track of these until they can be put to better use?"

"Certainly, but who then might be this possible common denominator?"

"A man who recently spoke here in London at the Savage Club," Sherlock Holmes answered as he blew out the flame.

"Who might that be?" I asked.

Sherlock Holmes thought for a moment as he smoked his long stemmed clay pipe and quietly said, "Mr. Samuel Clemens, better known throughout the world as Mark Twain."

Chapter 3

January 22nd, 1896 9:45am

221 B Baker Street, London, England

I AROSE LATE THE NEXT MORNING, as was my custom, to find my friend Sherlock Holmes had already eaten his breakfast and was preparing to take his leave for the day.

"Ah, good morning, my dear Dr. Watson," Sherlock Holmes said cheerfully, as he draped his Inverness cape over his arm and headed toward our front door. "You may ring the bell for your coffee and breakfast of eggs and rashers; I suspect I shall be gone much of the day."

"Where are you off to this morning?" I asked, still not yet fully awake.

"The list I requested from the Queen, identifying the ten mint employees who had access to one or both of the vaults, arrived by special courier at 8:30 this morning, as I anticipated. I had already hired a carriage and have since mapped out a route across London affording me the benefit of laying eyes upon each of their homes or flats before arriving at the Royal Mint this afternoon. There I will be requesting to speak privately with each of these ten employees."

"I can see where you might benefit by observing if any of these mint employees appear to be living beyond their means," said

I as I sat upon the sofa and retrieved the well-read Daily Telegraph morning newspaper from the coffee table. Continuing I said, "but are you not concerned that if this is an inside job, won't the suspected mint employee tip off the mastermind behind this caper, if indeed there is one?"

"That is precisely the behavior I intend to hasten," Sherlock Holmes replied. "One or more of the ten employees identified on this list will tip their hand when they go to inform whomever is behind this criminal conspiracy. Upon leaving the mint this very evening, they will be entirely unaware they are being followed by one of my Baker Street Irregulars. I shall be notified this evening if any of these men deviates from their most natural route home. Oh, by the way, might I trouble you for the velvet bag containing the gold coins given us last night by the Queen?"

"Certainly," said I as I walked over to the left side of the brick fireplace and removed a loose brick retrieving the burgundy colored bag from a concealed compartment which had been cleverly built into the fireplace. I then handed the bag with the gold coins to Sherlock Holmes.

"Thank you," he said as he stuffed the velvet bag into his cape pocket.

"This evening I shall look forward to hearing what you have learned," said I as I rang the bell to notify Mrs. Hudson I was ready for my breakfast. I asked of my roommate as he retrieved his deerstalker hat from our coatrack, "Is there anything I should be doing today to assist you in this matter?"

"Indeed there is," Sherlock Holmes replied as he stopped at our front door and turned toward me to ask, "Have you ever wanted to visit the Colonies?"

"The United States?" I asked, "Whatever for?" I added recalling the many stories of how wild and uncultured our adventurous friends are across the pond and how rustic their travel accommodations are reported to be.

"If you have time today," Sherlock Holmes asked as stood before our front door to put on his cape, "could you please look into the departure dates and times for the White Star Line steamship RMS Republic out of Liverpool?"

"Certainly, I would be happy to do so, anything else?"

"Yes; if you don't mind perhaps you could stop by the Royal Bank of England and make a sizable even numbered withdrawal from our newly established joint account which was to have been arranged for this morning by Prime Minister Salisbury?"

"Certainly," said I, "How much money do you suppose we might need?"

"Enough to accommodate several months of extended travel for the two of us abroad," Sherlock Holmes said, adding, "Ah, it sounds as if Mrs. Hudson is about to arrive with your breakfast." He opened the door swiftly to see Mrs. Hudson balancing a serving tray in one hand while preparing to knock upon our door with the other, and then said, "And while you're at it Dr. Watson, could you please pay Mrs. Hudson our rent for the next six months in advance; we don't want her to toss our belongings out into the street and lease our rooms to some other boarders do we?"

"What a pleasant thought that might be," Mrs. Hudson said as she entered our sitting room with my breakfast tray.

"It sounds as if we might be gone for some time, Mrs. Hudson," said I.

"I might rather enjoy some peace and quiet around here in your absence," Mrs. Hudson muttered aloud, although we all three knew she meant something quite the opposite.

"Very well then," Sherlock Holmes said, as he placed his deer stalker hat upon his head, "we shall mail you a postcard once we have arrived stateside, Mrs. Hudson, in the event you need to reach us or forward any important correspondence during our journey abroad. And now I bid you both a good day."

January 22nd, 1896 9:55pm
221 B Baker Street, London

IT WAS WELL AFTER DARK when I heard the key enter the lock to our front door. I sat the evening Daily News aside and watched as the door opened. Sherlock Holmes burst into our sitting room, draped his cape and hat over the nearest armchair and set immediately upon the apple pie and small block of sharp cheddar cheese Mrs. Hudson had set out upon our cupboard.

"Please forgive me Dr. Watson;" Sherlock Holmes said as he began to devour the food and explained between mouthfuls, "I am rather famished for I have been so consumed with our case today I hadn't taken time away to eat since breakfast this morning."

"Did you learn anything of interest during your inspection of the ten Royal Mint employee's homes?"

"I did indeed," he replied as he held up what remained of the crisp apple pie and cheddar cheese and asked, "Do you want any of this before I finish it off?"

"No, please finish, I ate earlier," said I, and watched as he placed the food upon our dining table and took a chair behind the table to face me before continuing.

"Seven of the Mint employees own their own homes or townhomes, two rent flats and one man lives with his older sister who is caring for their elderly parents. None of the employees appear to be living beyond their means; however, the most important piece to the puzzle I learned this morning was the most direct route home each of them would likely travel upon leaving their place of employment, the Royal Mint. At noon I met with Billy to ensure that he and eight of his Baker Street

Irregulars would be positioned across the street from the Mint when these ten employees got off duty and started home at the end of their work day."

"What about the other two employees?"

"We planned for Billy to follow the ninth employee to leave work and I would follow the tenth man to his home. We had arranged for Billy and the other eight Baker Street Irregulars to meet me at Trafalgar Square at 8pm so they could each report to me on what they had learned in following their targets home and receive payment from me for their services; an 1893 Queen Victoria-Jubilee Head Two Pound Gold Double Sovereign. I kept the one counterfeit coin and the coin pouch," he said as he walked to our fireplace, removed the loose brick concealing the secret compartment and returned the velvet bag to its hiding place.

"That was a very generous payment, I can well imagine they were delighted to each receive a Two Pound Gold Double Sovereign," I commented as Sherlock replaced the brick back into the fireplace.

"They were thrilled; most of the younger boys had never held a gold coin in their lives. I explained the coins came from a wealthy benefactor and their payment was based more on need than services rendered. Besides, for my surveillance purposes they each performed admirably."

"How were these young boys to know who it was they were to follow?" asked I.

"A good question," Sherlock Holmes replied as he returned to our table and finished off the cheese and then pushed the plate aside. "Since I would have spoken personally with each of these men just a few hours previous, I would know what they looked like and what they were wearing when they left the mint. All mint employees are required to pass through security located just inside the front entrance as they leave work at the end of their shifts. I planned to be standing just outside the front entrance of the mint and would walk up to each employee as he departed, remove my hat, reach inside it to retrieve a business card tucked in the hatband and hand to them. Then I'd explained that if he thought of anything useful to please contact me here at our Baker Street address written on the back of my card. This gesture would tip Billy to assign one of his assistants to follow the man who accepted my business card; a well-rehearsed tactic we have deployed successfully on many occasions. Billy was concealed across the street where he could see me and signal one of his young assistants to follow each of the mint employees to ascertain if they went immediately home or made any stops along the way."

"Hold on a moment, I wish to chronical what you learned when you spoke to each of the ten employees," said I as I retrieved my leather-bound notebook from my bedroom and took a seat at the dining room table across from Sherlock Holmes. I opened my pocket notebook to a blank page and began to write. "When you spoke to each of the ten employees earlier this afternoon did any of them tell you anything of importance?" I asked.

"It is not what any of them said that was of importance, but how they said what they said that interests me most," Sherlock Holmes explained as he finished off the last piece of apple pie and confessed earnestly, "I am dearly going to miss Mrs. Hudson's cooking while we're abroad, but please don't let on, she thinks I find her cooking only somewhat above tolerable."

"She is a wonderful cook," said I in agreement, then encouraged my friend to continue reporting his investigative findings as I documented notes carefully upon the next several pages.

"I began my brief inquiries at 2:30 this afternoon, starting with the three senior mint employees who had the combinations for both vaults; including, the smaller vault which holds the coin dies and the larger vault containing the genuine and counterfeit gold coins. My initial assessment of these three men agreed with what the boys at the Yard had previously concluded; these top men are of impeccable character and completely trustworthy. Of the other seven employees who had access to one vault or the other, but not both, five also gave the appearance of being perfectly trustworthy; however, two men proved of considerable interest to me."

"What are their names?" I asked, turning to a fresh page in my notebook.

"Thomas Leadbedder and Robert Coyne."

"That second name, Coyne, sounds somewhat familiar," said I as I looked up from my notetaking to see a smile on my friend's face.

"I thought it might. It turns out he is the brother of Stanley Coyne, also known as Shady Coyne, who has found himself in considerable trouble with the law for many years. When I asked Robert if he were related in any way to Stanley Coyne he repeated my question aloud and then answered in an evasive way suggesting they were brothers who have long since been estranged."

"Why was his repeating your question of interest?" asked I.

"The primary reason anyone repeats a question during an interrogation is to buy themselves more time in fabricating whatever it is they are going to lie to you about; truthful people do not need additional time as the response is already set factually in their minds."

"What is it you think he lied to you about?"

"In two specific areas of inquiry; 'when was the last time you saw your brother' and 'do you know how the counterfeit coins were produced'."

"Did this Thomas Leadbedder also repeat your questions before answering?"

"No, but he was clearly evasive, especially when I asked three questions of him in rapid succession. His physical reactions were also very telling."

"How so?"

"Unless someone is a habitual liar, or a much practiced one, it is difficult to tell three lies in a row. I also noticed his upper lip had begun to sweat and he avoided making eye contact on specific key questions; such as 'do you know how the counterfeit coins were produced'; however, on the other more routine questions he consistently maintained eye contact. Any physical deviation from a pattern of behavior during critical questions is noteworthy."

"Don't you need to write notes yourself so you don't forget any details?" said I as I continued to write on the pages of my notebook so I would not forget anything of importance.

"My mind works differently than most," Sherlock Holmes said, as he retrieved the K encyclopedia from our bookshelf, turned the pages rapidly and then stopped to point to the word Kinetoscope. "Thomas Edison is responsible for the invention of a motion picture camera and has been producing films for public viewing. I have trained my mind to record events, both visually and with sound, as they occur. Then when I wish to recall a specific detail for any investigation I simply rewind the film reel in my mind, stop at the point in question, and then play that portion of the event over in my mind; either in slow or fast motion, as many times as necessary to extract specific details. This recall has proven much faster for me than referring to handwritten notes and more detailed since the mind captures both what is seen and every word spoken. Most people only use a small portion of their brain. I suspect in time you might train yourself to recall the details of every patient you ever attended to, as well as their medical treatment; although this experiment might prove beneficial with a larger sampling size."

"I see," said I, not taking the bait Sherlock Holmes dangled in front of me trying to get a rise out of me for having few patients. I continued taking notes and asked, "Did you confront either Leadbedder or Coyne about your suspicions that they were departing from the truth?"

"No, today was simply a preliminary investigative inquiry; however, it is reassuring to know these other Mint employees appear credible and trustworthy. The Mint has taken the precaution to change the combinations on both vaults and further limit the number of employees who have access to the combinations of these two and other vaults within the Royal Mint."

"Very well. Now, what did you learn when you met with the Baker Street Irregulars this evening at Trafalgar Square; did any of the ten employees deviate from their natural routes home after work?"

"Four employees did make departures from what would appear to be their most direct or natural route home. One went a few blocks out of his way to pick up shirts at a neighborhood laundry, another stopped by a cobbler to drop off a pair of shoes that appeared to be much in need of new soles. And then there was Mr. Robert Coyne, who dropped by a bakery to pick up a loaf of French bread and a bottle of red wine before stopping by to see an apparent lady friend who lives off of Cannon Lane. He remained there an hour and twenty-six minutes before arriving at his home, empty-handed, to a wife with three small children who were awaiting him for dinner."

"I can see how that behavior might make Coyne a cad, but it does not necessarily make him a crook," said I.

"Agreed; however, it might make him susceptible to blackmail."

"I see," said I as I made a note next to his name and continued, knowing my friend had likely held the most interesting facts for last. "And now, please tell me what you learned from your meeting at Trafalgar Square with the Baker Street Irregulars regarding the forth employee who deviated from his normal route home this evening."

"Ah, and here the plot thickens," Sherlock Holmes replied as he rubbed is hands together and nodded toward the set of thick encyclopedias in the bookcase, "Would you please be so kind as to return the K and hand me the W?"

"Certainly," said I, and did as requested. I watched as Sherlock Holmes flipped quickly through the pages, settled midway through the thick book and ran his long slender index finger down the page.

"Here it is, the Whitechapel Bell Foundry," Sherlock Holmes announced triumphantly, as he tapped on the page and pushed the heavy book in front of me on the table before he continued, "Mr. Thomas Leadbedder, upon leaving his employer this evening at 5:30pm went immediately to the business district of the Tower Hamlets and arrived at the Whitechapel Bell Foundry at precisely 6:10pm. Despite the factory already being closed, he rang the front bell. The door was opened by a short heavyset older man wearing a leather apron. Mr. Leadbedder was allowed inside where he remained until 6:25pm. Upon his departure Leadbedder looked around to see if he was being followed and then went immediately to the nearest pub, where he remained for 45 minutes before going home."

"Completely unaware he was being followed?" I asked.

"Completely," Sherlock Holmes emphasized and then added, "No self-respecting criminal could conceive he was being followed by an 11-year-old boy of the streets; which is what makes the Baker Street Irregulars such perfect agents for undercover operations.

"But why a bell foundry?" I asked completely in the dark.

"Does it not strike you as odd that not one of the counterfeit coins has surfaced?"

"Indeed it does," I agreed.

"This only serves to reinforce my premise that the genuine gold coins are no longer coins and whoever is behind this caper runs a well-disciplined criminal enterprise. Please read aloud what the encyclopedia has to teach us."

"The Whitechapel Bell Foundry dates back to 1570 and is the oldest manufacturing company in Great Britain. The bell foundry has been casting bells for over 350 years and has been at its present site for 150 years. The foundry primarily makes church bells, along with various fittings, clappers and accessories, although it also produces tolling bells, carillon bells and handbells. The foundry is best known for being the original manufacturer of the Liberty Bell, a famous symbol of American Independence. The foundry is also well known for re-casting Big Ben, which rings on the quarter hour from the north clock tower of the Houses of Parliament in London."

"Isn't that extraordinary?" Sherlock Holmes proclaimed.

"Isn't what extraordinary? That Big Ben chimes on the quarter hour?" I asked failing to make any connection between our case of the counterfeit gold coins and an old bell foundry.

"The audacity of it all."

"The audacity of what all?" I asked still mystified.

"Don't you see," Sherlock Holmes replied as he stood, retrieved his Stradivarius violin from the fireplace mantel and began to pace around in front of the fireplace as he explained his reasoning. "Nearly ten percent of the 1893 Jubilee gold coins housed inside the Royal Mint, amounting to nearly 6,000 authentic Two Pounds Gold Double Sovereign coins, have, in the last year, been removed from the Royal Mint and replaced with counterfeit coins. These counterfeit coins are of such high quality, that other than being struck on brass rather than on gold coin planchets, they are nearly undetectable; which implies they must have been struck using the original coin dies."

"But, why then, haven't the genuine gold coins flooded the market place," I asked scratching my head and then confessed, "I fail to see how then these crooks are profiting in the least bit from their illegal activities?"

"The only way for these authentic 1893 Jubilee Gold Double Sovereigns to have not flooded the marketplace is that they are no longer gold coins."

"If they are no longer gold coins," asked I, "What are they then?"

"Gold bells," Sherlock Holmes explained and then continued, "I surmise most, if not all, of these 6,000 stolen Two Pound 1893 Jubilee Gold Double Sovereign gold coins have been melted down and recast into four 65-pound gold bells."

"What? 65-pound gold bells?" I asked entirely perplexed, "Who would want a 65-pound gold bell? Why, each one alone would cost a king's ransom."

"Indeed. Four 65-pound fire bells, cast of 999+ fine pure gold, would be equivalent to approximately ten percent of the 1893 Jubilee Gold Double Sovereign gold coins inventoried during the 1894 end of year audit at the Royal Mint. At the end of the 1895 calendar year the annual audit revealed 1 in 10 of the 1893 Jubilee real gold coins is now counterfeit."

"Very well," I conceded, "I see where those figures might calculate, but why fire bells weighing 65-pounds each and who on earth would want a gold fire bell, let alone four?"

"Someone who wants to smuggle huge quantities of stolen gold out of the country undetected."

"But where on earth would they possibly ship these huge gold fire bells to?"

"Back to where the gold originated," Sherlock Holmes replied as he tucked his violin under his arm, unfolded a map of the United States with his free hand and spread it out upon our dining room table. Then he pointed with the tip of his violin bow to the center of the map and said, "The four gold fire bells were shipped here, to the Greatest Gold Camp on earth, a quaint little mining town high in the mountains of Colorado, a place called Cripple Creek."

"How can you possibly know that?" I asked, perhaps sounding a little incredulous.

"Because I spoke with the stevedore who has the route which includes the Whitechapel Bell Foundry and he complained mightily about having to ship four heavy 65-pound crated fire bells, one a month for the past four months, from the back door of the Whitechapel Foundry to the port of Liverpool, where each crate was to be loaded aboard the…" Sherlock Holmes stopped himself midsentence and turned to look at me, waiting for me to complete his sentence.

"RMS Republic," said I.

"And shipped to?" Sherlock Holmes asked in prompting me to complete his sentence again.

"The Cripple Creek Fire Department," I replied, playing along, "but I fail to see how these crooks are making any money whatsoever from their criminal endeavors."

"By returning the gold back to where it was first mined from the earth, they can melt the gold bells down into gold bricks or ingots and then blend the stolen gold in with the other newly minted gold bars undetected."

"Some of which is very likely to have been sold back to the Royal Mint to replace their stolen gold coins."

"Exactly; completely unaware, the Royal Mint is buying back their stolen gold as a raw material to mint new British gold coins," Sherlock Holmes replied and then asked of me, "So, Dr. Watson, when do we ourselves leave for the States aboard the RMS Republic?"

"In four weeks," I replied as I sat back in my armchair for a moment in complete astonishment, once again, in awe of my friend's most unique investigative abilities. "The next departure of the RMS Republic for the States," said I checking the note I had made in my pocket notebook, "is February 26th at ten o'clock in the morning. I will purchase our tickets first thing tomorrow morning."

"Thank you my good man," Sherlock Holmes replied as he tuned his violin with his eyes closed.

"Tell me Dr. Watson, do you recall the name of the engineer with the severed thumb you brought around to me in the summer of '89?"

"I do indeed, Mr. Victor Hatherley, a hydraulic engineer."

"Correct. Mr. Hatherley had the misfortunate of being hired by an exceedingly thin man who had introduced himself as a Colonel Lysander Stark. Our Mr. Stark turned out to be in collaboration with a group of coin counterfeiters. They were operating at the time out of a secluded house in Berkshire, outside of Reading. This house was leased to a short heavy set Englishman who gave his name upon the lease as Dr. Becher."

"Yes, I remember asking around of my medical colleagues. No one had ever heard of this Dr. Becher," said I.

"This is because, I now believe, he is not a medical doctor, but a geologist with a Ph.D.," Sherlock Holmes explained, adding, "thus explaining the cover story he told Mr. Hatherley involving Fuller's earth, and as to his last name, it is no doubt an alias, but his vain use of the title doctor is noteworthy."

"How so," asked I.

"Because the three bedroom flat on Cannon Lane, where

Robert Coyne stopped by to visit his lady friend, is leased by a short heavy set older Englishman calling himself Dr. Bakerslee. Upon inquiring of the nosy landlady who lives next door to Dr. Bakerslee, the other two tenants, an exceedingly slender man and a woman appearing slightly younger than he, both have heavy German accents."

"Which matches perfectly the description of the three counterfeiters who fled the secluded house in Berkshire, with several bulky boxes in the back of a wagon," said I. "I do recall this case in considerable detail, for having written about it at the time and for it being only one of two investigations where you were not able to bring the villains to justice."

"Not able to bring the villains to justice, yet," Sherlock Holmes said, with an emphasis on the word "yet". "As you recall, these three counterfeiters not only fled in the middle of the night, after one of them tried to kill your patient with a meat clever, but then the house was set ablaze to conceal their illegal activities. Remember too, another hydraulic engineer from London, a 26-year-old Jeremiah Hayling, had mysteriously disappeared the year previous."

"This is a murderous gang of thieves, no doubt. One thing that has always bothered me about this case," said I, "was why that woman, who tried to warn Mr. Hatherley of his perilous position, why she would remain in the company of these two evil men? If she was married to one of the two, presumably the younger man who also had a heavy German accent, why would she not simply leave him, and go immediately to the police and then file for divorce?"

"Because she is not his wife, but likely his younger sister," Sherlock Holmes replied. "As you may recall, when Mr. Hatherley said they were arguing, she called him 'Fritz' and he called her 'Elise' which are quite likely their real first names; both are common names in the German language I should mention for your recordkeeping. Her brother Fritz is also quite possibly her only means of financial support; further, I suspect she may have been criminally involved somehow in this counterfeiting operation. I have learned it is far easier for a pretty woman to pass off fake coins than a man; especially a man with a German accent who is as remarkable in appearance as what Mr. Hatherley describes of this Colonel Stark; appearing almost 'fleshless'—as if his skin were draped over his bones."

"So, you alone managed to crack this case in less than 24 hours when the best minds at Scotland Yard, aided by the senior leadership at the Royal Mint, failed to do in over a month?"

"I wasn't alone, remember," Sherlock Holmes replied and then added with a wry smile, "I was aided by nine boys from the Baker Street Irregulars."

"Will you not hand this case off to Scotland Yard so these three suspects on Cannon Lane can be arrested?"

"No, our investigation is far from over; Fritz, if that is his real name, hasn't been seen by the next door landlady for nearly a month, which, she said is not entirely unusual. I suspect he may be escorting the golden bells to the States, probably with one or more hired thugs. If we act prematurely and nab the woman and possibly the older man at the Whitechapel Bell Foundry now, we may alert whoever else is involved that we're on to them; besides, we lack sufficient physical evidence to ensure prosecutors a conviction on the counterfeiting charges; barring an unlikely confession. And we have no evidence whatsoever that would convict these three culprits of the murder of young Mr. Hayling or harder still, the murder of 002. These three criminals, and whoever their counterparts are in the States, if not convicted will likely go underground only to surface a year or two from now engaged in even more sinister and sophisticated counterfeiting endeavors. This case is far from being over or ready to be handed off to Scotland Yard."

"Indeed," said I, amazed once again at how the answer to my own questions appear to have been right in front of me all along, and yet when explained by Sherlock Holmes, the answers had escaped me and anyone else involved. I ran though the small inputs I had to offer through my mind and then said, "I have another question."

"Yes?"

"Should I purchase our tickets aboard the RMS Republic in first-class?"

"First-class, if you please."

"Are there any other travel or lodging accommodations you wish for me to make once we arrive in the States?"

"Yes, please, I would like for us to spend a few days in New York City, visiting with Mark Twain about the much needed advancements in the field of forensic science related to fingerprint identification and collection methods. Mr. Twain also knows both Thomas Edison and Nikola Tesla personally. I am hoping he will be good enough to introduce us to these two gentlemen so we might set to rest this dubious business of alchemy. By the way, do you happen to have any medical colleagues presently residing in the high mountain state of Colorado?"

"In fact I do," I replied, while making myself a growing list of things to do tomorrow, including writing a letter to my friend Dr. William Bell. "When we last corresponded he was treating a growing number of tuberculous patients. Dr. William Bell and his wife Cara helped establish a small town, named Manitou Springs as I recall, at the foot of some mountain he had become quite fond of, I believe he referred to it as 'Pike's Peak' or some such appellation."

"Sounds quaint," Sherlock Holmes replied, as he tucked his

Stradivarius beneath his chin and drew the bow lightly across the strings.

"Anything else?" I inquired as I prepared to retire to my room for a good night's sleep.

"One more small request, my good man," Sherlock Holmes said as he turned away.

"Yes?"

"While we are in the States, I think I should like to take in an opera," Sherlock Holmes said, as he began to play his violin without waiting for my reply.

I glanced toward the framed picture of "The Woman" on the left side of the fireplace mantel and observed it had been moved to where Sherlock Holmes now stood with his eyes closed. As I shut my bedroom door I heard him playing his violin ever so softly and mournfully, no doubt recalling, as he once said, "the face of the most beautiful of women with the mind of the most resolute of men." I wondered where this adventure would lead us, recalling in my mind the beautiful voice of Irene Adler, one of the most talented opera singers of our time and a well-known adventuress to men, including once, the King of Bohemia.

I fell asleep that night listening to Sherlock Holmes playing the soft silvery tones that only a Stradivarius can make, as I recalled the details of the case of *A Scandal in Bohemia*, which had brought Irene Adler into our lives. I have seldom heard my friend mention her since her hasty marriage to her attorney, Mr. Godfrey Norton, before the two newlyweds sailed for the States some years ago. Under an odd set of circumstances, wearing a disguise, Sherlock Holmes had served as best man as the couple tied the knot. Although she is now a married woman, I know in the eyes of my friend Sherlock Holmes the beautiful Irene Adler still eclipses the whole of her sex and to him she will always be known, respectfully, as The Woman.

February 26th, 1896 8:45am
Liverpool, England

As we stepped out of the hansom cab I stared up and marveled at the sheer size and beauty of the majestic steam-powered ocean liner, the RMS Republic, docked before us at the Liverpool pier. The cloudless azure sky provided the perfect backdrop for the 570 foot long flag ship of the White Star Line, adorned by a red banner emblazoned with the lone white star painted toward the top of the multistoried single smoke stack positioned at the center of the ship. The water was perfectly calm as far as one could see and there was so much excitement you could feel it in the air as the RMS Republic was being prepared to take her leave for the United States.

Sherlock Holmes walked up beside me and said, "I understand she can carry 2,830 passengers, plus a crew of 300, along with unfathomable quantities of coal, fresh water and stores of food and cargo; including, with any luck at all, a wooden crate containing a 65-pound gold fire bell bound for Cripple Creek, located high the Rocky Mountains of Colorado."

I looked around as hundreds of well-dressed passengers emerged from immaculate horse-drawn carriages and began streaming up the first-class boarding ramps, followed by hundreds of muscular stevedores loading heavy steamer trunks packed with fine clothing, expensive jewelry and other priceless valuables one simply could not find or purchase in America at any price.

"I see why they call her the Millionaires Ship," said I to my travel mate, as he finished paying our driver and giving instructions to a stevedore unloading our four large steamer trunks; Sherlock Holmes' three trunks and my one.

Sherlock Holmes pulled me gently by the arm back out of

harm's way; avoiding my being trampled by a group of a half dozen excited young people, each carrying a single piece of carry-on luggage. As they rushed pass on their way to the third-class ramp toward the back of the ship, one young teenage girl with flowing red hair looked back and shouted gleefully, "Sorry!" meant as an apology for their group.

"Well, I don't imagine every passenger coming aboard is a millionaire," Sherlock Holmes said and then added with a smile, "although I suspect most do come aboard with dreams of becoming one in America, the land of endless milk and honey."

As we made our way toward the first-class ramp I looked back to ensure the stevedore with our luggage was following. Everywhere you looked there were hundreds of people laughing and crying and hugging their loved ones, many perhaps knowingly for the last time. As we made our way up the ramp, our progress was slowed by the frequent stops of passengers on the ramp ahead of us, stopping sporadically to waive goodbye to family and friends below.

At the top of the ramp stood a tall bearded officer wearing a crisp blue uniform waiting to check our tickets. "Welcome aboard the RMS Republic, Mr. Holmes and Dr. Watson," he said upon punching our tickets. "I am ship's third-mate Joel Ziegler," said he with a tip of his white hat adorned with an impressive embroidered gold braid on the bill. "James here will show you to your quarters," he said as an athletic-looking black porter wearing a spotless white uniform stepped forward and received instructions from the officer.

"The Victorian Staterooms, very well, this way if you please, gentlemen," the porter said as he guided us toward our first-class cabin amid ship. "My name is James Mercier, I am from Abu Dhabi. I will be at your service during this ten-day transatlantic crossing. If there is anything at all I can do to make your trip more enjoyable please do not hesitate to let me know."

Sherlock Holmes stepped forward to walk alongside James and handed him a tip. James looked down at the gold coin in his hand, smiled and said, "It's a pleasure to have you aboard Sir."

"Mercier," I heard Sherlock Holmes say casually to James, "From your surname I take it your family were traders, Bedouins perhaps?"

"Yes," James said with a huge smile accentuated by gleaming white teeth, "on my father's side. The men in my mother's family were all pearl divers."

I followed along, one step behind my travel mate and two steps ahead of the stevedore pushing the heavy cart laden with our four large trunks, once again, amazed at the depth of my friend's worldly knowledge and ease of connecting almost immediately with nearly anyone at any time.

"Ah, here we are gentlemen, the Victorian Suite," James said as he unlocked the door to our cabin, stepped inside to hold the door open for us and the stevedore and handed me a set of keys. I noticed the stateroom and the keys were not numbered; the cabin being identified by a brass nameplate as "The Victorian" and the keys likewise marked with a matching heavy brass key tag. As the stevedore began to unload the trunks from the handcart, James showed us around our luxurious living room and slid open the glass doors leading out onto our private balcony. "I'm sure you will be most comfortable here, The Victorian is one of our finest luxury cabins. I will be delighted to serve you tea or coffee each morning out here on your deck if you wish. Most first-class passengers enjoy taking their meals in one of our five restaurants, located on this floor or on the two levels above us; however, room service is also available 24-hours a day; just ring the bell there by the front door. Please, allow me to show you to your separate bedrooms, each with private bathrooms, walk-in closets and two large portholes to enjoy the ocean views during our voyage."

"Very nice," said I as I thought back to my time aboard the smelly hospital ship HMS Orontes and compared that memory to the opulence of our two staterooms, each decorated with a large bouquet of fresh cut flowers in a cut-glass crystal vase.

"As you can see," James said as he flipped on a switch in the bathroom, "each of your suites has electricity and running water."

"I'll take this room," Sherlock Holmes announced, "If it is alright with you of course, Dr. Watson."

"Certainly," said I, unable to discern any distinction between the two luxurious bedroom suites.

"Thank you, James, I'm sure we will be most comfortable and I will be looking forward to becoming better acquainted with you during our crossing," Sherlock Holmes said, as he walked our porter to the door and shook hands, slipping another tip to James.

James did not open his hand to look down at the second gold coin Sherlock Holmes had pressed into his palm, but I suspect the weight of the large gold coin may be what drew another wide smile from our porter as he was leaving. Sherlock Holmes then turned his attention to our stevedore, "These three trunks go in my room there," he said politely. "Dr. Watson's single trunk you can place in his room over here," Sherlock Holmes said.

I took a seat on the sofa in the living room to wait as Sherlock Holmes finished directing the stevedore where to place our steamer trunks in our respective bedrooms. When they finished and returned to the living room, Sherlock Holmes asked the man, "Were you able to confirm the wooden crate containing the 65-pound fire bell was loaded aboard with us this morning?"

"Yes sir," the stevedore replied, "I picked it up myself, at the Whitechapel Bell Foundry noon yesterday, just like you asked, and personally stowed it aboard the cargo hold of this ship first thing this morning."

"Very good," Sherlock Holmes replied, as he handed the man a large stack of folded currency. "Will this cover the payment for your shipping services, along with your tip?"

"Yes sir," the man said, as he counted the money he had been handed, then added with a smile, "You are most generous."

Sherlock Holmes then handed the stevedore an additional Two Pounds gold sovereign, along with his business card, and said, "You will receive another of these every time you notify me through this address, confidentially, of any future orders being shipped from the Whitechapel Bell Foundry addressed to the Cripple Creek Fire Department in the U.S. state of Colorado."

"I will be certain to let you know Mr. Holmes," the stevedore said as he stuffed the money and business card in his pocket and commented as he was leaving, "But I fail to see how anyone has such an interest in fire bells."

"Well," Sherlock replied as he held the door open for the stevedore, "one can never put too much emphasis on the value of fire safety."

Once we were alone I handed one of the two cabin door keys to my friend and asked, "Would you care to join me for a stroll about the ship and perhaps we can watch from the starboard deck as we separate from the dock and get underway?"

"That sounds delightful," Sherlock Holmes said, as he opened the cabin door, "lead the way my good man."

We strolled casually around the upper decks, making small talk with a few of the other first-class passengers. We watched from the railing as the ship's officers shouted orders to the dock hands on the pier below, casting off the lines and preparing the massive seagoing vessel to get underway. Sherlock Holmes wanted to see where the first-class lifeboats were stowed, a wise precaution anytime one sets out to sea. After that we stood among the other passengers leaning against the solid railing on the starboard side of the ship and watched as passengers waived merrily at their family and friends below. A loud blare of the ship's horn prompted shouts from the passengers and spectators alike, as colorful paper streamers fluttered down from the ship to the throngs of people below on the crowded pier.

Three tugboats pushed us away from the pier and guided us toward the open waters of the Atlantic Ocean. I stood clinging to the railing; all the while wondering if this might have been the very spot where Sherlock Holmes' predecessor, 002, may have stood to watch the English coast disappear into the distance.

In a low voice, so as not to be overheard by the handful of passengers who still lingered on deck, I said to Sherlock Holmes standing next to me, "Now that we are underway will you attempt to locate the wooden crate containing the fire bell in the cargo hold below? I can imagine you would want to confirm it was indeed cast with 65 pounds of gold and not of brass."

"It is tempting, to be sure," Sherlock Holmes said, as he glanced back toward the rear of the ship where the freight cargo had been brought on board. "However, I suspect that crate is more than likely under the watchful eye of some menacing agent. A previous gold bell could very well have been the cheese that drew 002 into a deadly trap. Besides, we have the benefit of knowing where the golden bell is headed, to the Greatest Gold Camp on Earth."

I watched as a school of dolphins rode beside us in our wake, very much at home in the icy waters of the Atlantic. "Brrr," said I, as a cold breeze made me shiver, "it has gotten considerably colder out here on deck now we're underway. I think that I shall retire to our cabin to unpack and perhaps ring James for a spot of tea. Care to join me?"

"No, thank you anyway," Sherlock Holmes replied as he turned up the collar on his top coat. "I think I shall wander around a bit to see what I might see and possibly learn more about whom and perhaps what is aboard this ship."

I watched my friend descend the stairwell leading toward the lower decks and felt another shiver run up my spine; though I did not know if it were from the cold in the air or the danger lurking about deep within the hull of this massive oceangoing vessel.

Chapter 4

March 2nd, 1896 5:30pm

RMS Republic, Twenty Miles off the Coast of Greenland

IT WAS OUR FIFTH NIGHT AT SEA and I was in my bedroom dressing for dinner when I heard Sherlock Holmes moving about in our adjoining sitting room. "Nice of Captain Smith to invite us to dine at his table this evening," said I as I tied my black bowtie. I checked myself in my bedroom mirror and straightened the tails on my tuxedo.

"It was," Sherlock Holmes replied as I stepped out of my bedroom to find my friend not wearing his tux; instead he was dressed in a tattered plaid shirt, patched trousers and a floppy knit cap. Stunned to see how sloppily my friend was attired, I stopped dead in my tracks and found myself utterly speechless in seeing his unshaven and rather slovenly appearance.

"I regret I won't be able to join you for dinner at the Captain's table this evening," he said as he tied a dirty red bandanna around his neck and answered the knock upon our cabin door.

"Ah, good evening James," I heard Sherlock Holmes say as he held the door open for our porter, James Mercier, to enter.

I nearly didn't recognize our porter, James, for oddly enough he was not wearing his white uniform; instead, he was dressed in ordinary street clothes and had a white towel draped around his neck. In his hand he carried a tin bucket; which I noticed to be empty except for a single large yellow sponge.

"Were you able to extend my apologies to Captain Smith for my not being able to join him at his table for dinner this evening?" Sherlock Holmes asked of James.

"Indeed I was and I was able to locate a suitable replacement," James replied, as he stepped inside and closed the door behind him, before he continued. "As luck would have it, Dr. Watson, there is another author aboard, perhaps you've heard of him, a Mr. Rudyard Kipling?"

"Rudyard Kipling!" said I in amazement. "Who hasn't heard of Rudyard Kipling, the best-selling author of *The Jungle Book*? I had heard he was making a world tour promoting his most recent bestseller, but did not know he was aboard our ship. I shall very much look forward to meeting him over dinner this evening, although I must confess my short stories of my friend here pale in comparison to Rudyard Kipling's fabulous contributions to English literature."

"I'm sure more of a reflection on my lack of talent as a consulting detective than your talents as a writer," Sherlock Holmes said with a mischievous grin.

I watched as Sherlock Holmes pulled on a tattered coat and prepared to leave with James. "Unless I miss my mark," said I, "it would appear you two might be headed to a boxing match?"

"You are most perceptive, Dr. Watson," Sherlock Holmes replied, "James informed me late this afternoon of a boxing match below deck in third-class where an Irish boxer from the States, fighting under the name the Boston Strong Boy, is taking on all bare-knuckle challengers. Naturally, I wanted to avail myself of this unique opportunity to sharpen my skills as a pugilist."

"I see," said I, as I watched my friend and our porter preparing to take their leave. "One moment please, before you go," I asked, as I retired to my bedroom for half a minute and returned shortly with four Two Pound Gold Sovereigns which I pressed into James's hand.

"I cannot accept this, Dr. Watson," James said as he looked down at the gold coins in the palm of his hand and explained, "Mr. Holmes has been more than generous with his gratuities."

"Oh, this is not a tip," I said, "It is a wager. Two gold sovereigns for me and two for you; I should like to wager on my friend here beating the Boston Strong Boy, although you are free to bet on whomever you choose."

"Thank you, Dr. Watson, while I have only known Sherlock Holmes five days now, and don't profess to know much about the sport of boxing," James replied as he slid the coins into the front pocket of his trousers, "I do know enough not to bet against someone with the strength of character and determination as I see in the face of Mr. Holmes."

"I do hope you enjoy dinner at the Captain's table this evening," Sherlock Holmes said as he straightened my bowtie, "and please extend my sincere regrets to our Captain Smith and Rudyard Kipling."

Same Day 6:10pm
Captain's Table, First-class Dining Room, RMS Republic

When I arrived for dinner I was escorted to the Captain's table by the maître d' dressed in a tailored black tuxedo every bit as nice as the new one I was wearing; which cost me a small fortune on Savile Row in London. The maître d' introduced me to the captain of our luxurious ship, 46-year-old Captain Edward John Smith, himself wearing his formal Captain's uniform adorned with a chest full of shining medals. Seeing as I was the last of his seven dinner guests to arrive at his table I felt an apology was in order.

"I am sorry in arriving a few minutes late for dinner, Captain Smith," said I, then added, "I am embarrassed to admit this but I got turned around again coming out of my cabin and got lost on your titanic ship."

"Please don't feel bad my dear Dr. Watson," Captain Smith said as he stood and shook my hand enthusiastically, "happens to me all the time!"

Everyone, including Captain Smith, roared with laughter. I felt the genuine warmth of his hospitality, putting me immediately at ease at his table. As I slipped into my tall-backed chair, across from the Captain, I glanced around the lavishly-set round dining table as he proceeded to introduce me to the other elegantly dressed passengers who too had been extended the honor of dining at the Captain's table this evening.

"Lady, and gentlemen," the Captain said, as he tapped his sterling silver spoon lightly against the crystal wine glass to the right of his china place setting, "may I introduce Dr. John H. Watson from London." The other guests smiled and nodded politely as Captain Smith continued, "Dr. Watson the gentleman on your right is Lieutenant Colonel Arthur Godfrey Peuchen."

"Pleasure to meet you Dr. Watson," Colonel Peuchen said as he shook my hand firmly. In glancing down at the inscription engraved on a medal worn on his red mess jacket, I read, "The Queen's Own Rifles of Canada - Established 1860."

Captain Smith continued, "Next to Colonel Peuchen are Mr. and Mrs. Andrew Carnegie." I nodded politely to Mr. and Mrs. Carnegie; thinking this truly is the Millionaires Ship.

"Please call me Louise," Mrs. Carnegie said with a pleasant smile.

"To my right here is Mr. Karl Friedrich Benz, an automotive engineer from Germany," Captain Smith said and then continued, "To his right is Mr. Samuel Pierpont Langley, Secretary of the

Smithsonian Institution in Washington, D.C., and lastly, it is my pleasure to make your acquaintance to the man seated on your left, a fellow author you may have read once or twice, Rudyard Kipling."

I shook hands with Rudyard Kipling, one of the best known authors of our time, and said sincerely, "It is an honor for me to meet all you this evening; especially you, Mr. Kipling, for I have been a fan of yours for some many years."

"That is very kind of you, Dr. Watson," Rudyard Kipling said. "I have read several of your fascinating short stories, chronicling your adventures with who many people claim to be the world's greatest consulting detective."

I nearly blushed in hearing this compliment about my writings coming from such an accomplished author as Rudyard Kipling; then I reminded myself it was not my writing deserving of his high praise; but the accomplishments of my most unique friend Sherlock Holmes.

Rudyard Kipling retrieved a Champagne bottle from a sterling ice bucket and said, "Care to join us for a glass of Champagne?"

"I would indeed," said I while taking note of the three other ice buckets each icing down three other opened bottles of Champagne. The immaculate table was set with beautiful white china plates bearing the red banner and white star logo of the White Star Line. Rows of gleaming silverware were arranged on both sides and above our dinner plates, each set upon a rich white cloth tablecloth with matching white cloth napkins. I placed my napkin in my lap and glanced down at my flatware reminding myself to start from the outside and work my way in toward the plate during the different courses.

Colonel Peuchen retrieved another bottle of Champagne from an ice bucket, topped off Mr. Carnegie's glass, and then his own, before reading from the gold label aloud, "Champagne

Krug, Makers of the World's Finest Champagne Since 1843, an excellent choice, thank you, Mr. and Mrs. Carnegie, here's to your health."

"Our pleasure," Mr. Carnegie said as we each held up our sparkling glasses to toast the Scottish-American industrialist who had become one of the richest men in America.

Colonel Peuchen leaned over toward me and whispered, "At twenty-four hundred dollars a bottle, as you can imagine, we don't drink a lot of this with the Queen's Own back home in Canada."

Doing the math in my head, I couldn't help but being astonished that among the eight of us we would be consuming $9,600 in Champagne with oysters served on-the-half shell, caviar and other assorted appetizers, all before dinner. I sipped my Champagne ever so lightly, for I was confident red and white wines would be served with dinner, followed no doubt by brandy or cognac or both during dessert followed yet by expensive cigars; most likely Cuban. The cost of this dinner would no doubt exceed my annual income. In any event I was determined to savor every sip of Champagne and not become lightheaded during what I was confident would become a very engaging dinner conversation certain to flow well into the evening.

"Before you joined us, Dr. Watson," Karl Benz commented, "Mr. Langley here was telling us how he believes man will fly before the end of this century."

"Tis true," Samuel Langley said, as he slurped a spoonful of the lobster bisque, then added. "If not before the end of this century, I have no doubts man is destined to fly within a few years into the dawn of the twentieth-century. Even within the next ninety days my team and I intend to launch the fifth unpiloted 25-pound model of an aeroplane off a boat out on the Potomac River. By our calculations it will fly ten times further than any previously demonstrated heavier-than-air flying machine."

"In a letter I received from Theodore Roosevelt," Rudyard Kipling said, cracking open a king crab leg, "my friend expressed every confidence in you and your team at the Smithsonian, Mr. Langley."

"That's very kind to hear," Mr. Langley replied, adding, "if man does take to the air, as I predict he will, if not in my lifetime, certainly in yours, Mr. Kipling, it will be due to the innovative advancements in aviation that will come not from the Smithsonian Institute or any other institution, but from the most unlikely of men."

"Who do you have your eyes on, Mr. Langley?" Karl Benz asked.

"Well, I am not at liberty to disclose any specific details, but I have been rather impressed with the Bishop's boys, two young bicycle mechanics from Ohio," Samuel Langley replied, then changed the subject, "But please share with us, Mr. Benz, what you can of your outlook for the burgeoning automotive industry."

"I have been following closely the direction of my new Board of Directors at Benz & Cie who have been encouraging us to build a less expensive automobile, one suitable for mass production, which can be driven by nearly anyone, including women."

"Tell me, Mr. Benz, does your wife drive one of your Motorwagens?" Louise Carnegie asked.

"Yes, my Bertha is a very accomplished driver of automobiles. In fact, below deck at this very moment is an 1895 Benz Velo, she has driven extensively. It is one of the 134 automobiles we built in Mannheim last year; I intend to race this auto in the States next month against other automotive manufacturers."

"A sense of German engineering pride perhaps?" Captain Smith asked.

"Well there is that," Karl Benz confessed with a smile. "However, we at Benz believe auto racing is the surest path to achieving the many technological breakthroughs required to advance the automotive industry worldwide."

"That has certainly proven to be the case with our Royal Canadian Yacht Club," Colonel Peuchen said, as the wait staff cleared our salad dishes and prepared to serve our main course. "This year the Lincoln Park Yacht Club of Chicago challenged the RCYC to a series of match races. The winners receive a large cash prize, along with a splendid trophy presented by Tiffany & Company headquartered in New York City. However, what we have found to be even more valuable than cash prizes, magnificent sterling trophies or bragging rights, are the technological advancements accelerated through spirited competition, not to mention the refined skills acquired by all those involved in any racing event."

"Tell me, Colonel Peuchen, if your racing proceeds were to generate unimaginable wealth, and you had no heirs, what would you do with your money?" Mr. Carnegie asked.

"I cannot imagine ever being in such a position personally," Colonel Peuchen replied with a smile, "remember, as a yachtsman I am guided by two ever-present principles. First, a boat is defined as a hole in the water into which you endlessly pour money into and secondly, anyone who has ever owned a boat will forever be in want of a bigger one!"

"I can relate to that," Captain Smith said with a righteous laugh, and then held up a bottle of Bordeaux to ask, "More red wine anyone?"

"Yes, please," Rudyard Kipling said, raising his wine glass in accepting the Captain's invitation. "How about you, Dr. Watson, if your Sherlock Holmes short stories and novels were to generate enormous personal wealth, and you had no heirs, what would you do if you had the burden of unimaginable wealth?"

"Well, I don't, as of yet have any heirs," said I, "but the first thing that comes to my mind would be the establishment of hundreds of free public libraries across Great Britain and the United States."

"Don't forget about Canada!" Colonel Peuchen said with a laugh, raising his wine glass in another toast to Mr. and Mrs. Carnegie.

"Speaking of yacht racing," Samuel Langley said to Captain Smith, "Do you anticipate us setting a transatlantic crossing record on this cruise?"

"We very well may do so," Captain Smith said with a smile. "With our two twin screws the RMS Republic is capable of generating speeds of up to 16 knots; depending upon the currents we may shave off nearly two hours by the time we reach the New York harbor."

"Are you not worried about colliding with another ship or an iceberg when traveling at those speeds in the northern Atlantic at night?" Colonel Peuchen asked.

"Heavens no," Captain Smith said dismissively, "we're not some flimsy yacht, like what you're use to racing. We have sharp lookouts positioned around the clock up in the crows' nests ever in search of another ocean liner. And we are equipped with the new Marconi wireless telegraph system and in case something catastrophic was to happen we can issue a distress signal using the newly established Morse code. With a tonnage in excess of 15,400 tons, I can assure you we don't have much to be concerned about even if we were to bump up against an iceberg."

Because he was sitting next to me, I was perhaps the only person at the table who may have sensed Colonel Peuchen's grimace at the Captain's casual reply.

"Are you traveling alone Dr. Watson?" Mrs. Carnegie asked, no doubt wanting to change the subject of a disaster at sea.

"Actually, I am traveling with my friend Sherlock Holmes," said I.

"Where is your friend, Sherlock Holmes, this evening?" Mr. Carnegie asked.

"One can only imagine," said I.

Same Day 7:20pm
Below Deck, Third-class Dining Hall, RMS Republic

THUMPT!
WAS THE SOUND of Sherlock Holmes' sweat-drenched body slamming against the dirty dining room floor during what appeared to be a very one-sided boxing match. Sensing the end was near, the raucous crowd rose to their feet and cheered with excitement on this the third time Sherlock Holmes had been knocked down. James Mercier pulled the blood-soaked towel from around his neck and started to throw it in between the boxers, signaling an end to this lopsided fight.

"Not so fast," Sherlock Holmes whispered softly to James, as he drew himself upright and spit blood into James's tin bucket. Then he turned and swung, with a wild right hook, at the bobbing head of his much larger opponent, fighting under the name; the Boston Strong Boy.

Another jab from the Boston's Strong Boy's right bare-knuckled fist to Sherlock Holmes's exposed ribcage, followed by a fierce left hook to the jaw, sent Sherlock Holmes sprawling across the floor once again.

"Twenty-to-one!" The ring announcer shouted, sensing this match would soon be at an end.

Sherlock Holmes looked out his one good eye at James and nodded his head, "I'll take that!" James shouted handing the fight promoter the four Two Pounds gold sovereigns.

"I'll be having some of that me-self!" another man shouted from across the dimly lit room.

Sherlock Holmes struggled to get to his feet, leaned against two sweaty intoxicated men in the crowd to get a look at the man wearing a pork pie hat who had placed the bet. Beneath the narrow rim of the hat Sherlock Holmes spotted a familiar face. It was none other than Robert Coyne's brother Stanley "Shady" Coyne, a former criminal from the streets of London who had on occasion acted as an informant and muscle for Sherlock Holmes.

Deciding his opponent was nearing his end the Boston Strong Boy closed in for a knock out. To his utter surprise, the smaller man caught him under the chin with a fierce upper cut, followed by a staccato of vicious blows to his body and head. The burly man staggered forward into a powerful right hook from Sherlock Holmes. The legs beneath the Boston Strong Boy wobbled and then gave way as the huge man crashed to the floor at the feet of Sherlock Holmes. The crowd went wild! Cheers went up from the few winners and boos erupted from the many losers.

Shady Coyne grabbed his winnings, tipped the short rim of his hat at Sherlock Holmes and headed toward the nearest exit.

James draped his bloodstained towel around Sherlock Holmes' neck, collected the prize money and led his bloodied fighter toward the stairwell that would eventually return them up to first-class. James had already coordinated their return with several of his other porter friends who would have otherwise blocked the entry of such an unsightly pair ascending the stairs to the first-class section of the ship.

Same Day - 10:20pm
Victorian Suite, RMS Republic

I UNLOCKED THE DOOR to our cabin with my heavy brass key and heard low voices coming from outside on our deck. Walking through our front room I picked up an empty bottle of Champagne from a sterling silver ice bucket and read the familiar gold label; 'Krug, Makers of the World's Finest Champagne Since 1843'. I walked through the sliding glass doors out onto our darkened deck to find Sherlock Holmes and James Mercier sitting comfortably in the two deck chairs smoking cigars. Another bottle of Krug Champagne was turned upside down in a tin bucket near the deck railing. By the faint light of the waning moon I could make out Sherlock Holmes was nursing a black eye.

"I trust you two gentlemen had a memorable evening," said I as I lifted the second bottle of Champagne from the tin bucket, confirming it too was empty.

"I fear we may have drunk all the Champagne," Sherlock Holmes said, then added as he held up a fresh cigar. "But, we saved you one of these."

I held the expensive hand-rolled Cuban cigar beneath my nose and inhaled deeply. "Ah, Cohibas," said I without needing to read the brand name printed boldly on the label. "I just finished two of these with brandy after dinner, so I will save this one for tomorrow." Looking at the empty Champagne bottle in my hand and the other in the tin bucket, I said, "I'm not sure how expensive cigars and $4,800 worth of Champagne will look on my expense report when we get back to London."

James stood up from the thickly-padded deck chair, stretched his arms above his head and then walked over to lean against the railing next to me. "I don't suspect that will be a much of a problem, Dr. Watson," said he as he picked up the empty bottle from the blood-spattered tin bucket and held the bottle out over the railing. "The trouble, you see, with transporting expensive bottles of liquor at sea," said he as he let the bottle slip gently from his hand into the sea below and continued, "is one can never account for breakage."

"I can see where that would present a problem," said I as I followed suit and tossed the second Champagne bottle over the railing into the dark rolling waves below.

"And when it comes to keeping track of cigars," James said, taking a last puff on his cigar before flipping the butt into the sea below, "well, they are inventoried by the case."

"Thank you for the tip and the fine cigar," said I as I held the Cohibas up to my nose for another whiff of the strong tobacco and then slipped the expensive cigar into my coat pocket.

"I think I best turn in gentlemen, I bid you both a pleasant evening," James said, adding as he headed back inside. "Oh, Dr. Watson, you will find your winnings on your dresser. My family and I sincerely appreciated you staking our twenty-to-one wagers on the boxing match this evening, a fight the passengers in third-class will no doubt be talking about for the rest of this transatlantic crossing."

"Good night, James," said I, as I looked at Sherlock Holmes holding a wet towel with ice up against his swollen black eye. "Would you like me to take a look at that?"

He pulled the towel away and I inspected the thin cut across his brow to confirm he did not need stitches. "I suspect you will live but you may want to keep ice on that until the swelling goes down."

"Please join me won't you?" Sherlock Holmes said in beckoning me to take a seat in the empty deck chair beside him, "there is a matter I would like to discuss."

"Very well," said I as I sat and waited patiently for him to say what was on his mind.

After a few minutes organizing his thoughts he began quietly, "I was gazing up at the stars while giving considerable thought to our discussion as we were departing from the port of Liverpool, about me avoiding the temptation to inspect the Cripple Creek fire bell in the cargo hold below; wanting to confirm it was indeed cast of gold. You may recall my saying at the time that a similar 65-pound fire bell may have been the cheese that drew 002 into a deadly trap?"

"I do recall our discussion," said I, adding, "And I specifically recall being relieved when you declared there was no need for you to risk going into the bowels of this massive vessel to search for and inspect the bell. I hasten to ask, have you changed your position?"

"Tomorrow night we will cross the threshold marking the midpoint of our journey to the States and yet we are no closer to solving the murder of the last man to die here on this ship in Her Majesty's Secret Service."

"You believe 002 is dead then?"

"Yes, and his lifeless body cast into the sea."

"What do you propose?"

"I have asked James to surreptitiously borrow a cargo manifest indicating where the wooden crate containing the Cripple Creek fire bell is stowed in the cargo hold below deck. Then, tomorrow night, and here is where I shall require your assistance, we will order room service and dine in our cabin. Afterwards, we will turn out our cabin lights, well before 10:30pm, appearing as if to turn in for the night. Then at precisely 11:15pm, I intend to sneak below under the cover of darkness, locate said crate, extract a slight sliver from the inside of the fire bell and return with it to our cabin for chemical testing purposes."

"How will you leave our cabin without being seen?"

"The portal windows in our bedrooms are large enough for a man to squeeze through; I know as I have done this every night since we came onboard. Located two levels directly below my bedroom window are three first-class port side lifeboats suspended on an apparatus designed to lower the lifeboats into open sea in case of an emergency."

"I wondered why you had selected that bedroom over the one you offered to me," said I, thinking back to when James first showed us around our cabin.

Sherlock Holmes then turned to look at me with his one good eye to make sure I was following his instructions, "In the top left drawer of my dresser you will find a 30-foot rope ladder that when lowered will allow us to descend two levels to reach the lifeboats below."

"What do you need me to do?"

"I will leave at precisely 11:15pm and you at 11:45pm, lowering yourself down the rope ladder, with your service revolver and ammunition secured in your pocket, and then you will conceal yourself under the tarp at the stern of the middle lifeboat."

"And then?"

"Unless I have misread our assassin he will wait to make certain it is the Cripple Creek fire bell I have taken an interest in and in not wanting to leave a blood trail near where the golden bell is secured, he will wait to attack a considerable distance away from where the gold bell is now stowed. I expect he will follow me until he sees an opening to attack, one that provides him easy access to the open sea where he will plan to toss my body overboard. In our deadly game tomorrow night, I will be the cheese and will lead him to you, while you lay waiting to spring the trap near the stern of the middle lifeboat."

"I will be waiting, with my revolver in hand, as you have instructed, but if you are not back by midnight I will come looking for you."

"If you have to use your revolver, aim for the lower extremities, I very much want this Fritz or whoever this assassin is taken alive. I need to interrogate him to confirm the identity of our English doctor and whoever that man works for at the top of this criminal enterprise."

"Who do you suspect this criminal mastermind to be?" asked I.

"The mastermind who protects nearly all of England's criminals in exchange for their obedience and a share of their ill-gotten gains."

"Professor Moriarty?"

"None other," Sherlock Holmes whispered, having vowed to never speak the name of his archrival aloud.

"Remember, the tricky part about placing the cheese in a mousetrap," said I; "is to make sure you yourself don't get caught."

"Indeed, a most deadly game of cat and mouse is afoot," Sherlock Holmes said, and then whispered assuredly, "Tomorrow night, before the stroke of midnight, we shall use a golden bell to catch us a rat; a deadly assassin who killed a British secret agent, a brave man who lost his life nobly in the service of our Queen and Country. His death is one that shall be avenged."

March 3rd, 1896 11:58pm
Starboard First-class Lifeboats, RMS Republic

THE ASSASSIN ATTACKED out of the dark on our sixth night at sea. He was dressed all in black and seemed to materialize out of the shadows. Sherlock Holmes must have felt his presence for I noticed my friend had quickened his pace considerably before turning around at the stern of the very lifeboat in which I was concealed, to face his attacker. The assassin pounced upon my friend with cat-like quickness. I threw back the tarp over my head, stood up and pointed my revolver at the thin man attempting to kill my best friend Sherlock Holmes. The only light was from a dim red emergency lantern above the lifeboat; I had no shot, for the two men were locked in mortal hand-to-hand combat.

I saw the flash of the assassin's knife blade and shouted, "Fritz!" The assassin, surprised to see me standing in the small boat suspended a few feet above him, was distracted for but an instant, which was all the time Sherlock Holmes needed to grab his knife by the blade. Although both men were struggling to control the knife, Sherlock Holmes managed to pivot his body away from the other man giving me a shot. POW! The moment my gun went off the assassin released his grip on the knife, spun around and in an instant had jumped over the railing.

"I didn't hear a splash," said I as I climbed down from the lifeboat and raced to the railing where Sherlock Holmes was standing looking overboard.

"You won't" said Sherlock Holmes holding up a slackened rope which had been tied to the railing, the other end flapping in the wind below. "I should have anticipated this," Sherlock Holmes said admonishing himself aloud for allowing his would-be assassin to escape.

"How could you possibly have known?"

"Since the location for the attack was one of his choosing, I should have anticipated he would have planned for a secondary escape route to avoid being captured."

"Sorry I missed him, he was so exceedingly thin there wasn't much of him to take aim at," said I as I searched the waves below hoping to see the body of a dead man floating away into the darkness.

"You didn't miss," Sherlock Holmes said, pointing to the fresh bloodstains on the deck where he and the assassin had been struggling.

"Perhaps I should have aimed a little higher."

"You did exactly as I had asked you to do, aim for the lower extremities, and you saved my life in doing so. It is unfortunate my predecessor did not have a Boswell, such as yourself, at his side, for this is quite possibly the very spot where he met his death."

"Shall we notify the Captain so he can order the ship searched for this wounded man?"

"No, it would be nearly impossible to find a man hiding in the depths of this behemoth vessel; besides, we have the benefit of knowing when and where he will surface again."

"When a 65-pound golden bell is delivered to the Cripple Creek Fire Department?"

"Precisely," Sherlock Holmes said as he held the knife up by the blade to the dim red light cast down by the emergency lantern pointing the way to the lifeboats where we stood, "let us retire to our cabin to see if our man was good enough to leave us the gift of his fingerprints on the handle of this knife."

"Look, you are bleeding, again!" said I as I saw a trickle of blood running down from his gloved hand, across his wrist and into his shirt sleeve.

"I am aware of that fact," Sherlock Holmes said as we walked down the deck away from the lifeboats. "The first rule of knife fighting is to accept the fact that you will be cut; once you have accepted that being cut is a given, it takes away the fear and you can concentrate upon disarming or killing your opponent."

As we started up the nearest stairwell, a sailor came running toward us carrying a pistol in one hand and an electric torch in the other, "Did either of you hear a gunshot a moment ago?"

"We did see two young boys shooting off pop-bottle rockets," Sherlock Holmes said as the sailor ran past us headed toward the lifeboats.

"At times you can be a most convincing liar," said I as we walked down the first-class hallway leading to the Victorian Stateroom.

"It wasn't a lie, which is what makes it convincing," Sherlock Holmes replied as I unlocked our cabin door with my brass key. "As you may recall, two nights ago we did observe two young boys shooting off pop-bottle rockets into the open sea. I simply did not elaborate on when it was that we witnessed this activity."

"I see," said I, as I closed and locked our cabin door behind us. "Now, come with me into my bathroom and remove your glove over my sink, I don't want to have to clean up the floor after you."

"You are too kind," Sherlock Holmes said, as he set the assassin's knife aside on the white marble sink in my bathroom and gingerly peeled off his blood-soaked glove.

I examined the deep knife wound to the palm of his hand, "This is rather deep and is going to require several stitches. Run the cold water over it and wait here as I retrieve my medical bag from my closet."

"If you insist, oh, and doctor?"

"Yes?"

"If you don't mind could you please retrieve my chemical bag from my closest?"

"Certainly," said I. When I returned to my bathroom, I saw he was examining the tiny sliver of gold he had extracted from the inside of the fire bell under the light above the marble sink.

"Within the hour we shall know for certain if this is indeed a bell made of gold, once you have finished applying your skills in patching me up and I am free to conduct my chemical test. From my initial observations I do believe we are dealing with a genuine pure gold fire bell."

"Do try to avoid getting any of your chemicals into your wound," said I as I opened a bottle of whiskey I had retrieved from our liquor cabinet to cleanse his open wound and my needle. I held his hand over the sink and poured the whisky directly over his open wound.

"Wait!" Sherlock Holmes exclaimed as he snatched the bottle from my hand.

"I know this must hurt," said I sympathetically, "but I really must sanitize your cut."

After holding the bottle up to the bathroom light for an instant Sherlock Holmes brought the whisky bottle to his lips and drank down two huge gulps and said, "This is 24-year-old Macallan Single Malt Whiskey man! James brought it to our liquor cabinet just yesterday and now I must endure the most painful part of this whole ordeal in watching you pour this liquid gold down the sink!"

I wrestled the whisky bottle from his grip, swallowed a large gulp myself and then poured a generous amount over his hand again along with a dowsing over my needle and thread. "Now, do try to hold still for just a minute or two."

Sherlock Holmes took another swallow from the bottle and said, "The only comfort in any of this is in knowing that somewhere in the depths of this seagoing behemoth lies an assassin possibly having to tend to his own gunshot wound; hopefully with a far more inferior liquid pain reliever and far less competent medical provider."

"Thank you, I will send you my bill in the morning, now hold still, I am about to finish tying a tidy little knot here at the end of the thread," said I as Sherlock Holmes winced in pain and I took another swig from his bottle.

March 7th, 1896 2pm
New York City, U.S.A.

As we sailed into the New York Harbor and passed by the patina-encrusted green Statue of Liberty, I found Sherlock

Holmes topside leaning against the starboard railing. "There she is my good Doctor," said he, pointing with his walking stick to Lady Liberty holding a golden torch above her head. "A gift from the French to the Americans, intended to serve as a symbol of freedom, welcoming immigrants from around the world for the last decade."

"Yes, it is quite impressive, especially for the French," said I as we passed beyond Ellis Island. "How is your hand feeling this morning?"

"Oh, I'm hoping it will mend well enough; although I did detect a strong odor of alcohol upon the breath of my physician as he tended my wound."

"It is hard to find good medical care when traveling abroad," said I as I leaned against the railing to watch a pod of dolphins below escorting the RMS Republic into the harbor.

"I do have a small request," Sherlock Holmes said.

"Yes?"

"Once we arrive in the city would you be so kind as to see if you can find an international bank where you might make an even numbered withdrawal from our account?"

"I will; yes, it would be good of us to notify the PM and thus the Queen we have arrived stateside safely and that everything is proceeding as well as can be expected," said I as I looked down at the bandage wrapped around my friend's hand. "I recommend you not try to lift anything too heavy with that hand for a few days, I don't want to have to stitch you up again if it can be avoided."

"I wouldn't want to be a bother," he said with a crooked smile upon his face. "Were you able to secure suitable accommodations for us in the city," he asked.

"I was. I spoke with Andrew Carnegie at breakfast this morning and he recommended a hotel in Manhattan. He suggested an upper floor suite overlooking a park of sorts. He even went so far as to send a telegraph ahead on our behalf to make reservations."

"That was very thoughtful of him," Sherlock Holmes replied. "I said our farewells to third mate Joel Ziegler and our able porter James earlier this morning and paid them both sufficiently to ensure our four steamer trunks are sent on to our hotel once we dock."

"Very well," said I, "I have a few things yet to retrieve from our cabin so I'll let James know which hotel to have our baggage delivered."

"What is the name of the hotel?"

"It is called the Waldorf Astoria, it is on Fifth Avenue."

"Did Mr. Carnegie happen to recommend a nice restaurant for dinner this evening?"

"He did; a newer place called Delmonico's. It, like our hotel, was built within the past three years and is also conveniently located on Fifth Avenue, in Midtown, Manhattan. Mr. Carnegie also offered to make reservations for us there as well."

"Excellent. Have you heard back from your telegram inviting Mark Twain to dine with us this evening at dinner?"

"In fact I have," said I, "Mr. Twain said in his reply he would be delighted to join us for dinner this evening and said he would meet us at Delmonico's at 7:30pm."

"Excellent. Looks as if we'll be docking soon," said I, "are you prepared to go ashore?"

"I am. I shall meet you at the ramps," Sherlock Holmes said.

As we stepped onto the concrete pier I relished the feel beneath my feet from being on solid ground again. We watched as hundreds of excited passengers disembarked from the ship rushing into the waiting arms of family and friends. As I started forward Sherlock Holmes pulled me back by the arm to avoid my being trampled over by a group of a half dozen young people, each carrying a single piece of carry-on luggage. As they rushed passed one familiar looking teenage girl with red hair glanced back over her shoulder and shouted gleefully, "Sorry! Again!"

"Welcome to America, Dr. Watson," said Sherlock Holmes.

Chapter 5

March 7th, 1896 7:30pm

Corner of Fifth Avenue and 44th Street, New York City

The luxurious Waldorf Astoria was all Mr. Carnegie said it would be and then some. After unpacking and freshening up a bit, Sherlock Holmes and I walked down Fifth Avenue to Delmonico's where the maître d' was expecting us.

"Your dinner guest has already been seated," said he, as I tipped him with a crisp U.S. twenty dollar bill that I had received three hours previous when I stopped by to make an even numbered withdrawal from the Bank of the Manhattan Company. I was yet unaccustomed to making the monetary conversions from British pounds to US dollars in my head and had no idea if a twenty dollar tip was customary. However, judging from the smile on his face I surmised the gratuity to be more than ample.

As we neared the back of the elegant restaurant we could hear the raucous laughter of Delmonico's well-dressed wait staff and diners clustered around one table where a man in his mid-sixties sat smoking a cigar. From his white suit, bushy white moustache and unkempt hair the man could only be the world acclaimed humorous; Mark Twain.

"Gentlemen," Mark Twain said as he stood to greet us with an outstretched hand and twinkle in his eye, "Welcome to America!"

"Thank you," Sherlock Holmes said as he shook Mark Twain's hand, "So good of you to come meet us this evening for dinner, especially on such short notice."

"My pleasure, I heard so much about your exploits from your brother Mycroft, when I spoke at the Savage Club a few months back." Then he turned to shake hands with me and said, "And thank you, Dr. Watson, for your telegram this morning. It is indeed an honor for me to meet a fellow author, especially one whose characters have become so well known around the world."

"The pleasure is all mine," I said to Mark Twain, adding, "Shall we be seated?"

"Was your wife not able to join us this evening?" Sherlock Holmes asked.

"Olivia and the girls left yesterday morning by train to visit her family in Elmira, that's in lower New York State. I have business here in the City for the next few days so the timing of your visit could not have been any better. Where are you staying?"

"Just down Fifth Avenue, at the Waldorf Astoria," Sherlock Holmes replied, adding, "It is very nice."

"I stayed there when it first opened," Mark Twain said and then added, "it used to be a nice hotel, but that proves nothing, I used to be a good boy."

I watched as a middle-aged man wearing a blue three-piece suit, white shirt and a yellow silk tie approached our table carrying three large menus.

"Ah, Lorenzo, my friend!" Mark Twain said loudly, as the tall dapper man with a black well-trimmed mustache stopped at our table, smiled and handed each of us a large menu. "May I introduce Mr. Sherlock Holmes and his intrepid companion Dr. John Watson?"

"Gentlemen, it is indeed a privilege to have you dine with us at Delmonico's this evening," Lorenzo Delmonico said.

"Lorenzo Delmonico, is the owner of this wonderful eatery," Mark Twain explained, then continued, "He has taken over the restaurant business from his uncles John and Peter Ticino, who came to America from Switzerland."

"What is this?" I asked, looking at the menu with an impressive list of dinner entrées.

"We at Delmonico's pride ourselves in being the first restaurant to offer dinner served a la carte as opposed to table d'hôtel," Lorenzo explained, and then he handed me a second smaller menu, before continuing, "and we are also the first restaurant to offer a separate wine list."

I picked up the wine list, featuring what appeared to be 30-40 selections, in one hand and glanced at the open menu in the other and commented, "With so many choices I am not sure where to begin."

"I highly recommend the Delmonico steak," Mark Twain said, handing his menu back to Lorenzo, adding, "Make mine medium-rare."

"I will have the same," Sherlock Holmes said, closing his menu, then adding as he looked at Mark Twain, "we came as visitors to a new land seeking your advice, we may as well begin with your dinner recommendation."

"I shall do the same," said I as I handed the large menu back to Lorenzo.

"Do you care to make a wine selection?" Lorenzo asked while offering the wine list to Mark Twain.

"No mystery there," Mark Twain said with a smile, "A bottle of your finest vino, a red if you please, Lorenzo."

"Excellent choices," Lorenzo said with a smile as he left our table and welcomed another pair of guests by name.

"The only way to keep your health," Mr. Twain said as he flipped the ash from the end of his cigar into a crystal ashtray, "is to eat what you don't want, drink what you don't like, and do what you'd rather not."

"Have you always wanted to be a writer, Mr. Twain?" I asked.

"No, not initially, you see I was born and bred along a bend in the Mississippi River," Mark Twain began, as he puffed on his cigar bringing it back to life before he continued, "and shared the common goal among all the young boys who were growing up at the time in my small hometown of Hannibal, Missouri, of wanting to one day become a riverboat pilot. Then the war came along and the boats stopped running."

"Did you serve in your military?" asked I.

"Briefly; I have always believed the institution of slavery to be abhorrent and when the war first broke out I felt compelled to enlist in the Union Army. My military service lasted but two weeks, for I found myself fatigued, brought on from the constant state of retreat. Then, in 1861, I began to realize there comes a time in every young man's life where he feels compelled to head off somewhere and dig up something; so I headed west to become a gold miner in the Territory of Nevada."

"Tell us about your experience in the gold fields," Sherlock Holmes asked casually, although I knew he was genuinely interested in learning what he could about the business of mining gold in the American West.

"Gold mining is a life filled with whiskey, fandangos and fist fights," Mark Twain explained.

"I can see where that lifestyle might appeal to some," said I as I looked across the table at Sherlock Holmes who refused to return my look.

"Do go on," Sherlock Holmes said, as a server arrived at our table with our dinner salads, followed by another waiter carrying a bottle of red wine. I watched as the second waiter poured a small sample into Mark Twain's wine glass, waited for him to taste the wine and nod his head in approval, before filling our wine glasses.

Mark Twain continued, "Like most gold miners, my partner and I found life owning a gold mine was one of hope, followed by desperation, followed by hope again, until the money eventually runs out. That's how I became a writer, Dr. Watson, out of desperation I took a job at $25 a week as a newspaper reporter in Carson and Virginia City; it was awful drudgery for a lazy man like me. As a reporter I saw the insides of many things; I learned that first you get the facts, and then you can distort them any way you please."

"That does seem to be common practice among most writers," Sherlock Holmes said as he glanced my way.

Mark Twain took a sip of wine and turned toward me to ask, "Tell me, Dr. Watson, I could use your advice as a fellow writer, people are constantly coming up to me asking how Tom Sawyer and Huck Finn are doing, completely unaware these two characters, of which I have written so much about, don't actually exist. When I tell them the truth, that these are but two fictional characters I created out of my own overactive imagination, they often walk away crestfallen and disappointed in me, almost as if I had killed off two of their beloved friends. The thing I wish to know, Dr. Watson, is it more ethical of me as an author to set these folks straight by confessing Tom Sawyer and Huckleberry Finn, whom so many people around the world have come to love, are but two fictional characters, created purely out of thin air, or is it better that I should allow them to remain content and live under the false assumption these two characters are indeed real people?"

"I can't imagine ever being in such a position myself, but I suppose there is little harm in allowing your readers to continue to believe your two characters are in fact real people," said I as I watched the efficient wait staff clear away our salad plates.

"Ah, here comes Lorenzo with our steaks," Mark Twain said as he held his cloth napkin up across the front of his chest. "You'll want to protect your clothes from the sizzle popping up from your steaks."

I held up my napkin as Mr. Twain demonstrated and watched as Lorenzo and two other waiters placed a large sizzling steak on the table in front of each of us. After Lorenzo and his assistants had returned to the kitchen we continued to hold our napkins between ourselves and the steaks until the hot splatters had subsided.

"They do smell wonderful," said I.

"I should have warned you, at Delmonico's you pay for both the steak and the sizzle," Mark Twain said.

After enjoying a delightful dinner and an unforgettable conversation filled with Mark Twain's wit and charm, we moved into the nearby lounge, found a secluded corner table and ordered brandy to enjoy with an expensive cigar.

"Tell me, Mr. Holmes," Mark Twain said, as he puffed on his cigar to get it going, "I don't suppose you and Dr. Watson here have traveled all the way across the Atlantic Ocean to talk about how I got my start as a writer. How Sir, may I be of service?"

"In two areas of interest," Sherlock Holmes replied, as he pulled a small 3x5 inch index card out of his inside coat pocket and handed it to Mark Twain.

"A partial latent fingerprint, double whorl, most unusual, should be identifiable," Mark Twain said as he studied the laminated card displaying the would-be assassin's fingerprint. "Did you lift this print yourself?"

"I did," Sherlock Holmes said.

"From what type of a surface?"

"The wooden handle of a jack knife."

"Thumbprint?"

"I believe so."

"Right-handed."

"It would appear."

"What chemical did you use?"

"Ninhydrin," Sherlock Holmes said, "as you may know it is a chemical that once applied is invisible to the naked eye in daylight; however, in the dark it fluoresces under ultraviolet or UV light, emitting a soft bluish light."

"I confess to not being familiar with ninhydrin," Mark Twain said as he wrote a note to himself on the back of an envelope with a fountain pen.

"Nor was I," Sherlock Holmes said then explained, "until a chance conversation last year at Oxford University with a German-English chemist, Siegfried Ruhemann, who happened to mention he had observed ninhydrin's reaction with amino acids. I suggested he consider using ninhydrin for the development of fingerprints since it is the amino acid being excreted from the pores of our skin between the ridges of a fingerprint that leaves behind this trace evidence."

"Ah, ninhydrin, I must give that a try sometime," Mark Twain said. "Thank you for sharing that technique."

"Certainly."

"You have an interest in finding whomever this fingerprint belongs to I suppose?"

"Indeed I do; he tried to kill me five nights ago aboard the RMS Republic. I suspect he may have killed another man on that very ship on its way here to the States."

"Do you have this suspected killer's name?" Mark Twain asked as he handed the fingerprint card back to my companion.

"I do not, he is using an alias," Sherlock Holmes explained, as he slid the card back into the inside pocket of his suit coat and continued, "and if I did have his name, as you well know, there is nothing to say he would not be using another alias while here in the States. Therein lies the problem and why I am here with you tonight, to propose a possible solution."

"How might I be of service?"

"I am aware of your strong support for the advancement of fingerprints as a forensic science."

"Yes, go on."

"I also understand you have some influence with the New York City Police Department."

"Yes, I suppose that is the case," Mark Twain said nodding his head in agreement, "I am very supportive of the use of fingerprints as a form of identification, including placing a criminal at the scene of a crime. And recently engaged in an hour long discussion with the President of the New York City Police Commissioners, Theodore Roosevelt, on that very subject."

"Was he supportive of this idea?" Sherlock Holmes asked.

"I believe so. Teddy's only been a Police Commissioner for two years now, but I think he is as sharp as a tack and has a bright political future ahead of him. The only thing I distinctly remember Teddy saying at the end of our conversation was, 'bully' – whatever that's supposed to mean – and then he slapped me on the back so hard I nearly spit my cigar across the room."

"In referring to the whorl fingerprint pattern on my fingerprint card, you obviously are familiar with the work of Sir Francis Galton published in 1892, where he described in detail his proposed classification system. I have been in communication with Sir Galton, Sir Edward Henry and others in Europe, concerning the adoption of what's being referred to as the Henry Classification System."

"I haven't read anything about this as of yet here in the States, but completely agree on the need to establish an international standard of some sort for fingerprint classification. How may I be of assistance?"

"With the sheer size of the New York City Police Department and Transit Authority, whichever system they adopt, the rest of the law enforcement agencies in the U.S. are sure to follow. The first favor I ask of you therefore, is, after an objective review of the data, if you should find the Henry Fingerprint Classification worthy of becoming the international standard, I ask you to consider using your influence with the New York Police Commissioners, including Theodore Roosevelt, to push for the adoption of the Henry Fingerprint Classification system?"

"Consider it done; however, I must tell you that it has been my finding that there is no distinctive criminal class, except of course for congress."

"And perhaps members of Parliament," said I.

"Ah, well said, Dr. Watson! And now, to your second favor?" Mark Twain asked.

"My colleague and I would very much appreciate the honor of you granting us a personal introduction to meet privately with Thomas Edison and then with Nikola Tesla, anytime in the next few days while we are here in New York City."

"Consider it done. I know both of these successful businessmen personally and will give them a call first thing in the morning to arrange your visit. I have always believed that if your job is to eat a frog, it's best to do it first thing in the morning. And if it's your job to eat two frogs, it's is best to eat the biggest one first. Can I reach you tomorrow at the Waldorf?"

"Yes, that would be perfect and thank you," Sherlock Holmes said as he finished the last of his brandy, "we are indebted to you for your support."

"I feel obliged to caution you both, if you are looking to invest your money in electrical technologies or to make your fortunes in the power industry, do not use me for an example. The only thing I know for certain is how to turn a large fortune into a smaller one."

"HA!" Sherlock Holmes laughed and then explained, "Not to worry, Mr. Twain, our mission is not for personal fame or fortune."

"While it is none of my business, so don't feel obligated to answer this question," Mark Twain said, "but I sensed ever since I read Dr. Watson's telegram that you would not be here in New York, nor would you have made this request to meet privately with Thomas Edison and Nikola Tesla, if there was not something of a global importance to your visit here to America."

"Confidentially, our purpose in requesting a meeting with these two American inventors, who are no doubt leading the world when it comes to the rapidly evolving science of electricity," Sherlock Holmes explained, "is to put to rest an apparent untruth that electrical generation can somehow turn baser metals into gold or vice versa."

"Alchemy?" Mark Twain asked, with raised eyebrows.

"We don't put much stock into this notion personally, that electricity can aid in the practice of alchemy," Sherlock Holmes explained, "However, there are powerful people in Great Britain who are most interested to learn the expert opinions of these two notable inventors here in the United States."

"I am certain your discussions with Tesla and Edison will put to rest any concerns your people back home may need to address," Mark Twain said as he stood to make his leave. "It has been my experience that a lie can travel half way around the world while the truth is putting on its shoes."

"Thank you," Sherlock Holmes said as he bid Mark Twain good night.

"It has been a privilege to meet you," said I, adding, "And I must thank you for all the wonderful books you have written and the unforgettable characters you have brought to life and given to the world. I wish you much continued success in all your writing endeavors."

"Thank you, Dr. Watson, and I wish you much continued success as you continue to chronical the important work of your most unique friend here," Mark Twain said as he shook my hand in farewell. "As for me, I intend to continue to write until my pen runs dry. Good night gentlemen."

March 8th, 1896 10:30am
Menlo Park, New Jersey

I WAS VERY MUCH LOOKING FORWARD to meeting the 49-year-old Wizard of Menlo Park, Thomas Edison, the holder of more than 400 U.S. patents, including the incandescent light bulb and the phonograph. We had taken the train from Grand Central Station in New York City to Menlo Park in Middlesex County, New Jersey, where Thomas Edison had built his home and research laboratory twenty years ago.

"It says here," said I, reading a magazine article to Sherlock Holmes, seated beside me in the hansom cab taking us to Menlo Park, "Thomas Edison claims his first major success was when Western Union paid him $10,000 for what he called the quadruplex telegraph. The profits were used to build his Menlo Park, the first institution built exclusively for the purpose of conducting technological innovation and improvement."

"It is much larger than I had anticipated," Sherlock Holmes said as he looked out the window of our cab at the sprawling complex.

"The article mentions how Menlo Park kept expanding until it occupied two full city blocks. The article quotes Thomas Edison in stating his intent was to 'have a stock of almost every conceivable material' and then the article goes on to claim the lab contains, 'eight thousand kinds of chemicals, every kind of screw made, every size of needle, every kind of cord or wire, hair of humans, horses, hogs, cows, rabbits, goats, minks, camels...silk in every texture, cocoons, various kinds of hoofs, shark's teeth, deer horns, tortoise shell...cork, resin, varnish and oil, ostrich feathers, a peacock's tail, amber, rubber, all ores...' and the list goes on and on."

"Sounds like heaven to me," Sherlock Holmes said; I looked over to see his eyes were closed and the expression on his face was that of him being in a dreamlike state. All too soon, I suspect for my friend, the carriage slowed to a halt at Menlo Park and my friend stirred out of his dream. When our driver opened the carriage door I paid the man and asked him to return to pick us up in three hours. We walked up the wide steps into the main office building and were soon being escorted by a young female assistant to a spacious laboratory located in a separate building where we met one of the most prolific inventors in America.

"Thank you for agreeing to meet with us, Mr. Edison," Sherlock Holmes said. "This is Dr. John Watson."

As we shook hands Thomas Edison said, "I was pleased to have received the call from my dear friend Mark Twain and I have been looking forward to meeting you, Dr. Watson, from my having a lifelong passion for reading and in meeting you, Mr. Holmes, as I understand it we share an unbridled passion for experimenting, especially with chemicals."

"We are delighted to meet you and were most fortunate to find you here at your lab," Sherlock Holmes said.

"I have been spending more time at my winter retreat, Seminole Lodge, in Fort Myers, Florida, which I purchased a few years back for my second wife Mina, her having found the winter months there much more tolerable than here in New Jersey. Come," Thomas Edison said, as he pulled on his heavy winter coat, "let me show you around Menlo."

As we walked in and out of the various buildings spread across the Menlo Park campus, he told us about the passing of his first wife Mary, in 1884, and how he married Mina, nineteen years his junior, two years later. Sherlock Holmes was most interested in watching the recording Thomas Edison had made on his Kinetoscope, of the 1894 Leonard-Cushing bout, consisting of six one-minute rounds. For two hours our conversations with Mr. Edison varied from his explaining why he opposed the gold standard to showing us his talking doll.

"You truly are a man ahead of your time," Sherlock Holmes said as a compliment.

Thomas Edison replied, "I have found that being ahead of your time is both a blessing and a curse. Take for instance, my idea for building a concrete house filled with concrete furniture; a foolish notation to most people, unless they happen to be living along the Florida coast watching a hurricane force wind rip the roof off their wooden framed house and deposit their expensive furniture two blocks away in some stranger's back yard pool. Naysayers pointed out how I, in owning the Portland Cement Company, stood to make a fortune from people buying into my idea. I tried to counter their argument by explaining that it was because I owned a concrete business that I knew something about building materials these critics knew nothing about; however, doubters rarely want to be confused with facts."

Sherlock Holmes told how he was interested in having Thomas Edison share his thoughts on how electricity could be used as a source of energy to communicate with people who are dead; a notion that would certainly have a profound impact on criminal cases involving murder.

"If we did all the things we are capable of, we would literally astound ourselves," Thomas Edison replied and shared personally how he would cherish even one more brief conversation with his beloved Mary.

Eventually Sherlock Holmes steered the conversation to asking Thomas Edison his thoughts of using the power of electricity to turn baser metals into gold.

"Alchemy?" Thomas Edison asked and watched as Sherlock Holmes nodded his head yes and then continued pointedly, "One of my first jobs was with Samuel Laws, at the Gold Indicator Company, nearly thirty years ago. I worked my way up to mechanical supervisor. That's where I first heard the term alchemy. When I first started experimenting with electricity, well things were pretty tight and resources were often hard to come by; but, for the past two decades I have had the benefit of being surrounded by the brightest minds graduating from the finest engineering schools across the United States. We have had at our fingertips the latest technological advancements science has to offer. It is my learned opinion, after considerable inquiries, that the subject of alchemy is, regrettably, but a myth."

"Thank you," Sherlock Holmes said as he shook Thomas Edison's hand, "We shall not take up any more of your time."

March 9th, 1896 2:30pm
46th and 48th East Houston Street, Manhattan, New York

"How old is Nikola Tesla?" I asked of Sherlock Holmes, as we walked along Houston Street and crossed 46th Street.

"Thirty-nine," Sherlock Holmes replied. "He moved his lab from Fifth Avenue to the sixth and seventh floors of this building just this past year.

"How long has he been in the States, do you know?" I asked as we walked toward the elevators.

"Yes, I made it my business to know," Sherlock Holmes said matter-of-factly. "He came to the States in 1884, as an employee of the Edison Machine Works," Sherlock Holmes answered as we entered the elevator.

"What floor?" the lift operator asked as he closed the door.

"Seventh floor please," Sherlock Holmes replied. When we stepped off the lift Sherlock Holmes continued in answering my previous question, "Nikola Tesla was born an ethnic Serb in the Austrian Empire; he became a naturalized U.S. citizen four years ago."

We approached a receptionist and Sherlock Holmes handed her his business card and said we should be expected. The receptionist made a quick phone call, and then smiled as she said, "follow me please."

She led us to a corner office where Nikola Tesla was standing behind a large wooden desk. We introduced ourselves and accepted a seat at a long conference table with a commanding view of the Hudson River.

"Gentlemen, how may I be of service?" Nikola Tesla asked getting immediately down to business.

"We appreciate you taking time from your busy schedule," Sherlock Holmes began.

"Not a problem," Nikola Tesla replied, "I have been looking forward to meeting you both ever since Mark Twain called me the day before yesterday explaining how he would consider it a personal favor were I to take a few minutes of my time to meet with you while you are here in New York."

"How long have you and Mark Twain been acquainted?" I asked, trying to buy a little more time for my companion to make his observations before we got down to business.

"I only met him three years ago, at a talk he was giving here in New York City, but I first became acquainted with him through his writings. When I was seventeen I contracted cholera and was bedridden for nine months, near my home town in Serbia. My doctors told my father I was close to death several times. When

I was finally able to leave the hospital I spent months rehabilitating in the mountains hunting and being in contact with nature, which is what I believe, made me stronger, both mentally and physically. During my lengthy recovery I read many of Mark Twain's books, which I believe, helped me make what my doctors called a miraculous recovery. I have also read a few of your books, Dr. Watson, and I believe you, Mr. Holmes, and I share something in common."

"What might that be?" Sherlock Holmes asked.

"I do not think there is any thrill that can go through the human heart like that felt by the inventor as he sees some creation of the brain unfolding to success," Mr. Tesla said, standing to look out the window. "Such emotions make a man forget food, sleep, friends, love, everything. That thrill is what I suspect you as an investigator and I as an inventor share in common."

"Indeed," Sherlock Holmes said, as he stood and walked to the window to look down upon the Hudson River. "Men like you and I abhor the dull routine of existence. We crave for mental exaltation. That is why I have chosen my own particular profession, or rather, in my case, created it, for I am the only one in the world. And why you are unique in your world."

Both men stood in silence for several minutes, lost in their own unique worlds. To break the silence I asked, "Mr. Tesla, I understand you are Serbian by birth?"

"Yes," Nikola Tesla said, as he turned away from the window and leaned against the back of an executive chair. "I am as equally proud of my Serbian origin, and Croatian homeland, as I am to being an American today."

"When did you first meet Thomas Edison?" Sherlock Holmes asked, taking over the questioning as he resumed his seat at the conference table.

"In the early 1880s I worked in the telephony and electric power industry. One of my first jobs included the installation of indoor incandescent lighting for Continental Edison in Paris. In 1884 my then manager, Charles Batchelor, was brought back to the United States to manage the Edison Machine Works and he asked that I should be brought with him to the States as well. I began working almost immediately, managing a staff of twenty field engineers with the Edison Machine Works, on Manhattan's Lower East Side."

"While you were working for the Edison Machine Works did you ever meet the founder, Thomas Edison?" Sherlock Holmes asked.

"Yes, although it is doubtful he would remember. I only met him on a few occasions, but one chance encounter stands out in my mind. I had worked all night repairing the damaged dynamos on the SS Oregon. Early the next morning, as I was leaving the ship, my manager Mr. Batchelor and Thomas Edison were coming aboard. Upon seeing me, my manager called out to me, referring to me as, "My Parisian," and suggested, in front of Mr. Edison, that I had been out on the town all night. When I explained that I had worked all night repairing the damaged dynamos on the ship, Mr. Edison pointed to me and said to Mr. Batchelor, 'this is a damned good man'. I understand, as of late Mr. Edison still refers to me as such, although I believe he now leaves out the word 'good'."

"Mr. Tesla," Sherlock Holmes said as he crossed his long legs and folded his hands in his lap, "We will come straight to the point. We are most interested in hearing your opinion on the matter of alchemy."

"Alchemy?" Nikola Tesla repeated with a raised eyebrow.

"Exactly," Sherlock Holmes said, adding, "as one of the world's leading researchers in electricity, and the world's foremost expert on the use of alternating current, do you believe it is possible to use electricity to turn baser metals, such as brass, into gold or conversely, to turn gold into brass."

"Absolutely not," Nikola Tesla said, as he turned and walked to the tall glass window looking out over the Manhattan skyline. He stood there momentarily and then turned around to look at the two of us sitting at the long conference table. "This mystical business of alchemy would have been better off had the notion been left behind centuries ago in the Middle Ages."

"Thank you," Sherlock Holmes said as he stood, shook hands with Nikola Tesla and said, "we thought as much, but wanted to hear it straight from you."

"Very well," Mr. Tesla said as he shook hands with me and walked us back out to where the receptionist sat. "Where are you two off to next?"

"Colorado Springs," said I.

"Colorado Springs?" Nikola Tesla repeated and then said, "I have heard of this town at the foot of the Rocky Mountains. I am looking for an out of the way place, with some altitude, where I may want to conduct a few of my electrical experiments. Would you please drop me a note to let me know what you think of the place?"

"I will," said I as I stepped into the lift next to Sherlock Holmes.

"Going down?" the lift operator asked, already knowing the answer.

"No doubt," Sherlock Holmes replied.

March 10th, 1896 6:30am
Peacock Alley, Waldorf Astoria, New York City

As I JOINED MY FRIEND Sherlock Holmes, at a table in the back of a quaint little restaurant, called Peacock Alley, located on the first floor of our hotel, I said, "After breakfast I will stop by the front desk to check us out and settle our bill." I checked the time on my pocket watch and said, "I have already made arrangements with the bell captain to have our four steamer trunks delivered to Grand Central Station by 10am."

"Very good," said Sherlock Holmes while not looking up from the New York Times he was reading.

The waiter came over to our table, warmed up my companion's coffee, while I ordered tea and read through the menu. "Perhaps you would like the eggs Benedict?" I asked.

"No," replied Sherlock Holmes, "I already ordered a poached egg on whole wheat toast," he replied barely glancing up over the morning newspaper at me.

"I am sorry we were unable to catch an opera while we were here in New York," said I probing further.

"That's quite alright," Sherlock Holmes replied, "perhaps we can catch one in Chicago or Denver."

"Or Cripple Creek?"

Sherlock Holmes set his newspaper aside; as the waiter placed our breakfast on the table before us. My friend looked at me as he cracked open his egg with a silver spoon. "Whatever do you mean?" he asked innocently.

"You know exactly what I mean," said I as I placed a printed placard on the table and pushed it across the table toward him. "The concierges caught up with me while I was at the front desk and asked that I give you this; the opera schedule for La Boheme, by Puccini, which as you know," said I as I pointed to the top of the announcement, "opened in Turin, Italy, in January 1896, followed by appearances here in New York City, in February, Chicago in March, Denver in April and of all places Cripple Creek, Colorado, in May."

"That would be a rather remarkable coincidence, wouldn't it?" my companion said as he buttered a slice of toast.

"Another remarkable coincidence I couldn't help but notice

the other night, while I was in your bedroom, when we were at sea?" said I.

"Whatever were you doing in my bedroom, at night, at sea?"

"Oh, it was the night you asked me to slip into your bedroom, retrieve the rope ladder from your dresser drawer, lower it out your portal window and then climb down myself out of your window – which was a terribly frightening experience I have been meaning to tell you – and then, let me see, where was I, ah yes, I found myself hiding under a mildewed tarp in a lifeboat while you lured an assassin to the very spot where he intended to kill you?"

"Ah, I do seem to remember that night," Sherlock Holmes said rubbing a fresh bandage he had wrapped around the palm of his hand. "And the coincidence you mentioned?"

"As I was lowering my derriere out your portal window, out over the open sea and in the middle of night I might add, I happen to notice the framed photograph of Irene Adler, a photo of one of the world's foremost opera singers, you know the framed photograph I am speaking about, the one the future King of Bohemia gave you, the photograph that once graced our fireplace mantel in our flat back in London? Oddly enough, I noticed that photograph was sitting on your bedroom dresser aboard the RMS Republic."

"Ah, I can see where that would seem a bit of a coincidence, wouldn't it?" Sherlock Holmes said as he continued eating his poached egg on toast.

"Do you think it wise that you see her again? I ask this question more as your doctor than as your friend."

"Whatever do you mean, Dr. Watson? Is it not enough that I occasionally enjoy a good opera?"

"You know exactly what I mean. I, as your friend I might ask if you having an obsession with a married woman is in any way healthy, while I as your doctor would remind you of the last time she sailed out of your life, I found you in an almost comatose state after you having spent nearly two weeks in an opium den. Neither of these two circumstances is in any way healthy for you, mentally or physically. This, again, I say this to you as my friend and as much as my patient."

"I assure you my good man; I have as much control over my emotions as I do my cocaine addiction."

"That's what concerns me!" said I.

"Tell me one thing, Dr. Watson," Sherlock Holmes said earnestly.

"Yes, what is it?" I asked.

"While you were snooping around into my private affairs this morning, did you happen to notice if I had any telegrams waiting at the front desk?"

Accepting the fact my friend had purposely changed the subject, I replied, "There were two telegrams waiting at the front desk; one for me from my friend Dr. William Bell, in Colorado, and one for you from Mrs. Hudson in London."

"Please, read aloud the one from Mrs. Hudson."

"To Mr. Sherlock Holmes, Waldorf Astoria, New York, NY Dated March 3, 1896 Dear Mr. Holmes (Stop) a burly stevedore came around late yesterday asking for you (Stop) said to tell you another 65-pound fire bell had been shipped to the same address as previous (Stop). He wouldn't leave until I paid him Two Pounds gold sovereign (Stop) P.S. you really must find a better place to hide your money than the Persian slipper on the fireplace mantel. (Stop). My compliments to Dr. Watson, (Signed) Mrs. H."

"What a lovely lady," Sherlock Holmes replied, "what does your telegram from your colleague Dr. Bell have to tell us?"

"Essentially that Dr. William Bell and his wife Cara will be on travel in San Francisco, California, until March 15th; however, he has made arrangements for us to stay with a friend of his, a General

William Jackson Palmer, at a place called Glen Eyrie."

"I have read some about this General Palmer, sounds like a very accomplished fellow; after the American Civil War he went west, made a fortune in the railroading business and has spent considerable time in England," said Sherlock Holmes.

"Dr. Bell's telegram suggests that when we get off the train we drop by the Antlers Hotel and inform the front desk clerk General Palmer is expecting us. I suspect once we get west of the Mississippi River, accommodations will become rather rustic," said I, envisioning the Antlers Hotel resembling more of a hunting lodge than a first-class hotel.

Sherlock Holmes handed me a small piece of folded paper and said, "If you would be so kind, I have a telegram of my own I wish for you to send."

I unfolded his note and read, "To PM at Number 10 Downing Street London, England (stop) all as expected with TE & NT (stop) presently off to Little London (stop). (Signed) SH."

"Certainly; I will drop your telegram to the Prime Minister off at the front desk, and then send a short one of my own to Mrs. Hudson advising her where she can reach us in Colorado staying at this Glen Eyrie with a General William Jackson Palmer.

March 12th, 1896 2:30pm

Denver & Rio Grande Train Depot, Colorado Springs, Colorado, U.S.A.

"Welcome to Colorado Springs," the conductor said as our train rolled to a stop.

I glanced out the window of our Pullman train car at the majestic snowcapped mountain and said to Sherlock Holmes, "It is beautiful here, reminds me somewhat of the Swiss Alps."

"It does indeed," Sherlock Holmes said, as he put on his hat and topcoat preparing to disembark from the train.

"The travelogue I was reading a moment ago," I said to my friend, "told how an American writer, a professor named Katharine Lee Bates, while teaching an English class here at Colorado College, during the summer of 1893, was so inspired after a trip to the summit of that 14,000 foot purple mountain, she hurriedly jotted down the words to America the Beautiful, evidently it is a popular patriotic poem here in the States. She was staying here in Colorado Springs, at the Antlers Hotel, which, if I'm not mistaken is the building straight ahead there," said I pointing out the coach door to the four story hotel a short half block away.

"You being such as stickler for documenting our travel expenses, I still find it hard to believe you leased an entire Pullman first-class train car for just the two of us to travel in from New York to Chicago to Denver and finally here to Colorado Springs," Sherlock Holmes said as we stepped down from the luxury coach onto the wooden train platform.

"It seemed a bargain after paying for our first-class passage on the RMS Republic, and settling the bill for our suite at the Waldorf Astoria," said I. "Nevertheless, I shall miss our Pullman; I understand the shortline from here to Cripple Creek is a narrow gauge railroad, the tracks being only three feet apart."

Sherlock Holmes pointed to where our steamer trunks were being offloaded onto the train platform. "Would you be so kind as to arrange for our baggage to be delivered to the bellman at the Antlers Hotel?" Sherlock Holmes asked, and added, "We can send for them later. There's a constable standing over there I would like to speak with?"

"Certainly," said I, noticing the policeman's uniform was remarkably similar to those worn by our constables back in London, including his distinctive dome-shaped Bobby's helmet.

After I had hired a man with a wagon to transport our four steamer trunks to the Antlers Hotel, I rejoined my friend who was shaking hands with the constable.

"Thank you, Officer Bish," Sherlock Holmes said, bidding the policeman a good day. My friend said to me, "Since the founding of Colorado Springs in 1871 it has become affectionately known as Little London, and if that officer is any example of the Colorado Springs police force, which I imagine he is, I suspect the police here are a very competent and dedicated lot."

"That is good to know," said I, "especially if we find we are in need of their services as your investigation unfolds. Shall we make our way up to the Antlers Hotel and see if we can locate this General Palmer?"

Same Day 3pm
Antlers Hotel, Colorado Springs, Colorado, U.S.A.

The lobby of the elegant Antlers Hotel was adorned with a large collection of massive elk and deer antlers, which the hotel owner, our General Palmer, had installed throughout the hotel. The front desk clerk was most proud to share that the hotel boasted 75 unique guest rooms, a Turkish bath, a music room, billiards room and a barber shop. Similar to the Waldorf Astoria, the Antlers Hotel also had gas lights, steam heat, hot and cold water and a hydraulic elevator.

"Except perhaps for its fewer number of rooms," the desk clerk explained proudly, "the Antlers Hotel is as luxurious as any hotel to be found anywhere in the American West. If you gentlemen care to relax in our lobby I will telephone Glen Eyrie to see if I can locate General Palmer."

As we sat upon one of the comfortable sofas in the lobby, I said to Sherlock Holmes sitting beside me, "Let me see your hand."

"Why?" My friend said as he reluctantly held out his bandaged hand.

"It's been 21 days now," said I as I unwrapped the bandage on his hand and retrieved a pair of tweezers and a small pair of scissors from my medical bag. "Your wound has healed nicely, see here—there's no infection—but these stitches need to come out."

"Let me order a whiskey first," my reluctant patient said as he raised his other hand to get the attention of a waiter across the hotel lobby. While he was distracted I snipped the knot on one end of the stitches with my scissors and with my tweezers I grabbed the knot at the other end and yanked the thread from the palm of his hand.

"Ouch!" Sherlock Holmes shouted, and jerked his hand away from me and rubbed the palm of his hand. "You rather enjoyed that, didn't you?"

"All done," said I, putting my medical instruments back into my medical bag. "Look here's the desk clerk now; your whiskey may have to wait."

The efficient desk clerk glanced down at Sherlock Holmes rubbing his hand and glaring at me and hesitantly said, "I don't mean to intrude gentlemen, but I have located General Palmer. He is presently at Colorado College finishing a meeting and has sent his driver, Jessie Bass, with a carriage to fetch you here in front of the hotel. Mr. Bass should be pulling up out front in just a few minutes."

Within ten minutes a beautiful open air carriage, drawn by a matching pair of black horses, pulled up in front of the hotel. The driver, a black man in his sixties, wearing a black suit, dismounted and approached us and said as he tipped the brim of his black derby hat, "Good afternoon gentlemen, my name is Jessie Bass, are you Dr. Watson and Mr. Holmes?"

"We are, thank you, Mr. Bass," said I, "We appreciate you coming to fetch us."

"My pleasure," our driver said as we got into the carriage. As he steered the carriage north on a wide street marked by a street sign on the corner as Cascade Avenue, Jessie Bass explained, "It's a short ride. Colorado College is but eight or so blocks north of downtown."

Same Day 4:15pm
Colorado College, Colorado Springs, Colorado, U.S.A.

"There is General Palmer now, coming from Cutler Hall," Jessie said, as the carriage rolled to a stop in front of the grand building located at the center of the Colorado College campus. "General Palmer is the shorter man at the top of the steps wearing the dark blue suit."

"Thank you, Mr. Bass," said I as Sherlock Holmes and I stepped down out of the carriage. "May I offer you payment or a gratuity for your services?"

Jessie touched the narrow brim of his hat and replied, "That is very kind of you Sir; however, I am fortunate enough to be in the fulltime employment of the General and as such am already well compensated for my services. Thank you."

As Sherlock Holmes and I walked along the wide walkway toward Cutler Hall, General Palmer waived at us and started down the stone steps to greet us. There were two other well-dressed men with him.

"Gentlemen, welcome to Little London," General Palmer said warmly, as he reached out to shake hands, starting with me. "You must be Dr. John Watson; our mutual friend Dr. William Bell has told me so much about you."

"It is a pleasure to meet you and thank you for hosting us while

Dr. and Mrs. Bell are away on travel," said I.

"It is my pleasure, I'm sure you will feel most at home at Glen Eyrie," General Palmer said as he turned to greet my companion, "And you must be Mr. Sherlock Holmes, of whom I have read so much about."

"I am Sir. It is a pleasure to meet you, General Palmer," Sherlock Holmes said, adding, "Glen Eyrie, if I am not mistaken, is Scottish meaning Valley of the Eagle's Nest?"

"You are not mistaken," said General Palmer with a smile. "May I have the pleasure of introducing you both to two of my business associates; Winfield Stratton and Irving Howbert?"

After the five of us exchanged pleasantries for a few minutes, Mr. Stratton and Mr. Howbert strolled off toward the downtown area of Colorado Springs while General Palmer gave us a short tour of the Colorado College campus. "Over there is the library," he explained, "and over here we are planning to build a new science building, which is the reason why Mr. Stratton and Mr. Howbert were here visiting with us this afternoon. I am one of the founding trustees for Colorado College and both Mr. Stratton and Mr. Howbert have been most generous with their financial support for various philanthropic endeavors here in the Colorado Springs area.

Bong! Bong! The bell in the bell tower above Cutler Hall chimed, announcing the time as 4:30pm.

Sherlock Holmes stopped walking and looked up at the large brass bell housed in the bell tower, "General Palmer, would you happen to know how much that bell weighs?"

"Two hundred and fifty pounds, I believe is what the architectural schematics called for," General Palmer replied, "Ah, there's Jessie now, let's ask him to drive us out to Glen Eyrie, shall we? We'll get you settled into your rooms, where you can freshen up a bit, and this evening the three of us will have an opportunity to become better acquainted over a nice supper."

Same Day 5:10pm
Glen Eyrie, Colorado, U.S.A.

A FEW MILES WEST OF COLORADO SPRINGS our carriage ascended a gradual sloping mesa where a spectacular view of Pikes Peak unfolded before us. An amazing red and white stone arrangement of towering rock formations standing upright came into view below.

"The Garden of the Gods," General Palmer said, "a sacred land visited for thousands of years by American Indians, including the Ute, Apache, Cheyenne, Arapahoe, Comanche and the Lakota. That opening there between the rocks is called the Gateway Rocks. The ranch you see there, off to the left, belongs to me, I call it the Rock Ledge Ranch. A friend of mine, Charles Perkins, owns most of the rest of the land adjoining the ranch, 480 acres. I understand he intends to deed his land to the City of Colorado Springs, to be set aside as a public park, after his death. My Glen Eyrie is off to the right there, in Queen's Canyon."

"Queen's Canyon?" asked I, recalling our meeting with Queen Victoria in the Tower of London, back in January.

"Yes, I named it for my late wife, Mary Mellen Palmer, her nickname was Queen. She passed two years ago in England, only 44 years of age, I miss her dearly, every day. She was fifteen years younger than me, when we first fell in love and married, I naturally assumed she would far out live me. Life can be such a fleeting thing, don't you agree?"

"I do," said I, thinking back to my time in the British military. "The Garden of the Gods is aptly named," I commented as I pulled the bear fur blanket Jessie had given us up to my chest, noticing Sherlock Holmes sitting beside me in the open carriage doing the same.

"It can get cold here in the springtime," General Palmer said, "especially once the sun has dipped down over the horizon. When I left for town afore noon, I had asked Jessie to harness an open air carriage for us to use today; I just love the fresh air and the unobstructed views. Dr. Watson, as you are probably aware, the fresh mountain air and dry climate is what brought so many wonderful people here to Colorado Springs, seeking a cure for tuberculosis."

"Yes, I was aware. In his last letter Dr. Bell wrote about the medical advancements being made in the treatment of tuberculosis here in Colorado Springs, most impressive."

"While we are far from a cure, we are making progress," General Palmer explained. "It is estimated that one in three people living in Colorado Springs today have tuberculosis, including my youngest daughter Marjorie, who was stricken with this dreadful disease a few years ago. Consumption, as some people call this horrific disease, is aptly named for it consumes its victims, young and old alike. Marjorie, along with her two older sisters, Dorothy and my eldest Elsie, are at present in Denver. The Denver Zoo opened just this year and the girls took the Nomad, that's my private train car, to Denver for a few days. They had been living in Kent, with their mother, when she passed away. The girls are living back here with me now, where I believe Marjorie may receive better medical care. We have several sanitariums and sanatoriums already well-established here in the area, with more on the way, and you may have noticed dozens of the houses you passed along Cascade Avenue serve as boarding houses, many feature large attached sunrooms."

As we descended the west side of the mesa, our horse-drawn carriage crossed over a picturesque rock bridge and then past a dairy on our left, which the General referred to as the Glen Eyrie Creamery. We then entered a tree lined lane which meandered between more spectacular red and white vertically standing rocky crags.

We began to hear a hum, "That's an electrical power generation station," General Palmer explained. "We had electrical lighting here in Glen Eyrie at the same moment the first electrical lights were turned on in New York City; which was the first city in the U.S. to get electricity."

Amber colored electric lights had been lit along the drive as we entered Queen's Canyon, illuminating the quaint pathway leading to General Palmer's home.

"There's your eagles nest," Sherlock Holmes said, pointing to a large nest built into a gray craggy sandstone formation off to our right. "You chose the name and location for your home here well General Palmer. When did you move here?"

"I first laid eyes upon Pike's Peak in the late sixties, while surveying the route for the Kansas Pacific Railroad, that's where Dr. William Bell and I first met; he was an important part of our survey crew."

"Was he your company's doctor?" asked I.

"Actually Dr. Bell was our photographer," General Palmer explained. "Although he had no photography experience, he took a two-week crash course on photography, purchased his own camera and portable darkroom and joined our survey crew near the Kansas-Colorado border. We were experiencing active fighting with the local Indians at the time and shortly after his arrival, Dr. Bell took a photograph of the mutilated body of Sergeant Frederick Wyllyams, a soldier with the U.S. 7th Cavalry, who had been brutally killed by the Indians. Harper's Weekly, a political magazine based in New York City, had published similar photos from the Civil War. Although many people objected to the publishing of such gruesome pictures, Harper's Weekly communicated the horrors of war and the brutality of slavery better than any other publication."

"I remember seeing the photograph of the body of Sergeant Wyllyams, some thirty years ago," said Sherlock Holmes. "Seeing the many arrows protruding from his mutilated corpse is what compelled me to promote the advantages of documenting the scenes of crime and autopsy of crime victims by photography with Scotland Yard."

"Dr. Bell has been very instrumental in helping me found Colorado Springs, which we had intended from the beginning to become a health resort. And I proudly supported him in the founding of Manitou Springs, a small town where he and Cara built their Briarhurst Manor; it's located on the west edge of the Garden of the Gods. When I was surveying for the railroad routes, I first rode through here on the roof of a stagecoach, it was at night and the moment I first saw this wonderful view, it was under the moonlight where I fell instantly in love with the Pikes Peak Region. I wrote to Queen and told her at the time, we weren't even married then, that this place would make for a beautiful home, fit for a Queen. I purchased the land in Queens Canyon from the first Sheriff of El Paso County, Rankin Scott Kelly; offered him a thousand dollars cash and was delighted he accepted my offer. He had acquired the land intending to build himself a grand home here one day; evidently, his plans changed and he rode off into the sunset. I understand Sheriff Kelly returned to try his hand at silver mining a few years back in Leadville. He hasn't seen Colorado Springs as of yet, but I hope he approves. The Colorado Silver Boom in 1879 made a lot of my friends rich men, including Irving Howbert and HAW Tabor, but gold is where Winfield Scott Stratton made his fortune; he was Cripple Creek's first millionaire."

I could tell my friend Sherlock Holmes wanted to ask a few follow-on questions, but just then the magnificent Glen Eyrie came into view. I could hardly believe my eyes! There before us, nestled tastefully into the beautiful red rock formations, stood a majestic three-story home complete with a castle tower. I looked up to see the British flag had been hoisted up a flagpole above the tower. It was a picture perfect moment and felt as if we had never left England.

"There she is gentlemen, welcome to Glen Eyrie," General Palmer said proudly as he stepped down from the carriage and guided us over a stone footbridge with a gesture of his hand, toward the main entrance.

"You fly the Union Jack?" asked I as I nodded to the welcoming British flag overhead.

"When we have honored guests here at Glen Eyrie we fly the flag of their country while they are staying with us in residence," General Palmer explained. "Come, let's get inside out of the cold."

Sherlock Holmes and I followed the General inside the majestic home, where we were met by his butler, Pryor Shelby, who led us upstairs and showed us to our adjoining bedrooms.

"I had your four steamer trunks placed there," Pryor said, pointing to where our baggage had been placed. "I lit the fire in both your bedroom fireplaces, you may want to toss another log on the fire before you turn in tonight; mornings can be rather brisk this time of year. Dinner will be served this evening at 6:30pm, in the dining room, located on the lower level; you should find it easily enough. Should there be anything you require before then, just press this button," he said showing us a small round button located beneath the light switch. "A bell will ring downstairs in the kitchen and either I or another of the staff will knock on your door within a minute or two to answer your call and attend to your needs."

"Thank you, Pryor," said I, "I hope I don't offend anyone for asking this, but for my edification, could you please tell me if gratuities, for either you or your staff, are acceptable."

"Thank you for asking," Pryor replied as he made his way to the front door, "as Mr. Bass may have mentioned, tips are not necessary. I and all of our staff at Glen Eyrie are also full-time employees of General Palmer. Many of us here were former slaves and the General has always made us feel as if we are all part of his family. You are his guests and therefore, we are all honored to have you here with us and are committed to making your stay as pleasant as possible. I shall look forward to serving you gentlemen at 6:30 for dinner in the dining room."

Once we were alone, I walked into my adjoining bedroom, admired the modern fixtures in my private bathroom, complete with running water, white marble sinks and modern electrical lighting. My fireplace was decorated with beautiful six-inch square white and blue titles, depicting a tranquil windmill scene. I recognized the ceramic tiles from our shopping two weeks ago at Tiffany's in New York City. The ornate tiles had been imported to New York City from Holland and then here to Colorado by rail, to be expertly installed around the fireplace in my guest suite. I wondered if this fireplace, like that in our flat back on Baker Street in London, also had a hidden vault where valuables could be concealed.

Clearly General and Mrs. Palmer had exquisite tastes, in addition to significant financial wealth at their disposal in building their beautiful Glen Eyrie. As I stood to warm myself in front of the fireplace, I touched the beautiful blue and white ceramic tiles and felt a smile forming on my face as I recalled our shopping at Tiffany's, on Fifth Avenue, in New York City. Sherlock Holmes had unexpectantly suggested we stop by on our way to Delmonico's to meet Mark Twain for dinner. As we were shopping my companion distracted me by drawing my attention to the display with these beautiful ceramic tiles from Holland depicting various landscape scenes.

While I was looking at the ceramic tile display I saw Sherlock Holmes had slipped away to where the China tea cups and saucers were being sold near the front window of Tiffany's. I watched from a distance as my friend purchased a beautiful tea set and discreetly filled out the paperwork. There was little doubt in my mind he was shipping the tea service from Tiffany & Company in New York City to Mrs. Hudson, 211 Baker Street, London, England; intended to replace the tea service he may have stained with his fingerprinting experiments.

When I walked back into Sherlock Holmes' bedroom, I observed he was unpacking one of his steamer trunks. I was drawn to the warmth of his fireplace and admired the craftsmanship of the wood panels framing the beautiful fireplace. The wallpaper, carpets, bedlinen, pillows and drapery were exquisite.

"Not the sort of rustic accommodations you were expecting, Dr. Watson?" Sherlock Holmes said as he laid out his clothes for dinner.

"I should say not," said I. "I could not have imagined such a place existed anywhere on earth; other than England or perhaps Eastern Europe, let alone out here in the American West. I shall have to send a note to Nikola Tesla informing him that Colorado Springs may serve him well as a place for his electrical experiments; especially once the Science Building is added to the Colorado College campus next year."

Sherlock Holmes held up his new charcoal gray three-piece suit we had tailor made at Brooks Brothers, the oldest men's clothier in the States. "We may want to dress for dinner," Sherlock Holmes said. "I've been looking for such an occasion to wear one of the new suits we had made for us while we were in Manhattan."

"Well, Brooks Brothers is not Savile Row in London," said I, "but our suits do appear to be very well made and I appreciate you wanting us to not stand out as foreigners. While we were being measured my tailor proudly shared how they had been in business since 1818, evidently 78 years is considered a long time here in America. My tailor also shared, with considerable pride, how Abraham Lincoln was wearing a Brooks Brothers suit and coat when he was assassinated."

"Well," said Sherlock Holmes, as he laid out a burgundy colored silk tie on the bed next to his charcoal colored suit, "let us hope the same cannot be said of us one day."

Same Day 6:30pm
Dining Room, Glen Eyrie, Colorado, U.S.A.

As we descended the stairway and approached the dining room, I saw Pryor Shelby was also wearing a perfectly tailored three piece suit and I was relieved Sherlock Holmes had suggested we wear our new Brooks Brothers suits. Entering the dining room I observed how all the wait staff was also tastefully attired in matching white uniforms, reminding me of our recent dining experiences at the Waldorf Astoria and Delmonico's in New York City. The dining room was located in the east wing and was elegant in every way. Along one wall a fire burned in a large stone fireplace. Two huge deer antlers racks hung to both sides, each a trophy.

The dining room could easily seat two dozen guests comfortably for supper; however, tonight there were only the three of us - Sherlock Holmes, myself and our gracious host General William Jackson Palmer who was sitting at the far end of the table. When he looked up from a book he was reading, he stood and greeted us warmly.

"I trust you gentlemen made yourselves comfortable in your bedroom suites," he said as he directed us to the two dining room chairs arranged to his left and right at the head of the massive dining table. There were three place settings arranged meticulously in front of each of our three chairs, reminding me of my dinner at the Captain's table aboard the RMS Republic. "Would either of you care for something to drink before dinner?"

"What are you drinking?" asked I, as we took our seats, noticing a small glass made of cut crystal filled with an amber liquid sitting in front of the General's plate.

"Oh, this?" said as he took a sip from his glass, "is just apple cider, I'm a bit of a teetotaler myself, but please order whatever you would like, Pryor keeps our wine cellar and liquor cabinet fairly well-stocked for the enjoyment of our guests here at Glen Eyrie."

"Gentlemen," Pryor said as he stepped forward, "what may I bring you to drink?"

"I believe I might enjoy a Scotch Whiskey this evening," Sherlock Holmes said, "Do you have any Single Malts by chance?"

"We do," Pryor replied, "several."

"Do you have a recommendation?" Sherlock Holmes asked, unfolding his cloth napkin across his lap.

"We have a nice 24-year-old Macallan you might approve of, although I find it a bit on the peaty side myself."

"That sounds like it might do," Sherlock Holmes replied, with a glance across the table to where I was seated. "I have only tried the 24-year-old Macallan once and really wasn't in a position to enjoy it at the time."

"I'll have the same, if you please, Pryor," said I, and then asked of our host, "General Palmer, I must admit how truly impressed I am with your Glen Eyrie. This is not at all what I expected to find here in the American West. Can you please tell us about your architectural design and manner of construction?"

"Certainly. I designed and built Glen Eyrie so my wife Queen would feel at home whenever she was here, we had also kept apartments in London and in New York City. I added on to the original home in 1888, including the tower to give it more of a castle look and feel. As my railroad and steel businesses have continued to flourish, I have given considerable thought to adding on again in a few years, perhaps adding a large Great Room to the second floor in the east wing and converting Glen Eyrie to even more of an English Tudor stone castle. I am very fortunate to have on my staff here a master carpenter, Charles Kneller, who did most of the wood work you see here at Glen Eyrie. Charles also did the carpentry work on my customized Pullman train car."

"What inspired you to want to build a castle?" asked I.

"During our Civil War I was taken prisoner and incarcerated for a time in the infamous Castle Thunder prison on Tobacco Row, in Richmond, Virginia. During my incarceration I had plenty of time to design a castle in my mind, trying to occupy my time. The process served as a distraction from my pending execution. You see there were some troubling accusations I was a spy for the Union Army, having been found out of uniform and uncomfortably behind enemy lines. I was fortunate to be involved in a prisoner of war exchange; otherwise, we would not be able to have this conversation this evening. To your health gentlemen," General Palmer said as he took a sip of his apple cider and we of our whiskeys Pryor had set before us on the table.

"Your architectural design and construction is certainly that of an English Tudor-style," said I, "most representative of what Mark Twain refers to as the Gilded Age."

"Thank you, the glen here offers a unique setting for a grand home, nestled in among the magnificent red sandstone formations. In a future expansion, in addition to a large great hall, I am considering adding a billiards room, a two-lane bowling alley in the basement and central vacuuming throughout the castle. I have two architects working on drawings now, including a young Scotsman named, Thomas MacLaren, who studied architecture at the Royal College of Art in London. To improve his health, Thomas moved from Denver to Colorado Springs in 1894, four years after his brother James passed away from tuberculosis. I believe Thomas will one day become a premier architect in our fair city."

"Tell me General," Sherlock Holmes asked, "how was it you, as an officer in the Union Army, being caught behind enemy lines and out of uniform, were able to avoid being put before a firing squad before a prisoner of war exchange could be orchestrated?"

"Two tactics proved particularly useful in the circumstance I found myself in; first, I had fabricated a somewhat believable cover story, I was a businessman from the north checking out my business holdings in the south when I was mistakenly taken into custody. Secondly, a cover story, supported by a series of telegrams and false newspaper articles, were released reporting my being in Washington D.C., at the same time I was being held prisoner. There was just the slightest element of doubt in the mind of my captors that when the offer to exchange prisoners came about they wanted their Confederate officer back much more than they wanted me shot."

"Very informative techniques to keep in mind, thank you for sharing," Sherlock Holmes replied.

"Ah, here comes Pryor and his staff with our supper," General Palmer announced. "Pryor, please share with us what you and your staff have prepared this evening."

"With pleasure, tonight we are serving elk medallions, covered in brown mushroom gravy, with trout almandine for your main course, fresh asparagus spears grown in our green house, canned baby carrots in a butter cream sauce, along with a lettuce wedge drizzled with creamy blue cheese dressing topped with bacon crumbles and for dessert we have peach cobbler, served hot out of the oven, topped with homemade vanilla ice cream and a warm caramel sauce. Would either of you gentlemen prefer red or white wine to drink with dinner?"

"Red for me," Sherlock replied.

"I would like white wine myself, to pair with the trout almondine," said I, "this is truly a marvelous dinner. Thank you again for hosting us, General. I'm not sure how we can ever repay you for your hospitality."

"My pleasure," General Palmer said, as we dined, "any friend of Dr. Bell is a friend of mine; you will always be welcome at Glen Eyrie. But tell me gentlemen," the General said as Pryor and his staff disappeared back into the kitchen, leaving the three of us alone for the first time since we met earlier that afternoon at Colorado College, "you two do not strike me as men being on vacation and from what I understand in reading of your work Mr. Holmes, you are most likely on a mission of some global importance, one that you may not be at liberty to disclose, sent here by a person of some high standing in your country. And while I would enjoy speaking endlessly about the architectural design and construction of Glen Eyrie, I feel compelled to ask if, confidentially of course, I might be of service—providing information perhaps?"

"You are most perceptive," said Sherlock Holmes, "no doubt from being in a similar position such as ours during your American Civil War. Information is golden as they say. Confidentially, I can share with you that we will be traveling to Cripple Creek in the morning and we would very much appreciate you telling us the brief history of what is today being called the Greatest

Gold Camp on Earth, along with the names of people who you think might be of importance for us to speak with about gold mining outputs and anyone connected to the Cripple Creek Fire Department."

"Well, in addition to suggesting that you speak privately with Winfield Scott Stratton, you will find him at the Mining Exchange Building in Colorado Springs, I would also suggest you speak with Bob Womack, although I cannot vouch for how confidential that conversation might be; Bob is known to enjoy a drink or two, but he is the man who deserves credit for the first discovery of gold in Cripple Creek in 1890. Then there are the two Jimmies, Burns and Doyle, both enterprising Colorado Springs firefighters who struck it rich in Victor; Cripple Creek's nearest neighbor. And I would highly recommend you make time to speak with Speck Penrose and his partner Charlie Tutt; both knowledgeable and trustworthy businessmen."

"Could you please tell us more about how Bob Womack made the initial discovery of gold and where we might find him?" Sherlock Holmes asked.

"Do either of you object to my taking notes," I asked as I retrieved my fountain pen and black leather-bound notebook from my coat pocket.

"Not at all," said General Palmer, "none of what I am going to tell you is particularly sensitive information, in fact most of what I am about to share is rather well known and fully documented in our local or state newspapers."

"Where might we locate Bob Womack?" Sherlock Holmes asked again, as we continued our dinner and I took notes between bites.

"He has a cabin, on Poverty Gulch, in Cripple Creek," General Palmer said, "if you don't find him on his ranch, you can probably find him at one of the bars in Cripple Creek or one of the saloons in Colorado City, that's located between Colorado Springs and Manitou Springs. If you buy Bob a drink he'll be happy to tell you all about his discovering gold along the creek on his ranch, rumored to have crippled a cow at some time or another; which is how the town of Cripple Creek got its name. What is important to note, is that while some people claim Bob Womack to be a town drunk, I do not share that opinion. He was smart enough to have recognized the importance of the Hayden geological surveys conducted by the federal government after the Civil War."

"Can you tell us more about this geological survey and who might have had access to this report?" asked Sherlock Holmes.

"These were official government surveys conducted by Dr. Ferdinand Vandeveer Hayden from 1873 until 1876 when Colorado became a state. Dr. Hayden's geological survey described the area beyond Pikes Peak as a volcanic formation composed of trachyte and sylvanite. When Bob Womack found ore samples which he suspected contained gold he tried to get people interested but he was ignored for several years until Professor Harry Lamb, a metallurgist professor from Colorado College, analyzed two of Bob's ore samples, which he assayed in at $250 to the ton. Womack filed a claim, for what he called the El Paso Mine; however, what became vitally important was the milling process to extract the gold from the ore. Bob continued to work his claims and in the fall of 1890, he began discovering high-grade gold ore that he had unearthed around the rim of what the Hayden survey had referred to as a volcanic formation. By 1891 other miners began prospecting the land around Poverty Gulch. What became commonly referred to as a 'Bowl of Gold' was confined to just a six square mile area. Other mines around the rim began producing millions of dollars' worth of gold, year after year and today, six years later, the Cripple Creek Gold

Rush has become America's greatest gold rush."

"Please tell us more about the Two Jimmies," Sherlock Holmes asked, as I finished my dinner and took more notes as I enjoyed my wine.

"As I mentioned, the Two Jimmies were industrious Colorado Springs firefighters, I don't know if they ever had any affiliation with the Cripple Creek Fire Department, but when Winfield Scott Stratton discovered a rich gold vein, at his Independence Mine, under Battle Mountain, just above Victor, Jimmy Doyle and Jimmy Burns also struck it rich at their Portland Mine. They helped establish the town of Victor. What all these men have in common was they were friends from the beginning, each willing to work hard and were determined to succeed."

"What can you tell us about Mr. Penrose and Tutt?" Sherlock Holmes asked.

"Both enterprising young men, friends long before gold was discovered in Cripple Creek. Charlie Tutt arrived here first from back east and then he convinced his friend, Spencer Penrose, who prefers to be called Speck, to join him mining for gold around the volcanic rim. They soon struck it rich; with a mine they named the C.O.D. Mine, which stands for Cash on Delivery. When Speck and Charlie sold the C.O.D., they invested a portion of their fortune in buying up other gold mining claims and other real estate holdings in the Cripple Creek business district. Their main headquarters building is easy to find on Bennett Avenue, the main street running through town. I have a lot of respect for both Spencer Penrose and Charlie Tutt."

"That's very helpful General Palmer," Sherlock Holmes said as Pryor quietly served our desserts, along with a brandy sniffer being warmed over an open flame, then he quietly slipped away again. "Is there anything else we should know before we leave in the morning?"

"Yes, you are welcome to leave your baggage here at Glen Eyrie, where your valuables will be safe, but I encourage you to use an abundance of caution. Cripple Creek is comprised of ten mining camps, reaching a population in the summer months of nearly fifty thousand people, but in reality it is a very small town, controlled by a miners union and mine owners constantly at odds with one another. Starting tomorrow, you will find this Bowl of Gold filled with very ambitious people from all walks of life and danger lurks around every corner and down every mine shaft."

Chapter 6

March 13th, 1896 3:30pm

Cripple Creek, Colorado, U.S.A.

Rather than taking the Short Line railroad from Colorado Springs to Cripple Creek General Palmer encouraged us to board a passenger car with the Midland Terminal Railway Company, which ran three times during the day and once at two in the morning. A Pullman service was available; however, we had released our Pullman car the previous day in Colorado Springs thinking the only rail service to Cripple Creek was by narrow gauge. At the Midland Train Depot I purchased round trip tickets for Sherlock Holmes and me, at a cost of two dollars each, which I duly noted in my black leather notebook chronicling the smallest details of this case, beginning with Mycroft's coded telegram arriving at our flat on Baker Street in January.

As I thought back to when this case first began it was hard for me to conceive that nearly three months had passed and that we had traveled halfway round the world to find ourselves now arriving in the gold mining town of Cripple Creek, which did not even exist four years ago. The "Greatest Gold Camp on Earth" was located 44 miles southwest of Colorado Springs, at an elevation of 9,494 feet above sea level. I was glad we had dressed for the cold weather. We had left our steamer trunks at

Glen Eyrie, as General Palmer had suggested; however, I had decided to carry my leather medical bag, which now concealed my service revolver and spare ammunition. I had hoped Sherlock Holmes would be able to complete his business here in this bustling mining town within a few days for I was looking forward to returning to Little London and from there returning to our flat in London sometime within the next month. Meanwhile, I was very much looking forward to learning more about the medical advancements being made in the treatment of tuberculosis from my friend, Dr. William Abraham Bell. He and Mrs. Bell were due to return to his home, the Briarhurst Manor, located in Manitou Springs near the west exit of the Garden of the Gods, the day after tomorrow.

When our train slowly pulled to a stop at the Midland Terminal Depot in Cripple Creek, we found the depot was still under construction. The three story brick building was situated at the eastern end of Bennett Avenue, the main street running east to west through town, and while construction on the Midland Train Depot was still not yet complete it had already become the central focal point of human activity. Newly arrived passengers were greeted by hundreds of townspeople who came to welcome family and friends or simply to watch the comings and goings of countless excited arrivals and departures.

One of the townspeople who enjoyed this pastime was Bob Womack, the rugged looking cowboy sitting on a nearby bench. Our conductor pointed out Bob and his white horse Whistler, as Sherlock Holmes and I stepped down from the train car.

"Don't you want to speak to him now?" asked I of my companion as we walked past the man sitting on the bench talking with people gathered round him, everyone excited to hear Bob share his story of discovering gold in Cripple Creek.

"No, too many people around at the moment," said Sherlock

Holmes. "But it is good to know what he and his horse look like," nodding his head toward the horse tied to a lamppost behind where the cowboy sat. "General Palmer mentioned Mr. Womack lives in a log cabin on Poverty Gulch; I would prefer to speak with Mr. Womack there if at all possible. Let us head on into town and see where the Cripple Creek Fire Department might be found."

As we walked along the uneven dirt street we soon observed a three-story red brick building on the north side of Bennett Avenue, bearing a sign at the top, "The Gold Mining Stock Exchange". Another sign on the brick building claimed it was built in 1895; however, most of the buildings located in the town of nearly 40,000 people, were of a wooden frame construction.

"There is City Hall and next to it the Fire Department," said I pointing to the two-story buildings adjacent to one another; the building on the right was identified as the Central Fire Station.

"With only one bell tower," Sherlock Holmes said, "therefore the Cripple Creek Fire department requires but one fire bell. It will be important for us to learn, if we can, where the fake fire bells went after they were received there at the Fire Department. If my preliminary investigative theory runs correct, the gold bells were melted down into gold bars somewhere nearby and then most likely reported as gold bullion on the Gold Mining Stock Exchange."

"Indeed," said I. After walking two more blocks further into the small town, I stopped and pointed across the street to a two story building identified with a sign toward the top of the elaborately painted wooden façade, identifying it as the Tutt Building.

"That building must be owned by Charles Tutt, the business partner of Speck Penrose whom General Palmer mentioned last night over dinner. Come, let us check out the inside," Sherlock Holmes said as we crossed the wide street and stopped to read the advertisements posted on the inside of the glass facing out toward the street.

"Says here," said I, in reading from the first advertisement, "the Tutt Building features call boards running private wires to the Colorado Springs, Pueblo, Denver, Chicago and New York Stock Exchanges. They boast private conference rooms and a finely stocked bar. I could certainly use a drink, how about you?" asked I turning to my friend standing next to me, leaving my invitation for a drink unanswered. I found Sherlock Holmes to be totally absorbed in an advertisement about a local bare knuckles boxing champion, named Dempsey, a mucker at the Portland Mine, who was fighting Saturday night under the boxing name of "Kid Blacky."

"Look at the size of his fists," said I as Sherlock Holmes moved to his left and I had an opportunity to read the advertisement and observe the photo of the boxer known as Kid Blacky. "I hope you're not planning on challenging this man, he'll beat you to a pulp," said I, turning once again to see why my friend had not answered my question. I found he was now busily reading the next advertisement promoting the four-part opera La Boheme. The poster shared how La Boheme was composed by Giacomo Puccini and premiered in February 1896 in Turin, Italy. It would be showing every Saturday in May at the Butte Opera House in Cripple Creek.

"Actually," my friend finally replied as he approached the front door to the Tutt Building, "I was thinking we may want to take in an opera Saturday night in Denver, La Boheme won't be here until next month."

"What a coincidence," said I, as I finished reading the advertisement, "this opera features a dramatic contralto, which is how many people in the business describe Irene Adler's operatic singing voice. You don't for a moment have aspirations of a romantic rendezvous with this now married woman, do you my dear Mr. Holmes?"

"My good Doctor, you know my admiration for this woman, beyond her unequaled talents as a world-class opera singer, lies simply in her wit and daring. If there were to be a chance encounter I have no intentions of allowing my emotions to stray from being anything other than that of a platonic relationship," said Sherlock Holmes as he opened and held the door for me to enter the Tutt Building. "Now, about that drink you promised?"

As we stepped inside I observed there were three rows of wooden chairs, four across, all facing to our left, in which sat nine well-dressed men. Another man in a tweed wool suit stood writing on a floor to ceiling chalk board positioned in front of these men, all of whom were absorbed in what I imagined were fluctuating stock prices being continuously updated on the call board. Behind a bar stood a man in his late sixties wearing a white apron and a black derby, another man in a suit was standing on this side of the bar drinking a beer. Half the men looked up briefly as we walked in and all turned away except for one, Winfield Scott Stratton, whom General Palmer had introduced us to yesterday in front of Colorado College.

"Gentlemen," Mr. Stratton said, as he stood and shook our hands. "Welcome to Cripple Creek. May I buy you a drink?"

"Yes, thank you," Sherlock Holmes said, as we followed Mr. Stratton to the bar.

"Rollie," Mr. Stratton said to the bartender, "I'll take a beer and a shot, and please add whatever these gentlemen are having to my tab."

"We'll have the same," Sherlock Holmes replied, answering for the both of us.

"When in Rome," I thought to myself, unaccustomed to drinking whiskey while chasing it with a beer.

Mr. Stratton pointed to the nearby cupboard with a nice assortment of breads, meats and cheeses arranged neatly on silver platter below a large mirror, "I was about to make myself a sandwich, care to join me?"

We followed Mr. Stratton to the cupboard where I made myself a thick ham and Swiss cheese sandwich with spicy mustard spread on freshly baked cracked wheat bread.

"I read on the front window where the Tutt Building has private conference rooms," Sherlock Holmes commented as we three finished making our sandwiches and looked for a place to sit.

"Yes," Mr. Stratton replied, "Rollie, could you please have our drinks delivered to the back room?"

Once we had settled into one of the private conference rooms on the main level, with our drinks and sandwiches, Sherlock Holmes said, "Mr. Stratton, I am sure you get this request all the time, but we would be most grateful in hearing from you your story about how it was you came to be Cripple Creek's first millionaire."

"I don't mind sharing my story with you," Mr. Stratton said, as he drank down his whiskey in one gulp and chased it with a long pull from his icy beer mug. "I arrived in the Colorado Springs area in 1868, just barely twenty-years-old. Like everyone else I came with dreams of striking it rich in silver or gold. I had heard there was gold here in the Cripple Creek area. I came up every year for twenty-three years in a row, prospecting. During the winter, when it got too cold up here to mine, I'd take odd jobs as a carpenter down in Colorado Springs, saving up enough money to fund another season prospecting. Then I'd make my way back up here in the spring, prospect for gold and then head back down once the snow fell. Broke. Year after year. Twenty-three years in a row. Then in 1891, I was up here with two other men, camped out for the night on the south slope of Pikes Peak. When I awoke from a dream the next morning, July 4th, and this is where some people think I'm a little touched in the head…"

"Please go on," said Sherlock Holmes encouragingly.

"Well, you see," Mr. Stratton continued softly, "in my dream, this angel came to me, when I was asleep there, in camp, and showed me where I should dig. I recognized the very spot instantly for I had been there before, t'was over near where the town of Victor stands today. So early the next morning, when I awoke, I didn't say nothin to the other two men. I knew they'd just laugh at me if I told them about being visited by an angel. At dawn I struck out on my own, walked right to the exact spot where the angel had pointed to in my dream and I began to dig. Almost immediately I struck gold, a thick rich vein of it, so I covered over where I had been digging, staked out a claim and made my way back into Colorado Springs to file my claim at the El Paso County Clerk and Recorders Office. I named my mine the Independence, recognizing it being filed on the Fourth of July. Now, this is where most folks ask how they can get rich themselves or offer to help me spend my money if'n I was to give them some, sort of like doing me a favor, taking as much of it off my hands as I was willing to let go."

"Well, we're not miners ourselves, and we're not interested in relieving you of your well-earned wealth," Sherlock Holmes replied as he finished his sandwich, folded his hands over his plate and leaned forward, "but we would be most interested to know, from your experience and intimate understanding of the mining operations here in the gold region, are there any mines that within the past year or two began producing large quantities of gold rather unexpectedly?"

"Well," Mr. Stratton said, after thinking about the question for a moment, "I know most of the mines round here of any consequence; Womack's Gold King Mine, the Mollie Kathleen, Anaconda, Pharmacist, the C.O.D. owned once by Spencer Penrose and Charlie Tutt, and the Portland over on Battle Mountain, owned by the Two Jimmies; but there are two mines here inside the bowl of gold that did truly surprise me; the Cracker Jack and the Tincup."

"Do you mind if I take notes?" I asked of Mr. Stratton.

"I don't mind you taking notes," he replied, "but please don't repeat what I'm a tellin you to anyone; you see, I've had more than my share of trouble with the miners' union."

"What can you tell us about the miners' union?" Sherlock asked.

"It all began in '94, when the owners of the Buena Vista increased their daily shift from eight hours to nine, with no increase in wages. Most of the other mine owners here in Cripple Creek started doing the same; dumb idea. I wouldn't have liked it neither. Spencer and Tutt sold their C.O.D. last year and wisely invested their profits in an ore processing plant down near Colorado City. Me and the Two Jimmies, Doyle and Burns, kept our shifts to eight hours. Other mine owners started hiring strikebreakers and scab labor. The union men resorted to harassing and threating the replacement laborers. The Panic of 1893 had caused the price of silver to plummet while the price of gold remained relatively steady. Out-of-work silver miners poured into the gold mines so hiring nonunion miners who were willing to cross the picket lines was not a problem; most just trying to feed their families. Strikers began setting off dynamite; blew up the shaft house at the Strong Mine on Battle Mountain and then the train depot down the street, killing several nonunion men and wounding dozens more. That's why we've had to build us a new train depot. Some of these men round here would just as soon kill you as look at you."

"Who started the miners' union?" Sherlock Holmes asked as I took notes.

"Well, there was this one fella, you mighta of known him, being he was from Scotland and all, named Calderwood. Said he had begun mining when he was just nine-years-old. Immigrated to the States, worked mining coal in Pennsylvania for a while and then moved west to Butte, Montana, where he somehow got himself on the wrong side of both the mine owners and the miners. He was instrumental in forming the Western Federation of Miners in '83, in Butte, and then he came here in '94 and began right off organizing our miners into the WFM labor organization. He intimidated most of the miners in the Poverty Gulch area, Anaconda and Victor to join the WFM. When Calderwood called for their first strike, five hundred miners walked out of the mines but seven hundred continued working."

"What happened next?" asked I.

"Tempers flared up between union and nonunion miners; then mine owners went to a district judge down in Colorado Springs, who granted them an injunction to prevent the WFM from interfering with mining operations. Mine owners had hired spies to infiltrate the union. When two of these spies were discovered, they were tortured and one was killed and throwed down a mine shaft, the other was taken to the edge of town and run off.

"Then in March '94, El Paso County Sheriff, Frank Bowers, caught up with Calderwood in Altman and served him with a restraining order. The sheriff left six deputies to keep the peace, but a mob captured three of the deputies and took 'em prisoner. Calderwood negotiated their release; but things never got much better, I'd encourage you both to use an abundance of caution while you're here asking questions, there are spies all around you here bouts and money talks. Everything is for sale in mining towns; booze, sex, cocaine, even information. Miners see the mine owners sitting back getting richer while they're breaking their backs down in the mines. Since the strike in '94, mine owners have been accusing the miners of high-grading."

"I don't know what high-grading means," I confessed.

"High-grading is when miners conceal the highest grade of ore in their lunch pail or on their person, and sneak it out of the mine," Sherlock Holmes replied.

"And then they fence the stolen gold ore on the black market," Mr. Stratton added.

"Can't they be searched when they're leaving the mines?" asked I incredulously.

"Yes," Mr. Stratton answered, "mine owners began requiring the miners to be strip-searched when they got off shift, which didn't go over well at all, as you can imagine. Some miners claimed the ore was planted on them, when they was caught, so Calderwood negotiated with the mine owners to allow one WFM representative to be present whenever a union member was searched; nevertheless, the policy of strip-searching everyone was very unpopular with the miners and a most unpleasant task for everyone involved. Most strip searches done now are supposedly random and what compounds things is high-graders are rarely prosecuted to the full extent of the law. They are usually just fired and then they move on to the next mine, where they're hired, often under an assumed name, so the process starts up all over again. Miners here in the Cripple Creek area are paid an average of three dollars a day, but miners can make an extra twenty dollars a day high-grading."

"Where is the ore from the Cracker Jack and Tincup mines processed?" Sherlock Holmes asked.

"The ore from the Cracker Jack is loaded onto the Midland railroad cars and hauled down to Tutt and Penrose's Colorado-Philadelphia Reduction Company outside of Colorado City, where the ore is processed. Once the gold is extracted it's melted and then poured into ingots or bricks. But the owners of the Tincup, some odd consortium of sorts from Switzerland, invested a boatload of cash to build their own processing plant up here after they bought the mine in '94."

"You mentioned you were surprised to see how the Cracker Jack and Tincup mines exceeded your expectations in gold output," Sherlock Holmes said.

"Yes, I may have misread the Cracker Jack, or maybe they got lucky and hit a rich vein, luck has a lot to do with gold mining, but I thought the Tincup was nearly played out. I don't know, maybe they're secretly bringing in ore from another local mine, sort of like salting the mine to artificially inflate the value of the mine, but these guys don't seem to be wanting to sell."

"Or they're high-grading?" I asked.

"That's always a possibility," Mr. Stratton said, "Either way, the Tincup is far out producing what they should be, at least in my book. I'd advise you gentlemen to shy away from the Tincup if you're looking to invest."

"Thank you, Mr. Stratton," Sherlock Holmes said as we began to take our leave, "we're not looking to invest, but we will be very cautious with the information you have provided."

"Well, I don't know how much help I have been to you gentlemen, but there is one favor I might ask of you," Mr. Stratton said.

"Certainly," Sherlock Holmes said.

"When you gentlemen get back to London could you keep your ear to the ground for any reputable investors who may be interested in buying my Independence Mine? I'm thinking it's about time I sold out and invested my wealth into some more worthwhile cause so people will stop hounding me all the time for my money."

"We will do that for you, Mr. Stratton, my brother Mycroft

runs in rather wealthy circles," Sherlock Holmes replied, "and now if it's not too much trouble could you please ask if Mr. Tutt or Mr. Penrose might be available to speak with us privately for a few minutes?"

Mr. Stratton led us upstairs where we found the door leading to Mr. Tutt's office standing open. His office was near the front of the building overlooking Bennett Avenue. Upon knocking on the office door, Mr. Stratton said, "Charlie there's a couple gentlemen here from London I'd like you to meet, Mr. Sherlock Holmes and Dr. John Watson."

Charles Tutt stepped around his large wooden desk and shook hands. As we took our seats, Mr. Stratton excused himself and closed the door on his way out. In short order we had learned that Charles Tutt and his friend Speck Penrose had been childhood friends growing up in Philadelphia. Tutt had moved to Colorado in '92 and convinced Speck to join him two years later in '94. Evidently Speck's brother Richard Penrose, a successful geologist, had read the mineralogical reports from the rocks around the Cripple Creek region and encouraged Speck to accept Tutt's offer to loan him the money so the two friends could go into business together. As Cripple Creek grew, the Tutt-Penrose real estate business also grew. They specialized in commercial properties; selling gold mines and business lots in downtown Cripple Creek. Mr. Tutt said the Cripple Creek business listings had now exceeded eight hundred businesses and the population was rapidly approaching forty-thousand. Speck Penrose was in Colorado Springs, so we didn't get to speak with him personally; but Mr. Tutt reaffirmed Mr. Stratton's suspicion that the gold output of the Tincup Mine and its milling operation far exceeded their expectations.

We left the Tutt Building through the back door, so as not to be noticed, and walked east up the alley to the corner of Bennett

Avenue and Second Street where we observed the bay doors standing open to the Cripple Creek Fire Department. Inside we found Cripple Creek's fire chief, Frank May, busily greasing the axel of a hose cart.

"Good afternoon," Sherlock Holmes said as we approached the fireman, "Please don't let us interrupt you, we happened to notice the doors to your station standing open and thought we'd inquire for a moment about your department."

"Gentlemen, please excuse my manners, I'd shake hands," the fireman said, "but my hands are covered with axel grease. I'm Fire Chief May, what can I do for you gentlemen?"

"We happen to be looking to invest in business property in town here and wish to inquire about the state of readiness for your department in case of a fire emergency."

"Well, you'll find your business in capable hands with us, I can assure you," Chief May said proudly. "Our city officials have invested in two water reservoirs; one located about two hundred yards uphill there," the fire chief said pointing with a greasy finger out the open bay door to the north of the station. "We have nearly three miles of underground water pipes, with fire hydrants on every corner; each fire hydrant has excellent water pressure that can easily reach the roof of our tallest three-storied buildings, in case of a fire on an upper floor."

"Do you have full-time firemen stationed here round the clock?" Sherlock Holmes asked as he glanced around at dozens of firemen jackets and helmets hung on coat hooks.

"I'm the only full-time paid member of the fire department, but we have one-hundred and seventy-five trained volunteers. Besides this one, we have two other new hose carts, a hook and ladder wagon with highly-trained members of the J.L. Lindsay Hose Company right behind them and we also have a state-of-the-art chemical engine. We cross-train monthly with the boys from the Victor Fire Department, they're only five miles away so we can transport our equipment and firemen by train should the occasion arise where we need to support them or them us on a big fire."

"Well, it is reassuring to know you are so well-equipped and trained," Sherlock Holmes said and then asked what it was he really wanted to know, "Does the Cripple Creek Fire Department have only the one bell tower?"

"That's all that's needed," Fire Chief May said as he wiped the grease off his hands with a red rag. "The city limits is under a mile and a half square; our fire bell can be easily heard from anywhere in town."

"You have just the one 65-pound fire bell then?" Sherlock Holmes asked.

"HA! We have just the one fire bell," Chief May said with a grunt as he lifted the heavy wooden spoke wheel back onto its axel and tightened the square nut with a large wrench. "But our fire bell weighs 600-pounds! I'm not sure who would want a 65-pound fire bell, couldn't be heard all that far away." The fire chief said as he stood up, wiped his hands again with the greasy red rag, stuffed it into the back pocket of his uniform pants and then pointed up to the mines on the nearby hillside with his wrench, "When our fire bell tolls it can be heard all the way up there, at the mines, almost three-quarters of a mile away."

"Is that the Tincup Mine?" Sherlock Holmes asked pointing to a mine on the ridgeline east of town.

"No, that's the Mollie Kathleen," Chief May replied, "that's the Tincup over there, on Battle Mountain."

"Thank you, Chief May," Sherlock Holmes said as we walked out the front bay doors and headed off in the direction of Battle Mountain.

Same Day 10:30pm
Tincup Mine, Battle Mountain, Cripple Creek, Colorado, U.S.A.

WE WAITED UNTIL DARK before approaching the hillside above the Tincup Mine. From there we watched for nearly an hour as a handful of workers departed the mine and milling plant, making their way down the hill into town. As we approached the mine's entrance it appeared there was only one night watchman on duty and he seemed more interested in the newspaper he was reading than with two well-dressed strangers sneaking past him into the entrance of the mine. Immediately inside the mine entrance Sherlock Holmes found two lanterns, which he lit with a Sulphur match, handing one to me, then we cautiously entered the dark mine.

"Over there," Sherlock Holmes said pointing to a pair of wire cage elevators suspended above the vertical mine shaft, "come, this way."

"Said the spider to the fly," I quipped as we stepped into one of the two flimsy elevator cars suspended by a steel cable over what appeared to be a bottomless pit.

"We don't need to search the entire mine," he said as he released the brake on the cable and began lowering us down the shaft. "I'm only interested to know if they're still actively working this mine or to confirm it is more likely a cover for their criminal activities.

"And how do we get ourselves back up?" asked I as I watched horizontal shafts pass as we continued to descend slowly down the vertical mine shaft.

"These elevator cars are normally operated under steam power but they also have a manual pulley system; see that block and tackle overhead?"

"Yes, but I suspect we're going to find it much harder going up than down."

"Perhaps," Sherlock Holmes said as we stopped at horizontal shaft, "that is why you're here." We opened the wire elevator door and as I held my lantern up we read by the dim light the number five painted on a crudely made metal sign.

"Level five," said I, then asked, "how far down are we?"

"I don't know," said he, "I'm guessing these horizontal shafts are perhaps thirty meters beneath one another, we may be down a hundred and fifty meters or more."

"From my limited understanding of mining," said I, "I understand miners dig the vertical shafts downwards first, then dig outwards with these horizontal shafts, hoping to hit a gold vein which they follow until it runs out and then one moves on to the next horizontal shaft or further down the main vertical shaft."

"I think that's about right, all I hope for us to accomplish tonight is to confirm the Tincup here is not producing any large quantities of gold ore. One thing for certain, they are not running twenty-four hour a day operations, like most of the other mines, so they're not operating at anywhere near capacity."

"Agreed," said I. "Other than that one night watchman, it appears as if we're the only ones down here. Wait, what's that sound?"

"It's the other elevator car," Sherlock Holmes said, "it is descending."

"Maybe it's the night watchman. Do you think he saw us?"

"I don't know, there might have been other watchmen uptop that we didn't see, or it could be a small crew of miners, whoever it is they haven't stopped at any of the other horizontal shafts above us. I think we are going to have to go deeper into the mine shaft and find a place to hide while we extinguish our lights."

We walked rapidly away from the elevator shaft, deeper into the mine, looking for a place to hide. "There, behind that pile of rocks," Sherlock Holmes said.

"I'm getting my new Brooks Brothers suit dirty," I complained quietly as I kneeled down behind the pile of loose rock, "and my new shoes are getting all scuffed up."

"Shhh, now, turn out your lantern," Sherlock Holmes whispered. As our lights went out I discovered a new definition of darkness. There was absolutely no light; this was total and absolute darkness and spooky.

"I think they have stopped here at level five," said I quietly.

"Quiet," whispered my friend whom I could not see although he was kneeling inches away from me. "They are coming this way; listen, I hear voices."

"It sounds as if they're arguing," said I. Then I heard a POW! "Is that a gunshot?" I asked, then "POW. POW!" Two more distinctive gunshots rang out and I thought I saw the muzzle flash of a gun, about a hundred meters down the shaft toward where the elevator cars were parked. "What's that?" said I seeing a faint light bouncing along the shaft coming toward us rapidly.

"Someone's running this way," Sherlock Holmes said, as he reached out and put his arm on my shoulder and whispered into my ear, "Now might be a proper occasion to retrieve your service revolver."

I felt for the latch on my medical bag at my feet, opened the top and felt around inside. I welcomed the familiar touch of my revolver, pulled the gun from my leather bag, but found I had no target. All I could see was the tiny white light, about five feet above the ground, growing larger as it was coming toward us. The shooting had stopped and it sounded as if the elevator car had started up again. Now there was no sound except for that of footfalls, running toward us. Sherlock Holmes pulled me to my feet. I heard the sound of a person laboring to breathe as the white light slowed and then illuminated Sherlock Holmes and me standing next to him; I shielded my eyes with my hand and pointed my gun toward the light.

"Don't shoot!" A man's voice shouted out, and he moved toward us, "Hurry, not a moment to loose!"

"Do as he says!" Sherlock Holmes commanded as the man rushed passed us.

"In there!" the man said as he pushed my friend and me toward a deep hole in the wall behind the pile of rocks. "Quickly, under here!" said he as we huddled beneath a heavy iron ore car leaning over on its side. "Help me pull it down on top of us," said this stranger wearing the headlamp of a miner attached to a helmet on his head.

The three of us lowered the heavy ore car over our heads; there was barely room enough for two men, let alone three and this now intimate stranger was not a small man. We were so close to one another I could smell the body odor of the two men clustered next to me. "What," I started to say, but before I could finish asking my questions the ground beneath us rumbled and began to move upwards and then I heard a loud explosion—KABOOM!

"Dynamite," the stranger sitting next me said, "they've sealed the entrance."

Rocks rained down upon the overturned ore cart under which we had taken refuge. Then the light on the miner's helmet went out. The ground shook violently for several seconds. I couldn't tell if the entire mountain had collapsed down on top of us or just loose rocks. No one spoke until the rocks had stopped falling. There we three sat in complete silence. Each man contemplating the same question in his mind, "Is this how my life will end?"

I felt movement coming from my friend, at least he was alive. Then I heard the sound and smelled the Sulphur of a match being lit. Sherlock Holmes held the match upright between the three of us to where we could see one another's faces. "Hello

Stanley," Sherlock Holmes said, "Long way from Piccadilly Circus aren't we?"

"Wishin I was back there now, I can tell you that much," the big man said.

"Dr. Watson," said Sherlock Holmes, "I don't believe you've met Stanley "Shady" Coyne, have you?"

"A pleasure, I'm sure," said I as the match went out. "I believe you're sitting on my hand Mr. Shady."

Sherlock Holmes lit another match.

"Here," Stanley Coyne said, as he pulled a small white candle from his pocket, "before the flame goes out again."

Sherlock Holmes lit the candle and said, "Let's see if we can lift this ore car off of us before we run out of oxygen."

We managed to tip the ore car over onto its side and slowly stood up. Fortunately, neither Sherlock Holmes nor I were seriously injured; however, by the light of the candle I could see blood on the trousers of Mr. Coyne.

"You are injured," said I, "drop your pants and let me take a look."

"Said the spider to the fly," Sherlock Holmes quipped as I borrowed the candle and examined Mr. Coyne's lower calf muscle to see where the blood was coming from.

"Sherlock," said I, "perhaps you could make yourself useful, see if you can locate my medical bag and maybe find one of our lanterns? I could use a better light here."

"I suspect it's a gunshot wound," Mr. Coyne said, as I probed the wound to the front and back of his leg under the candlelight.

"I believe you are correct," said I as Sherlock Holmes approached with a lit lantern.

"I'm afraid the other lantern is broken," Sherlock Holmes said, "And, unfortunately, your medical bag here has seen its better days." I glanced over to see where he had set my expensive brown leather medical bag on the ground at my feet. "I'm sorry to say it was crushed under a handful of large rocks along with your hat."

"Lovely," said I as I placed my flattened hat upon my head and opened my ruined medical bag, "Look, it's all scuffed up now. I had just bought this bag before we left London, to match my new brown leather wingtip shoes."

"Well, if it's any consolation Dr. Watson," Mr. Coyne said, as he pointed down to my dirt covered shoes, "Your scuffed up bag still matches your shoes."

"And look here," said I, "the knees of my trousers are torn too, and the cuff here is ripped half way off. I'm a mess."

"You would have looked more of a mess had Stanley Coyne not come along when he did," Sherlock Holmes replied. "Just how was it that you happened to be here at our hour of need?"

"Well, OUCH! That hurts Doc!"

"He does that to me all the time; you really must work on your bedside manners, Dr. Watson," Sherlock Holmes said as he struggled to repair the broken lantern.

"Try to hold still," said I, as I continued to debride the gunshot wound in the man's leg, "The bullet exited the front of your leg here, but I will need to clean the wound track, best I can in this unsterile environment, least you run the risk of infection over the next week or two."

"That may be the least of his problems," Sherlock Holmes said as he managed to get the broken lantern lit and held it up toward where the tons of rock that had fallen into the mine shaft between ourselves and the elevator shaft. "We appear to be trapped some hundreds of feet below ground and I don't expect anyone up top will be interested in mounting a rescue effort for us anytime soon."

"You are correct there, Mr. Holmes," Mr. Coyne said, "That dynamite explosion was meant to kill you and me both. When I saw you boxing there on the RMS Republic, knowing that golden fire bell from Whitechapel was on the same ship as us, well, I figured it was just a matter of time a 'fore you found yourself here to Cripple Creek."

"But why would they want to kill you?" asked I as I finished wrapping a white bandage around his leg. "Were you not one of them?"

"Three days ago I got a telegram from my sister-in-law back in London, telling me my brother, Robert, was dead. Said he'd been run over by a freight wagon over on Cannon Lane. She didn't know why he was there and the driver of the freight wagon didn't stick around at the scene of the accident, so I got to wondering if it really was an accident. Tonight I was at Johnny Nolan's Saloon, and I bought a couple rounds for the other guy who came across the pond with me. I don't know his real name; he just goes by 'Stark" or "Colonel" a real skinny bloke, mid-forties I'm guessing. Anyways, Stark had hired me back in London to help him make sure this wooden crate containing a fire bell got delivered here to the Cripple Creek Fire Department. Funny thing Doc, one night, when we was at sea, Stark came limping back to our cabin and he himself had gotten shot in the leg."

"Served him right, I'm sure," said I.

"Does this Stark work alone or is there someone else involved?" Sherlock asked.

"There's another guy, an English doctor, but he's not a real doctor like you, Dr. Watson."

"What does he look like?" Sherlock asked.

"Real short fella, a bit older than Stark, from his waistline he looks like he never was one to miss a meal. He was involved in some counterfeiting operation back in England that went wrong. They may have killed a man outside of Reading, from what I was able to pick up. This English doctor, I don't know his name, he never liked me, he thought I was just Cockney trash, my coming from the Cheapside of London, anyways he came here to Cripple Creek a month or two before I got here with Stark. Stark had been here a couple times before."

"Do you know where they're staying?" Sherlock Holmes asked.

"They have rooms on the upper floor of the Central Dance Hall, on the south side of Myers Avenue," Shady said as he pulled his pants back up and buckled his belt.

"Do you know who Stark and this English doctor work for?" Sherlock Holmes asked.

"I never met him and never heard a name, but the night Stark got shot on the boat he took to drinking real heavily afterwards, to deal with the pain of trying to doctor himself up, he let slip that The Professor owes him big time for taking a bullet. Whoever this Professor is he's been here in Cripple Creek before and he's got spies everywhere. According to Stark, one of these spies told the English doctor about two well-dressed men with English accents, asking questions around this afternoon at the Fire Department about a 65-pound fire bell. I didn't know these two men had English accents until I stepped off the elevator at Level Five with Stark. He went over to the dynamite locker and that's when Stark told me these two men with English accents, who had been asking about the fire bell, had been followed here to the Tincup Mine and had slipped past the night watchman. What you two didn't know was the man who had followed you had informed Stark, who had told that English doctor, you two was a down here. When I asked Stark what he was gonna do with the dynamite, that's when he pulled his gun on me and said, 'accidents happen' which also confirmed to me in my mind that my brother, Robert's death was no accident. That's when I took off running, down the shaft here, to warn you what Stark was a fixing to do, Mr. Holmes. That's when I got shot in the leg."

"Thank you, Shady, I will remember what you've done. How long had Robert worked at the Royal Mint?" Sherlock Holmes asked.

"Several years now, t'was a good job for 'em. Things was going really well there for a spell for me brother. Robert had a good job at the Mint, pretty wife, growing family, then one night after work he stopped by a pub on the way home with a coworker for a pint and his friend introduced him to this floozy. Robert told me his wife, Sophia—she was a good catholic girl—had told him she didn't want no more kids and so she cut him off. But she had one more kid, a tow-headed boy, didn't look nothin like Robert. Last Christmas, I'd had a wee bit too much of the whisky in me and suggested to Robert, in front of his wife, maybe the boy's birth was another Immaculate Conception. Robert threw me outta da house. Can't rightly blame him."

"What was Robert's girlfriend's name?" Sherlock Holmes asked.

"He never told me her name, but he did say she had a German accent and was real hard to understand, especially when she got excited, if you know what I means."

"How about the coworker who introduced Robert to this woman at the pub? What was his name?" Sherlock Holmes asked.

"I only met him once, but I remember his first name was Thomas, cause that was me own father's name."

"Thomas Leadbedder?" Sherlock Holmes asked.

"Yeah, that's the bloke!" Mr. Coyne replied.

"All that's for not if we don't get out of here," said I, trying not to sound as desperate as I felt.

"I'm sure there must be a way out," Shady said, "one of the first things miners do underground is make sure they dig themselves an exit in case there's a cave in; our difficulty is in finding it."

"No difficulty there," Sherlock Holmes said, pointing to how the yellow flame burning atop the candle was leaning to one side, "we just follow the draft to lead us to fresh air."

"We best get busy then," Shady said, "it's a long way up and it's gonna require some considerable effort."

"Considerable effort" turned out to be an understatement. It took the three of us three hours of tracing and retracing the horizontal shafts just to find access to Level Four. Then when we found the elevator cars for that level the elevators were also inoperable, no doubt sabotaged by Colonel Stark from above. Then we had to go back searching for the secondary access to Level Three, then to Level Two and so forth before we finally reached ground level some twenty-two hours later. Mr. Coyne showed us a back way out of the milling plant so as not to be seen by the night watchman. From there we hiked five miles to the neighboring town of Victor wanting to avoid being spotted by the Professor's spies in Cripple Creek; though it was doubtful anyone would recognize us in our filthy condition and state of dress, resembling most of the miners.

March 14th, 1896 11:30pm
Victor, Colorado, U.S.A.

We rested on a hillside, above the train tracks leading from Victor to Colorado City. I laid on my back, staring up at the glistening stars. It was a cold, clear night.

"Won't be daylight for at least six more hours," Sherlock Holmes said.

"I guess we should count our lucky stars to be alive," said I. "I don't recall ever seeing a night sky more filled with stars than what's above us right now."

"There's the Milky Way. The stars look much closer at this altitude," Sherlock Holmes said pointing; he was lying on his back as well, positioned to the right of me, while Shady Coyne snoozed on and off about twenty yards to the left of me. Sherlock Holmes remained quiet for some time; I thought he too may have fallen asleep when finally he spoke in a low voice so as not to be overheard by Shady Coyne, "My dear Doctor Watson, I owe you an apology."

"An apology?" I asked, "Whatever for?"

"For nearly getting us killed."

"Why? You did nothing wrong," said I.

"I did everything wrong, which is what nearly got us killed." Sherlock Holmes said in a most sincere tone. "We had been warned about there being spies all around us and yet I allowed us to walk into the devil's den wearing nothing more than an American-made suit to conceal our identity. I underestimated my opponent, a capital mistake. I was distracted by my wanting to test my skills as a pugilist, in facing this professional boxer named Dempsey, and worse, the worst mistake of all, I allowed my romantic thoughts of seeing The Woman again to cloud my better judgement. For those egregious errors I offer you my most humble and sincere apology."

"Apology accepted," said I. "But I knew the inherent risks when we boarded that ship back in Liverpool."

"If you are still game," Sherlock Holmes said and paused for my reply.

"You know me, I am always game," I answered.

"Good, you may want to write my requests down."

"Hold on," said I as I found my notebook and a pencil and sat upright so I could write down his instructions under the moonlight. "Go on, I'm ready."

"First, I need you and Shady to hop aboard the next outbound freight train and make your way back to Colorado Springs, without buying a ticket; you must avoid being detected by any spies hanging about the nearby train depots. You will need to pass yourself off as a hobo."

"Well I'm certainly dressed the part," said I as I looked

down at the tattered condition of what was my favorite Brooks Brothers suit.

"And don't speak to anyone other than Shady; you must not allow your English accent to betray you until you get back to Glen Eyrie. Do you remember the two tactics General Palmer shared with us that helped him from being executed when he was taken prisoner during their Civil War?"

"Yes, he had a believable cover story and word spread about Washington D.C. reporting his presence in their Nation's Capital, suggesting he could not be the man being held in prison."

"Precisely, your cover story, until you reach the safety of Glen Eyrie, is that you are a deaf mute who tried his hand at gold mining and are now trying to make your way back home to San Francisco."

"Why San Francisco?" asked I.

"Because, once we leave Colorado, if for some reason, you and I were to become separated for more than two weeks; you will know where to go so that we can meet up."

"But why San Francisco?"

"Because there is a pattern to all this; raw gold being mined from the ground and being processed nearby, and like Denver, San Francisco also has a U.S. Mint."

"Where in San Francisco do I meet you? I understand it's a rather large city."

"Fisherman's Wharf. Go there at noon to feed the pigeons for ten days in a row, if I am not there on the eleventh day make your way back to London without me."

"Understood, but how am I to make our presence known in Colorado Springs when you are here and not there with me?"

"I'm sure General Palmer can help you with that ruse, make your presence known riding about town in a carriage, with one of Palmer's trusted employees dressed up as me, make dinner reservations for two under my name, then cancel at the last minute, you might send a telegram or two to me at the Antlers Hotel."

"Very well," said I, making notations on the pages of my notebook.

"Speaking of telegrams," Sherlock Holmes said.

"Yes, go on."

"Please send one to Lestrade and Gregson at the Yard, asking that Thomas Leadbedder be taken into protective custody and held until I return to London."

"Very well, what else?" said I looking over to make sure Shady was still asleep.

"Make an odd number withdraw from our joint account at your earliest opportunity."

"Yes, a wise decision," said I.

"Not only is it a wise decision to alert the PM things have gone astray, but I'm going to need you to give me whatever money you presently have on your person."

I handed Sherlock Holmes all my money and said, "What else?"

"This investigation may require considerably more pains than I had at first anticipated. I will have to remain here, alone, and go deep undercover as a miner. This could take considerable time. Do you think you can occupy yourself around Colorado Springs for a month or so?"

"Certainly, I have wanted to spend some time with my friend and colleague Dr. Bell to learn of the medical advancements being made here in the treatment of consumption."

"Excellent. One last request," Sherlock Holmes said.

"Yes," said I ready to make myself a note.

"Buy yourself a new suit, you look rather a mess."

March 15th, 1896 2:40am
Gold Camp Road, El Paso County, Colorado, U.S.A.

SHADY COYNE SHOWED ME HOW TO HOP a freight car, which was much more difficult than he made it look. As we rode the train hauling tons of gold ore from the Cripple Creek goldfields to the smelters below near Colorado Springs, I worried about my friend Sherlock Holmes, going deep undercover as a miner in the Greatest Gold Camp on Earth. I was less concerned about his being discovered, knowing how adept he was in disguising himself, but what concerned me the most was himself. Not only as his friend, but as his doctor, I knew all too well the ever-present temptations brought on by his addiction to cocaine, fueled by his alcohol consumption, but this time his calculating mind would be clouded with thoughts of The Woman, Irene Adler.

"They're coming," Shady whispered.

"Who?" asked I, as our train approached the entrance to a tunnel up ahead.

"Railroad dicks," Shady said, "I was hoping we might avoid them, we may need to hop off when we comes out of this tunnel."

"Hopefully they'll slow the train down to let us off."

"Wishful think'n," said he as he looked ahead to where the tracks exited the tunnel and made a bend around a hillside with a slightly even grade. "That might be our best bet, they'll have to slow down a goin round that bend. Git yurself a ready to jump."

"You two!" shouted the railroad detective, with a thick Irish brogue. He shined his electric torch on Shady and me hanging on to the side railing of the freight car. "Where do you think you're going? Don't make me chase you to the next car!"

While trying to cradle my crumbled up medical bag in one hand, and holding onto the railing in the other, I made a feeble attempt to use sign language, in keeping with my cover to be an out-of-luck deaf mute. To my amazement the railroad detective signed back to me. I had no idea what he was trying to communicate until he spoke.

"That's the poorest excuse for sign language I ever did see," said the railroad detective as he pulled his Billy club from his back pocket. "What I was a signing you was my little brother, in Colorado Springs, is a deaf mute, but you couldn't understand me cause you ain't one are you?"

The jig was up so I decided my best option was to try to reason with the big angry man. "My apologies constable," said I, "truth be told I'm trying to make my way back to Glen Eyrie where I'm staying as a guest of General Palmer."

"The President of the Denver & Rio Grande?" asked the railroad detective.

"Yes," said I, hanging onto the railing between Shady and the railroad detective.

"And I suppose you arrived here in Little London aboard your own private Pullman car, did you?" said he.

"As a matter of fact we did," said I, "all the way from New York City." I breathed a sigh of relief in knowing the man with the Billy club was beginning to understand we weren't hobos, despite the shoddy way we were dressed and riding a freight car in the middle of the night.

"Off you go," said the railroad detective as he tapped his Billy club on the railing above my knuckles. "If there's one thing I can't tolerate, even more than someone who can't tell the truth, is someone pretending to be deaf or handicapped in some way when they ain't."

"Come on, Doc, train's a slowed down as much as it's going to," said Shady, "this might be the best place to hop off."

I watched as Shady released his grip and rolled down the embankment away from the tracks.

"Off you go!" said the railroad detective, as he reached out and pushed me from the train.

I dropped my medical bag, as I rolled down the dirt embankment, finally coming to rest beneath some thorny bushes. As the train lumbered past and disappeared into the dark of night I saw by the moon's light Shady picking up my doctors bag and a handful of my scattered medical equipment which had fallen out of my bag.

"Come, Doctor Watson," said Shady, pointing down below, "We might be in luck."

"How so?" said I, as I stood up, tried to brush the dirt off my completely ruined suit and questioned in my mind how things could get any worse.

"There's a campfire a burning down below there," Shady said, as he handed me my tattered medical bag and whatever instruments he managed to see in the dim moonlight. "It won't be light for another four hours, let's make our way down to dat camp where we'll be safe."

"Safe?" said I, looking about, "safe from what?"

"Da bears," said Shady, "they're coming out of hibernation this time of year and they'll be right hungry."

"Let's go," said I, as I followed close behind the big man. Sherlock Holmes had told me privately that Stanley "Shady" Coyne was one of his many informants on the streets of London.

"Once the sun comes up," Shady said, as we neared the firelight, "You'll be on your own."

"Where are you going?"

"I'll be making my way to Colorado Springs, there's a fella named Clark I worked with once afore. I'll try to make enough money to make me way back to London, see if there's anything I can do to help my sister-in-law and her kids. My brother Robert had a pretty good paying job there at the Royal Mint, but he was never one to save up much money."

"I don't have any money on me right now, but if you can wait until later in the day I can make a withdrawal at one of the banks in Colorado Springs. I feel I owe you something for saving my and Sherlock Holmes' life back there in the mine."

"You and Mr. Holmes saved my life too; Stark would have shot me dead had I not turned and run to warn you when I did; sides, I watched you two workin just as hard as I did, diggin our way out from under that mountain, it wouldn't be right for me to take any money from yous."

"Here," said I, as I handed Shady my pocket watch, "maybe you can pawn this in Colorado Springs to give yourself a little walking around money. Take it; you can pay me back once we get back to London."

"Thank you, Dr. Watson," Shady said as he reluctantly accepted the only thing of value I had on me at the time. "I will pay you back for this. Now, let's see if we can gets invited into the camp, we don't want to get shot sneaking in unannounced."

"Speaking of which, you may want to get your gunshot wound looked at once you get to Colorado Springs, make sure it's not getting infected."

"Will do, thanks Doc," said Shady, and then shouted, "Hello the camp!"

"Hello yourself," came the reply from a man's voice in the dark. "Come on in."

"Thank you," said Shady as we approached the campfire. There were two hobos, dressed similarly to us, roasting a turkey around an open fire. "My name is Shady, this here's my buddy, Stinky Eddie, he's a deaf mute," Shady said, I waved keeping up the appearance I couldn't talk.

"Welcome," said the hobo turning the turkey on the spit over the fire. "I'm Tom, that's Jerry, we're about to have ourselves a feast here, you're welcome to join us if you're hungry."

"Thank you, that's mighty kind," Shady said as we sat down around the fire.

"Care for a snort?" Jerry asked, as he took a swig from a bottle and passed it around.

Shady took a drink and then handed me the liquor bottle, which I passed to Tom without taking a drink.

"Too good to drink with us?" Jerry asked, obviously intoxicated.

"No, he's trying to quit," Shady said.

"Ain't easy," Tom said as he pulled the turkey legs off the carcass and handed one to Jerry and one to me.

I hadn't realized how hungry I was until I smelled the turkey roasting over the open fire."

"I want that one," Jerry said as he reached for my turkey leg.

"No, this one's mine," said I holding my delicacy away from the drunken hobo and blowing my cover of being a deaf mute once again, adding, "Tom gave it to me!"

"I want it!" Jerry said as he lunged for my turkey leg, "You're no deaf mute." Next thing I knew I was rolling on the ground trying to keep this stranger from wrestling a turkey leg from my hand.

"Hold it you two! Why do you want that one, Jerry?" asked Tom, trying to separate the two men rolling on the ground.

"Left-handed turkey legs taste better," Jerry said.

"I done gave you the left one, Jerry, see?" Tom said pointing to the turkey leg Jerry had laid on a rock by the fire.

"Oh, sorry 'bout that," Jerry said as he went back over, picked up his turkey leg, and wandered off to eat his meal in solitude.

"He ain't been right since he got kicked in the head by a mule a while back," Tom explained as he cut slices of white meat from the turkey with a sharp knife.

"Maybe we best be goin," Shady said, as he accepted a piece of the turkey from Tom and we made our way away from the hobo camp.

"Thanks for the hospitality," said I as I held up my turkey leg in one hand, my battered medical bag in the other and walked with Shady away from the warmth of the camp fire.

"I can see why Mr. Holmes didn't want you being with him up in Cripple Creek," Shady said, "you can't stay in character more than ten minutes."

I didn't respond, as I finished my turkey leg, but had to agree, being undercover is harder than it might at first appear; especially when strong emotions are involved.

A couple of hours later, Shady said, "Sun will be up soon. Best we be on our separate ways. I'm headed down there," he said nodding to the lights of Colorado Springs below to our right. "If you stick to this logging road you'll come to Manitou Springs, you should be able to find your way from there. Good day to you, Doc, maybe I'll see you one day back in London."

"Good luck to you, Shady," said I as I buttoned the top button on my coat and watched him walk away toward the flickering lights of Little London.

Chapter 7

March 15th, 1896 11:30am

Manitou Springs, Colorado, U.S.A.

After leaving the hobo camp, I followed Shady's advise and headed north on the upper Gold Camp Road until I spotted the standing red rocks of the Garden of the Gods off in the distance. The first glint of sunlight reflecting off the tall red rocks was truly a breathtaking sight. I recalled General Palmer mentioning the Briarhurst Manor, the home of my friend Dr. Bell, being located at the west end of the Garden of the Gods, near the small town of Manitou Springs. Since the distance from my vantage point appeared to be considerably less to Manitou Springs, than Glen Eyrie, I decided to make my way to the Briarhurst Manor to inquire if Dr. Bell had yet returned from his trip to San Francisco, California.

With each step that drew me closer to Manitou Springs, where I would find safety and personal comfort with the help of friends, I was painfully aware I was leaving my best friend, Sherlock Holmes, further behind to face the dangers and his demons alone in the Greatest Gold Camp on Earth. I had little doubt Sherlock Holmes would be successful in locating a prospector, down on his luck and eager to sell his clothing, mining equipment and donkey to anyone with ready cash. This time, rather than two men with English accents, arriving by train, wearing expensive American three-piece-suits and asking questions about a 65-pound fire bell; Sherlock Holmes would simply slip into Cripple Creek unnoticed, dressed like the hundreds of gold prospectors and leading a donkey burdened down with well-used prospecting equipment.

Blending in with the crowd, and taking his time to craft a convincing cover story, I felt the inherent risks to Sherlock Holmes from his undercover investigation would likely pale as compared to his personal vices he will have to confront. Thinking of his cocaine addiction, unchecked alcohol consumption and the intoxicating adrenalin rush he receives whenever he enters a boxing ring against a worthy opponent; what troubled me the most, was his unbridled passion for The Woman. In six weeks Irene Adler, performing under a stage name and wearing an elaborate costume, would be starring in La Boheme at the Butte Opera House in Cripple Creek. I had every expectation that sitting all alone in a box seat on opening night would be, my friend, Sherlock Holmes.

As I walked into the outskirts of the small town of Manitou Springs, I observed a beautiful Victorian stone manor house. A large brass plaque on the stone column to the left of the gate read, "Briarhurst Manor" while the one on the right read "Established 1888". The majestic home of Dr. and Mrs. Bell was constructed using pink colored stone and trimmed in light blue lattice work. It had a stylish gray slate gabled roof topped with tall terra cotta colored fireplace chimneys that blended perfectly into the red rocks behind their home. The elegant house sat at the base of a hill, surrounded by tall evergreen trees. The landscaping was immaculate. A narrow stone bridge crossed over a babbling brook creating an idyllic setting rivaling any manor house set in the English countryside. I crossed the stone bridge and followed the winding path that led gracefully to a grand entrance.

A pair of English Foxhounds brayed nearby as I rapped the heavy brass door knocker upon the large brass plate and stepped back from the front door to await someone in answering my knock. For the first time since the sun had risen, I looked down at myself; Sherlock Holmes was correct, I looked affright! My suit and I were absolutely filthy. My topcoat was ripped and my hat was crushed. One pant cuff had been nearly torn from my pants leg and was hanging down around my ankle. My custom made shoes were scuffed beyond repair. My medical bag had been ruined; although, it was much lighter to carry since half my medical instruments had been lost when Shady and I were thrown from the train. The front door opened and a heavyset housekeeper wearing a spotless white uniform appeared.

"If it's somethin ta eat you're a after, you'll have ta go round ta the back door of the kitchen," she said with an unmistakable Irish brogue.

"Madam," said I, as she looked down her nose at me, "You don't understand, Dr. Bell is expecting me, could you please tell him Dr. Watson is here to see him?"

"You? A doctor? I hardly think so," she said as she started to close the door.

"Wait," said I, as I searched my pockets for a calling card. I reached inside my coat pocket and retrieved one of my last two embossed business cards from the inside pocket of my black leather notebook. "Here, please present my card to Dr. Bell."

"Wait here," the housekeeper said, suspiciously reading my name printed on the calling card aloud, "John H. Watson, M.D., London," as she closed the thick wooden door.

Within a few minutes the front door began to open and I heard the voice of Dr. Bell begin to say, "Why Dr. Watson, it's good to see..." his voice trailed off when he saw me. He looked from me to my business card he was holding in his hand and then back up at me.

"It is I, John Watson," said I, hoping he might recognize my voice. "I apologize for appearing so unsightly. The past two days have been rather harrowing."

"Good lord man," Dr. Bell said as he stepped down onto the stone front steps.

"Who is it dear?" I heard a woman's voice say, as a small woman appeared at the front door, followed by the much larger Irish maid.

"Cara, you remember Dr. Watson, don't you dear?" Dr. Bell said, as he handed his wife my business card.

"I'm not sure that I do," Cara said as she struggled to see any possible familiarity.

"I'm not sure I would recognize myself at the moment," said I, removing my crumbled hat and setting my distressed medical bag on the flagstone porch.

"What has happened to you my good man?" Dr. Bell asked, as he began to look me over more closely and asked, "Are you hurt?"

"Miraculously, I don't believe I am hurt. However, in the past two days I have been buried underground by a dynamite explosion beneath the Tincup Mine, thrown from a moving train by a railroad detective for pretending to be a deaf mute when I wasn't and then I got into a fight over a turkey leg at a hobo camp; other than that things have been going rather well since my friend Sherlock Holmes and I got off the train in Little London. If it's not an imposition, might I trouble you for a lift to Glen Eyrie?"

"Certainly, my good man, I will drive you there myself," Dr. Bell said as he instructed the maid to have a carriage brought around.

"Where is Mr. Holmes now?" Cara asked, looking around to see that I was alone.

"One can only imagine," said I.

March 17th, 1896 8:30am
Glen Eyrie, Colorado, U.S.A.

AFTER DR. BELL HAD DRIVEN ME back to Glen Eyrie, I took a long hot bath, ate an egg salad sandwich, chased by three fingers of whiskey and slept for nearly two straight days. When I awoke, I dressed in my remaining Brooks Brothers suit and walked downstairs to find to my pleasant surprise, that General Palmer had invited my friend Dr. Bell to join us for breakfast in the music room on the main floor of his grand home.

"Good morning, Dr. Watson, you look much better than you did the last time I saw you," Dr. Bell said as he stood to shake my hand.

"I feel a new man," said I as I shook his hand and took a seat at the table.

"We are relieved to see you have recovered from your first trip to Cripple Creek," General Palmer said, as he laid the morning newspaper aside.

"Would you care for either tea or coffee?" Pryor Shelby, General Palmer's efficient butler asked.

"Coffee, please, with cream," said I, adding, "I hope I haven't been a bother to anyone."

"Not at all," General Palmer said, "we are delighted to see you up and around this morning."

"I feel remarkably well rested and am most anxious to spend some quality time over the next few days learning about the extraordinary advances in medicine being made in the treatment of tuberculosis patients here in Little London."

"It will be my pleasure to show you around," Dr. Bell said, "I don't know that I mentioned my reason for being in San Francisco was to attend the annual conference for the American Medical Association. The AMA has asked me to serve on an international committee being organized to issue a report on tuberculous management and treatment. Starting tomorrow morning I shall be visiting many of our local sanitariums, to interview their physicians and nursing staffs, you are welcome to join me if you wish."

"I would be delighted," said I. "Perhaps I can purchase a replacement medical bag somewhere along the way."

"I have taken care of that for you," Dr. Bell said as he stood and retrieved a beautiful new burgundy leather medical bag from the piano stool and sat the bag on an empty chair next to me. "A gift from Cara and me, I had just bought this physicians bag last week in San Francisco, from a local medical supplier who had a large booth at the AMA conference. You should find everything in here to be state-of-the-art, including a new stethoscope similar to the one Rene Laennec patented for the treatment of TB."

"This bag is a Cole Brothers from England," said I.

"It is," Dr. Bell said, "it's the Gladstone, their newest model. I'm sure you will put it to good use."

"I bought myself a new physician's bag before we left England; I looked at one at Cole Brothers but the price on a Gladstone equipped like this one was $250 dollars; that's more than I earn in three months from my modest practice in London. May I at least pay you for the bag?"

"No, this is a gift. After I returned to the Briarhurst from dropping you off here at Glen Eyrie, day before yesterday, Cara reminded me I had bought this new bag when we were in San Francisco last week. She ordered a second one for me, it should be here within three days, the medical supplier has an express delivery service," Dr. Bell said as he sipped his coffee.

"This is very thoughtful of you and Cara," said I as I marveled at the craftsmanship of the beautiful leather bag and the state-of-the-art medical equipment inside, "I thank you both."

"Please take no offense, Dr. Watson, but Cara and I agreed we can't have you showing up at all our local sanitariums with that crushed bag you were carrying when you showed up on our front door step, you wouldn't be making a very positive first impression of us English doctors," Dr. Bell said with a kindly smile.

"Can't say that I would blame anyone, besides half my equipment had been lost along the way," said I. "Thank you, I will think fondly of you and Cara every time I open my doctors bag to treat a sick or injured patient."

"You are most welcome," Dr. Bell said. "By the way if either of you are ever looking for a place to stay in San Francisco I highly recommend the Palace Hotel. That was where the AMA held their annual conference, it was very nice."

"Thank you, I will keep that in mind," said I admiring the contents of my medical equipment housed in separate customized compartments inside my new Gladstone.

"Breakfast, gentlemen," Pryor said as he entered the music room and signaled for the kitchen staff to serve our meal. "This morning's breakfast consists of a ham and cheese English quiche served with French crepes stuffed with apple or cherry fillings."

"This looks absolutely wonderful, Pryor," General Palmer said, "We thank you and your staff."

"I am famished," said I, "I believe I may have to try one of each."

After Pryor had plated our quiche and crepes he topped off our coffees and said with a smile, "Enjoy. Please ring the bell if you need anything." When I looked up from my breakfast I saw that Pryor and his kitchen staff had disappeared.

"How do they do that?" I asked.

"Do what?" General Palmer asked.

"Your staff always seems to magically vanish into thin air," said I.

"No magic involved, I had my master carpenter, Charles Kneller, build a series of hidden chambers into Glen Eyrie's interior to allow the wait staff to walk about without being seen or heard pushing service carts throughout the main halls," General Palmer explained. "Pryor tells me your clothing was beyond repair Dr. Watson, but we have a fine tailor in Colorado Springs, if you like I can make an introduction for you."

"Thank you," said I, "fortunately Mr. Holmes and I had two suits tailor made for each of us when we were in Manhattan, along with a second pair of shoes, a topcoat and hat. I should be good for the time being with this second suit I'm wearing, but I will definitely keep your offer in mind if my stay extends beyond the next two or three weeks. Again, please do let me know if my stay here gets to be too much of a burden."

"No bother at all," General Palmer explained, "the bedrooms you and Mr. Holmes are staying in were recently remodeled as guest suites. I wish Queen could have seen how they came out, I know she would have enjoyed how our home is beginning to look more like a castle."

"These French crepes are delicious," said Dr. Bell, wishing to change the subject in knowing how much General Palmer missed his departed wife, Queen. At least the General was comforted now in having his three daughters living with him at Glen Eyrie. "I will have to ask Pryor to share this recipe with Cara; although she doesn't have to do so anymore, she still enjoys spending time in the kitchen. Sunday brunch is one of her favorite meals for us to enjoy with friends, you will both have to join us one Sunday for brunch."

"I would love to join you for a Sunday brunch, perhaps the next time I won't appear as distressed as the last time I appeared at the front door of your Briarhurst Manor," said I adding, "These crepes are delightful, the French have always been exceptionally talented chefs."

"Besides the French being wonderful chefs," General Palmer said, "As you may know they are making considerable headway in the treatment of tuberculosis. Until his passing last year, I had been in correspondence with Louis Pasteur and we have adopted his pasteurization process in its entirety here at the Glen Eyrie Creamery."

"I remember," said I, thinking of my friend, "Sherlock Holmes quoting Louie Pasteur more than once, in saying, 'In the field of observation, chance favors only the prepared mind' which my friend claims to also apply to the field of criminal investigation."

"We are still building upon the groundbreaking work of the French doctor Rene Laennec," Dr. Bell acknowledged, "what a tragic loss the entire medical profession suffered when he contracted the disease himself while treating his patients. He was only 45 when he died. Another French physician, Jean-Antoine Villemin, demonstrated that tuberculosis was an infectious disease back in 1865—thirty some years ago—yet we are still experiencing difficulty convincing many doctors and midwives to wash their hands before delivering babies."

"Unfortunately," said I in thinking of Sherlock Holmes, "the portrayals of Dumas and Murger, with their operatic depictions of consumption as a romantic disease, namely in Verdi's La Traviata and Puccini's La Boheme, have not helped our cause in the containment of TB."

"And our politicians and public health physicians are all too quick to blame the poor for the spread of this horrific disease," said General Palmer. "The indigenous people of South and North America have all suffered catastrophic losses with the spread of small pox and cholera, beginning with the first contact with the

Europeans in the 15th Century. Tragically, Native Americans had no immunity or medicine to treat these deadly contagious diseases. Now, here at the close of the 19th Century, our American Indians suffer five times the mortality rates; while our greedy politicians in Denver and Washington DC look at this health epidemic as a way to solve what some refer to as the 'Indian problem'."

"Robert Koch, a Prussian physician, proved beyond doubt the causal agent for the White Plague is mycobacterium, better known as Koch's bacillus," Dr. Bell said, "let us pray an inoculation to prevent TB in the first place will soon be on the horizon. Meanwhile, Hermann Brehmer, a German physician, continues to share his research that tuberculosis arose from the difficulty of the heart to properly irrigate the lungs. Dr. Koch was the first to establish an anti-tuberculosis sanatorium above 6,000 feet in elevation, proving the high mountain air offers a health benefit for TB patients. He had been encouraged by his professor of medicine, Johann Lukas Schonlien and the famous German explorer Alexander von Humboldt, to explore the health advantages of breathing air at a higher altitude. That was in 1854; forty-two years ago."

"With our elevation of 6,000 feet above sea level, dry climate, abundant sunshine, mineral spring waters and fresh mountain air, Little London has attracted physicians, patients and their families from all over the world," General Palmer said. "As you may know, Dr. Watson, sanitariums have more of a hospital setting, whereas sanatoriums are intended to be more of a health spa or resort. We have several of each here in Little London, which has helped us become well known around the world as a place where millionaires, artists, musicians, dancers and poets can come to seek the cure from this dreadful disease."

"And gunfighters," said I, remembering a story I had read in a dime-novel on the train about famous western folk heroes; including the legendary lawman and gunfighter, Wild Bill Hickok, who was shot and killed during a poker game in Deadwood, Dakota Territory. It was hard for me to imagine such a wild and uncultured place existed in today's Glided Age. "From what I read about Wyatt Earp's friend, Doc Holiday, after being diagnosed with tuberculous he traveled to Glenwood Springs, west of Denver, to seek the reputed curative power of the waters."

"Unfortunately," said General Palmer, "the sulfurous fumes from Glenwood's hot springs may have done his lungs more harm than good. You will observe that several of our sanatoriums throughout the Pikes Peak region, well known for their luxury spas, have easy rules and frequent parties. Sexual affairs have become commonplace among their patients, many of whom refer to one another affectionately as fellow 'lungers' who often adopt the attitude it is better for them to cram as much living as possible into every single day for they may not live to see tomorrow."

"Well, starting tomorrow morning," Dr. Bell announced, "you and I will begin our tour of the larger sanatoriums in Colorado Springs and Manitou Springs. We will not be able to visit all the smaller private sanitariums, such as the Red Crags Sanitarium, which I founded a few years ago or the short-lived Cascade Villas, founded in 1874 by Dr. Thomas Horn or the many smaller clinics run by visiting nurses or the Sisters of Charity. However, I am quite confident there is much you will be able to learn and take back with you to England. I will pick you up here in my carriage tomorrow morning at 8:30."

"Very well," said I, "I will look forward to seeing you tomorrow and thank you, and please thank Cara, for my wonderful new physician's bag, I shall put it to good use."

After Dr. Bell had departed Glen Eyrie I retired to my upstairs bedroom where I spent the rest of the morning familiarizing myself with the contents of my new Cole Brothers of England doctor's bag and cleaned my service revolver, which fit snuggly inside the Gladstone, along with spare ammunition. After lunch I decided to take a long walk through the nearby Garden of the Gods and in not wanting to carry my heavy service revolver and leather notebook, for fear one or both might inadvertently fall out of my pocket as I scampered over the rocks, I looked about my bedroom to see if I might find a suitable place to hide these two small items. I trusted General Palmer's staff explicitly; however, Sherlock Holmes had cautioned me that our enemies might learn where we were staying at Glen Eyrie and attempt to search our rooms. Besides, I thought it only responsible of me to avoid the risk of my firearm coming into the hands of small children who might innocently wander into my bedroom while I was away.

In looking around my bedroom, I was drawn once again to the fireplace adorned with the white and blue square tiles with the scene of windmills from Holland. Standing in front of the fireplace I recalled the hidden compartment cleverly concealed behind the loose brick of our fireplace on Baker Street in London. There were three decorative wooden panels above the fireplace mantle, each measuring about six inches in height. The center panel was about thirty-six inches in width and the panels positioned on the left and right twelve inches in width. I felt around the center and right panels, which felt secure. However, when I tugged gently on the left panel I found it was cleverly hinged at the top and concealed a secret compartment of about twelve inches in depth – the perfect place to hide my pocket notebook and service revolver. After catching up on my journal entries, I placed my notebook and handgun inside the hidden compartment and pushed the front panel closed.

The craftsmanship of this hidden compartment was truly extraordinary and I suspected was the handiwork of Charles Kneller,

General Palmer's master carpenter. I would not have known to search for this hidden compartment except for my having seen a concealed small vault built into our fireplace on Baker Street in London. I felt assured my service revolver and black leather notebook would be safe until I returned from my walk in the nearby Garden of the Gods.

March 18th, 1896 10:30am
St. Francis Sanatorium, Colorado, U.S.A.

"THE ST. FRANCIS SANATORIUM WAS BUILT in 1887," Dr. Bell explained as he drew our carriage horses to a halt in front of the largest of the buildings located on the south side of Pikes Peak Avenue at Prospect Street. "It was our city's first hospital and today treats patients with other health issues, in addition to tuberculosis. A small handful of Sisters from the St. Francis of Perpetual Adoration, located in Lafayette, Indiana, came here to Colorado Springs when our St. Francis was just a small clinic being built for the Colorado Midland Railroad employees and their families. Shortly after the arrival of the Sisters we suffered a fatal train accident which brought sixty injured people instantly into their care. Afterwards the Sisters went door to door throughout El Paso County raising money to build a bigger hospital and to feed the poor."

"The Sisters are exceptionally good fundraisers," said I.

"Ha," Dr. Bell laughed, "it is hard to say 'no' to a Sister, even if you're not Catholic. Sister Mary Huberta Duennebacke served as the first administrator for the hospital and she proved to be highly competent."

"Is she still here, I would like very much to meet her?" said I.

"No, she was sent on to establish St. Anthony Hospital in Denver, which opened three years ago. A crematorium was built over there," Dr. Bell said, pointing to a tall smoke stack located a block to the east and across Pikes Peak Avenue. "It is used to cremate the bodies of the people who die locally here of tuberculosis. Cremation of the bodies, as you may well know, helps prevent the spread of this highly contagious disease."

"I understand the bodies of people who died centuries ago from tuberculosis can still be found to contain the deadly disease."

"Yes, that is true," reaffirmed Dr. Bell. "It's one of the major concerns we have for archeologists who go to great lengths to unearth Egyptian mummies or careless adventurers who dig up Native American graves here in the American West in search of artifacts. There was an article in the latest issue of JAMA, the Journal for the American Medical Association, suggesting that if, or when, as I choose to believe, we find a vaccine to eradicate this deadly disease from the face of the planet, that perhaps two hundred years from now someone might unearth the body of a person who had died from tuberculosis and once again this deadly plague will be spread around the world. But for now, let us go inside where I can introduce you to a few of the dedicated Sisters of St. Francis."

March 25th, 1896 8:30am

National Deaconess Sanitarium, Colorado Springs, Colorado, U.S.A.

"The National Deaconess Sanitarium is another of our hospital-like medical facilities dedicated solely to the treatment of tuberculosis," said Dr. Bell as he guided our horse drawn carriage up to the main building located adjacent to the Deaf and Blind School. "Many doctors in the eastern cities of America have been advising their patients to come to Colorado to regain their health. Our neighboring city to the north, Denver, didn't know how to manage this massive influx of sick people, many of who were homeless, so they put these ill people in jail; which of course, only served to spread this deadly disease to other inmates and jailers.

Some fifteen years ago Denver had earned itself the nickname The World's Sanitarium. By the time many of these sick people made their way from Denver to Colorado Springs to seek the cure they were so ill they soon died."

"What does it cost for patients to stay in the sanitariums?" asked I, as I lifted my burgundy leather Gladstone medical bag from the back of the carriage.

"The poor often have to stay in open-air tents, but the nicer sanatoriums charge patients about $7 per day. Luxury accommodations can cost upwards of $50 per week. There is a lot of money to be made in health care today in America; even more so in the years to come, I suspect; as the financial focus for many medical providers is, unfortunately, on the management of health care rather than prevention. Some of our sanitariums claim a cure rate of about sixty percent, a wonderful marketing ploy; however, as you and I know the treatment of patients is not our ultimate goal. As doctors we must continually seek a cure for this horrific disease. Like most doctors, I believe prevention, through inoculation, should be our ultimate end game."

"I agree," said I. "Who runs the National Deaconess Sanitarium?"

"This sanitarium is run by Eleanor Collier, with the aid of about thirty very dedicated women. They began administering aid to TB patients back in 1888. Then in 1890, with the support of a group of physicians, it grew into the Bellevue Sanitarium. The house physician here is Dr. S. Edwin Solly; let's go in, I will introduce you to Dr. Solly and perhaps we can join him as he makes his rounds to see his patients."

April 2nd, 1896 10am
Glockner Tuberculosis Sanitarium, Colorado Springs, Colorado, U.S.A.

"The Glockner Tuberculosis Sanitarium owes it founding

to one person, Marie Gwynne Glockner, a 22-year-old widow," Dr. Bell shared as we walked into the front lobby of one of the largest sanitariums in Colorado Springs. "Her husband died here in Colorado Springs from tuberculous when he was just 31-years-of-age. The Glockner Family helped fund the development of the Glockner Sanitarium in 1893. The first superintendent was a friend of mine, Dr. Boswell P. Anderson; he was the former Colorado Midland Railroad physician. His assistant, Dr. Charles Fox Gardiner, along with the head nurse at the time, Sarah Callahan, were equally dedicated to the treatment of tuberculosis patients here on the North End of Colorado Springs. Come out back with me, I want to show you the inside of one of our modern tuberculosis huts."

April 9th, 1896 9:30am
Union Printers Home, Colorado Springs, Colorado, U.S.A.

As we rode in Dr. Bell's open air carriage, east on Pikes Peak Avenue to the Union Printers Home, I noticed the thick black smoke being emitted from the tall smoke stack of the crematorium located below the Deaf and Blind School. I wondered silently how many bodies were being cremated this morning and if any of those bodies were physicians, like me and my friend Dr. Bell seated beside me, or nurses or one of the selfless Sisters of St. Francis. As I contemplated the inherent risks of treating patients with infectious diseases, I was painfully aware it had been three weeks since I had seen Sherlock Holmes and worried constantly if he were even alive. How would I ever know if my friend had already met an untimely death? Could the body of Sherlock Holmes at this very moment be buried somewhere down a deep mine shaft beneath the rim of the Bowl of Gold?

Thankfully, Dr. Bell broke into my demure thoughts to say,

"General Palmer was the original land-grantor of several institutions, including the Colorado School for the Deaf and Blind. It was built in 1874, three years after we founded the City of Colorado Springs."

"General Palmer has been most generous in sharing his wealth with the citizens of Colorado Springs," said I.

Dr. Bell pointed to the large stone building and said, "This is the Childs-Drexel Home for Union Printers. It was founded to treat union members suffering from tuberculosis and black lung disease contracted from breathing carbon-based ink used in the printing process. The home has its own dairy, a large vegetable garden and raises chickens and pigs. And then every year they plant some 200 acres of wheat."

"Most impressive," said I, as I glanced to the western horizon, trying to shake off my mounting worries for Sherlock Holmes located somewhere on the backside of Pikes Peak, in the Greatest Gold Camp on Earth.

April 17th, 1896 10:30am
Montcalm Sanitarium, Manitou Springs, Colorado, U.S.A.

"CONSTRUCTION ON THE MIRAMONT CASTLE," Dr. Bell said, "began last year, as a private home for Father Jean Baptist Francolon, a French-born Catholic priest. With thirty rooms it is so large he invited the Sisters of Mercy to share the property with him as a treatment facility. The Montcalm Sanitarium focus today is on offering less ill tuberculous patients clean lodging and abundant quantities of good food to compensate for a patient's weight loss. Montcalm's first patients arrived just last August and since then they have begun teaching music."

"It is a rather unique architectural example of the Victorian Era," said I looking up at the rather eclectic castle. "It almost looks out of place, located here at the foot of Pikes Peak, but then again I am not certain where else it would fit in, if not here in Manitou Springs."

"It is rather unique," said Dr. Bell. "Father Francolon and the contractor, two brothers, Angus and Archie Gillis, tried to blend the architectural styles, from the Byzantine to Tudor. Construction is expected to be finished later this year."

"Fascinating," said I, trying to decide I if liked the outcome of the architectural design or not.

"Dr. Watson?" Dr. Bell said as we sat next to one another in his carriage parked in front of the Montcalm Sanatorium.

"Yes?" said I.

"There is something I have been meaning to say."

"Yes?" said I, recalling the countless hours we have talked over the five weeks since we began the tour of the sanitariums and sanatoriums in Little London.

"I turn 55 later this month and General Palmer will be 60-years-old in September. When one looks back upon the decisions they made in life, that led you down the path you are on today, one cannot but wonder about how much time remains of this life and what might be the best use of the time we have remaining on this earth. General Palmer and I are both dedicating more of our time and financial resources toward philanthropic endeavors. I was in my mid-twenties, and he in his late-twenties, when we first met, surveying a route west for the Kansas Pacific Railroad. Together, General Palmer and I have been involved in more than two dozen businesses—he always serving as company President and I as Vice-president—going into business with him was the best business decision I ever made in my life. William Jackson Palmer is, and will always be one of my dearest friends, a friendship, I suspect, not unlike your friendship with Sherlock Holmes."

"Yes, Sherlock Holmes and I have become quite close, in spite of his peculiar habits."

"I have begun to divest my business holdings here in the States and eventually Cara and I will relocate permanently back to England. I have watched how you interact with other medical care providers and witnessed first-hand your compassion for the sick people we came in contact with over the past month we have spent together. You truly care about people who are ill and are dedicated to improving their health as a physician."

"Yes? Go on," said I wondering where this intimate conversation was leading.

"Dr. Watson," Dr. Bell said as he turned to look me in the eye before continuing, "I have a business proposition for you; would you please give some serious consideration to eventually taking over my medical practice here in Little London?"

"Why, Dr. Bell, I am flattered by your offer," said I, being completely taken by surprise at his invitation. "While it is hard for me to imagine my not residing in England, it is even harder for me to imagine living apart from Sherlock Holmes and I know how difficult it would be for him professionally to not be located in London. Although he complains about their ineptness all the time, Sherlock Holmes is quite fond of Scotland Yard. I believe his biggest challenge would be in not finding enough to do to keep him occupied professionally here in the states." Aside from those expressed concerns, I was privately aware from my intimate relationship in living with Sherlock Holmes over the past several years, how his frequent alcohol consumption and cocaine addiction will too often fully consume him when he is not gainfully employed.

"You could stay on a while, here in Little London, to see how it suits you," said Dr. Bell.

"I must admit the thought of my being involved at the cutting edge of medical research in the treatment of tuberculous is rather exciting. What will you do with your Briarhurst Manor when you leave for England?"

"I have two trusted long-term employees," Dr. Bell said, "I will leave the Briarhurst in their care. Please do give my offer some serious consideration, won't you?"

April 25th, 1896 Saturday 12:55pm
Glen Eyrie, Colorado, U.S.A.

It was Saturday shortly after noon when word reached us of a major fire that had broken out in Cripple Creek. I knew instantly the life of my friend Sherlock Holmes was in great peril.

"General Palmer is downstairs on the phone," Pryor said, as I answered his excited knock upon my bedroom door. "He asks that you come at once."

I grabbed my cane and followed Pryor quickly down the stairs to where the phone booth was located under the stairwell near the front entrance. General Palmer's three daughters; Elsie, Dorothy and Marjorie were standing nearby with worried looks upon their young faces. General Palmer hung up the phone and stepped out of the phone booth.

"I just spoke with Winfield Scott Stratton," General Palmer explained, "details are still sketchy, seems a fire broke out at noon on Myers Avenue and quickly spread from building to building."

"How did it start?" asked Elsie.

"A young couple staying at the Central Dance Hall may have knocked over a gas stove which reportedly started the fire," General Palmer replied. "A strong wind spread the fire rapidly to the nearby buildings. Firemen, including nearly all of the men with the J.L. Lindsey Hose Company, are trying desperately to contain the blaze to the south side of Myers Avenue; however, one of their two hoses has broken and the smoke is so thick now they can't see to fight the fire. The smoke can be seen in Victor and firemen from there will be responding with their equipment by train to assist, but as of now the fire is completely out of control."

"What can we do to help?" asked I.

"Mr. Stratton is organizing a special train to leave Colorado Springs by three o'clock, with food, clothing and additional firemen and firefighting equipment. He has also written a $250 check to help cover initial emergency expenses, there haven't been any reported deaths as of yet, but there are injuries."

"I'll grab my medical bag," said I.

"I will have Jessie Bass bring a carriage around to drive you to the train depot," said General Palmer.

As I returned upstairs to my bedroom, I began packing a few things into my Gladstone medical bag, including my service revolver and spare ammunition. I jotted down a couple quick notes in my notebook before stuffing it into the secret compartment above the fireplace mantel. Saturday, being a weekend, I had taken a break from visiting patients and the medical staff at the local sanitariums. We had just finished lunch with General Palmer and his three daughters and I had been planning to take a long walk through the Garden of the Gods. I was intending the walk to clear my head so I could think over Dr. Bell's enticing offer to assume his medical practice; however, the only thing I found constantly on my mind was the fact I had not heard from Sherlock Holmes in over a month. I was also very much aware that next Saturday, one week from today, Irene Adler would be appearing on stage for the opening of La Boheme at the Butte Opera House in Cripple Creek. She may very well be in Cripple Creek at this very moment, and I surmised a dress rehearsal would certainly precede opening night. To my way of thinking, the likelihood of her, Sherlock Holmes, an assassin who twice tried to kill him and this raging inferno somehow not being interrelated was simply unimaginable.

April 25th, 1896 Saturday 6:10pm
Bennett Avenue, Cripple Creek, Colorado, U.S.A.

As our relief train pulled into the Midland Train Depot, we could see where the fire had broken out at the Central Dance Hall, located on the north side of Myers Avenue, and where it had spread north to other buildings on Bennett Avenue. As I walked further into town, I saw where the fire had crossed Bennett and soon learned The Topic Theater, owned by Spencer Penrose and Charles Tutt, had been among the first buildings to go up. The Topic Theater was followed shortly by the Butte Opera House where Irene Adler was to perform next Saturday.

Within minutes, the intense flames, continually fanned by the strong winds blowing in from the south, had spread to every surrounding dance hall and parlor house. I blended into the crowd and watched with the other spectators standing on the dirt street, as the post office went up in flames, sending a half dozen dedicated postal workers out into the street, leaving behind bags of undelivered mail.

Firemen were using the high masonry wall on Bennett Avenue, between Third and Fourth Streets, as a firebreak. One loud KABOOM! Followed by another, followed by a third, drew the gasps and attention of the crowd to the buildings nearest the blaze which was burning out of control around Third and Myers Avenue. "What was that?" one man shouted, "They're using dynamite to blow up the buildings, the firemen are attempting to establish a firebreak to keep the fire from spreading!" Another man in the crowd shouted. "Good luck with that!" another man shouted while a woman pointing toward the sky as the wind blew, said, "Look, the wind's carrying hot embers across to the rooftops over yonder!"

I stood among the frantic crowd and watched as huge plumes of black smoke billowed into the air and the raging fire spread further north, consuming whatever stood in its way. As if alive, the fire leapt across Carr Avenue and in an instant consumed the Episcopal, Baptist and Congregational churches before crossing further north to Eaton Avenue. The newly built Sisters of Mercy Hospital, located onto the south side of Eaton Avenue, stood alone in its path of destruction. Another loud KABOOM went off as wood and parts of another building were thrown over a hundred feet into the air. Debris rained down on the streets below, engulfing a handful of firemen and merchants struggling to carry out whatever merchandise they thought might have been most valuable from inside the buildings.

Suspecting there would be injured people in need of emergency medical care, I raced up Eaton Avenue, through the thick smoke toward the Sisters of Mercy Hospital, to find the Sisters wrapping their patients in blankets and evacuating them from the hospital to nearby homes.

"I'm a doctor," said I to two of the Sisters carrying a patient on a stretcher from the hospital. "Where can I help?"

"Over there," one of the Sisters shouted, nodding toward a tuberculous tent with a crude red cross hand-painted on the canvas nearest the door. "That's our emergency room; Dr. Anderson is inside doing triage."

"Thank you," I shouted to the Sister as I made my way to the tent. I could hear the cries and moans of injured people coming from inside, reminding me of my time serving in military field hospitals in the Middle East. Scattered on cots and laying prone upon the ground were eighteen to twenty injured people, being attended to by one doctor wearing a blood-spattered white lab coat, while being assisted by three Sisters of Mercy wearing long black habits.

"Where do you need me?" said I to the one doctor bent over a badly burned patient lying on a canvas cot. I laid my new doctors bag on the ground, took off my suit coat and began to roll up the sleeves of my white shirt.

The doctor, who looked to be in his mid-to-late sixties, glanced quickly at my medical bag and then up at me to ask, "Do you have any morphine?"

"Yes, several vials."

"Good, let's start with him," the doctor said, "I ran out thirty minutes ago."

As I injected the needle into the patients arm, the other doctor held the patient's arm still to keep him from thrashing about and breaking the needle off in his arm. "Glad you arrived when you did," he said. "I'm Doctor Wes Anderson with the Sisters of Mercy Hospital, who are you and where on earth did you come from?"

"I'm Doctor John Watson, I just arrived a few minutes ago on a special relief train from Colorado Springs," said I. "Mr. Stratton sent a train up the Short Line loaded with blankets, food and medical supplies.

"Sister Mary," he said to the nearest sister, "could you please go down to the Midland Train Depot and see if you can direct some of the medical supplies and blankets up here? Thank you," he added as she slipped quickly out of the tent.

"Well, Dr. Watson, you and the supply train arrived just in time," said Doctor Anderson, as our struggling patient relaxed his body as the effects of the morphine took effect. "Over here, he's next," Doctor Anderson said directing me to the patient sitting on the next cot, holding his upper arm covered in blood. "What do we have here?" he asked as he laid the man back gently on the cot and cut away his bloody shirt sleeve with a pair of scissors and slowly loosened a bloody tourniquet.

"I think me arm is broke," the man said, squirming in pain. As Doctor Anderson rotated the man's arm so we could get a better look at his wound, a spurt of blood from a severed artery shot across the front of my clean white shirt and blue silk tie.

"Clamp," said Dr. Anderson, without looking at me.

"Clamp," said I as I handed him the piece of medical equipment from my bag.

"This looks bad," Dr. Anderson whispered to me, "We may have to amputate. Do you have a bone saw?" he asked nodding his head toward my medical bag.

"NO!" shouted the man, "I makes me livin as a black jack dealer at Johnny Nolan's, I'll never gets me job back if I has only one arm."

"Johnny Nolan's is gone," Doctor Anderson said, "We'll do what we can to save your arm. Doctor Watson is going to give you a shot of morphine to ease your pain. Hold still now."

When the black jack dealer dropped off to sleep, we moved quickly to the next patient and then the next, giving morphine to ease their pain where necessary. "When Sister Mary comes back, I'm going to have to operate on our black jack dealer, can you manage to care for the rest of our patients on your own until I finish?" asked Dr. Anderson.

"Yes," said I, holding my doctor's bag, "my bag is fairly well equipped, I should be able to manage."

"Nice bag, is it a Cole Brothers of England?" Dr. Anderson asked.

"It is," I said.

"I read an advertisement in JAMA about the Gladstone. I was thinking about ordering one, but equipped like yours they cost about $250, that's more than I make in six months working here with the Sisters of Mercy."

"Take whatever you need," said I, as I held open my medical bag and watched as Dr. Anderson selected two small stainless steel clamps, a razor sharp scalpel, a bone saw and a handful of clean bandages.

"Thank you," he said gratefully. "The last few pieces of medical equipment I bought I paid $3 out of my own pocket, to a hobo who came to the hospital a couple weeks back, said he found them scattered along the railroad tracks, but I'm sure they were probably stolen."

"No doubt. Where did you learn to use a bone saw?" asked I, cutting immediately to the core of his bona fides.

"Gettysburg. Yourself?"

"Afghanistan."

Dr. Anderson nodded his head respectfully and turned to go about the grim task of amputating a man's limb to save his life. Two hours later, about the time I thought we were getting a handle on the patients lying about the ER tent, the canvas door flap to our makeshift emergency room flipped opened and a fireman with a thick handlebar mustache burst in carrying an injured fireman cradled over his shoulder in a hold I recognized as the fireman's carry.

"Lay him down here," I said to the first fireman and helped him lower the injured fireman onto our only empty cot. The injured fireman began coughing and I wiped the smoke and dirt from his face with a wet washcloth. The other fireman helped me remove the injured fireman's heavy coat and helmet. I opened my medical bag and retrieved my stethoscope and plugged the earpieces into my ears and held the other end to his chest. "Try to take a deep breath," said I. He did as instructed and coughed again. I could hear wheezing in both lungs. "I think he is just overcome with exhaustion and smoke inhalation; he should be alright in a few hours."

"Thank you doctor, I see you have a new medical bag," said the fireman with the handlebar mustache.

I recognized the familiar voice and looked beneath the wide brim of his fireman's helmet to see the soot-covered face of my friend Sherlock Holmes smiling back at me. "Sher," I began to say, but he placed the palm of his dirty hand against my mouth before I could finish saying his name. "You're alive," I whispered, nearly overcome with emotion.

"Indeed I am," said he.

"Irene?"

"She is safe."

"Where?"

"I will explain later. Right now you and I both have work to do."

"How will I find you?" asked I as he turned to leave.

"You won't, I will find you," Sherlock Holmes said as he slipped out of the tent.

It was after sunset, when the winds finally calmed down and the firemen were able to contain the fire. They continued to pour water on the hot embers until well after midnight. Our steady stream of injured people slowly tapered off about 2am. By the time the sun rose Sunday morning the Sisters of Mercy had already started moving patients back into their hospital where they could receive better care.

"Dr. Watson, why don't you go get yourself some coffee and something to eat?" Dr. Anderson said, as he put his arm around my shoulder and whispered in my ear, "You've done enough, thank you, John. We can take the watch from here."

I rolled down the sleeves of my bloodstained dirty shirt, and then put on my coat and hat. As I turned to leave I rummaged through my medical bag to see what supplies I might leave behind. I removed my last two vials of morphine, my last sterile syringe and a handful of clean bandages, which I handed to Sister Mary on my way out of the tent.

"Thank you, Doctor Watson," Sister Mary said with a smile, "You coming when you did was an answer to a prayer. May you go in peace."

April 26th, 1896 Sunday 8:20am
Bennett Avenue, Cripple Creek, Colorado, U.S.A.

I WALKED DOWN THE HILL, away from the Sisters of Mercy Hospital, and through the smoldering ruins of the buildings on Bennett Avenue. I learned from a passing fireman that nearly thirty percent of the town had been burnt to the ground. The *Cripple Creek Morning Times* had somehow managed to print the morning's newspaper, quoting town officials estimating the property damage would be at least half a million dollars. The First National Bank was open for business and welcoming people inside for warmth and something hot to eat. I walked inside and stood in line behind a small group of firemen waiting in front of me to accept a free cup of coffee and a hot breakfast. I carried my scrambled eggs, bacon, sourdough toast and coffee outside, found an empty bench and sat down for the first time in fourteen hours.

"This seat taken?" a fireman, carrying a fire axe in one hand and a tin cup of coffee in the other, asked.

"Please, join me," I said to the fireman with the bushy handlebar mustache. He sat next to me as I took the first sip of my coffee and said, "Rumor on the street claims this fire may have been intentionally set."

"That rumor is true, this fire was definitely arson," Sherlock Holmes replied.

"How can you be sure?" asked I.

"There were three points of origin with pour patterns of a

flammable liquid detectible at each site."

"Someone said the fire started on the upper floor of the Central Dance Hall on Myers Avenue?" I asked.

"Correct again," Sherlock Holmes replied. "The very place where Shady Coyne said Colonel Stark and our English geologist were staying. This fire was no accident. While there may never be a way for us to prove our two deadly counterfeiters were involved, this crime does fit their modus operandi in destroying the evidence of their deadly crimes with fire."

"Do you think Stark and Bakerslee are still here in Cripple Creek or do you think they fled town when the fire was raging?"

"I do not yet know," Sherlock Holmes replied as he drank his coffee. He looked down Bennett and Myers Avenues at the burnt out buildings. "Without knowing which buildings were their intended target it is not possible for me to determine if they accomplished their objective. Using dynamite to create a firebreak, by blowing up the buildings that stood in the path of the fire, may or may not have been effective in suppressing the fire, but that act of desperation was almost certainly not an anticipated event."

"That was a bold decision on the part of Fire Chief May," said I, "while controversial with the business owners, he may have saved the rest of the town."

"That decision was not made by Fire Chief Frank May, as he was unable to participate in fighting this fire, Police Chief James Marshall, acting as both the police and fire chief, gave the order to use the dynamite."

"Why wasn't Fire Chief May here to fight the fire?" asked I.

"Tragically, his infant son died yesterday morning. Chief May was at home grieving with his wife over the death of their infant child."

"You don't suspect Colonel Stark or Doctor Bakerslee had anything to do with the death of their child do you?"

"No, while I suspect they have killed at least two and quite possibly more people to cover up their crimes, one would hope the killing of an infant is beneath even the most desperate of criminals."

"So you think the death of the Fire Chief's son was simply a coincidence?"

"You know I don't believe in coincidences," Sherlock Holmes said as he finished his coffee. "While I cannot completely eliminate random chance from entering into my deductive reasoning, I believe a more likely scenario may have been that the absence of Chief May, in not being on duty yesterday, an absence caused by the death of his infant son, simply presented our counterfeiting culprits a convenient window of opportunity to cover up their criminal acts."

"Do you think they realized they were not successful in killing us and Shady in the explosion at the Tincup Mine?"

"Possibly," Sherlock Holmes said. "Having a police chief, as opposed to a well-trained fire chief, in charge of extinguishing a major fire, is almost certain to result in a less effective fire suppression effort. The only thing most police officers are any good at, when we firemen are busy fighting a fire, is to keep spectators from trampling over the hose."

"I see, spoken like a true fireman," said I, as two other fireman walked past on their way to get something to eat inside the bank. "How is it that none of these real firemen recognized you as an imposter?"

"Easy; the firemen who came here from Victor assumed I was with the Cripple Creek Fire Department and the firemen from the Cripple Creek Fire Department assumed I was with the Victor Fire Department."

"I am sorry you did not get to see Irene Adler perform in La Boheme," said I, looking down Bennett Avenue where the ruins of the beautiful Butte Opera House lay smoldering.

"Ah, but I did," said my friend as he reached inside his firefighters coat and handed me a program for La Boheme.

"This program is for the opening night, which was not supposed to happen until this coming Saturday night," said I confused.

"I was present two nights ago for the first full dress rehearsal," my friend said as he closed his eyes and smiled, savoring the memory.

"Did she know you were there," asked I.

"I don't know if she knew it was I sitting there when she first stepped out on stage," Sherlock Holmes said. "I was the only person in the audience, still dressed as a miner, when the curtain went up. I had made arrangements for a dozen red roses to be delivered to her dressing room after each act, with a note—signed 'from an admirer'—by the time the curtain dropped after the fourth act she had sent me a note inviting me to her dressing room adorned with four dozen red roses. She did not seem at all surprised the flowers were from me."

"And how was that experience for you, seeing her again after all these years?" asked I.

"Why, Dr. Watson," Sherlock Holmes said with as warm a smile as I ever recall seeing on my friend's face, "as you can well imagine, there are those private moments in two people's lives too tender to share with even their most intimate of friends, but I can confirm that whoever said there is nothing so sweet as forbidden love, clearly had to have been speaking from experience."

"Will you see her again?"

"I hope to, have you ever wanted to visit New Mexico?" asked my friend.

"New Mexico? Heavens no; why, is that where The Women is presently?" I asked.

"She is on her way to Santa Fe."

"Where is Santa Fe?"

"It is a quaint old Spanish town in northern New Mexico."

"Is she traveling alone?"

"No, while she could probably manage, I thought it safer for her to have an escort. I hired Bernie Dempsey and two of his younger brothers to escort her."

"Dempsey? The heavyweight boxer fighting under the name Kid Blacky?"

"Turns out Kid Blacky is the name all the Dempsey brothers use whenever any one of them step into the ring."

"How did you get to know the Dempsey brothers?"

"The two older brothers work in the local mines, Bernie at the Molly Kathleen and John at the Portland. Soon after I became a mucker at the Portland, John introduced me to Bernie and I became his sparring partner. He took me home with him several times for dinner, where I met the other Dempsey brothers and their parents. Their father, Hyrum, raised all his children to work hard and taught the older boys how to fight. They in turn taught the younger boys the art of boxing. Each of the younger boys became better boxers by being taught the sport by their older brothers. The youngest brother, Jack, is just a year old but from everything I have seen of the Dempsey brothers, young Jack Dempsey will have all the makings of a true champion."

"What do we do now?"

"I must remain here, my work is not yet be finished," Sherlock Holmes said as he opened his eyes and looked around at the people who were already starting to rebuild the businesses in Cripple Creek. "You, my friend, must return to Colorado Springs."

"Irene?"

Sherlock Holmes replied in a voice slightly above a whisper, "In Santa Fe there is a small chapel, run by the Sisters of Loretto, with a miraculous staircase that attracts visitors from all over the world. I would very much like to see it one day, in the company of The Woman."

April 26th, 1896 Sunday 11:30am

Denver & Rio Grande Train Depot, Colorado Springs, Colorado, U.S.A.

When I stepped off the train at the depot in downtown Colorado Springs I noticed two Pullman cars being coupled to an engine preparing to leave the station. One of the Pullmans I recognized was the Nomad, belonging to General Palmer, the other belonged to Dr. Bell. The train consisted of two engines, a coal car, the two Pullmans, followed by three other boxcars being loaded with supplies and a red caboose at the end. I recognized three well-dressed men standing at the back of the caboose speaking to a fourth man as the train started to pull away from the station. It was apparent this was another supply train headed to Cripple Creek.

The three men turned toward me as I approached them in my exhausted condition with bloodstains visible across my white shirt and soiled blue tie.

"Good God man, are you hurt?" General Palmer said as he rushed up and embraced me by the shoulders.

"No, I'm fine," said I, "just a little tired, but there are dozens of injured people who are in need of medical supplies in Cripple Creek."

"That's where this relief train is headed," said Winfield Scott Stratton. "Speck Penrose will make sure the supplies get distributed where needed, along with the food and other items that Charles Tutt requested in his telegram this morning. General Palmer and Dr. Bell here have volunteered their Pullman cars to help serve as temporary businesses or housing as needed."

I sat my doctor's bag on the ground and reached for my wallet. I handed Dr. Bell $250 in cash and asked, "Would it be possible for you to order another Gladstone, equipped the same as this one, and have it delivered as soon as possible to Dr. Wesley Anderson at the Sisters of Mercy Hospital in Cripple Creek?"

"I will take care of it immediately," said Dr. Bell. "I will put a rush on the order; it should arrive within 72-hours. Should I add a note to let Dr. Anderson know it is from you?"

"No need," said I, "he'll know."

"Come," General Palmer said, "Jessie is over there with my carriage, let's get you back to Glen Eyrie where we can get you cleaned up, fed and rested up again. At least you don't look as worse for wear as you did the last time you came back from Cripple Creek."

"At least this time I didn't get thrown off the train by a railroad detective," I said adding, "And General Palmer, if it's not terribly inconvenient, on our way back to Glen Eyrie would it be possible for us to stop by that tailor shop you mentioned? I find I am in need of a new shirt and tie and I might as well get measured for another new suit, I don't believe I will ever get the smell of smoke out of this one."

Chapter 8

April 29th, 1896 1:30pm

Glen Eyrie, Colorado, U.S.A.

FOUR DAYS AFTER THE FIRST FIRE, the Cripple Creek fire bell rang again as a second fire broke out in the kitchen of the Windsor Hotel. Like all the other buildings in the downtown business district of Cripple Creek, the spectacular four-year-old Windsor Hotel, standing at the northeast corner of Myers Avenue and Second Street, was built entirely of wood. By the time firefighters could begin pouring water on the once grand Windsor Hotel, the building was completely engulfed in flame. Fueled by a strong wind coming again out of the south, this fire soon spread north across the street as hot embers landed on the roof of the Wright Hardware store.

I was in Glen Eyrie's music room, carefully documenting the first fire in my black leather pocket notebook, when General Palmer's butler rushed into the room to deliver the tragic news.

"This fire sounds worse than the first," Pryor said as I followed him to the phone booth near the front entrance.

"How is that even possible?" I questioned aloud, as Pryor and I waited for General Palmer to finish talking on the phone with the desk clerk at his Antlers Hotel.

"The fire is out of control," General Palmer said as he hung up the phone.

"Any deaths or injuries?" asked I, worried about my friend, Sherlock Holmes, who I had left behind, four days ago, in the Greatest Gold Camp on Earth.

"There are reports of injuries and at least two deaths," General Palmer said, "it sounds as if your services will be needed once again Doctor Watson."

"I will get my doctors bag," said I.

"You have time," General Palmer said and explained, "The Victor Fire Department has been called in to help battle the blaze, they may already be there by now, and Winfield Stratton is organizing another relief effort. Speck Penrose is on his way to the Midland Train Depot to prioritize the cargo to be loaded onto the first train to leave the station. From the last fire we have a better idea what is needed, and when, but his effort to gather supplies and load them in boxcars will require at least two hours. I will have Jessie bring a carriage around in half an hour so you can make arrangements to be on the first train to depart for Cripple Creek."

"Any other details?" asked I.

General Palmer looked down at his notes and read, "The roof on the Windsor Hotel has collapsed; sounds as if it will be a total loss. The Palace Hotel and Pharmacy are both gone. Ammunition in the storeroom of the Wright Hardware store has been exploding, keeping firemen at bay. Fire Chief May is back from his son's funeral and there's widespread speculation he may order the firemen to use dynamite again to establish a firebreak by blowing up the buildings standing in the path of the fire."

"Any details on those who have been killed?" asked I, searching for any scrap of information letting me know Sherlock Holmes might still be alive.

"One man was shot dead, by Floyd Thompson, who witnessed the man intentionally setting fire to a pile of trash in an alley. I don't think the dead man is our Sherlock Holmes. The man who was shot was carried to the Sisters of Mercy Hospital, where he was pronounced dead-on-arrival. He did not have any identification on him; however, he is described as being very tall, with a pale completion and is said to be exceedingly thin, appearing somewhat emaciated."

"STARK!" I thought to myself as I rushed upstairs to my bedroom where I scribbled down a few notes in my pocket notebook and tucked my black leather notebook into the secret compartment behind the panel above the fireplace mantel for safekeeping. I grabbed my coat, hat and doctors bag and left Glen Eyrie enroute once again to the Greatest Gold Camp on Earth.

April 29th, 1896 9pm
Cripple Creek, Colorado, U.S.A.

THE FLAMES HAD BEEN EXTINGUISHED by the time our relief train pulled into the Midland Train Depot at the east end of Cripple Creek. Nearly all the buildings along the main street of Bennett Avenue had now been destroyed; a handful were standing smoldering hulks in what had been a thriving downtown business district just four days ago. The adjacent homes immediately north of the downtown, along Eaton and Carr Avenues, had also been completely destroyed, as were many of the houses along Golden Avenue. More than five thousand people were now homeless. The First National Bank building and the Cripple Creek fire station had burnt to the ground. The Fire Department's 600-pound brass fire bell lay on its side, partially buried under the charred rubble. Property losses were already being estimated to exceed two million dollars.

As I stepped down from the train car onto the platform I observed Sister Mary standing resolutely beneath a nearby street lamp. Under the artificial light, dressed in her long black habit, the casual observer could have mistaken the sister for a religious statue. I suspected she had been standing there for some time; praying and waiting ever patiently to direct blankets, food and medical supplies to the Sisters of Mercy Hospital and elsewhere about the town as needed.

"Another answer to a prayer?" I asked as I approached Sister Mary and respectfully removed my hat.

"Two prayers actually," she said with a slight smile, "one for these supplies and a special by-name request for you, Dr. Watson."

"I am, once again, at your service," said I. "Doctor Anderson is at the hospital I presume?"

"He is, he's been at it non-stop. You will find him in the ER tent. He is deciding which patients are to be moved back inside the hospital, now that the fire is out, and which ones might be released tonight or first thing in the morning."

"How many dead and injured?"

"Six dead, many more injured, including half a dozen volunteer firemen who were hurt when dynamite went off prematurely in front of a building, while they were fighting the fire at the back of the building," Sister Mary said as she clutched the small wooden cross she wore on a chain around her neck. "I'm sure Dr. Anderson will be able to give you a more thorough report; I have been here waiting for the train to arrive for the past forty-five minutes so I am not at all current on our causalities. Please go on without me, Doctor Watson, I will be along shortly."

The TB tent in front of the hospital had once again been transformed into a makeshift emergency room. I spotted Dr. Anderson toward the back of the tent. He was bent over a patient lying on a cot, the end of his new stethoscope pressed against the patient's chest. Dr. Anderson did not see me until I placed my doctors' bag on the ground next to an identical burgundy leather

Gladstone beside him.

"Nice bag," said I softly, after he had finished listening to the heartbeat of his patient and pulled the stethoscope earpieces from his ears.

"It arrived just this morning, thank you," Dr. Anderson said, as he looked down at his new doctor's bag and then glanced back up at me. "I've already put your gift to good use; the patients started arriving shortly after two o'clock this afternoon. It had been a steady stream until about an hour ago. I think the worst is behind us now."

"You need a break?" asked I, noticing how it appeared as if Dr. Anderson, who was not that much older than me, seemed to have aged ten years since I had last seen him four days ago.

"I'm okay for the moment, thank you," Dr. Anderson said, "I want to finish taking the vital signs on these other three patients; then I can decide who to move inside for the night."

"Very well, let me know when you need me to relieve you, I'll take the midnight shift so you can get some sleep. Meanwhile, could you please direct me to where the dead are housed?"

"They're in the small toolshed, behind the hospital; it's far from ideal but I didn't have anywhere else to store them. Four of the bodies have been identified; one of those has already been claimed by family. I'm not sure who the other two people are; here," Dr. Anderson said as he handed me a small battery operated electric torch, "you are going to need this. Looking for anyone in particular?"

"Two men, one a friend," said I as I tested the light on the electric torch, picked up my medical bag and headed out behind the Sisters of Mercy Hospital into the dark of the night.

As I approached the small rickety wooden toolshed, I laid my medical bag on the ground and withdrew my service revolver. I didn't think I would need to shoot anyone inside – these people were already dead—but holding the heavy revolver in my hand helped steel my nerves. I held the electric torch in one hand, my handgun in the other and took a deep breath as I flipped on the handheld light and stepped inside. The pungent odor of death greeted me. The roof was low causing me to bend over to avoid knocking off my hat. The five bodies were stacked on narrow wooden shelfs; two on the left side and three on the right.

A quick glance at how the sheets were draped over the dead bodies indicated the victims had all been carried into the tool-shed headfirst; their feet closest to me. The distance between the bodies on the left to those on the right was less than three feet; if a person turned sideways they could walk down the narrow aisle between the dead. From the smell I knew at least one of the dead had been severely burned. I did not look forward to the gruesome task that lay before me.

To free up a hand, I slid my service revolver into the outer pocket of my topcoat and bent down to slowly pull back the white sheet from the body located on the bottom right shelf. Praying silently I would not see the face of my friend, Sherlock Holmes, I held my breath and directed the light beam from the electric torch into the face of a middle-aged man with flaming red hair. The bright color of his hair reminded me of our case with the Redheaded League. I whispered a prayer and pulled the sheet back up over his face.

Then I moved on to the next body located on the middle shelf above the redheaded dead man. I pulled a blanket down from over its head and shined my light into the face of an elderly woman with gray hair. "Poor dear," said I to myself. Oddly enough in the dim torch light it had appeared as if she was smiling. At moments like these, surrounded by death—three dead people in front of me and the bodies of two more dead people behind me—I have often questioned that when these unfortunate souls awoke this morning, a day not unlike any other in their lives, that when they put on their shoes could they possibly have had any premonition that today, this day, would be their last? I looked down one last time at the surreal smile on her angelic face, pulled the stiff wool blanket gently back over her face and moved to the next body on the top shelf.

The white cotton sheet covering this body was blood-soaked and oddly misshaped. When I pulled the sheet back, and shined my light to where the face should have been, I saw why this body looked so irregular – it had no head! Suddenly, I felt a hand clamp down upon my shoulder and I jumped bumping my head on the low ceiling! I felt the presence of a man standing close behind me, turned suddenly and shined my electric torch light into the face of Sherlock Holmes.

"Don't do that!" I shouted, overcome at once with the emotions of fright, embarrassment and relief all coming out at the same instance. Sherlock Holmes was dressed the same as the last time I had seen him; wearing a fireman's heavy coat, red suspenders, black high-topped boots and a fireman's yellow helmet.

"George Griffith," Sherlock Holmes said calmly, "He was a volunteer fireman, when he wasn't training horses for one of the local ranchers. Poor George lost his head the instant his fellow firemen dynamited a building without realizing there were other firefighters battling the blaze from the back alley."

"How did you know I was here?"

"Simple enough, yet I hesitate to explain for fear that every time I do you or whoever else I take the time to explain my methods, people go from believing I'm a rather clever fellow to someone who possesses only slightly above average abilities in my deductive reasoning."

"Please do explain," said I, always anxious to learn more about the peculiar habits of my rather unique friend.

"Very well; I knew you would do everything you could to be on the first relief train from Colorado Springs. I saw the train pull into the station a few minutes ago. From your last trip here to Cripple Creek I knew you would head straight to the Sisters of Mercy Hospital and from there, in having been informed there were multiple deaths, you would come immediately here, to this temporary morgue, looking for me, which is where I found you just now. I knew this tool shed had been designated as the morgue because I had helped another fireman carry George's body in here earlier this afternoon. When I arrived here a moment ago I observed your doctors' bag sitting in front of the tool shed door and therefore knew you would be found inside."

"I suppose that is a rather simple deduction, but tell me then, since you are so clever, do you suppose one of these two bodies is that of our Colonel Stark, or whatever his real name might be?" said I, shining my electric torch on to the two covered bodies.

"We will know soon enough," Sherlock Holmes said as he quickly pulled the white sheet away from the body lying on the middle shelf. The man's face was as white as the sheet itself and his skin appeared as if it had been literally draped over a human skeleton. The dead man, who appeared to be in his mid-forties, was so extraordinarily paper-thin it appeared as if he had no flesh between his skin and his bones.

"He is tall enough and thin enough, I will grant you that," said I as I examined the two bullet holes in the front of his vest, the cause of his demise.

"Let us see if he has an older gunshot wound to either of his legs," Sherlock Holmes said holding up my doctors' bag by the handle, "Here, I thought you might need this."

"Thank you," said I as I shined my light inside my bag and located a pair of scissors. "I believe I shot him in the upper right thigh," said I as I handed Sherlock Holmes the electric torch.

"Make yourself useful, won't you?" said I as I reached over the dead man's body and cut open the man's trousers exposing his upper right leg from his knee to his crotch. "Ah, what have we here?" said I as I probed the front of the man's right thigh muscle.

"Looks to be a bullet exit wound," Sherlock Holmes said, "how old would you estimate his wound to be, doctor?"

"I'd say about two months and from the grayish-green discoloration around the scar it looks as if the wound track was not cleaned properly."

"I have heard rather poor reports about many doctors found aboard cruise ships," he said as he rubbed the palm of his hand where he had been cut by the man now lying dead before us.

"So this is our assassin?"

"We'll know in a moment," said my friend, "may I borrow your fountain pen?"

I handed him my pen and watched as he walked over to the nearby workbench where he shined the light beam on the tools and then selected an 18-inch wood saw from the tools hanging from nails above the work space. He laid the saw on the workbench and squirted all the black ink from the barrel of my fountain pen onto one spot on in the middle of the saw blade.

"Hold his right thumb up here, would you please?" Sherlock Holmes said, as he handed me back my empty fountain pen.

I did as he instructed and watched as my friend held the saw blade out for me to press the man's stiff thumb against the wet indigo ink on the metal saw blade. Once the inside of the dead man's thumb was completely covered with black ink, Sherlock Holmes tossed the wood saw back onto the work bench and rummaged through my doctors bag.

"This will do," he said finally as he ripped open a sterile suture pack, removed the white cardboard backing and discarded the now unsterile thread into the bottom of my medical bag.

"Please, help yourself to anything you need," said I, still holding the dead man's thumb upright as if he were hailing a ride from a cab.

"Thank you," he said, unphased that I was trying to be sarcastic. "Here roll his thumb across the cardboard paper."

I did as he said and watched as Sherlock Holmes directed the light from the electric torch to illuminate a perfect black ink imprint of the dead man's thumb silhouetted against the white cardboard backing from the suture pack.

"You can let go of his thumb, if you care to," Sherlock Holmes said as we walked back over to the workbench. "Now, could you please shine our light onto his inked thumbprint here?"

I again did as he instructed and watched as he placed a second fingerprint card on the workbench alongside the first.

"Is that the fingerprint you lifted from the handle of the assassin's knife?"

"It is," he said as he pulled a round magnifying glass from the inside coat pocket of the fireman's coat he was wearing. Sherlock Holmes motioned for the electric torch, bent over the dusty workbench and carefully compared both prints. "A double-whorl, most unusual, humm," he murmured softly. Then I heard him counting quietly, "nine, ten, eleven, nine ten, eleven." I stepped closer to peer over his shoulder. He continued counting, "seven, eight, nine, seven, eight, nine. "HA!" he announced loudly as he slapped the palm of his hand on the workbench, startling me once again. "A perfect match!"

"So this is the assassin who tried to kill you and likely 002 aboard the RMS Republic?"

"And severed the thumb of your hydraulic engineer, Mr. Victor Hatherley, with a meat cleaver and possibly murdered 26-year-old Jeremiah Hayling, the first hydraulic engineer from London who went missing after having been summoned to repair a hydraulic press being used to strike large quantities of counterfeit silver coins outside of Reading."

"So you believe this fire, which burnt down 70% of the town of Cripple Creek, was intentionally set by Colonel Stark or Fritz or whatever our dead man's real name is, to cover up evidence of an international counterfeiting ring?" asked I.

"I have no doubt."

"As well as the first fire four days ago?"

"Yes," Sherlock Holmes said resolutely.

"Why two fires?"

"Because the first fire failed to destroy the intended target."

"Which was?"

"The Cripple Creek Fire Department."

"What evidence could possibly have been at the Cripple Creek Fire Department?"

"We won't know for certain, since the evidence has now been destroyed, but I suspect it may have included one or more bills of lading confirming multiple deliveries of 65-pound fire bells."

"Who do you think signed for the deliveries of the golden bells?"

"Again, we may never know for certain, but I question if the volunteer fireman who signed for one or more shipments of the priceless golden bells might have been our headless horseman here."

"George? You think this man on the top shelf was in on this caper too?" asked I.

"I don't know that he was part of their counterfeiting operation. It is more likely George may have simply have had the misfortune of being on duty when one or more of the 65-pound fire bells were delivered to the fire station. Therefore he may have known who claimed the bells or where they went next. I do question how the dynamite explosion was detonated prematurely, killing poor George. Was the detonation intentional or was he possibly already dead and the explosion intended to make his death appear accidental? I am leaning toward another murder for as we know this criminal organization does not leave any loose ends behind when they are forced to relocate and they seem to consistently cover their murderous ways with fire."

"Do you think our pudgy Dr. Bakerslee or whatever his name is, might still be here in what's left of Cripple Creek?" asked I.

"Doubtful," Sherlock Holmes replied, "it would be much harder for him to hide now, plus he is a far less capable criminal without his right-hand man, a seasoned assassin. I think they are finished here in Cripple Creek and will be relocating their operation elsewhere."

"What of Elise, Robert Coyne's German girlfriend? Was she here too or is she still back in London?"

"There may be another woman involved in all this somehow; but I don't believe our Elise was ever here in the states. She may have moved from her Cannon Lane flat after Shady's brother, Robert Coyne, was killed in the hit-and-run accident, which of course, was no accident.

"Now what?" asked I.

"Whenever your medical services are no longer required here in Cripple Creek, please return to Glen Eyrie and I will contact you there within the next two to three weeks."

"And you?"

"First, I need to drop by the Dempsey family's cabin to say farewell and to ensure The Woman made it safely to Santa Fe, New Mexico and eventually I will also need to relocate to Colorado Springs."

"Why Colorado Springs?"

"Because our Little London is the nearest town of any size where the English geologist, Dr. Bakerslee, might attempt to hire a replacement assassin."

"Good help is hard to find," said I.

"Don't I know," said my friend, adding, "Could you please cover up our dead assassin and get the door?"

May 20th, 1896 1:30pm
Glen Eyrie, Colorado, U.S.A.

Mining production never declined one ounce after the Cripple Creek fires destroyed most of the town. A wealthy Cripple Creek businessman, J.M. Roseberry, financed the rebuilding of the town's commercial center, built this time entirely of brick. Mr. Parker rebuilt his First National Bank; his financing wasn't a challenge for listed among his shareholders were the names: Winfield Scott Stratton, Spencer Penrose and Charles Tutt. A new business was added to the business district: Cripple Creek's first undertaking service; featuring on-site coffin sales, embalming, funeral and burial services. One of the local firemen, L.M. McBride, went on to become an explosive engineer and would later write, "In both fires explosives were used to excess, recklessly, and without concerted action, organization or plan and the use probably assisted the fire as much as retarded it."

I continued to record details of our investigation en bloc in my black pocket notebook.

June 14th, 1896 4pm
Old Colorado City, Colorado, U.S.A.

Meadow Muffins was a three-story pub located in the 2600 block of West Colorado Avenue, across the street from Thunder and Buttons, another of the nearly two dozen bars, saloons and dance parlors in the raucous little town known as Colorado City.

This town was situated between Colorado Springs and Manitou Springs, both of which were referred to as "dry towns" since they didn't serve any liquor. The Midland Railroad Terminal, Tutt-Penrose's Colorado-Philadelphia Reduction Company, the Upper and Lower Gold Camp Roads and the mouth of Ute Pass all converged here within one square mile.

Colorado City was the place where thirsty gold miners, cattle ranchers, teamsters and businessmen alike headed to buy a drink or the companionship of a woman. It was also the place where my friend Sherlock Holmes went in search of information on our counterfeiting ring. He had taken a position as a bartender and lived upstairs in a corner room with two windows that overlooked the main street, Colorado Avenue, below. He worked the evening shift, from 4pm to 2am, serving drinks to intoxicated men, listening to hear word of a counterfeiting ring or of an English doctor looking to hire muscle. During the day Sherlock Holmes sat at his second-story window hoping to spot a short fat man matching the description of our geologist with a Ph.D.

I busied myself visiting more local sanatoriums, documenting the advancements being made in the treatment of TB and contemplating Dr. Bell's enticing offer to take over his medical practice in this beautiful country. I had not yet mentioned Dr. Bell's offer to Sherlock Holmes, he had enough to worry about without the thought of me staying behind in Little London when he eventually returns to England. But there was another worry I held for my friend; for I was aware that just one block west of Meadow Muffins was located Sam Wah's Laundry, with a notorious opium den in the basement.

I had rarely seen Sherlock Holmes, in the month since the second Cripple Creek fire, so I was excited to get his invitation to buy me a drink at Meadow Muffins this afternoon at 4pm. I had asked Jessie Bass, General Palmer's driver, to drop me off on the corner of 30th and Pikes Peak Avenue; I would walk the rest of the way making sure I wasn't being followed. I walked into the bar, finding it nearly deserted, and took a seat on a barstool at the far end of the bar. A bartender wearing a black derby, thick eyeglasses and a white apron approached to take my drink order. He had a full gray beard so I closed my eyes and waited for him to speak.

"Afraid we're all out of 24-year-old Macallan partner, but the beer's cold," the bartender said with a slight Irish brogue.

I smiled when I recognized the voice of Sherlock Holmes and opened my eyes to see my friend standing on the other side of the bar wiping a beer mug out with a dirty bar rag.

"A cold beer sounds good," said I loudly, then added a little more quietly, "I must say this is one of your better disguises but your accent could use a little polishing."

"You are looking well," he said, as he poured my beer and slid the mug across the slick bar, coming to a stop in front of me, "I believe you have put on five pounds since I saw you last."

"Not more than three, I assure you, but you are looking fit as well. How is Irene?"

"She's well; I understand she may be auditioning for a role with the Santa Fe Opera."

"I didn't know Santa Fe had an Opera House."

"Yes, the people of Santa Fe may appear a little rough around the edges; but they are a much more cultured community than one might imagine at first glance, I think you might fit in there rather nicely."

"You think our time here in Little London may soon be coming to an end?"

"Possibly, Shady Coyne and another man, named Clark, have been in here a few times for drinks. I don't think Shady recognized me; they usually sit in a back booth rather than up here at the bar. They were joined one night by a short round man that was so fat he could hardly fit into the booth. But I haven't seen them in here or on the street for over a week now. The coppers come in here to drink, mostly the Colorado City police officers, but occasionally they are joined by a two or three of the Colorado Springs town constables."

"What do you hear from them?"

"Nothing directly. They are pretty guarded with any details concerning their ongoing investigations, but if I pour them enough free drinks I can occasionally overhear snippets of their conversation, if they're sitting here at the bar. They were in here last night; apparently one of the Colorado Springs police officers, a Samuel Agard, got jumped while making his rounds the other night, by two guys who roughed him up pretty good and stole his service revolver."

"Do they know who did this?"

"No, but there's been a string of hold-ups over the last several weeks, the victims are usually men walking home alone after a night of drinking, the crooks steal wallets or jewelry. Two stolen pocket watches and one ring were pawned at the Silver Dollar Pawn Shop in Colorado Springs. The two suspects generally match the description of Shady Coyne and the other man, Clark, a former Canon City inmate. Clark is employed locally as a wagon driver. At least that's what I've been told by the other bartenders here at Meadow Muffins or across the street at Thunder and Buttons."

"Do you want me to try to talk to Shady?"

"Why? Do you think he would tell you anything?"

"He might," said I. "We were getting along fairly well; Shady said getting thrown off a moving train by a railroad dick can bring a couple blokes together. A lot of Londoners look down on Shady's class; they've been labelled as Cockney's, but from what

I've seen they have given us our crack Volunteer regiments and turn out more sportsmen and fine athletes than any other body of men in Great Britain."

"Let's hold off talking to Shady for now, word might get back to our Dr. Bakerslee, could spook him off and one thing we've learned is that once they think someone is on to them they will flee immediately and won't leave any loose ends behind. If we don't learn anything of significance about this counterfeiting ring by, let's say July 4th, let's revisit the possibility of one or both of us speaking with Shady Coyne."

"Agreed," said I. "But what is special about the 4th of July?"

"Evidently it is a date the Americans celebrate, they call it Independence Day."

"Independence Day? Independence from whom?" said I as I finished my beer and sat my glass mug heavily upon the bar.

"Independence from England," Sherlock Holmes said.

"How can that be something to celebrate?" said I as I flipped a silver half dollar on the bar and walked out the front door.

June 28th, 1896 8:30am
Glen Eyrie, Colorado, U.S.A.

General Palmer and I had just finished breakfast and were enjoying a nice cup of English breakfast tea in his comfortable den when Pryor rushed into the room carrying a copy of the Colorado Springs Weekly Gazette newspaper special edition.

"You're going to want to read this General," Pryor said as he handed General Palmer the newspaper announcing the death of Officer Benjamin Bish.

"The most sensational affair that has happened in Colorado Springs occurred at about 10:30pm last evening," General Palmer read aloud from the full-page account of the tragic affair. He continued to scan the article and summarized the details, "Benjamin Franklin Bish, a 33-year old junior officer had just been appointed to the department two months ago by the Colorado Springs City Council whose members include officer Bish's brother Gordon. The Bish family, originally from Missouri, has been here in the city for several years. Officer Bish, a U.S. veteran from the Indian Wars, had previously been employed as a trolley car conductor before entering law enforcement. He is married and he and his wife have one child, a daughter."

"Poor dear," Pryor said.

"Pryor's brother, Horace Shelby, is a Colorado Springs police officer," General Palmer explained. "City council hired him in 1888, Shelby was our first black officer. "What else does the paper say?" asked I.

"At about 10 o'clock on the fateful night that would be his last, Bish reported for duty in the alley bounded by Tejon Street and Cascade Avenue on the east and west, respectively, and by Pikes Peak Avenue and Huerfano Avenue on the north and south, respectfully. Twenty minutes later, gunshots were heard, and two men were seen running from the alley. There, Constable Bish was found lying mortally wounded with his own revolver in his hand and another lying under him. His service revolver was still smoking, from the one shot Officer Bish managed to fire after being wounded. He died about half an hour later."

"Anything else?" asked I.

"Says here," General Palmer continued to read, "Fellow officers immediately began combing the scene for his assassins. From a dark courtyard area just off the alley, another shot rang out. Opening the door to a nearby coal bin, they found the body of a man, his revolver clutched in his hand. He was identified as William Clark, a former inmate from Canon City, who was working locally as a wagon driver. Once Clark was identified officers began searching for his friend and coworker, Stanley Coyne, whom they took into custody at 2am at a local boarding house where he shared a room with Clark. Coyne initially denied any involvement until he learned Clark had killed himself, and then he changed his story and confessed that he and this Clark were involved in a series of hold-ups over the past several months. In fact, the second handgun found at the scene of Bish's murder was one Coyne had stolen from another policeman during an assault on the officer just two weeks earlier."

"I believe I better go see him," said I.

"Stanley Coyne? You know this man?" General Palmer asked somewhat surprised.

"Yes, Sherlock Holmes and I know him, he's also from London," said I.

"Perhaps there has been some mistake?" General Palmer suggested.

"Not likely," said I, "could you please ask Jessie Bass to drive me down to where ever prisoners are held?"

"By all means," General Palmer said, "Pryor?"

"I will see to it," Pryor said as he went off to find General Palmer's driver.

"I best get my medical bag and take care of a few things up in my room," said I to General Palmer as I rushed upstairs. Once I was alone in my bedroom I opened the secret compartment behind the decorative panels above the fireplace mantel, removed my service revolver and tucked it into my Gladstone doctor's bag. I double-checked to make sure my bag contained spare ammunition and ensured my medical equipment was in place. I laid my topcoat across my bag, set my hat on top of those to make sure I had everything bundled together as I prepared to hurry down the stairs to the horse-drawn carriage outside.

I removed my black leather pocket notebook from the inside

pocket of my top coat and the last thing I did before tucking it into the secret compartment in the fireplace, was to scribble down a few quick notes and wrote the names in capital letters —SHADY COYNE & DR. BAKERSLEE—next to the date June 28, 1896.

Monday April 6th, 2020 4:30pm
Modern-day Glen Eyrie Castle, Colorado Springs, Colorado, U.S.A.

LITTLE DID DOCTOR WATSON KNOW he would never return to Glen Eyrie or ever see his black leather pocket notebook again.

"Dr. Fletcher, look what I found!" Joseph Sanchez said as he rushed into the Glen Eyrie music room and handed the black pocket notebook to Samuel Fletcher. For over three decades Dr. Fletcher has been the historian for the Navigators, a worldwide Christian ministry founded in 1933 by the late Dawson Trotman. The evangelist Billy Graham had convinced Dawson Trotman to purchase the 65-room castle in 1953. For over sixty years the Navigators have used Glen Eyrie as the headquarters for their worldwide organization as well as a conference and retreat center. Recently, Dr. Fletcher had been overseeing the remodel of the Castle's music room and three of the upstairs bedrooms, as well as the nearby Carriage House being converted into a bookstore.

"What did you find?" Dr. Fletcher asked of Joseph, a 28-year-old skilled carpenter who has been a fulltime craftsman for nine years with the Special Projects Division of the GE Johnson Construction Company, also headquartered in Colorado Springs.

"It's a journal or a diary or something," Joseph said. "I think it's really old. It didn't have any money in it; but there's a business card inside the front pocket.

Dr. Fletcher removed the business card and read the name embossed on the card aloud, "John H. Watson, M.D., London."

Then he read the first entry in the notebook, "January 20, 1896 2:30pm 221 B Baker Street, London, England." Repeating at the address aloud, he thought to himself, "that address sounds vaguely familiar."

"1896! Do you think this notebook has been hidden away here in the castle for over a hundred years?" Joseph asked as Dr. Fletcher examined the first several pages.

"Possibly, it seems to be quite old; the handwriting was done in cursive using a fountain pen and was written when the General was alive and living here in the castle with his daughters. This Dr. Watson may have been a guest of General Palmer's and accidently left his notebook."

"What's the date on the last entry?" Joseph asked.

Dr. Fletcher thumbed through the pages and stopped about three-quarters of the way toward the back cover and read the date of the last entry, "June 28th, 1896."

"What does it say?" Joseph asked as he looked over Dr. Fletcher's shoulder.

"The last entry was written in capital letters, SHADY COYNE and DR. BAKERSLEE," Dr. Fletcher said, "What a fascinating mystery! Where did you find this?"

"Behind a wooden panel above the fireplace mantel in Dr. Watt's bedroom," Joseph said, "I was repairing those six-inch white and blue square tiles around the fireplace, like you asked me to do, and I noticed one of the wood panels above the mantel was slightly crooked, I believe the castle may be settling slightly. When I tried to straighten the panel I pulled up on the bottom and found the panel was concealing a secret compartment. When I looked inside I saw there was something hidden in there so I reached in and that's when I found this leather notebook."

"Was there anything else inside?"

"No, just the notebook. The compartment is about twelve-inches deep; I put my hand all the way in to the back and felt around, there was nothing else in there; just this old black leather notebook. Want to come see where I found it?"

"Lead the way!" Dr. Fletcher said excitedly as he followed Joseph up the grand staircase and down the hall to the last bedroom on the right.

"See, there, just above the fireplace mantel," Joseph said, pointing at the three decorative panels; the one on the left was standing open revealing a secret compartment. "This panel is attached to a pair of hinges at the top and screwed into the wood. That's some really fine carpentry work there, I can tell you that; whoever built this knew what he was doing, he had to have been a cabinet maker or a master woodworker for sure."

"We have records of General Palmer having a master carpenter on staff, a Charles Kneller. Do you have a tape measure?" Dr. Fletcher asked. Joseph reached into his leather carpenters belt and handed him a tape measure. "Hum, twelve-inches wide, six-inches in height, and like you said, it's about twelve-inches deep," Dr. Fletcher said, and then he measured the pocket notebook. "Four inches by nine inches and it's about three-quarters of an inch thick." Then he gently lowered the panel back into place above the mantel. "It does blend in perfectly," he said. "Dr. Watt used this room when he was General Palmer's resident physician, after the General broke his back from being thrown from a horse in the Garden of the Gods. Had you not accidently discovered this secret compartment Joseph, no one would ever have known it was here; this notebook could have been hidden away in there for another hundred years. Are the other two panels securely fastened or do they also open?"

"No, they don't open, I tried them too, but there would have been plenty of room to put something else in this one, like a wallet or jewelry," Joseph said. "I'll be extra careful when I finish re-caulking around the rest of the decorative tiles below the fireplace mantel."

"Thank you for bringing this to my attention, Joseph," said Dr. Fletcher, "I will look into this more first thing in the morning. I think your discovery might turn out to be really important."

Saturday April 11th, 2020 6:30pm

Modern-day 221 B Baker Street, Sherlock Holmes Museum, London, England

JUDITH HUDSON, A 78-YEAR-OLD retired English teacher and docent at the Sherlock Holmes Museum in London, followed the last two visitors to the front door and thanked the elderly couple from Denmark for visiting. She locked the front door and returned to the sitting room. She placed another log in the fireplace and watched as the flames came back to life. She sat down in the comfortable chair behind the large wooden desk and opened the express package that had been delivered earlier in the afternoon. From the package she removed a one-inch thick stack of 8.5x11 inch documents, photocopied on both sides, along with a handwritten note.

The notecard had the Glen Eyrie logo embossed in the top left corner and the address printed at the bottom: 3820 North 30th Street, Colorado Springs, CO 80904. The handwritten note was dated April 7, 2020 and read, "Dear Ms. Hudson, please find enclosed a photocopy of the pocket notebook discovered yesterday in Glen Eyrie Castle. I also included a photocopy of the business card for John H. Watson, M.D., London, found inside the front pocket. As I mentioned in my email, once you have had an opportunity to research this on your end, to determine the artifact's authenticity, we can discuss where this notebook, along with the business card, should be housed or put on permanent loan for display purposes. Sincerely, Samuel Fletcher, Ph.D., Historian, The Navigators."

Ms. Hudson studied the photocopy of the business card then placed it on the upper left corner of the antique desk, alongside a 19th century business card from their collection which also read, "John H. Watson, M.D., London." After studying the print closely with a large round magnifying glass, another 19th century artifact from the museum's Sherlock Holmes private collection, she said to herself, "Well, the typeface and font do appear to be identical."

Then she carefully laid the original handwritten manuscript for Dr. Watson's 1892 novel, *Silver Blaze*, on the upper right corner of her desk and compared Doctor Watson's known handwriting against the handwriting on the photocopied pages of the notebook in question. After a few minutes she put the magnifying glass aside and thought to herself, "I believe they match. Should we be fortunate enough to ever see the original notebook, perhaps one of the forensic handwriting experts from Scotland Yard might grant us an opinion; but to me as a lay person with no formal training, the handwriting does look remarkably similar."

As she read the date at the top of the first page, January 20th, 1896, and the location, 221 B Baker Street, London, England, the hand of the great-granddaughter of Mrs. Hudson—who originally owned the building that today houses the Sherlock Holmes Museum—began to tremble with excitement. The pages of the notebook had been copied two to a page, double-sided, made it a little slow to read the notebook in landscape format; but soon she was flipping rapidly through the stack of papers. She read about the cryptic telegram Sherlock Holmes received from his brother Mycroft, and the mysterious meeting with Queen Victoria, who had passed away on January 22, 1901, at age 81.

Ms. Hudson stared at the flames dancing in the fireplace for a moment savoring what might be a primary source of someone who had met privately with Queen Victoria. She read Dr. Watson's description of the ocean crossing aboard the RMS Republic and having dinner at the Captain's Table with Rudyard Kipling, a first edition copy of *The Jungle Book*, stood in a bookshelf nearby. Then she read of the assassin's attempt to kill Sherlock Holmes. As a retired English teacher, the dinner Dr. Watson and Sherlock Holmes enjoyed with Mark Twain at Delmonico's in New York City, was the first section in the journal where she stopped and placed a sticky note to mark the page so she could return to read this section again more slowly.

She read with excitement about Sherlock Holmes and Dr. Watson chasing a ring of counterfeiters to America. She enjoyed reading the details about their arrival in Little London, staying at Glen Eyrie and of their first visit to the Greatest Gold Camp on Earth. Dr. Watson's penmanship was easy to read and it felt to her as if she were there with these two men, in the Rocky Mountains of Colorado. "If this is true," she thought to herself, "this adventure could make an extraordinary contribution to the Cannon of Sherlock Holmes written by Sir Arthur Conan Doyle."

Judith Hudson found herself skimming through the pages more quickly now; following the account of Dr. Watson, Sherlock Holmes and Shady Coyne being buried alive in the mine explosion beneath Battle Mountain and of the two fires in Cripple Creek. She also marked those pages with a sticky note, pledging to return for a more comprehensive read. A lump formed in her throat when she read about the murder of the 33-year-old policeman Benjamin Franklin Bish, and wondered what had become of the constable's widow and young daughter. Then, all too quickly, she turned to the last copied page of the notebook, dated June 28th, 1896 8:30am, Glen Eyrie, Colorado, U.S.A., and read about the secret compartment behind the panel above the fireplace mantel where Dr. Watson placed his pocket notebook for safekeeping.

The last entry was unusual for it was only two names and written in capital letters and underlined: SHADY COYNE and DR. BAKERSLEE. "I wonder whatever became of these two men?" she questioned aloud, as she set the copied papers aside.

Judith Hudson stared at the flames burning in the fireplace in the very sitting room where Sherlock Holmes and Dr. Watson discussed their many cases. She got up and added another log to the cozy fire, noticing the antique clock on the fireplace mantel to the right of the Persian slipper showed the time to be 8:25. She could hardly believe she had been reading a copy of the journal for nearly two hours; it seemed more like twenty minutes. She returned to the desk and once again read the handwritten note from the Glen Eyrie historian. "Fletcher," she said to herself, thinking, "Now, there's an Old English surname for you; as I recall the fletchers were arrowsmiths, ancient craftsmen who applied the feathers to arrows."

As she thought about the shape of an arrowhead, a distant childhood memory slowly formed in her mind. The memory of seeing a tiny arrowhead carved into one of the bricks of this very fireplace. "Could it be possible?" Judith Hudson said softly as she stood up from her leather chair, steadied herself against the heavy wooden desk for a moment as her mind raced and then she walked slowly back to the fireplace. She studied the red fireplace bricks, the same fireplace she had sat in front of countless times as a little girl, seventy-some years ago. She felt the warmth of the fire on her legs and closed her eyes and recalled the voice of her great-grandmother reading her the many stories about the adventures of her two famous boarders, Sherlock Holmes and Dr. John Watson.

The building that included the flat with the famous address,

221 B Baker Street, London, England, had been passed down from Judith Hudson's Great-grandmother to her only son. Then to his only surviving son—his eldest son, Judith's uncle—had been killed serving in the RAF during WWII. Having never been married, Judith Hudson had no heirs and she had left her family's estate to a non-profit organization founded to maintain the Sherlock Holmes Museum. As a docent, Judith Hudson volunteered three days a week, Thursday-Saturday; the museum is closed on Sunday and Monday. The thought of waiting until Tuesday for her to search the fireplace for a secret compartment never crossed her mind.

As Judith Hudson inspected the fireplace bricks she recalled Dr. Watson mentioning in his notebook about a small compartment concealed behind the bricks on the left side of the fireplace. Carefully tracing the surface of every brick gently with her fingers, Judith Hudson came across one brick, at about eye level that was different from all the rest for it had a small indentation in the shape of an arrowhead pointing up, just like she remembered. She wiggled the brick above where the arrowhead pointed and discovered it was loose. She felt beneath the brick and discovered a small slit on the underside of the brick. She inserted her fingertips into the slot and gently pulled the loose brick free from the fireplace revealing an opening – a secret compartment! She looked inside, it was dark, but she could see something. Her heart raced as she reached her hand into the small compartment and removed a dusty sealed yellow envelope.

"Oh my, what do we have here?" Judith Hudson said as she carried the musty smelling envelope back to the desk and sat down in the chair. She removed an antique jackknife from the top desk drawer that she often used as a letter opener and sliced open the top of the envelope. She folded the single knife blade into the handle; a second knife blade had been broken off long ago. She had been tempted to throw this old knife with the broken blade away a dozen times; however, she rationalized it still had one useful blade and often wondered what stories the knife could tell. She poured the contents of the old yellow envelope out onto the desk.

Judith Hudson stared at the two items that now lay before her, a brown leather pocket notebook and a small 2-inch tan colored envelope. She wondered if it were possible that neither of these items had seen the light of day in over a century. From her museum experience she recognized the small envelope as being the same size, paperweight and color that had been used at the British Royal Mint to house coins. She opened the coin flip first, turned it upside down and watched as a heavy gold coin slid out from the envelope and landed face up on the desk. She picked up the round magnifying glass and read the date.

"1893! That's the date of the fake coins, but this is a real Queen Victoria-Jubilee Head Two Pound Gold Double Sovereign Coin," she said aloud. Then she turned her attention to the brown leather pocket notebook and felt the same rush of excitement pulsing through her aging body as if she were a little girl again. It was the same thrill she experienced every time her great-grandmother sat and read her one of Conan Doyle's short stories or one of his four novels.

Judith Hudson held her breath as she turned to the first page of the brown leather notebook. She read the date and location handwritten at the top of the first page. She compared the handwriting to the known handwriting of Dr. Watson, from his handwritten novel *Silver Blaze*, to the handwriting on the photocopied pages of the notebook discovered at Glen Eyrie Castle, in Colorado Springs, a town once known as Little London.

"These were both written by the same hand!" Judith Hudson said with astonishment. "I am sure of it; this is the same cursive handwriting, same style of journal entries and the dates match." She looked at the face of the clock on the fireplace mantel. "How can it be 9 o'clock already," she said to herself, "I should be upstairs readying myself for bed, but I am too excited to sleep. Let's crack on to see what happened to SHADY CONYNE and DR. BAKERSLEE!"

June 28th, 1896 10:30am
El Paso County Jail, Colorado Springs, Colorado, U.S.A.

THE INTIMIDATING THREE-STORY red brick building had originally been built 21 years ago, in 1875, to serve as a Colorado Territorial Jail. It was located two blocks south of General Palmer's Antler's Hotel in downtown Little London. A ten-foot tall wrought iron fence with spikes at the top encircled the jail where Shady Coyne was being incarcerated. Sherlock Holmes was sitting on a park bench across the street when I stepped out of the carriage. I told Jessie Bass not to wait. Without speaking, Sherlock Holmes and I walked through the front gate together, entered the jailhouse and approached a middle-aged deputy wearing a brown uniform behind the counter.

"We're here to see Stanley Coyne," Sherlock Holmes said to the deputy sheriff.

"Are you his attorneys?" the deputy asked.

"No, I am his doctor," said I holding up my medical bag, "this is his brother."

"You can't take that bag in here unless I search it first," the deputy said.

"No need," said I, "is there someplace I may secure it while we are in visiting him?"

"There's a locker there behind you," the deputy said pointing with the eraser end of stubby pencil. "Just put your bag and any weapons you're carrying inside, lock the door and take the key with you."

Sherlock Holmes and I soon found ourselves being admitted inside, but not until we had been thoroughly searched, down to the soles of our shoes. We were led to a small attorney's interview room where we waited for nearly half an hour before inmate Coyne was finally let into the room, his wrists and legs were shackled together in chains. It was obvious he had been beaten. When the door was shut and locked, Sherlock Holmes stood up, put his index finger to his lips, signaling us to remain quiet, and then peered out the small slot in the door to make sure no one was listening.

"Keep your voices low," he cautioned, as he sat on the bench next to me and across the table from the inmate wearing a black and white striped jail uniform.

"You've been hurt," said I as I reached over to inspect the fresh cuts and abrasions to his face, "let me look at you."

Shady pushed my hand away and said, "I'm okay Doc."

"Did the police do this to you?" asked I.

"Doesn't matter," said Shady, as he stared at the concrete slab floor and shook his head, "Don't blame 'em, this man was one of their own, I'd a done the same. I wondered who my doctor and brother were," Shady said, "especially since me only brother, Robert, is departed. Thanks for comin' to see me, Mr. Holmes, Doctor Watson; but, I don't suppose you being here will do me no good at all."

"Shady, can you tell us what happened?" asked I in a low voice.

"Last time we was together Doc, you and me up there on Gold Camp Road," Shady began in a low voice, while staring at the gray concrete floor, "I mentioned I was headed down to Colorado Springs, to meet up with this bloke named Clark?"

"I remember you mentioning him, yes," said I, "the newspaper this morning said he was a former inmate from Canon City, working locally as a wagon driver."

"Yea, that's him," Shady said. "Dr. Bakerslee had hired Clark before me and Colonel Stark got here, to haul freight from the train depot down here in Colorado Springs up to Cripple Creek, or elsewhere about the goldfields around Cripple Creek."

"Did this William Clark know what was inside the crates he was hauling in his wagon?" asked Sherlock Holmes.

"He never mentioned it if he did," Shady said, "but being he was a convicted felon, he wasn't too particular in whatever work came his way. Clark and I met with Bakerslee a couple times after the fires, hoping to find work. Bought us a few drinks, he did, in a bar over on the Westside. He slipped us a few bucks now and again, just to string us along, claiming he might need our services once he decided where to move his operation. Dr. Bakerslee claimed he knew nothing about Stark setting off the dynamite explosion beneath the Tincup Mine that could of killed the three of us, don't know if what he was a saying was true or if he was just shining me on; but I stayed in touch with him all the same, hoping to find out who might a killed me brother Robert. Things got kinda tight after the second fire; Bakerslee told me and Clark not to go back up there on account of some folks knowing the fires were set on purpose. We couldn't find much work down here, that's when we started holdin up a few blokes, for their cash and valuables. Oh, that reminds me, Doc, I pawned your silver pocket watch down at the Silver Dollar Pawn Shop; it might still be there if you want to try to buy it back, if'n it had any sentimental value."

"That's okay Shady," said I.

"Can you tell us what happened last night?" Sherlock Holmes asked, after looking out the small window again to make sure no one was standing nearby listening in on our conversation.

"Sure, as I mentioned, me and Clark, we'd done a couple small time hold-ups together, mostly rolling drunks headed home after a night out on the town. We never intended to hurt no one. Then one night, couple weeks back, this policeman making his rounds spotted us walking down the sidewalk, it was after midnight, he musta recognized Clark being a former inmate and called us over. When he went to frisk us, Clark, being a convicted felon and all, knew it was illegal for him to carry a gun. He'd told me once before he was never goin back to jail. So Clark got to wrestlin' with this constable, this was a couple weeks ago, and I jumped in fearin' Clark would pull his gun and shoot the policeman, so I got a hold of the policeman's service revolver and wrapped him over the head with it; knockin him out. Then Clark and me tooks off running."

"Go on," Sherlock Holmes said, "Tell us about last night."

"Same thing happened, last night, this other policeman, I never knew his name but his badge number was 7, you learn to take notice of things like that in my line of work, anyways, this copper spotted Clark and me in an alley, I'm guessin' it was nearing on 10 o'clock, we'd been drinkin pretty heavy since mid-afternoon. The copper had his gun out and pointed it at us and told us we was to put our hands in the air. When we did he approached me first and when he searched me he found the other policeman's service revolver tucked in me belt. Clark and me both knew the jig was up. Clark pulled his gun and shot the policeman. The policeman fired one shot, but the bullet missed Clark. Clark and me took off running down the alley, when we hit the street he ran one way and I ran the other."

"What happened next?" Sherlock Holmes asked.

"I went back to this apartment we had been renting to wait for Clark. He never showed up. So about midnight I went to sleep. Then around 2am these three policemen burst into my apartment and arrested me for the murder of that police officer. I denied it at first, then they told me they found Clark dead in a coal bin, apparently he shot himself in the head, when they was closing in on him. I knew that first policeman would be able to identify me from two weeks previous when we stole his gun. I surly got what's comin' to me; I should have ignored Bakerslee when he asked me to hang around till he decided where to relocate his ring. I should have headed to Denver weeks ago, after we split up on Gold Camp Road, Doctor Watson."

"Do you know what kind of doctor this Bakerslee is?" asked Sherlock Holmes.

"Doctor Bakerslee wasn't a real doctor, not like Dr. Watson; he was more into rocks and such; a geologist is what Clark called him, but he was always trying to impress blokes with big words. I think Bakerslee might have been a college professor at one time in one of those smaller universities back home in England. Don't guess I'll ever step foot in Ole England ever again."

"Did you find out anything from Dr. Bakerslee about Robert's murder?" Sherlock Holmes asked.

"No, he was pretty tightlipped about all that," Shady said. "I think the head guy above Dr. Bakerslee might have also been a college professor, but that's mostly speculation on Clark's part, he tends to get things mixed up when he's been drinking, which was pretty much all the time. The morning of the first Cripple Creek fire, Clark told me Bakerslee hired him to haul four heavy wooden crates from the Tincup Mine in Cripple Creek to the North End here in Colorado Springs."

"Do you know where Clark delivered those four wooden crates?" asked Sherlock Holmes.

"Not exactly, Clark said he put them in a carriage house behind one of those big houses up on the north end near the Glockner

Sanatorium. I had been there once before, I think Dr. Bakerslee was renting a room temporarily there in the big house."

"Could you draw us a map?" asked I.

"Wouldn't do no good," Shady said. "Clark told me he hauled those four crates from the carriage house to the Denver & Rio Grande Railroad depot late yesterday afternoon."

"Did he say where they were being shipped?" asked Sherlock Holmes.

"To Santa Fe, New Mexico," Shady replied, "Clark said Dr. Bakerslee told him last night he was leaving this afternoon, on the 12:15 train to Santa Fe, said he had some loose ends to take care of in New Mexico."

"We gotta go!" Sherlock Holmes said as he jumped up from the table and banged loudly on the cell door to get the attention of the jailer. "What time is it?"

I reached for my vest pocket where I kept my watch, finding my pocket empty, I inadvertently glanced at Shady Coyne.

Shady shrugged his shoulders and mouthed, "Sorry Doc."

"Must be well past 12 noon," said I, waiting next to Sherlock Holmes for the jailer to open the door.

"Thank you, Shady," Sherlock Holmes said as the jailer unlocked the heavy metal door, "Anything we can do for you?"

"You could check in on Robert's widow for me, when you gets back to London."

"Good luck, Shady," said I as I followed behind Sherlock Holmes. We were escorted to the front of the jailhouse.

"Don't forget your doctor's bag," the jailer said as we walked rapidly though the front lobby.

"Where are we going?' asked I as I struggled to keep up with Sherlock Holmes walking at a brisk pace.

"The train depot," he said.

"Why?" I asked as he headed down the street toward the depot.

"Santa Fe is where the Dempsey brothers escorted The Woman," Sherlock Holmes said as he trotted toward the ticket window to ask the Ticket Master if the Santa Fe 12:15 had already departed.

"You think Irene is the loose end Bakerslee said he needs to take care of in Santa Fe?"

"No doubt," Sherlock Holmes replied as he raced ahead to the ticket window.

"Just missed it," I heard the Ticket Master say as he turned his head toward the south and nodded at the empty set of railroad tracks.

"When's the next train to Santa Fe?" Sherlock Holmes asked.

"Next passenger train doesn't leave until 6:20 this evening," the Ticket Master replied.

"Where's that train going?" Sherlock Holmes asked, pointing to a freight car getting ready to pull away from the station southbound.

"It's going to Trinidad, that's a small town just this side of the New Mexico border," the Ticket Master replied, "you might be able to catch a train from there to get you on into Santa Fe afore evening."

"Thanks," Sherlock Holmes said, as he grabbed me by the arm and dragged me over to the freight car as it was starting to roll away from the station. "Hop in," he said as he tossed my medical bag inside, and lifted me up by the arm to help me inside. When we stood up inside the dusty freight car, our eyes slowly adjusted to the dim light. Then I heard the clucking of excited chicks. The freight car was stacked nearly floor to ceiling with wooden crates carrying hundreds of chickens. As the train picked up speed the chicken feathers began to swirl around inside the freight car. For several minutes it looked as if Sherlock Holmes and I were participating in a pillow fight.

"What's that smell?" asked I stepping toward the open door for fresh air.

"Money," replied Sherlock Holmes.

"Money?" asked I.

"You may have noticed the three cars ahead of this one were loaded with cattle."

"I hadn't noticed," said I, looking around for any place to sit down.

"When I was talking with Bob Womack, at his ranch up in Cripple Creek, a newspaper man from Boston stopped by to interview with him for an article. When he asked Bob how he handles the smell of fresh manure wafting up from Bob's barnyard to his cabin, Womack told him the smell wasn't at all offensive to him because it reminds him of money on the hoof."

"Charming," said I as I poked my head out the open boxcar door to see Colorado Springs shrinking into the distance. "I don't mean to complain but I couldn't help noticing we are leaving Little London in a slightly less luxurious train car then the one we arrived in a few months ago."

"Here," said Sherlock Holmes as he tossed a 50-pound burlap bag of chicken feed on the floor of the boxcar in front of the crates with the cackling chickens. "Sit here, lean your back against those crates." Then he tossed another heavy burlap bag alongside the first and sat down next to me, "See, like this," he said demonstrating by sitting down on the sack of chicken feed and leaned back against the chicken crates. Sherlock Holmes noticed me clutching my Gladstone medical bag, to keep it from getting dirty on the floor. "I don't suppose you have anything to drink in there do you Doctor, strictly for medicinal purposes of course?"

I opened my bag and handed him my silver flask, "You might find this to your liking."

He unscrewed the top, took a big swig and handed the flask back to me, "Ah, 24-year-old single malt, Macallan? Is it not?"

I took a big swallow myself and handed the flask back to my travel mate, "Indeed. Compliments of General Palmer's butler, Pryor Shelby."

"Ah, to Pryor and General Palmer and to your good health," Sherlock Holmes said as he took another big gulp and handed me back the near empty flask. Then he pulled his hat down over his eyes and said, "Could you please wake me when we reach the outskirts of Trinidad?"

"Certainly, I'm sure I'll be awake," said I as the chorus of cackling chickens continued over my shoulder. "One thing I would like to know before you drop off?"

"Yes?"

"How are we to find The Woman when we reach Santa Fe?"

"She's checked into the La Fonda Hotel."

"Certainly not under the name Irene Adler," said I.

"No, the Dempsey brothers told me they registered The Woman under their dear mother's maiden name."

"Which is?"

"Mary Smoot."

"And how did Doctor Bakerslee know Irene was staying at the La Fonda in Santa Fe?"

"That's what I intend to find out," Sherlock Holmes said as he drifted off to sleep.

I took one more small drink and placed the empty silver flask back into my doctor's bag. Two of the chickens poked their heads out of the crate and were looking over my shoulder at the floor where a handful of chicken feed had spilled out near my foot. I filled the palm of my hand and let the chickens peck cracked corn from my hand as I stared out the open door of the freight car. Half an hour later I watched as an enormous black building with tall smoke stacks from General Palmer's CF&I steel mill came into view as we rolled through the small town of Pueblo, Colorado. Then, twenty minutes later, the snowcapped Spanish Peaks came into view on the right side of our smelly freight car, full of chicken coops and chicken poop. I closed my eyes and dreamt that when I opened my eyes our private Pullman would be pulling into Paddington Station.

Chapter 9

June 28th, 1896 2:50pm

Trinidad, Colorado, U.S.A.

The shrill of the train's whistle approaching the Trinidad train depot caused my travel companion, Sherlock Holmes to open his eyes for the first time since leaving Little London.

"Are we there yet?" he asked as he sat up and stretched. He seemed as well rested as if he had slept the night in a fluffy feather bed at the Waldorf Astoria rather than two hours sleeping on top of a 50-pound sack of chicken feed aboard a slow moving freight train.

"Yes, if you are referring to being there as in Trinidad, Colorado," said I looking out the open door at the sleepy little town in Southern Colorado now coming into view, "No, if you are referring to Paddington Station."

"Come, Watson, we haven't then a moment to lose," said Sherlock Holmes as he stood at the door waiting for our train car to roll to a stop a hundred yards or so short of the small red brick terminal building. I hopped down and followed Sherlock Holmes to the ticket window and listened over his shoulder.

"May I help you?" asked the ticket master.

"Yes," Sherlock Holmes replied, "can you please tell us when the next train for Santa Fe departs?"

"The next passenger train departs for Santa Fe at 6:30pm. Would you care to purchase a ticket?"

"No, we haven't that much time," Sherlock Holmes said as he looked across the steel railroad tracks at the only other train in the vicinity of the depot. "Where is that train headed?"

"To Albuquerque, it will stop in Santa Fe to take on coal and deliver the mail, but that's a freight train," the ticket master said, stating the obvious.

"When does it leave?" Sherlock Holmes asked.

"It was supposed to leave twenty minutes ago, but the fireman hasn't shown up yet. It won't be going anywhere unless you two want to shovel coal."

"Very well," Sherlock Holmes said to the ticket master and headed toward the train. I followed along as Sherlock Holmes approached the engineer standing to the side the train engine, holding his pocket watch in one hand and an oil can with a long spout in the other."

"I understand you are in need of someone to shovel coal and we are in need of passage to Santa Fe, New Mexico, might we reach an accord?" Sherlock Holmes asked the man in the striped blue bib overalls with a large red bandana tied around his neck.

"Well, I don't know if that would be allowable," the conductor said looking to see if his tardy fireman was anywhere in sight.

Sherlock Holmes reached into his wallet and handed the engineer a crispy U.S. $50 bill, "What would you say if we sweetened the pot?"

"I'd say, all aboard!" the engineer replied with a wide grin.

I climbed aboard the train engine, behind Sherlock Holmes and the engineer, who appeared more than happy to be finally underway, especially with a new fifty in his wallet.

"You can stash your belongings over there," the engineer said and then he opened the metal door to the furnace. "There's only one shovel," the engineer said, holding up the large coal shovel, "so you'll have to take turns shoveling from the coal car back there into the furnace."

"No worries," said Sherlock Holmes, as he accepted the shovel and handed it to me, "I'll spell you when you get tired." Then he looked over the engineer's shoulder at the myriad of levers and gauges and said, "I've always been fascinated with trains, it looks so complex, can you please tell me how you make it go?"

"It's really quite straightforward," said the engineer as he began explaining the levers and gauges to Sherlock Holmes, while I began shoveling the black coal into the fiery furnace.

"I've always wanted to blow a train whistle! May I give it a try, Bernie?" I overheard Sherlock Holmes say to his new best friend; already on a first-name basis with the engineer before I had shoveled four shovels full of heavy black coal into the roaring furnace.

"I was the same way, ever since I was a young lad," the engineer said, letting go of the overhead cord and offering Sherlock Holmes the honors of blowing the train whistle announcing our departure from the Trinidad terminal, "here, Sherlock, give this a good tug."

As the train whistle blew, the train lurched forward; I steadied myself and continued to shovel coal into the maw of the furnace, while Bernie the Engineer and Sherlock Holmes acted as if they were two boys who had been given a new train set for Christmas.

"That's Raton Pass up head," I heard the engineer say to Sherlock Holmes as I lost count of how many shovels full of coal I had poured into the blast furnace. It was a hot summer's day and I had already worked up a good sweat shoveling heavy shovels full of coal into the red hot furnace. Unaccustomed to such rigorous exercise I could feel the muscles in my back, arms and legs protest as my friend and his friend hung their heads out the window and felt the cool breeze upon their faces.

"Is that sufficient?" I finally asked the engineer, pointing to the fiery orange flames in the blistering hot furnace.

"I'll close the door when you can stop," the engineer said, taking notice of how I had leaned momentarily against the handle of the shovel for a short break.

"He'll close the door," Sherlock Holmes repeated, then drew the attention of the engineer back to the open window and the beautiful passing scenery. "Bernie, do you happen to know the elevation of Raton Pass?"

"I do," said the conductor proudly, as he pointed to an approaching white sign with black letters on the right side of the tracks near the summit, "7,634 feet. Welcome to New Mexico, Sherlock!"

"What fun!" Sherlock Holmes shouted as he pulled the cord on the train whistle two more times, announcing our arrival in New Mexico.

I returned to my solitary chore of shoveling black coal into the red hot furnace.

June 28th, 1896 4:30pm
Santa Fe, New Mexico, U.S.A.

As OUR TRAIN ROLLED TO A STOP at the Santa Fe train depot Bernie pointed toward the town square, a half mile to the west, "You'll find the La Fonda Hotel on the Plaza, across from the Cathedral Basilica of St. Francis of Assisi, it's been nice traveling with you two gents."

"Thanks for the lift, Bernie," Sherlock Holmes said as we stepped down from the train engine.

"A new best friend?" I asked carrying my suit coat and wrinkled silk tie slug over one arm and my medical bag in the other.

"You will always be my Boswell, but as you know a person can learn much more from someone once you are on a friendly basis," Sherlock Holmes explained as we walked toward the terminal building.

"Such as?" asked I.

"Well for one, Santa Fe was founded by the Spaniards in 1607," Sherlock Holmes said as we stopped in front of the terminal building and took in our unfamiliar surroundings.

"Okay, and two?" asked I.

"And two," Sherlock Holmes said as he nodded his head slightly toward a wood frame warehouse behind the ticket office, "when freight is off loaded here at the depot and no one is standing here to claim the cargo, it is moved into that warehouse building until it is claimed."

"You think Dr. Bakerslee's four wooden crates are inside that warehouse right now?"

"Quite possibly, but first things first," Sherlock Holmes said as he studied the train schedule written in white chalk upon the slate blackboard nailed to the wall. "I need to go to the La Fonda Hotel to ascertain if The Woman, is still registered there as Mary Smoot."

"And me?"

"You need to purchase three first-class tickets aboard the 7:15 to San Francisco and after you purchase our tickets, please stop by the nearest bank and make an odd number withdraw from our joint account."

"Wise decision," said I, "to alert Downing Street where we are and that things are yet unsettled. Do I meet you back here at the depot?"

"No, meet me at the Loretto Chapel, near the spiral staircase."

"Why there?" asked I.

"The Miraculous Staircase has an intriguing legend behind it; who built it and how it was constructed using no nails, Bernie confirmed it is the 'must see' attraction in Santa Fe."

"Very well," said I as I prepared to walk away.

"Before you enter the Chapel," Sherlock Holmes said as he looked at my slovenly appearance. "You may want to stop at a public restroom and freshen up a bit; you don't want the Sisters of Loretto thinking you're a vagabond."

"I think myself a vagabond," said I as I set off toward the ticket office, "ever since you and I left Liverpool."

June 28th, 1896 5:50pm
Loretto Chapel, Santa Fe, New Mexico, U.S.A.

"WE WILL BE CLOSING IN TEN MINUTES," the sister announced quietly to the handful of people inside the chapel. I gave up on Sherlock Holmes joining me inside and walked out of the chapel to see if I might spot my friend approaching the chapel. There was only one bench nearby, so I decided to wait there in the shade where I could watch the front door. A Mexican wearing a multicolored serape, with a large straw sombrero pulled down over his face, was taking a siesta. I sat down next to him, trying not to disturb his late afternoon nap.

"Señor?" he said without looking up.

I turned my head toward the sleeping man sitting next to me, "Are you speaking to me?"

"Si," he said.

"Yes, what is it?" I asked as I looked across the street to see if I could spot Sherlock Holmes approaching from the throng of people mingling about the town square.

"We will need only two of those first-class train tickets," Sherlock Holmes said, as he lifted the wide brim on the sombrero. I turned and noticed a worried look upon on his face.

"What's wrong?" I asked.

"Mary Smoot checked out earlier this afternoon."

"Where did she go?"

"I don't know, quite possibly she is on her way to California."

"You think she's in trouble?"

"I fear so," he said as he looked across the plaza no doubt hoping to see the beautiful face of The Woman.

"Why do you believe that to be the case?"

"Within an hour of her checking out of her room and taking a hansom cab to the train station, a short portly man with an English accent appeared at the front desk of the hotel asking questions about a woman matching her description."

"The front desk clerk remembered the man saying this woman may have been connected to the opera. When he learned a woman matching the description of The Woman had checked out and hailed a cab to the train depot, he too grabbed a cab and headed off toward the Santa Fe train depot. Only one passenger train was scheduled to leave Santa Fe this afternoon, the 2:20 to Los Angeles, we just missed that train by two hours."

"Los Angeles, the City of Angels," said I.

"No place for our Dr. Bakerslee," Sherlock Holmes replied. "Hopefully The Woman will be travelling in disguise, possibly as a young man, for they very well may be on the same train headed to the west coast. Once there she or they could head anywhere up or down the coast."

"Our train doesn't leave for another hour and a half," I said, looking across the street at the town clock in the plaza, "but, how will we possibly know which way to go once we get off the train in Los Angeles?"

"We follow Dr. Bakerslee's four wooden crates stored in the warehouse behind the Santa Fe ticket office."

"Locating four wooden crates bound for California should be easy enough for us to find in the small warehouse behind the train depot here in the little town of Santa Fe, but how can we possibly follow the crates once they arrive in Los Angeles?"

"We will have to trace them," Sherlock Holmes said as he stood up and looked across the street at the dozens of businesses that encircled the town square.

"How can we possibly trace four crates once they are offloaded from our train and become intermingled with the hundreds or thousands of other crates at the train depot in Los Angeles?" said I, as I stood next to Sherlock Holmes to try to see what he was looking for among the dozens of businesses facing the plaza.

"Because our four wooden crates will be marked," he said as he started walking down the board walk.

"Marked? With what?"

"With an invisible chemical dye," he said as we crossed the street.

"Ninhydrin!" said I, remembering our discussion with Mark Twain at Delmonico's.

"But where on earth are we going to find ninhydrin," asked I as we stopped walking in front of a photography shop. From the advertisement painted on the window, the business specialized in selling photographs of tourists wearing western attire.

"In there, ninhydrin is used in most modern dark rooms," Sherlock Holmes said, looking through the front window. "Professional photographers today are trying to make a few extra dollars experimenting in chromatography, which uses ninhydrin as one of the chemicals in the development process. Were you able to make an odd numbered withdrawal from one of the local banks?"

"Yes," said I, pointing to the large adobe style bank on the corner, "I made a withdrawal of $1201 from the First National Bank of Santa Fe."

"Excellent, please give me two hundred dollars and then go

in to see if you can purchase a small quantity of ninhydrin."

"Aren't you coming in?" asked I, as I handed him the money.

"No, I'm going next door," my friend replied. I looked at the sign in front of the business advertising women's and men's clothing. "You don't expect me to travel first-class to the City of Angels dressed like this do you?"

"No, I suppose that wouldn't do," said I.

"You might want to join me, once you're finished purchasing our invisible powder," Sherlock Holmes said, "We might try to find you something off-the-rack, you are rather hard on fine clothing."

I watched as my friend walked away and went into the clothing shop next door. Then I entered the photography shop and approached the middle-aged man seated on a stool behind the front counter, "May I please speak with the proprietor?"

"That would be me," he said as he held a glass plate up to the light.

"Would you happen to have any ninhydrin?"

"Yes, I just purchased a small bottle last week," he said, putting the glass plate aside. "But I only have a small amount and it's very expensive."

I opened my wallet and placed two crisp hundred dollar bills on top of the glass counter.

"But I will be happy to share," he said with a smile. He went to the dark room and within a minute returned to the front of the camera shop where he shook about half the white chemical powder from a small vial into a small envelope and handed me the glass vial. I thanked the man and walked next door to the clothing store in search of my friend Sherlock Holmes.

"There you are!" Sherlock Holmes said, as he stepped out of a fitting room dressed as a cowboy. "Here, these are for you," he said, pointing to a stack of western clothing piled on a nearby chair. "Levi jeans, western shirt and belt, and I am thinking you will look best in a silver Stetson cowboy hat and black Tony Lama boots; you're a size ten and a half aren't you?"

"I don't know," said I hesitantly, looking at the cowboy boots with the pointed toes he was wearing.

"Come, you will fit right in," Sherlock Holmes said, as he handed me the stack of clothing and pointed to the dressing room. "Hurry, we haven't much time. Oh, you can leave your other clothing behind. We'll be traveling light from here on, Tex."

"Tex," I mumbled to myself in the fitting room as I cast my dirty tailored suit, shirt and tie on the floor next to Sherlock Holmes' Mexican clothing and straw sombrero. When I walked up to the front of the store I found my friend talking to a well-dressed Mexican man standing behind the counter.

"Will two hundred dollars pay for everything, Ernesto?" Sherlock Holmes asked the man with a wide smile on his face.

"Si, señor," he said, "You are most generous."

"Worth every halfpenny," Sherlock Holmes said to the man as both men looked at me dressed as if I had just stepped out of a western Americana catalogue. "Come along, Tex, and don't forget your Gladstone," he said as we headed toward the Santa Fe train depot.

"Don't you want to see the Miraculous Staircase?" asked I as we headed for the depot.

"I have already been there, while you were at the bank," Sherlock Holmes replied, "besides, we have less than an hour before someone will start loading the cargo from the warehouse onto the 7:15; do you have the ninhydrin?"

"Yes, but I was only able to purchase a small quantity," said I, fighting the urge to tuck my thumbs into my belt as I walked; as I had seen all the other cowboys do here in the West.

"We won't need very much," Sherlock Holmes said as we approached the depot.

June 28th, 1896 6:45pm
Train Depot, Santa Fe, New Mexico, U.S.A.

"HAND ME THE NINHYDRIN," Sherlock Holmes whispered after he had picked the padlock on the warehouse door and we had stepped inside.

"How will we ever find Bakerslee's four wooden crates?" asked I looking at the stacks of wooden crates inside the dusty warehouse.

"Because they will be stacked together near the front door waiting to be loaded onto the Los Angeles 7:15 and most likely marked FOB," Sherlock Holmes said as we both began searching the wooden crates stacked closest to the front door.

"Over here," said I, seeing only four crates stacked together near the front door. "The shipping labels on these four are addressed to Dr. Hiram Bakerslee, Los Angeles, California, and marked FOB. Freight on Board I suppose?"

"Or Free on Board," Sherlock Holmes said as he lifted each wooden crate and arranged them on the floor. "Meaning these creates will be paid for when they are claimed on the other end, in Los Angeles." Then he looked at my medical bag and as if he were a surgeon about to perform an operation as he held out his hand and said, "Scissors."

"Scissors," I repeated as I opened my doctor's bag and handed him a pair of my scissors.

"Suture pack," he said.

"I assume you only want the paper backing again," asked I.

"Correct," said he. I watched as he opened the sterile package, removed the cardboard backing and handed me back the thread in a heap. Next he folded the stiff paper lengthwise and used my scissors to cut a section out of the center and handed me back the scissors. His behavior reminded me of how children go about cutting paper dolls out of paper. I watched as he opened the folded paper to reveal the shape of a four-inch arrowhead, comprised of a tang and two barbs meeting at the point.

"A broad arrow?" I asked, recognizing the symbol used by the British government to mark government property.

"Exactly," he said as he removed his clay pipe from his pocket.

"Most fitting," said I in agreement.

"Ninhydrin," he commanded, as he held the stiff paper up against the front of the first wooden crate and held the stem of his clay pipe in his mouth with his teeth and pulled the bowl away from the pipe and set it aside. "Open the glass vial and hold it just in front of the paper template."

I did as instructed and watched as he blew air through the stem of his clay pipe across the opening of the glass vial containing the ninhydrin. As he blew moist air through the stem of his pipe small particles of the white powdery chemical were picked up and sprayed onto the wooden crate. When he stopped blowing he pulled the cardboard paper away from the wooden crate.

"I can't see anything," said I, looking over his shoulder.

"That's the idea," he said as he moved to the next crate.

"Oh," said I, remembering how ninhydrin was invisible to the naked eye. "Very clever."

"Now this one," he said as he held the paper template up to front of the next wooden crate and we repeated the process.

"I still can't see anything," said I, adding, "How do we know if this is working?"

"It's working," Sherlock Holmes said as he moved to the third crate, "how much of the chemical remains in your glass vital?"

"It is half gone," said I, "It is working."

"Last one," Sherlock Holmes said.

"The vial is empty," said I after he had finished marking the last crate with an invisible symbol of an English broad arrow.

"I want to look inside this one," Sherlock Holmes said, "There's a workbench over there, see if you can find something for me to pry open the lid?"

"Here," said I handing him a pry bar from the workbench.

"Make sure no one's coming," he said as he pried open the lid to the heavy crate.

As I approached the door I could see the smoke coming from the engine at the front of the train starting to expand as they were preparing the engine to depart the station. Then I noticed two large workmen headed our way from the depot. "Hurry, someone is coming!"

"Out the back," he said as he hammered the lid back in place on the forth wooden crate.

We slipped out the back door of the warehouse just as the front door opened. We walked around the building and headed toward the passenger loading platform. I handed the conductor two of our first-class tickets.

"May I please have our third ticket?" Sherlock Holmes asked.

I watched as my friend approached a young mother struggling to carry a baby in one arm and a heavy bundle in the other. She appeared to be Native America and wore a beautiful woven red blanket wrapped around her and her baby. The mother could not have been more than eighteen years of age and the baby but a few months. I could not hear what Sherlock Holmes said as he tipped his hat and handed her the first-class ticket. She smiled and handed Sherlock Holmes the bundle she was carrying. He escorted the young mother to the first-class passenger car where she presented the conductor her ticket and I followed them into the train car.

After we were all aboard Sherlock Holmes held the sleeping baby for a moment until the young mother had gotten settled into her seat across the aisle from our seats. Sherlock Holmes held the baby out away from his body and could not have appeared any more uncomfortable had he been holding a sleeping baby alligator. I chose the seat next to the window, leaving the aisle for my friend and said nothing when he sat down after witnessing his compassionate act of kindness.

"You have a grand gift for silence Watson," Sherlock Holmes said after a few minutes, then added as he pulled the brim of his cowboy hat down over his eyes, "It makes you quite invaluable as a travel companion."

As soon as our train was underway, I looked across the aisle to see the young mother nursing her baby beneath the red blanket. The next time I looked over, she, her baby and Sherlock Holmes were all three sound asleep.

An hour later the conductor announced as he walked down the aisle, "Next stop Albuquerque," and then he headed toward the next car. I felt my friend stir in his seat.

"Before you doze off again," I said quietly to Sherlock Holmes as he settled back in his seat and pulled the wide brim of his cowboy hat down again over his eyes, "I am dying of curiosity to know what it was you found inside that last wooden crate.

"It was full of these," Sherlock Holmes reached into the pocket of his cowboy vest and handed me a coin.

"1893 Queen Victoria-Jubilee Head Two Pound Gold Double Sovereign, no doubt heading somewhere to be melted down and minted into some less noble gold coin."

"I wanted to confirm my premise that not all of the 6,000 stolen gold sovereigns were melted down and turned into golden bells. You may keep that coin, if you wish," Sherlock Holmes said, then added before he slipped off to sleep, "a souvenir from our adventure out here in the American West."

June 29th, 1896 10:45am
Train Depot, Flagstaff, Arizona, U.S.A.

I HAD WATCHED SHERLOCK HOLMES help the young mother with her baby when they got off the train in Albuquerque. They were met by over a dozen American Indians of varying ages, all happy to meet what appeared to be the newest addition to their large family. Several of the men and women were wearing beautiful red woven blankets with similar designs to the one the young mother wore. When Sherlock Holmes got back on the train he said they were from the Navajo tribe and this was their ancestral homeland. I never could have imagined a more immense and diverse landscape than what passed beyond our train window as we traveled from New Mexico and into Arizona. We slept on and off throughout the night and enjoyed ham and cheese omelets, served with mild red chili salsa, for breakfast the next morning in the first-class dining car.

"What does it say about Flagstaff?" Sherlock Holmes asked, noticing I was reading a travel gazetteer about the state of Arizona I had picked up while refreshing my coffee.

"Flagstaff is the largest city between Albuquerque and the west coast," said I, as I read aloud, "The region is known for its proximity to the Grand Canyon and for having an abundance of timber, sheep and cattle."

"Dressed as we are we should fit right in," Sherlock Holmes said as he looked up from a note he was writing to look out at the beautiful forested countryside rolling past our window.

"Fit in? Are we getting off the train here in Flagstaff?"

"Briefly, yes. There should be sufficient time for you to drop by a local bank and make a modest withdrawal."

"Odd or even?" asked I.

"Even, I suppose things are going as well as could be expected," he replied.

"I suppose that is true enough, one of us could be shoveling coal."

"Or being mistaken for a hobo and tossed off the train," Sherlock Holmes said with a slight grin.

"You know these cowboy boots are rather comfortable," said I as I looked down at my feet and admired my new Tony Lama cowboy boots. "I might become rather accustomed to wearing western attire. What will you be doing while I am finding a bank?"

"Sending this telegram," Sherlock Holmes said as he handed me the note he had been writing. I saw it was a draft for a telegram and read it to myself, "To: Inspectors Lestrade and Gregson, Scotland Yard, London (Stop). Scheduled to arrive Los Angeles Train Depot tomorrow evening on 8:15 from Flagstaff (Stop). Request PM arrange for U.S. Secret Service agent to meet us where cargo is off loaded (Stop). Bring black light (Stop). S.H. (Stop).

"Do you think the detectives at Scotland Yard will recognize why we need a black light?"

"They should, late last year I had suggested they consider using ninhydrin to track criminals and counterfeit paper money. I demonstrated how the chemical emits a fluorescent ultraviolet blue-green light. The staining dye cyanine, as you may know, derives its name from the Greek word cyanides which means dark blue. It will be critically important for us to trace our four wooden crates once they leave this train and begin to travel throughout the immense railroad transportation network to their next destination, where they will be claimed by our Dr. Bakerslee or one of his nefarious agents."

June 30th, 1896 8:15pm
Train Depot, Los Angeles, California, U.S.A.

THE PLAINCLOTHES U.S. SECRET SERVICE AGENT, who appeared to be in his early-to-mid twenties, looked at Sherlock Holmes and I with a measured degree of skepticism, not expecting to be meeting anyone from England dressed as we were in western clothing.

"I am Sherlock Holmes," my friend said as he shook hands with the young Secret Service agent wearing a dark gray three-piece suit, white shirt and burgundy colored tie.

"A.J. Pinkerton, U.S. Secret Service," the clean-shaven federal agent said as he shook hands with Sherlock Holmes.

"Pinkerton? Are you Allen J. Pinkerton's grandson?" my friend asked.

"Great-grandson," the young man said, "I was named after him."

"Ah, it is a pleasure to meet you; may I introduce you to my travel companion, Dr. John Watson?"

"Dr. Watson, it is a pleasure to meet you as well, I have read several of your books," the young man said as we shook hands. "I am sure you were expecting a much older man then me, Mr. Holmes, how did you know I was the man you were to meet?"

"True, I was expecting a more experienced detective; however, you, standing here where you are, an equal distance between the only two freight cars attached to this passenger train, suggests you are more interested in cargo than passengers. Your appearance bespoke of you being a professional man, your bearing suggests you are well-educated and your self-confident posture implies you are well trained in self-defense, in either military or police work. Besides," Sherlock Holmes said as he nodded at the black leather attaché case at the young man's feet, "You brought the equipment I had requested. Obviously your superiors have confidence in you for this assignment; therefore I will trust you as well. Now, may I ask you two questions?"

"Certainly."

"First, and I don't mean to ask a personal or sensitive question of you, but why are you not employed with the Pinkerton's National Detective Agency, your family's business? That is where I would be if I were your age and interested in a career in detective work; and secondly, has there been any cargo unloaded from either of these two freight cars?"

"I get that first question asked of me all the time; my father and I agreed it would be best if I were to gain some practical investigative experience in a federal law enforcement agency prior to assuming a position within the family business. To your second question; no, I was standing here when this train came to a stop just a minute or two before you walked up to me and there has not been any freight unloaded as of yet. As you can see both double doors are still closed and padlocks are yet secured on both the car doors."

"Very well," Sherlock Holmes replied, "the cargo we are most interested in tracing must therefore still be on the train. I suggest we step away from these cars and watch from a distance to see if anyone comes to claim the four wooden crates of interest. If someone does come for these four crates, especially if it is a short portly English fellow, he has been implicated in a number of crimes including murder. I assume you are armed?"

"Always," replied the agent as he opened his suit coat revealing a butt of the large caliber revolver carried in a shoulder holster, a silver star-shaped badge was pinned to the front of the holster. "We will be less visible back here," he said as he guided us to a secluded area from which we could watch the cargo as it was being unloaded from the freight cars.

"Are you originally from Los Angeles?" I asked of Agent Pinkerton as we waited.

"No, I was born in Chicago, but I was transferred to the LA office shortly after I completed my formal training in New York."

"Does the U.S. Secret Service still investigate a fair number of counterfeiting cases?" Sherlock Holmes asked.

"Yes, as you probably know, Mr. Holmes, my great-grandfather got his start in the detective business when he broke up a counterfeiting ring before he helped found the U.S. Secret Service in the late 1860's. At one time nearly a third of the U.S. money was thought to be counterfeit. Today, in addition to protecting the current and former Presidents of the United States, their families and a handful of other government officials, the investigation of counterfeiting operations remains one of our primary missions. Is counterfeiting the crime that has brought you to Los Angeles this evening, Mr. Holmes?"

"Yes, there are four wooden crates on one of those two freight cars that will be unloaded here on this dock momentarily. Should they be claimed by the Englishman I described then we shall need your assistance to take him into custody for crimes against the British government, which includes the counterfeiting of British coinage, but more importantly he has been implicated in the murder of at least two British citizens."

"There," said I, pointing to the handful of dock workers who unlocked the doors on the two freight cars and began unloading dozens of wooden crates and a half dozen wooden whiskey barrels. Sherlock Holmes, Agent Pinkerton and I watched as two other workmen with a cart claimed the six whiskey barrels, loaded them on the handcart and wheeled them away."

"Looks like our four crates are being unloaded now," said I.

"It appears as if they are not going to be claimed here on the dock, let's follow the crates inside the warehouse," Sherlock Holmes said.

Once inside Agent Pinkerton showed his badge to the warehouse supervisor and checked to see that the shipping labels were addressed to Dr. Hiram Bakerslee.

"Let's have these four crates moved to a more secure area," Agent Pinkerton suggested and then spoke with the supervisor again.

Sherlock Holmes and I followed behind the four wooden crates that had been loaded onto a handcart and pulled by a workman to a secure room toward the back of the warehouse. The workman went inside, turned on a light switch and began moving the wooden crates inside the storeroom. After the four crates were unloaded from the cart, and placed on the floor, the workman left pulling his cart behind him.

"Agent Pinkerton, would you please activate your black light?" Sherlock Holmes requested as he closed the door and placed his hand on the light switch. When Agent Pinkerton activated the black light Sherlock Holmes turned off the light in the storeroom. The room was completely dark except for the faint blue light being emitted from the handheld black light.

"What are we looking for?" Agent Pinkerton asked.

"Here," said Sherlock Holmes, directing the black light onto the front of one of the wooden crates. "This symbol is a British broad arrow, claiming the contents of this crate to be property of the British government," Sherlock Holmes explained and then directed the black light in Agent Pinkerton's hand to shine upon the front of the other three wooden crates illuminating three more broad arrow symbols on the front of each crate. "Now," said Sherlock Holmes as he turned back on the electric light bulb above our heads, "Agent Pinkerton you can turn off and store your black light now, thank you, and, Dr. Watson, if you would be so kind as to search around the warehouse for something to open the lid to this first wooden crate I would like to explain its contents to Agent Pinkerton and make an official request."

I found a claw hammer which I was able to use to pry open the lid. Sherlock Holmes pushed aside the straw packing material to reveal the contents of the wooden crate consisted of two dozen smaller wooden boxes, stacked three rows deep. Then he opened one of the boxes on the top row and showed it housed nine rows of stacked gold coins. Taking one of the gold coins from the box he handed it to Agent Pinkerton.

"Beautiful," he said, as he held the coin up to the light and asked, "are they all alike?"

"In this box yes, I believe so," Sherlock Holmes said, then explained, "While I have only had an opportunity to do a random sampling I believe the coins in this crate are all genuine 1893 Queen Victoria-Jubilee Head Two Pound Gold Double Sovereigns."

"These gold coins must be worth a fortune," Agent Pinkerton said as he handed the gold sovereign back to Sherlock Holmes. "Are the other three crates also filled with gold coins?"

"No, just this one I etched with a small 'V' on the top right corner. I believe what is in the other three crates are the raw materials and tools necessary to counterfeit fake coins including 1893 Queen Victoria-Jubilee Head Two Pound Gold Double Sovereigns."

"What do you propose us to do?" Agent Pinkerton asked.

"My request, as a confidential representative of the British government, to you as a representative of the U.S. government, is for you to take possession of the contents of this crate and see that these gold sovereigns are delivered to Number 10 Downing Street, London."

"I can do that," Agent Pinkerton said confidently. "What are you going to do?"

"First," Sherlock Holmes said, "we need to transfer these gold sovereigns into another box, then replace them with something of similar weight and then reseal the crate. Then if Dr. Hiram Bakerslee or someone else comes here to claim this cargo we request you take them into custody and notify me and Scotland Yard. I don't believe that is going to happen. I suspect this Dr. Bakerslee or whoever he is working for will pay to have these four crates shipped to another location, possibly somewhere in San Francisco. If you or another agent from the Secret Service could contact me whenever they are moved, Dr. Watson and I will follow them to where ever they are shipped to next and see who claims them on the other end."

"Where do I contact you?" Agent Pinkerton asked.

"Doctor Watson?" Sherlock Holmes asked of me.

"The Palace Hotel in San Francisco," said I.

"Very good," said Agent Pinkerton, "Let me speak with the warehouse supervisor about what we've discussed, without mentioning the contents of any of these crates, and I will be back momentarily."

"Seems like a competent young detective," said I to my friend while waiting for the Secret Service agent to return.

"He certainly comes from a good family," Sherlock Holmes said as he pulled out his clay pipe and sat down on one of the wooden crates to wait for the young agent to return.

"Tell me again why you are so certain Dr. Bakerslee and the four crates are headed to San Francisco?"

"I am not certain Bakerslee even knows where the four crates will be sent next, he may be taking orders from someone back in England; but San Francisco seems a reasonable deduction since California and Colorado have a Gold Rush in common and each have a government mint producing gold coins; the Denver Mint in Colorado and the San Francisco Mint in California."

"That does seem to be a logical deduction," said I.

"This ought to do," Agent Pinkerton said as he returned to the storeroom pushing a handcart with a stack of red bricks and a similar sized wooden crate. "The warehouse supervisor pointed out on the bill of laden these crates weigh between 95-110 pounds each. These bricks weigh about 4 pounds each, so I brought 24 bricks that we can stack in three rows of eight to balance the load. The supervisor promised to contact me immediately if someone comes here to claim this cargo or directs this shipment to another location. He also offered to hold up the shipment for a day or two until confirmation can be made that I have been notified and given the opportunity to contact you to let you know where the crates are to be shipped."

"Someone is going to be very upset when they open this box up to find these bricks inside," said I.

"Livid, I should hope," Sherlock Holmes said, "Their emotions might cause them to do something out of character, which might tip their hand as to who is behind this organization."

"Would you like me to write you a receipt for these gold coins I am taking with me?" asked Agent Pinkerton as he nailed the lid shut on the crate now containing a small fortune in 1893 Queen Victoria-Jubilee Head Two Pound Gold Double Sovereigns.

"That won't be necessary A.J.," Sherlock Holmes said, "If we can't trust you as a federal agent of the U.S. government who can we trust?"

July 13th, 1896 12:15pm
Fisherman's Wharf, San Francisco, California, U.S.A.

It had been two weeks since Sherlock Holmes and I had checked into San Francisco's elegant Palace Hotel. I had not seen my friend in the past five days. As had been our previous agreement, I had come to Fisherman's Wharf every day at 12 noon to feed the pigeons, waiting for him to contact me. With each passing day my anxiety rose, for I believed Irene Adler was also here in the city of San Francisco, a growing international city struggling to blend countless diverse cultures from all around the world. My biggest worry was not only of my friend spending time with a married woman, nor was it of his determination to work the streets of San Francisco in seeking information on our counterfeiting ring. My chief worry was in questioning if one of these city streets might lead him to Chinatown where he would find his drug of choice—opium.

I purchased a bag of popcorn, selected a bench near the waterfront where I could sit to feed the pigeons. I watched the passing of tall-masted ships entering the harbor or heading out to some distant port across the Pacific Ocean. It occurred to me that from the time Sherlock Holmes and I had stepped ashore in New York City we had literally traveled entirely across the North America continent; from the Atlantic Ocean on the east coast to here, the Pacific Ocean on the west coast, and yet the end to our investigation was nowhere in sight.

A Chinaman pushing a peddler's cart overflowing with pots and pans and a sundry of kitchen items approached. He parked his cart in front of my bench, took a seat near me and began stuffing loose tobacco into his long-stemmed clay pipe. After tamping down the tobacco in the bowl of his pipe with his thumb, he began a futile search of his pockets for a match. Finding none he removed the pipe from his mouth and stared out to the open sea. Feeling sorry for him I removed a small box of matches from my vest pocket and handed them to him in hopes he would finish his smoke, go on about his day and my friend Sherlock Holmes might come along.

"Thank you, Doctor Watson," the Chinaman said, after he lit his pipe and blew a puff of smoke into the air. I recognized the familiar voice of my friend and was stunned to see the man sitting next to me wearing a disguise was none other than Sherlock Holmes.

"There you are," said I, "I have been worried sick about you."

"I am well," Sherlock Holmes said as he handed me back my matches.

"And how is Irene?"

"She is fine," my friend replied with a smile, "you saw her yourself just yesterday."

"Where?"

"Here, on this very bench."

"I do not remember speaking to any woman while I was sitting here yesterday."

"That's because she was disguised as a young man," Sherlock Holmes said, "I understand the two of you had a memorable conversation about the feeding habits of sea lions."

"I do remember that conversation; that was Irene? How did she know I would be here?"

"Because she had followed me here the day before, she said she wanted to see you one last time before she left the country."

"Left the county? Where is she going?"

"Down under."

"Down under? Down under what?"

"Australia."

"Why Australia?"

"To escape the grasp of Dr. Bakerslee and begin a search for another opera."

"When does she leave?"

"She sailed this morning."

"Did you find out how Dr. Bakerslee discovered Irene was staying at the La Fonda in Santa Fe?"

"From her husband Mr. Godfrey Norton."

"Her husband?" asked I in astonishment, "Why would he tell Dr. Bakerslee where Irene was staying in New Mexico, do you think he wanted her killed?"

"While she admits their marriage has been on the rocks since the start, I doubt he would wish her dead. The Woman knows of no connection between her husband and Dr. Bakerslee, which is why she felt it safe telling him where she was staying at the La Fonda. The connection is more than likely with a third party in London, someone who knows Mr. Godfrey Norton, Dr. Bakerslee and The Woman."

"Professor Moriarty?" asked I.

"I fear so," Sherlock Holmes replied.

"Why would Moriarty wish Irene dead?"

"While she was careful not to make any admissions or confessions to me, I suspect she may have helped pass some of the counterfeit silver coins in Reading and may have been prepared to do the same in Cripple Creek. However, there is an alternative theory that she wasn't involved in passing off the fake coins but somehow learned of Bakerslee's counterfeiting operation and was perhaps blackmailing him to buy her silence."

"Irene Adler is indeed a very complex woman," said I.

"And a very clever one, perhaps too clever for her own good," Sherlock Holmes said.

"Do you think she has realized there is a possible link between Dr. Bakerslee and Professor Moriarty?"

"She knows now, for I have advised her of such, and she will no doubt be more cautious when communicating her whereabouts with her estranged husband."

"What now?"

"There is word on the streets of San Francisco of gold being discovered in the Klondike region of the Yukon, in north-western Canada. If these rumors prove true, we will see a Klondike Gold Rush which would be the perfect place for Dr. Bakerslee to relocate his counterfeiting operation. If my hypothesis holds true tens of thousands of prospectors will start flooding into Canada and Alaska and Bakerslee's superior will direct him to immediately relocate their international counterfeiting operation there to take advantage of the chaos. I expect that within the next 24-48 hours we will receive word from the U.S. Secret Service that our four wooden crates are on the move again. Meanwhile I have to get back to work. I will join you this evening for supper at the Palace Hotel," Sherlock Holmes said as he assumed his role of a Chinese street peddler and resumed pushing his handcart along the merchant's row of Fisherman's Wharf.

July 14th, 1896 8:15am
The Palace Hotel, San Francisco, California, U.S.A.

"Good morning, A.J., won't you join us for breakfast?" Sherlock Holmes said as he stood to greet the young Secret Service agent approaching our table.

Agent Pinkerton shook hands with Sherlock Holmes and me and then sat down noticing the breakfast table had been set for three. "It appears you were expecting me?"

"We were; however, I was not certain what time you would arrive so we already ordered our breakfast," Sherlock Holmes said as the waiter sat our breakfast selection of French toast, scrambled eggs and thick-cut bacon in front of my friend and I.

"Would you care for anything, Sir?," the waiter asked.

"Just a cup of tea for me, Earl Gray if you please," Agent Pinkerton said to the waiter, then commented to us, "I ate breakfast on the train from Los Angeles this morning. I use to drink coffee with breakfast but ever since I returned from London I find myself drinking more tea and less coffee in my morning routine."

"Your first trip to England?" Sherlock Holmes asked.

"It was," Agent Pinkerton said. "The Director of the Secret Service thought it a good idea for me and a handful of other

Secret Service agents to personally deliver the wooden crate you requested to be shipped to Number 10 Downing Street in London. He thought it might strain diplomatic relationship if the wooden crate were to be lost along the way. I was pleased the Director selected me to lead our team for I have wanted to visit Scotland Yard. Your Prime Minister Salisbury was most grateful when he opened the box to find it contained 299 1893 Queen Victoria-Jubilee Head Two Pound Gold Double Sovereign coins. When the other Secret Service agents and I returned to our office in Los Angeles we found a commendation signed by your Queen Victoria had already been placed in each of our personnel files."

"A most deserving accolade," Sherlock Holmes said as he poured hot maple syrup on his French toast, then offered the syrup bottle to me and commented, "Care for some maple syrup, Dr. Watson?"

"Yes please," said I as I read the large lettering printed on the label "Did you know seventy percent of the syrup produced annually in the world comes from the Canadian providence of Quebec?"

"I did not," Sherlock Holmes replied, "but now that you mentioned it I will do everything I can to forget it."

Agent Pinkerton smiled as he waited patiently for his English breakfast tea to seep.

"I take it by your presence at breakfast this morning our four wooden crates will soon be on their way to Canada?" asked Sherlock Holmes of Agent Pinkerton as he stirred cream into his tea.

"Correct. I received word last night your four wooden crates will be shipped from the port of Los Angeles tomorrow morning aboard the Gloria Scott II bound for a gold camp being referred to as Dawson City. This gold camp is being established along the Klondike River, in the Yukon. The Gloria Scott II will make one short shop here, at Pier 53 in the port of San Francisco at noon to take on a cargo of forty whiskey barrels, before sailing on to Canada."

"Thank you, A.J.," Sherlock Holmes said, "Your investigative assistance, and that of the United States Secret Service, will not be forgotten."

Chapter 10

July 16th, 1896 10am

Three Miles off the Oregon Coast, USA

I LEANED AGAINST the weathered starboard railing of the Gloria Scott II, a three-masted barque, and watched for any recognizable landmarks on the rugged coastline on the horizon. A pod of curious dolphins swam up to the ship's wooden hull, reminding me of the dolphins who escorted us into the New York City harbor. The Gloria Scott II was an aging cargo ship nearing the end of her useful life, as was her captain, to whom Sherlock Holmes had paid an insane amount of money to provide us passage to the Klondike Region of Canada.

Thankfully the waves were less choppy than last night. Sherlock Holmes and I had to bunk with members of the ship's crew below deck in hammocks suspended from the wooden ceiling. It was difficult for me to decide who snored the loudest, Melville, the ship's cook, sleeping in the hammock below me, or my friend Sherlock Holmes sleeping in the swaying hammock suspended inches above my nose. The dreary day was identical to yesterday, gray and overcast, with intermittent rain, reminding me of home.

"Good morning, Dr. Watson," Sherlock Holmes said cheerily, as he climbed up the wooden stairwell balancing a steaming tin cup in each hand. "Your morning tea, compliments of Chef

Melville," he said handing me a hot tin cup. I quietly resented how my travel companion appeared as comfortable and well rested as if we were traveling once again aboard the luxury ocean liner RMS Republic. The Gloria Scott II, an old wooden sailing ship, leaked so severely her bilge pumps ran continually pumping murky water from below her deck out into the gray ocean. It was a race against the forces of nature; a race the Gloria Scott II could not win.

"Thank you," said I as I accepted the hot tin cup, took a sip and forced it down. "That's awful! Tastes like kerosene! What is in this tea?"

"Melville referred to it as the hair of the dog that bit you," Sherlock Holmes said with a smile. "You seemed to grow rather fond of this liquid elixir last night. How did you fair at the poker game?"

"Poorly, and, for the record, I don't believe One-Eyed-Willie is a real poker game," said I, trying to recall some of the hazy details about last night's extracurricular activities. "I believe I lost twenty American dollars, six British pounds, plus the naming rights to my first born son, to Captain Scofield, should I ever have any male children."

"Does the Captain wish your son to be named Herman, after him?"

"No, that old sea dog wants me to name my first born son Ishmael, so he will spend his life telling everyone he meets, 'call me Ishmael' – evidently our captain is a fan of *Moby-Dick* the 1850's novel that went out of print a couple years back. I doubt you've read it; it is about an obsessive quest by Captain Ahab in pursuit of a giant sperm whale that had bitten off Ahab's leg at the knee. The storyline reminds me of an obsessive quest a friend of mine once undertook, let's see, how did that end again, oh yes, I know somewhere in the wilds of Canada, only I believe it was a Grizzly Bear that bit off my friend's leg."

"Melville told me the Gloria Scott II was a whaling ship in a past life," Sherlock Holmes said.

"That would explain the stench," said I, taking a whiff of my new suit I had purchased in San Francisco, when we swapped our western attire for something more suitable for the Palace Hotel. "Oh no, I think I'm going to be sick again."

"Don't look at the waves, look at the horizon," Sherlock Holmes said.

"How about you; how did you fair last night?"

"I won seventeen American dollars, eight Indian rupees, one keg of whiskey, an old pocketknife and this," Sherlock Holmes said as he opened his palm to show me a large brass key.

"What is it to?" asked I, as I finished the dregs of my tea.

"It fits the lock on the door of the storeroom where Bakerslee's four wooden crates are presently housed below deck. Shall we go have a peek?"

"Lead the way, Ishmael," said I as I attempted to find my sea-legs to walk on the swaying deck without having to cling to a railing.

"I might request," Sherlock Holmes said as we descended the dim stairwell to the cargo hold below the waterline of the leaky ship, "when we dock in Dawson City tomorrow, could you please see if you can locate a telegraph office? I am thinking we may as well send a telegram to General Palmer at Glen Eyrie requesting he arrange to have our four steamer trunks shipped home to Mrs. Hudson in London. I doubt we'll be returning to Little London anytime soon and we may as well unburden ourselves with concerns about our baggage."

"And my black pocket notebook?" asked I.

"I think it safer where it is, in the secret compartment above the fireplace mantel," Sherlock Holmes said, adding, "at least for the time being. We don't want to risk your notebook falling into the wrong hands until our investigation has run its course."

"I have been keeping a daily journal in my replacement notebook since our leaving Little London," said I as I patted my inside suitcoat pocket to ensure my brown leather notebook was securely in place. "But I doubt I will be able to recall accurately any of the details required to properly document this investigation without acquiring my first notebook."

"No rush, remember we promised not to publish anything about our investigation until at least one year after the death of Queen Victoria," Sherlock Holmes said.

"Long live the Queen," we both said in unison as Sherlock Holmes stopped in front of a large wooden door secured with a heavy padlock. The Roman numeral III was scratched crudely in the wooden frame above the door. I watched as he inserted the key and unlocked the door.

"Here, we will need this," Sherlock Holmes said as he handed me an electric torch and pulled open the door. We stepped inside the dark locker room and I turned on the handheld light. "Most of the cargo in this hold is supposed to be round wooden whiskey kegs, so we won't need a black light to find Bakerslee's four rectangular wooden crates; besides, Melville said they should be stacked just to the right of the doorway toward the front."

"There, that's them," said I, shining the beam of light on the four wooden crates stacked on top of one another. "What do you propose we do?"

"I propose we unburden Dr. Bakerslee of his excess baggage. Let us leave the one crate containing the red bricks here and carry the other three crates topside where we can inspect the contents in the light of day before tossing them overboard. Agreed?"

"Capital idea," said I as I grabbed one end of the top crate and helped Sherlock Holmes carry it up the rickety stairwell where we laid the crate on the deck and returned to the cargo hold for the next crate. We repeated the process with the second crate, stacking it on top of the first and returned below to collect the third crate. As we lifted the third crate off of the bottom Sherlock Holmes motioned for us to set it aside.

"Shine your light over here on this bottom crate for a minute," Sherlock Holmes said, as he pulled an old pocket knife from his coat pocket and began using it to pry the lid off the remaining wooden crate.

SNAP!

"What happened?" said I as I shined the light on the pocket knife Sherlock Holmes held in his hand.

"I broke the blade," he said, looking at the jack knife.

"Did you cut yourself?"

"No, so you won't have an opportunity to practice your suturing skills on me this time," my friend said as he inspected his hand. "Fortunately, this knife has a second blade."

Sherlock Holmes used the knife to carefully pry off the lid and announced, "Two dozen red clay 5-pound bricks," he said as he used the heal of his fist to loosely tap the lid back into place.

"It looks as if it has been opened," said I, observing the lid to not appear to be as secure as before.

"As intended; however, just to make certain the point is not lost," Sherlock Holmes said as he used the pocketknife he had won in last night's poker game to carve a large symbol into the lid of the wooden crate that once held the genuine 1893 Queen Victoria-Jubilee Head Two Pound Gold Double Sovereign coins.

"What is it you have engraved?" I said as I watched over his shoulder.

"There," he proclaimed proudly, as he brushed away the wood

shavings and showed me the symbol he had carved into the lid of the wooden crate.

"Fitting," said I as I shined my light upon the eight-inch symbol carved into the lid, "A broad arrow, identifying the contents to be the property of the British government. I would like to see Dr. Bakerslee's reaction when he finds he has been duped."

"And you shall, it has all been arranged with Captain Scofield, when we dock day after tomorrow. Now, let us go topside and finish unburdening Dr. Bakerslee," Sherlock Holmes said as he closed and relocked the door to the cargo hold.

After Sherlock Holmes had pried the lids off the other three wooden crates we inspected the contents.

"This first crate contains the components for a portable hydraulic press," Sherlock Holmes said as I helped him toss it over the rail and into the open sea, where it made a big splash and sank like a ship's anchor beneath the white-capped gray waves.

"What is in the second one?" I asked as my friend inspected the contents.

"These are copper, brass and silver planchets, coin blanks waiting to be stamped into fake coins," Sherlock Holmes replied as we dumped the crate upside down over the railing, tossed the empty wooden crate into the ocean and watched it trail off in the wake of our ship.

"Let's see what's in this third box," Sherlock Holmes said as he began inspecting the contents. "This one contains tools and coin dies for counterfeiting coins of various countries; including silver dollars from the U.S., silver half dollars from Canada and gold coins from Great Britain. Ah, Eureka! Here's the one we want – the obverse die for the 1893 Queen Victoria's Jubilee Head Two Pound Gold Double Sovereign. I shall retain this one as evidence for having been stolen from the vault inside the Royal Mint," Sherlock Holmes said as he slipped the coin die into his coat pocket.

"So this is how Dr. Bakerslee had his four wooden crates organized," said I as we tossed the contents of the third box overboard into the gray waters of the Pacific Ocean. "One box held a portable hydraulic press to produce the more fake coins. The second box contained additional coin blanks and the third box held the counterfeit dies and tools. And the forth crate once held the genuine 1893 Queen Victoria-Jubilee Head Two Pound Gold Double Sovereign coins stolen from the Royal Mint, which were replaced with the counterfeit brass coins."

"Correct, and the genuine gold coins have now been replaced with genuine red clay bricks," said Sherlock Holmes as we leaned against the ship's weathered railing. I tried to imagine the contents of the first three wooden boxes lying scattered now across the floor of the ocean untold leagues below the hull of our ship. "It pleases me to say our Dr. Bakerslee is now officially out of the counterfeiting business. Come, I have worked up an appetite. Melville tells me he is fixing squid stew for lunch. Aren't you coming?"

"No," said I as I leaned over the railing my stomach feeling queasy again, "You go on without me."

July 18th, 1896 4:30pm
Dawson City, Yukon, Canada

Sherlock Holmes and I were the first to disembark from the Gloria Scott II, once she had tied up to the flimsy dock at Dawson City. More than a dozen ships lie at anchor in the harbor. Another half dozen ships of various sizes and descriptions had been run aground and marooned by their crews, stricken with gold fever. They had come to this remote part of Canada to participate in the Yukon Gold Rush. Sherlock Holmes walked fifty feet ahead of me, carrying the twenty-five pound wooden whiskey keg over his shoulder that he had won in the One-Eyed-Willie poker game night before last.

I carried my doctor's bag and hummed an annoying little drinking song the crew sang that I couldn't get out of my head, something about a sailorman eating spinach, and followed as Sherlock Holmes turned into the first building on the right. The wood frame building was a two-story pub with a hand-painted sign above the door identifying the establishment as the Bucksnort Saloon. Countless dogs roamed free on the streets, barking at me, at each other and at nothing at all as I crossed the muddy street. In places the mud was twelve inches deep and I curled my toes to keep my shoes from being sucked off my feet. I followed my friend inside the Bucksnort Saloon and watched from across the crowded smoke filled room as Sherlock Holmes sat the whiskey keg on the bar.

"Compliments of Captain Scofield," Sherlock Holmes announced to the Aleut bartender with a spiral tattoo across his face, a white bone pierced through his nose and large brass looped earrings dangled from both earlobes.

"Omniglot!" said the bartender, as he smiled and sampled the contents of the wooden barrel. "Quagaasakung," he said with a satisfying grunt.

"He says thank you," a Scotsman sitting at the bar said. "You arrived in the nick of time mate. We ran out of whiskey yesterday afternoon. He's been trying to satisfy us with cool beer and hot buttered rum." The bartender uttered something with a grin on his face, which according to the Scotsman serving as our impromptu Aleut interpreter, meant, "He wants to know if you care for anything, compliments of the house?" The bartender nodded at two dancehall girls wearing colorful hooped skirts sauntering by, giving my friend and me a look over.

"Just two beers if you please," said Sherlock Holmes. "And perhaps you can ask him if Captain Scofield's usual room is available upstairs?"

The bartender slid two beer mugs across the bar followed by a room key marked which a brass label bearing the number 9.

"We'll take these upstairs," Sherlock Holmes said as he handed me one of the cold mugs and I followed him up the stairs.

Sherlock Holmes inserted the key into the lock of the door identified by a brass number 6 and unlocked the door.

"I thought we were looking for room 9?" said I.

Sherlock Holmes smiled and turned the loose brass number 6 attached to the door, right-side up to display the number 9 attached to the door with a single nail at the bottom. We walked inside, shut the door and went to the window overlooking the wooden pier where the Gloria Scott II was being unloaded by the crew. Six crew members were transferring dozens of whiskey barrels from the ship and stacking them on the dock.

"This shouldn't take too long," Sherlock Holmes said as he moved two wooden chairs up to the window, sat down and sipped his beer.

I sat next to him and watched as the crew of the Gloria Scott II continued to unload cargo and stack it haphazardly on the wooden dock which appeared as if it would collapse at any moment. Captain Scofield stood on the dock with a clipboard in hand directing the crew where to stack the cargo, including the growing mound of wooden whiskey barrels. Several men from the town were making their way up the dock to claim cargo; of particular interest were the whiskey kegs. Captain Scofield had the men initial the paperwork on his clipboard before allowing them to cart off barrels of whiskey. This went on for fifteen or twenty minutes then we saw the ship's cook, Melville, carry a heavy wooden crate from the ship and set it on the dock by the Captain.

Within minutes we observed a short portly fellow, who I guessed was closer to age sixty than fifty, making his way up the dock toward the one wooden crate sitting on the dock next to the Captain. The man glanced briefly at the wooden crate and then began speaking with Captain Scofield, no doubt inquiring as to the whereabouts of his other three wooden crates.

"Dr. Bakerslee I presume?" said I.

"We shall know in a moment, but from here he looks to be the same man who I saw at Meadow Muffins in Colorado City buying drinks for Shady Coyne and William Clark," said Sherlock Holmes. We watched from our window perch as the short round man began to show his frustration. We could not hear what was being said, but at one time we saw the short man hold up four fingers, then point at the one wooden crate sitting on the dock. Captain Scofield shrugged his shoulders and pointed from his clipboard to the one wooden crate on the deck. The short man's frustration grew into anger as he stomped his boot upon the dock and then made the mistake of jabbing the Captain in the chest with his index finger.

Captain Scofield may have been an aging man, but he had spent every day of his adult life engaged in physical labor at sea, including the tying of knots with his calloused hands. He grabbed the short portly man's index finger and twisted it as if he were snapping a twig from a tree. The little man howled in pain and hopped around the wooden dock as Melville and two other crewmen came up and stood behind their Captain.

"That would be our Dr. Bakerslee," Sherlock Holmes said as a satisfied grin grew across his unshaven face.

We watched as Dr. Bakerslee struggled to pick up the heavy wooden crate, a task made even more difficult with a broken index finger. He had not taken more than twenty steps when he dropped the crate upon the dock as if it had given him an electric shock.

"Appears as if he got your message," said I, recalling the eight-inch symbol of the broad arrow Sherlock Holmes had carved into the wooden lid.

When the wooden crate hit the dock the bottom of the crate broke open and two dozen red clay bricks spilt out onto the dock. We watched as Dr. Bakerslee stared in disbelief at the bricks, as if frozen with his mouth open. He slowly reached down, picked up one of the red bricks, examined it briefly, and then tossed it angrily into the bay. Then he kicked the pile of bricks with his boot and we watched as the fat little man hopped around the dock on one leg.

"Looks like Bakerslee now has a broken toe to match his broken finger," said I.

"The jig is up," Sherlock Holmes said, as the short fat man stopped dancing around on one foot and began looking over his shoulder to see if anyone was approaching to take him into custody. Seeing no one coming his way, Dr. Bakerslee began limping hurriedly down the dock headed our way.

"Give me twenty minutes, and then come downstairs," Sherlock Holmes said as he left our room.

I reached for my pocket watch, to mark the time, before remembering I no longer had a pocket watch. "Thanks Shady," I said to myself.

The raucous laughter and loud piano music reminded me of our days in Cripple Creek. I could not help but wonder if the Yukon was destined to become the next Greatest Gold Camp on Earth. Through a thick cloud of cigar smoke, I observed Sherlock Holmes sitting at a card table, across from Dr. Bakerslee. I ordered a beer and slowly made my way over to the poker table. There was one open chair; it was located to the left of my friend.

"Soapy Smith is my name and five-card stud is the game," the dealer said to me as he shuffled the deck of well-worn cards. "Care to buy in?"

"Don't mind if I do," said I as I took a seat and sat my Gladstone on the floor next to my leg. I placed a U.S. twenty dollar bill on the green felt poker table. Soapy Smith pushed a stack of blue, red and white poker chips across the table to me and began dealing the cards. I checked my hole card, the three of clubs, and watched as the next card was dealt face up; the nine of hearts. Sherlock Holmes raised the pot fifty cents. I folded my hand, sipped my beer and looked casually across the table as Dr. Bakerslee drank down a shot of whiskey and slammed the empty glass on the table. The man's face was sweating profusely and he was in obvious pain. His right index finger was bent at an unnatural angle making it difficult for him to hold his cards.

"Bar keep! Another round," shouted Soapy Smith as he finished dealing out the hand. Sherlock Holmes folded on the fourth card, after a raise from Dr. Bakerslee. I detected an unmistakable English accent as Dr. Bakerslee cursed and threw his cards on the table after losing the hand to another player.

Twenty minutes later I had lost half my chips, while Sherlock Holmes had accumulated a large stack of chips in front of him and Dr. Bakerslee was reaching into his wallet again, angrily buying more chips from Soapy Smith. Sherlock Holmes paid for a round of drinks out of his winnings, making him the most popular man at the table. Half an hour later I was down to my last two dollars in chips. Dr. Bakerslee raised the pot five dollars and I folded with a pair of threes. Sherlock Holmes was the only player who had not folded his hand.

"I raise you five dollars," Sherlock Holmes said to Dr. Bakerslee, as he tossed a stack of blue poker chips into the large pot at the center of the table. Dr. Bakerslee had a pair of black eights showing along with the Ace of Clubs. Sherlock Holmes had a pair of red Queens showing. Only the two men knew what their holes cards were.

"I'm all in," Dr. Bakerslee said as he pushed his remaining chips, silver coins and paper money into the center of the pot and drank down his last shot of whiskey.

I felt Sherlock Holmes' left hand under the table tap my right coat pocket where my service revolver was concealed. I slowly pulled my handgun out of my pocket, placed it across my lap and waited.

"I call," Sherlock Holmes said as he tossed the metallic coin die for the 1893 Queen Victoria-Jubilee Head Two Pound Gold Double Sovereigns into the center of the pot scattering poker chips across the green felt card table.

Dr. Bakerslee grabbed the coin die from the center of the table, examined the date briefly, and then stood up and began to draw his revolver from a shoulder holster beneath his coat.

"You!" Dr. Bakerslee shouted at Sherlock Holmes as the barrel of his revolver cleared the holster with a lightening quick draw. Fortunately, he was slowed in firing from having a broken trigger finger.

Soapy Smith and the other men at the table dove for cover as the piano music abruptly stopped playing. Sherlock Holmes remained seated in his chair and stared, unflinching, across the green felt table into the red eyes of the deadly Dr. Bakerslee.

KABOOM! Was the familiar roar my revolver made the instant I pulled the trigger. My bullet struck Bakerslee in the center of his chest, right where I had aimed. The international counterfeiter that we had chased halfway around the world was dead before he hit the floor.

Several bar patrons gathered around the body of Dr. Bakerslee and confirmed he had passed his last fake coin.

"Righteous shooting if there ever was one!" Soapy Smith announced as he resumed his seat at the table and reached for Bakerslee's hole card. He turned the card over and said, "Ace of Spades; black aces and eights.

"The Dead Man's Hand," several players at the table whispered reverently.

Sherlock Holmes slowly turned over his hole card, the Queen of Spades, and laid it alongside the pair of red queens.

"Three queens," Soapy Smith announced, "you're the winner, the pot is yours mister?"

"Holmes," my friend said as he stood, picked up the coin die that had been stolen from the Royal Mint and tucked it into his coat pocket. "Sherlock Holmes."

I shoveled half the silver coins and folding paper money into my hat and pushed the rest of the pot over to Soapy Smith, "Another round for the house!"

The piano music resumed as Sherlock Holmes and I made our way to the front of the bar. I looked back to see the Aleut bartender dragging the body of Dr. Bakerslee out the back door.

"Thank you," Sherlock Holmes said as we began walking toward where the Gloria Scott II was tied up to the pier.

"You are welcome," I replied walking next to my friend and feeling no regrets whatsoever that I had just killed another man.

Captain Scofield was walking our way, heading to the Bucksnort Saloon.

"Gentlemen," the captain said as we met on the dock. "Your business already finished here in town?"

"It is," Sherlock Holmes said. "We have more unfinished business back in England; but first we must find a way home. Where are you sailing off to next Captain?"

"The Gloria Scott II and me are headed to Kodiak Island first thing in the morning. You are welcome to take passage with us. From there you should be able to catch a fishing trawler down the Aleutian Islands and across the Bearing Sea. From there into the Sea of Japan," the Captain said as he stroked his white beard. "From Tokyo you shouldn't have any trouble securing passage on a freighter bound for China or India and from there up the Red Sea and into the Mediterranean Sea. Once in the Med I'd suggest you head for Rome and then maybe catch the train to Paris."

"How long is that going to take us?" said I, anxious to get back to our warm flat on Baker Street.

"I would imagine it would take you no more than four or six weeks."

"How about going back through San Francisco?" Sherlock Holmes asked.

"It's about the same distance, but the trouble is," Captain Scofield said as he nodded at the abandoned ships anchored in the bay and those that had been discarded along the shoreline, "most of these ships came here one way, their crews are now scattered across the Yukon, no telling when the next ship will be headed back down the coast."

"You agreeable to head to Kodiak Island, Doctor Watson?" Sherlock Holmes asked.

"I'm with you all the way," I said, "at least we will be headed in the right direction."

"You are welcome to sleep aboard the Gloria Scott II tonight if you wish," Captain Scofield said, "As for me, I intend to wet me whistle a bit and sleep in a real bed tonight."

"Here," said I as I handed the captain a fistful of paper money and silver coins I had collected from the poker table, "please allow us to buy your first drink and dinner tonight at the Bucksnort and let me know if this does not cover our passage to Kodiak Island."

"I'm sure this will do fine," the captain said without looking at how much money I had given him. "It will be a pleasure having you gentlemen aboard the Gloria Scott II once again. We set sail first thing in the morning. Oh, I almost forgot, I hope you're hungry because Melville is serving squid stew again for dinner this evening."

Chapter 11

September 5th, 1896 5:30pm

221 B Baker Street, London, England

DURING OUR RETURN TRIP home I made modest even numbered withdraws from international banks in Tokyo, Hong Kong, Rome and lastly in Paris, alerting the authorities in London where we were at the time and advising them our mission had been successful. I had not been to the British colony of Hong Kong before, neither had Sherlock Holmes, who expressed some interest in learning more about the Second Opium War; I kept a close eye on my friend in knowing he was struggling with his own personal opium war. We stayed over another three days in Paris.

The layover in France was intended to allow us to rest up from our international travels; however, I knew the primary reason was to afford Sherlock Holmes an opportunity to visit Gustave Eiffel. Neither of us had seen Eiffel's Tower before, which now stands as the tallest structure ever constructed with human hands, surpassing even the ancient pyramids of Egypt.

The Eiffel Tower was built to serve as a grand entrance for the 1889 World's Fair. Listed among its famous visitors were the Prince of Wales, "Buffalo Bill" Cody and Thomas Edison who had presented Gustave Eiffel with one of his new inventions, a phonograph, which became another of the highlights of the exposition. Gustave Eiffel and his daughter kept an apartment at the top of the tower where he conducted scientific experiments, including studies on the weather and the effects on falling objects from altitude. Sherlock Holmes had telegraphed Gustave Eiffel requesting an opportunity to conduct an experiment of his own, to determine the effects elevation might have on human blood falling from great heights.

I stood on the ground beneath the Eiffel Tower as Sherlock Holmes dripped droplets of blood from the top of the tower onto a large piece of white cardboard. I did not have to ask Sherlock Holmes where he had obtained the human blood for his experiment—the fresh bandage on my friend's hand answered that question—reminding me of the first day when we met, in a hospital chemical laboratory where he was conducting an experiment on haemoglobin, using human blood, his own. It was fascinating to listen to Sherlock Holmes and Gustave Eiffel reach the same conclusion that once a drop of blood had attained its terminal velocity in flight, it would maintain that constant speed until impacting upon an intervening surface.

Sherlock Holmes and I also visited the Louvre Museum, where, in a rare display of affection my friend commented on how the smile on Leonardo da Vinci's Mona Lisa reminded him of a certain opera singer who once starred in La Boheme. I knew he missed being with Irene Adler; however complicated their relationship was in her being married and opposed to divorce. I secured our travel aboard the South Eastern Railway's Boulogne-sur-Mer-Folkestone route to the Calais-Dover crossing over the Channel back to England and sent a telegram to Mrs. Hudson letting her know to expect us home on the evening of September 5th.

"Oh, Mrs. Hudson, we're home!" Sherlock Holmes sang out

as we entered the front door of 221 B Baker Street. "What's for supper?"

"Whatever made you think I would be fixing your supper?" Mrs. Hudson said after she rushed to the front door to welcome us home with a warm embrace and kiss on the cheek.

"Something smells passably good," Sherlock Holmes said as he bound up our stairs and opened the door to our flat. Mrs. Hudson followed my friend upstairs, picking up his deerstalker hat and Inverness cape he had deposited along the way. I trailed behind the two of them listening fondly to their customary bantering back and forth. In the past nine months we had travelled completely around the globe and yet when I stepped into our warm sitting room it felt as if we had never left. Mrs. Hudson had built a fire in the fireplace and had set our dining table for two.

"We are going to need a third place setting," Sherlock Holmes said to Mrs. Hudson, adding, "Unless, of course, you have already eaten."

"I have not eaten," Mrs. Hudson replied with a surprised smile, "and I would very much enjoy dining with Dr. Watson and you, Mr. Holmes, this evening."

I noticed the teacups and saucers she had set out on the table were new. I turned one of the teacups upside down to read the label, "Tiffany and Company, New York, New York" printed elegantly in gold lettering across the bottom.

"Thank you," Mrs. Hudson whispered to me.

"I had nothing to do with this, it was all him," I said softly, pointing to Sherlock Holmes who was sorting through a large stack of mail Mrs. Hudson had piled upon his desk in front of the fireplace.

Mrs. Hudson smiled at Sherlock Holmes who had turned away pretending not to notice.

"Something does smell delicious," said I, "what is it you have prepared for supper?"

"A new recipe I have wanted to try, for Beef Wellington with brown mushroom gravy, served with creamed corn, roasted potatoes and baby carrots served in a nice Devonshire butter sauce. For dessert I made sticky-toffee pudding."

"Sounds delightful," said I, rubbing my hands together in front of the fire. "It does feel wonderful to be home."

"Here is your mail," Mrs. Hudson said, handing me a half dozen envelopes and a small package. "Your steamer trunks arrived a few weeks back from the States. I had them taken to the basement until you are ready to unpack. Now if you give me twenty minutes I will be back with our suppers and when I return I wish to hear all about your trip to the Colonies."

"Not much exciting to report," Sherlock Holmes said, thumbing through his large stack of mail and setting aside a handful of correspondence to read first; including letters from Mark Twain, Thomas Edison, Police Commissioner Theodore Roosevelt, Edmond Locard, General William Palmer, Kid Blacky and Agent A.J. Pinkerton.

I stood in front of the warm glow of our fireplace and flipped casually through my few pieces of mail. I noticed Sherlock Holmes was using the pocket knife he had won in the One-Eyed-Willie poker game aboard the Gloria Scott II as a letter opener.

"May I borrow your knife?" I asked.

"The one blade is broken, but it still has one good blade," Sherlock Holmes said, "I can't see throwing it away."

I used the knife as a letter opener and opened my mail to find a note from Nikola Tesla, thanking me for letting him know Colorado Springs might serve his needs for high-altitude electrical experiments. The small package contained an autographed copy of *The Jungle Book*, from Rudyard Kipling. There was a personal invitation from Captain Edward Smith, inviting us on a two-week "invitation only" cruise to Australia, culminating with a layover in Sydney to celebrate the New Year 1897. And then there was a small envelope containing a notecard from Dr. William Bell, postmarked New York City, New York. I used the jack knife to open Dr. Bell's envelope and handed the knife back to Sherlock Holmes. I read in Dr. Bell's note where he and Cara were planning to be in London over the Christmas holidays and was hoping to meet to discuss his business proposition of my acquiring his medical practice in Little London.

"Tomorrow I shall be in want of your able assistance," Sherlock Holmes said. "We have a few loose ends of our own to tidy up on this case and from first glance at this correspondence we have a handful of cases waiting for us in the wings. There is an intriguing letter here from a woman, from Lambeth, who has a mysterious lodger who constantly wears a veil; however, I don't believe this adventure is likely to be a pressing criminal matter and suspect we can hold off a bit longer. In the morning I intend to drop by to see Robert Coyne's widow and perhaps you might contact your former patient, Mr. Victor Hatherley, the hydraulic engineer, to inform him the man who severed his thumb with a meat clever has since passed on."

"Certainly, I will happy to deliver that message," said I, recalling the ghastly wound Mr. Hatherley had suffered when Colonel Stark tried to kill him, all the while imagining what it might be like to have a normal life and a regular medical practice back in the states.

"Good. Then I will send word to the boys at Scotland Yard that we will need to interview Thomas Leadbedder, who I presume is still in protective custody. At some point I suspect we will be forced to make a full report to officials at the Royal Mint and the Prime Minister's office, hopefully this can be done at the same time. I do despise the administrative side of these lengthy investigations. If you have time tomorrow afternoon I would very much like you to accompany me to visit Elise, whom I believe to be the younger sister of our departed Colonel Stark. That is unless you have other pressing matters of your own requiring your attention."

"Nothing that cannot wait," said I as I laid Dr. Bell's letter on top of the burning logs in the fireplace and watched as the yellow flames caught the paper on fire and all thoughts of my leaving my friend's side went up the chimney in smoke.

September 6th, 1896 3:30pm
Cannon Lane, London, England

SHERLOCK HOLMES WALKED to where I stood on Cannon Lane, across the street from Robert Coyne's former girlfriend's apartment, and announced, "The landlady said her young tenant was dressed as if she was going to the market and believes she would be home within the hour."

"How is Robert Coyne's widow getting along without him?" asked I.

"Sophia seems to have recovered sufficiently from her time in mourning; another man has already moved in with her, presumably the father of the tow-headed boy Shady mentioned. I handed her a modest bundle of British currency and told her it was from an insurance policy Robert had taken out during his employment with the Royal Mint. She told me she needed to buy herself a new hat. It was money I would have paid Shady Coyne for his assistance back in the States."

"He did save our lives," said I, recalling the horror of being trapped underground beneath the Tincup Mine. "Did you tell her of her brother-in-law's incarceration back in the States?"

"No, she already holds a low enough opinion of him, no need to add fuel to the fire. How did Mr. Hatherley react to hearing the news his would be assassin was now dead?"

"He was very much relieved," said I. "Said he could stop looking over his shoulder whenever he went out on a job in the countryside."

Sherlock Holmes pointed across the street toward a young woman carrying a grocery sack with a loaf of French bread sticking out the top. "That might be her now, let us go break the news."

We crossed the street and arrived just as the young woman had opened her front door with a key. She was balancing a grocery bag in one arm and cradling her purse in the other.

"Elise?" Sherlock Holmes said.

"Yes?" she replied instinctively, and then turned to see two strangers standing behind her.

"I am afraid we are the bearers of bad news," Sherlock Holmes said as he respectfully removed his hat.

"What is it?"

"Fritz won't be coming home," Sherlock Holmes said.

"He's dead isn't he?" Elise said as her eyes began to well up with tears.

"Yes," Sherlock Holmes said as Elise dropped her bag of groceries and backed unsteadily into her flat.

"May we come in?" Sherlock Holmes said as he picked up her bag of groceries.

"Yes," she said as she sat down heavily upon her sofa.

Sherlock Holmes handed me the bag of groceries, nodded toward the kitchen table and sat down on the floral print sofa next to her, "Was Fritz your older brother?"

"He was," she said, as she started to cry. Sherlock Holmes tried to comfort her as I sat the bag of groceries on the table and then took a seat in a well-worn armchair across from the sofa. She pulled a white handkerchief from her purse and tried to stem the flow of tears streaming down her pretty face. "I felt this was coming. He was supposed to be home last month and when I got no word whatsoever from him I knew something horrible had happened."

"Do you know where he was or who he was with?" Sherlock Holmes asked.

"Why? Are you with Scotland Yard?" she said as she stopped crying and looked us both over suspiciously. Her heavy German accent was unmistakable.

"No, my name is Sherlock Holmes; this is my friend Dr. Watson. I have the distinction of being one of the men your brother tried to kill and lived to tell about it; other men were not as fortunate as I. You tried to help one of those men that your brother tried to murder, a young hydraulic engineer, which is the only reason we are not here this afternoon with detectives from Scotland Yard. You need to understand that how truthful you are with me at this very moment will determine my actions when we leave here this afternoon. Do you understand?"

"Yes," she said as she wiped the tears from her eyes.

"If you lie to me, I will know. Do you understand?"

"Yes," she said as she wiped her eyes again.

"First, tell us your brother's full name and where you are from," Sherlock Holmes said as he motioned for me to start taking notes. I removed my fountain pen and brown leather notebook from the inside pocket of my suit coat and began jotting down what was said.

"His name is Fritz Hume Goring; we are from Heidelberg, Germany."

"Who was he working for?"

"An English geology professor; he said his name was Dr. Hiram Bakerslee, but I knew that wasn't his real name. He insisted

Fritz use an alias as well."

"What alias did Fritz use?"

"He called himself Colonel Lysander Stark, but Fritz was never in the military. He studied military history for a year at the University of Heidelberg, that's where he got involved with Dr. Bakerslee, who was teaching geology at the University."

"Describe this Dr. Bakerslee," Sherlock Holmes asked.

"He was a short, heavyset English man, about ten years older than Fritz, who is or was ten years older than me," Elise said, with a show of sorrow in referring to her departed brother for the first time in the past-tense.

"What did you know of their criminal organization?"

"Nothing at first," she said earnestly. "Fritz tried to hide all that from me, said he was offered a good job in Great Britain, working for Dr. Bakerslee and another college professor, doing metallurgy of some sort, is what he told me at first. Then Dr. Bakerslee started asking me to buy groceries and such for us in town, we were renting a big estate outside of Reading at the time. Bakerslee would give me British silver coins of larger denominations and always ask for the change back. I hadn't been in England very long and didn't know what British coins looked or felt like. Then one time, while I was in town buying mutton for our supper, the butcher looked at the coin Dr. Bakerslee had given me and said it was no good, he said it was a fake. I told Fritz what had happened and Dr. Bakerslee got very angry, said he'd have to tell the other professor. Wasn't long until we moved again."

"Do you know who this other professor was?" Sherlock Holmes asked.

"No, neither Fritz nor Dr. Bakerslee ever mentioned his name, I'm not sure if Fritz ever met him, but Dr. Bakerslee seemed rather afraid of him, this other professor was who sent them to the United States. Fritz said I would be better off staying here in London. He sent me money a few times, the envelopes were postmarked from somewhere in Colorado, Cripple Stream or some such, but the money Fritz sent me ran out days ago. I'm down to my last few halfpennies. Don't know how I will ever pay for my rent. I have no family here in England."

"Do you have family back in Germany?" Sherlock Holmes asked.

"Yes," Elise said, contemplating her future, "My father has passed on and my mother is quite elderly, she lives with my younger brother Wilhelm Goring, in Heidelberg. I suppose I could stay with them until I can find me a job and gets back on my feet.

"Elise, here is what's going to happen, listen carefully," Sherlock Holmes said as he stood up and started toward the front door. "My friend here is going to give you sufficient money to get back to Heidelberg and we will pay your landlady the rent money you owe. The day after tomorrow we will be meeting with Scotland Yard about your brother and Dr. Bakerslee; you have a 24-hour head start to leave London and return to Germany."

"Those are better terms then I would have expected under the circumstances. Why are you doing this?" Elise asked as she stopped crying.

"Because there is a young man in London, a hydraulic engineer with but one thumb, who may not be alive today had you not intervened to save his life. Your single act of human kindness has bought you 24-hours to leave Great Britain and never return."

"What if Dr. Bakerslee returns before I can leave London?"

"He won't be returning," said I as I handed her an envelope containing enough money to pay for her passage back to Germany and followed my friend Sherlock Holmes out the door.

September 8th, 1896 11:45am
10 Downing Street, London, England

As we departed the Prime Minister's residence, Sherlock Holmes stood next to me at the curb in front of 10 Downing Street and said, "That went as well as I could have expected."

"That went better than I had expected," said I as Sherlock Holmes hailed a hansom.

"It certainly helped that Prime Minister Salisbury arranged to have a senior representative from the Royal Mint present during our meeting and Inspector Grayson and Lestrade kept their questions to only three each," said Sherlock Holmes as the carriage got underway.

"I was relieved no one asked for a specific financial accounting on what we had spent on this investigation," said I, fearing that without my first pocket notebook I would not be able to provide sufficient details and we might be asked to reimburse the British government for what we had spent in the last nine months during our extensive travels abroad.

"I suppose their financial worries were relieved somewhat when young A.J. Pinkerton arrived unannounced at the PM's front door with an unexpected treasure chest full of 1893 Queen Victoria-Jubilee Head Two Pound Gold Double Sovereign coins. Here," Sherlock Holmes said as he handed me one of the gold coins wrapped in a small coin envelope, "you may keep this one the Prime Minister presented to me as a souvenir of our little adventure together."

"Thank you, I will give the other gold coin you gave me while we were on the train in Arizona to Mrs. Hudson as a Christmas gift from the two of us." I slipped the gold sovereign into my vest pocket which once held my silver pocket watch. "I must remember to buy myself a new pocket watch," said I as I wondered how inmate Stanley Coyne was getting along in prison back in Colorado. "The mint officials were certainly delighted when you handed them the genuine coin die you had recovered aboard the Gloria Scott II headed into the Yukon. Were you at all surprised Lestrade and Grayson did not ask more questions than they did during our meeting with the PM?"

"No, I suspect they were simply following orders given them by their supervisors at The Yard in preparation of their attending our briefing with Lord Salisbury. Besides," Sherlock Holmes said as he glanced out the carriage window to see where we were on the streets of London before continuing on with his thoughts, "Scotland Yard's official counterfeiting investigation was simplified considerably when Thomas Leadbedder's legal counsel arranged for him to plead guilty to the lesser charge of theft in exchange for his full cooperation. Leadbedder did not know who Bakerslee worked for but his confession helped the authorities confirm there were not more conspirators within the Royal Mint or at the Whitechapel Bell Foundry. With Colonel Stark, Dr. Bakerslee and Robert Coyne being dead now, and Elise Goring leaving the country, there simply is no one left to prosecute."

"A prosecution they did not want to see made public anyway," said I in remembering our solemn obligation not to disclose anything publically about this investigation until at least a year after the death of our beloved Queen Victoria."

"Precisely," Sherlock Holmes said.

"Where are we going for afternoon tea?"

"The Café Royal," Sherlock Holmes said as our carriage came to a graceful stop in front of one of London's most opulent hotels, located at 68 Regent Street in Piccadilly. "I made reservations for six; you, me and four very special guests."

September 8th, 1896 2pm
The Café Royal, London, England

"FOUR SPECIAL GUESTS?" asked I as we entered London's luxurious The Café Royal. The Café Royal had been in existence since 1865 and had become *the place* for afternoon tea in London. The restaurant had been made famous in March of last year from a well-publicized meeting where Frank Harris tried to persuade Oscar Wilde to drop his charge of criminal libel against the Marquess of Queensberry. Sherlock Holmes had followed closely the Marquess of Queensberry's endorsement of the code of conduct governing the sport of boxing, which have since become known as the as Queensbury Rules. The Marquess of Queensberry was eventually acquitted of all criminal charges and Oscar Wilde himself was tried, convicted and imprisoned. Our reservations for afternoon tea were in what has become known as the Oscar Wilde Room.

"Welcome Mr. Holmes, your guests arrived a few minutes ago," said the maître d' as he led us through the café to a burgundy padded velvet booth where a beautiful well-dressed woman in her mid-thirties, wearing a pink hat, and three lovely young girls wearing new dresses, waited patiently with their white-gloved hands folded in their laps.

"Ms. Sellers?" Sherlock Holmes asked as he shook the hand of the lady in the pink hat. "I am Sherlock Holmes, so good of you to join us for afternoon tea."

"So nice to meet you, Mr. Holmes and to receive your invitation for tea," she said adding, "My sister had given me your name in the event I was ever in need of your assistance."

"May I introduce my friend, Dr. John Watson?" Sherlock Holmes said as I shook hands with the lady in the pink hat.

"Nice to meet you, Dr. Watson," she said. "May I introduce my three daughters; Isabella, Iris and Irene."

The three young girls stood up and curtsied politely and then returned to their seats.

"Very pleased to meet you," Sherlock Holmes said. "May we join you, Ms. Sellers?"

"Yes, please," said the lady, "but do call me Andrea."

"Very well, Andrea, your sister asked me to tell you she is well and to give you this," Sherlock Holmes said as he handed her a printed program for an opera.

"La Boheme," said Andrea, as she read the cover, "Featured every Saturday night in May at the Butte Opera House in Cripple Creek, Colorado."

"Is that where Aunt Irene is singing," asked one of the girls.

"That is where she had been scheduled to perform last May," explained Sherlock Holmes, "unfortunately; circumstances beyond her control caused the opera in the U.S. to be cancelled."

"Where is my sister now?" asked Andrea.

"She is in Europe," Sherlock Holmes replied.

"What was La Boheme about?" asked the older girl of her mother.

"I was there for opening night, in Turin, Italy. Your Aunt Irene played Mimi, a poor seamstress, who asks a young man, named Rodolfo, to light her candle, and then they fall in love."

"I wish we could have seen it," replied Andrea's middle daughter.

"It would not have been appropriate for girls as young as you," their mother said, adding, "Mimi dies of tuberculous in the end."

"How sad," said Andrea's youngest daughter.

"Your sister said she will be starring under a stage name in a new opera, La poupee, which opens at the Theatre de la Gaite, in Paris, next month," Sherlock Holmes said.

"What is that opera about, mama?" asked the youngest girl.

"I read it is about a friar who falsely promises to marry his rich uncle's daughter, to trick his uncle into giving money to the monastery. The friar never intended to marry his uncle's daughter, because he would have to leave the monastery, but the girl makes a doll that looks like her and tricks the friar into marrying her in the end. La poupee would be a much more appropriate opera for you three to see," said the girls' mother.

"Can we go mama, please?" the oldest daughter pleaded.

"We would love to see Aunt Irene again," the middle daughter said.

"Please, you know how much I love dolls," the youngest daughter added.

"Your sister wants you to have these," Sherlock Holmes said as he handed Andrea an envelope containing four box seat tickets for the opening night in Paris, on October 21, 1896. "Your tickets come with an invitation to join her backstage. She also sent Dr. Watson and I two tickets for the opening night and asked that if you decide to go the two of us are to serve as your escorts."

"How exiting!" the girls replied, and then began pleading again with their mother, "Can we go, mama? Please?"

"Your sister is performing under a stage name of Emily Smoot and thought it best if your visit to Paris were kept strictly confidential," Sherlock Holmes said.

"Well, if Mr. Holmes and Dr. Watson are willing to serve as our escorts, I suppose we can go, but you three must promise to keep our seeing your Aunt Irene a family secret, otherwise we won't be able to go. Do you promise?"

"Yes, mama," each of the girls replied, "we won't tell anyone."

"Thank you, Mr. Holmes, Dr. Watson," Andrea said. "It will be wonderful to see my sister again and for her to see how much her three nieces have grown. Now, shall we enjoy our afternoon tea?"

Our afternoon tea consisted of an 1865 signature English breakfast tea, traditional scones with Devonshire butter, smoked salmon, roast Aberdeen Angus beef with horseradish dressing and crunchy watercress sandwiches, with an air-mousse-like lemon verbena, marbled white chocolate slate and strawberry eclairs which were the favorite dessert of Irene Adler's three nieces and of me. What I sensed Sherlock Holmes enjoyed most of all during our afternoon tea was simply getting to know Irene Adler better by being with her sister and three nieces. I will long remember afternoon tea at The Café Royal with Irene's beautiful sister and three lovely nieces for being one of the rare occasions where my extraordinary friend, Sherlock Holmes, seemed well, almost, ordinary.

Chapter 12

November 12th, 1896 8pm

Buckingham Palace, Westminster, England

"I BELIEVE WE ARE BEING DRIVEN around to the back entrance," said I to my friend Sherlock Holmes sitting beside me in the older horse-drawn carriage.

"As I would have expected, we will attract far less attention this way," said Sherlock Holmes.

"But I would have thought someone who is about to receive their knighthood from the Queen would at least be escorted through the front door. And I don't mean to complain, but I was expecting that a somewhat nicer hansom would have been sent to fetch us, wouldn't you?"

"On the contrary, my good Doctor, this is the exact carriage I was expecting to pick us up in front of our flat on Baker Street," Sherlock Holmes said as the driver stepped down from his seat and opened the hansom door. As my friend stepped out of the black carriage, he asked the driver wearing a long black cape, "Excuse me my good man; do you happen to have the time?"

"Sir," the driver replied, coming naturally to attention as he withdrew his pocket watch from his vest pocket. He held his timepiece up to the dim light cast by the carriage lantern and said, "I read the time to be precisely 8 o'clock."

"Thank you, Sergeant," Sherlock Holmes replied as he tipped his top hat respectfully, adding, "We have an important meeting and wouldn't want to be tardy."

"No sir, that simply wouldn't do," the driver said as he slipped his pocket watch back in his vest pocket, slid the small tin door on the carriage lantern shut and turned his attention to adjusting the well-worn carriage harnesses.

I glanced at the silver ring on the driver's finger and recognized the crest for the 1st Battalion of the Coldstream Guards. I smiled as I realized this was indeed the Queen's carriage. I walked with Sherlock Holmes up the long walkway to the rear entrance of the three-story palace which had been built for the first Duke of Buckingham and Normandy in 1703. Once known as the "Queen's House" Buckingham Palace has become the principal royal residence of Queen Victoria since her accession to the throne in 1837. Buckingham Palace is also where Queen Victoria chose to conduct many of her official investitures, including the knighthood of my friend Sherlock Holmes this evening.

"Welcome to Buckingham Palace, Mr. Holmes and Dr. Watson," said a young officer wearing the military dress uniform of the Fourth Queen's Own Hussars. He held open the door to the palace and introduced himself as he showed us inside. "I am Second Lieutenant Winston Churchill, recently returned from Bombay, British India. I joined the military just last year; however, my commanding officer knew how much I enjoy literature, including your writings, Dr. Watson, and reading of your investigations, Mr. Holmes. I was honored to have been granted the distinct privilege of welcoming you here to Buckingham Palace this evening on the occasion of your knighthood, Mr. Holmes."

"Thank you, Lieutenant Churchill," said Sherlock Holmes as we followed the young officer into the enormous palace.

"You may hang your topcoats and hats in the cloakroom here," said Lt. Churchill.

"Thank you," said Sherlock Holmes. After hanging up our coats the young officer led us down the grand hallway deeper into the interior of Buckingham Palace. "I believe you were born at Blenheim Palace in Oxfordshire, your family's ancestral home, were you not, Lieutenant?"

"I was," said Lt. Churchill proudly. "Construction on Blenheim Palace began two years after Buckingham Palace, which, as you may know, has been added onto several times since. Today it holds 775 rooms, including 188 staff bedrooms, 78 bathrooms, 92 offices, a post office, jeweler's workshop, cinema, swimming pool and the largest private garden in all of London. My paternal grandfather, John Spencer-Churchill, was the 7th Duke of Marlborough, and my mother, Jennie Churchill, was from an American family. I understand you gentlemen recently returned yourselves from America?"

"We have," said I. "I found America to be an astonishing immense and unexpectantly grand country; but above all I was most fascinated with the diversity of the American people."

"I have always said what an extraordinary people the Americans are," said Lt. Churchill as we turned off the grand hallway into a large anteroom. "This is the Green Drawing Room; it serves as an anteroom to the Throne Room. You will wait here, Mr. Holmes. Colonel Nelson of the Coldstream Guards will come to fetch you when the Queen is ready. There is a washroom beyond those doors over there, if you need to freshen up a bit. Now, Dr. Watson, if you will please follow me I will escort you to your seat.

We left Sherlock Holmes alone in the Green Drawing Room and I followed Lt. Churchill into the Throne Room. A lone master bagpiper marched in front of us playing *The Wearing of the Green*. Queen Victoria sat upright on her throne, which had been draped in gold. She was wearing a beautiful scarlet colored robe, trimmed with white fur, and atop her head she wore her Imperial State Crown, a Maltese cross adorned the top. She was as small in size as I remembered from our first visit in the Tower of London nearly a year ago, yet she still held the commanding presence of a Monarch who served as Queen to nearly a quarter of the world's population.

As Lt. Churchill and I stopped before the Queen she smiled and offered me her hand. I bowed and kissed the back of her hand; which had become the custom when greeting Queen Victoria as opposed to kissing her on the check. Queen Victoria was only 18-years-old when she inherited the throne and many people felt it was not proper for so many older men to kiss the cheek of such a young single woman. The tradition of kissing the back of her hand remains the custom, although she was now in her late seventies. I waited for Her Majesty to speak first.

"It is nice to see you again Dr. Watson," Queen Victoria said.

"Thank you my Queen," said I. "I was honored to receive your invitation to be here this evening to witness the knighthood of my friend Sherlock Holmes."

"My Dear Doctor Watson, in recognition of your faithful service to the Crown, I have extended your medical pension until your natural death." The Queen nodded toward the Prime Minister who was seated off to my left, "Further, I have directed Lord Salisbury to properly compensate you and Mr. Holmes for your professional services this past year in eliminating what had been a significant threat to the British government and the world's economy."

"Thank you my Queen," said I, as I bowed again and was escorted to my chair seated to the right of Prime Minister Salisbury. I noticed the PM was also wearing a black tuxedo with a white-tie. Sherlock Holmes and I had been given the choice of wearing either a black-tie or white-tie, to this formal occasion; I chose white-tie, as Sherlock Holmes prefers black.

"It is nice to see you again," Prime Minister Salisbury said as he stood to greet me.

"And you Lord Salisbury," said I in shaking his hand. Once we were seated I leaned over and said quietly to the PM, "I am deeply appreciative of the Queen's kind gesture to change my monthly compensation to a lifetime pension. Thank you for overseeing to that administrative procedure, this adjustment will greatly relieve my financial concerns for the future."

"You are most welcome and deserving," said the Prime Minister. "To further compensate you and Mr. Holmes for this yearlong investigation I have made a suitable deposit into your and Mr. Holmes' joint bank account. We are deeply appreciative of the fact this major international counterfeiting organization has been brought down and the men responsible for the murder of our secret agent have been brought to justice. We also recognized this yearlong investigation has prohibited you and Mr. Holmes from seeking financial compensation elsewhere with your professional services. One might also consider this recent deposit into your account as somewhat of a finder's fee for the unexpected return of the chest full of 1893 Queen Victoria-Jubilee Head Two Pound Gold Double Sovereign coins. We never expected to see any of those gold coins ever again. I was quite surprised when young Agent Pinkerton appeared unannounced on my doorstep with this treasure chest full of gold coins. He told me they were being presented compliments of you and Mr. Holmes. Oh look, here he comes now, shall we stand?"

A lone master bagpiper began playing Scotland the Brave; bringing our small party to their feet; except of course for the Queen, who remained seated on her regal throne. I stood alongside Lord Salisbury and watched as my friend Sherlock Holmes was escorted down the long isle of the Throne Room by Colonel Nelson, being led now by four more bagpipers and a drummer who had joined in the formal march.

The bagpipers and drummer stopped playing when they stood before the Queen, then marched off to the side as Sherlock Holmes stopped and bowed his head before the Queen. Then he touched the crown with one hand and kissed the back of her hand with his other hand. She spoke softly to Sherlock Holmes, words meant only for him, then she stood and stepped forward as Colonel Nelson positioned the kneeling stool in front of my friend.

While Sherlock Holmes knelt, Mycroft Holmes, wearing a black tuxedo with a white tie, appeared carrying a royal blue velvet pillow. Upon the pillow glistened a military sword.

"That sword belonged to Colonel Nelson's grandfather, Vice-Admiral Horatio Nelson, 1st Duke of Bronte," Lord Salisbury explained. "As you know Admiral Lord Nelson led the fleet of twenty-seven British ships of the line when they defeated thirty-three Spanish ships off the southwest coast of Spain, west of Cape Trafalgar. The battle was a major victory for the British Royal Navy, sinking twenty-two enemy ships, while the British lost none. Unfortunately, Admiral Lord Nelson was killed during the naval battle, while aboard his flagship the HMS Victory, carrying that sword. Now the Queen will bestow the Code of Knightly Honor upon Mr. Holmes."

Colonel Nelson picked the shiny sword up from the pillow and handed it to Queen Victoria who said, "Sherlock Holmes, do you promise and swear to be fearless to the strong, humble to the weak and show chivalry toward all women, of high or low degree?"

"I do," Sherlock Holmes replied.

"I knight you Sir Sherlock Holmes," said the Queen as she

tapped him lightly on each shoulder with the broad edge of the sword. "Please rise and attend to your duties."

Sherlock Holmes rose and stood alongside Colonel Nelson who retrieved the sword from the Queen and placed it back on the pillow as the Queen retired from the Throne Room.

"There will be a small reception in the Guard Room, Dr. Watson." Lord Salisbury said. "Come, I will show you the way. I believe the Guard Room is one of the most beautiful rooms in Buckingham Palace. It contains the white marble statues of Queen Victoria and Prince Albert, the husband of Queen Victoria who passed away in 1861. It is unfortunate your friend will not be able to use the title Sir Sherlock Holmes publically until after the death of Queen Victoria."

"Knowing Sherlock Holmes as I do, I doubt he will ever use the distinguished title of Sir," said I to Lord Salisbury as I followed behind Sherlock and Mycroft Holmes, who were being escorted to the Guard Room by Colonel Nelson and Lieutenant Winston Churchill.

"Lt. Churchill seems like a bright young officer," said I to the Prime Minister.

"He is," said Lord Salisbury, "I would not be at all surprised if he were to receive a knighthood himself one day."

December 24th, 1896 6:30pm
221 B Baker Street, London, England

Sherlock Holmes and I had agreed to exchange gifts after dinner in our flat on Christmas Eve. Mrs. Hudson was staying over Christmas Eve to celebrate Christmas with her son and his family. Before she left she prepared us a lovely supper for our evening meal and baked a nice quiche Lorraine for our breakfast Christmas morning.

Our supper was a delicious yet modest affair. Mrs. Hudson had hung a cast iron kettle of hearty beef stew near the fire to keep warm through the afternoon and into the evening. She had also baked a loaf of fresh whole wheat bread, served with a pad of Devonshire butter and laid out an assortment of brightly decorated Christmas cookies, fudge and fruitcake for desert.

"Dr. Watson," Sherlock Holmes said, as we finished our supper, "Do you happen to know what time it is?"

Instinctively I reached for my vest pocket, where for years I had carried a pocket watch, to once again find my pocket empty. "I keep forgetting to buy myself another watch," said I, as I looked up to see Sherlock Holmes smiling as he handed me a small neatly wrapped present.

"Merry Christmas my dear Dr. Watson," he said warmly.

"Thank you, it is so beautifully wrapped I hesitate to open it."

"It won't do you much good if you don't."

I tore open the paper to find a small white box. When I lifted the lid I observed a beautiful silver pocket watch and chain. I picked up the watch and read the name "Tiffany & Company" printed elegantly on the watch face.

"Open it," he said.

I did as instructed and observed the inside of the watch cover was engraved with the initials "SH" and "JW" and the year 1896.

"I wanted you to always remember the memorable time we shared this past year."

"Thank you, this is most thoughtful of you," said I as I handed Sherlock Holmes a box wrapped in white paper with a royal blue ribbon.

He untied the bow, unwrapped the paper and then opened a sturdy box to find a commemorative engraved bottle of 24-year-old Macallan single-malt scotch whiskey.

"Perfect," he said. "Might you care to join me in front of the fire for a toast?"

"I would be delighted," said I as I moved to a comfortable padded armchair in front of the fireplace and watched as my friend opened the bottle, poured two glasses of scotch whiskey neat and then took a seat on the sofa near me.

"To 1896," said Sherlock Holmes as he handed me a glass and raised his, "and long live the Queen."

"To 1896 and long live the Queen," I repeated as I took a sip of the scotch. I stood and walked over to our fireplace and gently removed the loose brick exposing the small hidden compartment. I removed my brown leather notebook and the small coin envelope containing the 1893 Queen Victoria-Jubilee Head Two Pound Gold Double Sovereign from my suit coat pocket and sealed both items in a yellow envelope. I tucked the sealed envelope into the secret compartment and carefully replaced the brick. When I stepped back I examined the mortar around the brick and commented, "This masonry work is so well done a person would never know this secret compartment was ever here unless you knew where to look. It would be unfortunate if no one ever knows about our trip to Little London in 1896."

"I will know, and you will know," Sherlock Holmes said as he sipped his scotch, "perhaps that is all who need to know."

"Perhaps," said I as I sat on the sofa next to my extraordinary friend and watched the flames in the fireplace dance across the logs and savored my glass of scotch. "I will be forever grateful to James Mercier for introducing us to this elixir of the gods."

"To Mr. James Mercier of Abu Dhabi," said Sherlock Holmes, as he gave another toast, then added, "I wonder where Mr. Mercier and the RMS Republic are tonight?"

"I do not know where they are tonight; however, I do know where they will be the day after Christmas."

"Where might that be?"

"Docked at the White Star Line port in Liverpool," said I. "May I ask you something?"

"Certainly, anything," my friend replied.

"Now that you have solved the mystery of the lady with the veil in Lambeth, do you think you might spare two weeks for a second less stressful voyage aboard the RMS Republic?"

"I suppose so," Sherlock Holmes replied. "As you know my business becomes rather slow during the Christmas Holidays and doesn't pick up again until a few weeks into the New Year. Why? What do you propose?"

"I have one more Christmas present for you," said I as I removed an envelope from the other pocket of my suit coat and handed it to Sherlock Holmes. "Merry Christmas, Sir Holmes."

"Whatever have you done, my dear Doctor Watson?" Sherlock Holmes said as he opened the envelope and removed three round-trip first-class tickets to Sydney, Australia, aboard the luxury ocean liner the RMS Republic.

"Why three tickets?"

"As it turns out La Boheme is scheduled to open New Year's Eve at the Sydney Opera House and the talented soprano who performs the role of Mimi was in need of transportation; I invited Irene to join us. Captain Smith promised to reserve the Victoria Suite for us, along with a stateroom across the hall for our travel companion."

"Sometimes you surprise me, Dr. Watson."

"Sometimes I surprise myself," said I as I raised my glass in salute of my friend.

"I thank you; I think this may be the most wonderful gift anyone has ever given me," Sherlock Holmes said as he stood stoically and walked to the fireplace. I watched as he placed the three tickets beneath the Persian slipper on our fireplace mantel, beside the picture of Irene Adler, and carefully picked up his violin. "And I have one more Christmas present for you."

I took another sip of my scotch and watched as Sherlock Holmes placed another log on the crackling fire and then tucked his violin beneath his chin and drew the bow gently across the strings of his Stradivarius.

"I had requested this piece be played on the bagpipes at Buckingham Palace on the evening of my knighthood," he said. "I knew it to be among your favorites when played on the bagpipes. I have been teaching myself to play it on the violin whenever you were out."

Savoring the scotch, and the moment, I closed my eyes to listen to Sherlock Holmes play *The Wearing of the Green*. I went to bed at midnight and dreamt that when I opened my eyes on Christmas morning we were back at Glen Eyrie and a gentle snow was falling over Little London.

Acknowledgments

I would like to express my sincere appreciation to my family; especially to my wife Brenda and daughter Laynie, for their understanding and support of me in becoming a full-time author. I want to thank my writing coach, Toni Robino, at Windward Literary Services, for seeing something in my writing and helping me advance in this profession. I want to thank my wonderful proofreaders, Dave and Ruth Spencer, Fred Leich, Karen Rhodes, Deb Bartos, Dwight Haverkorn, and my dedicated proofreader, Ginger Hipszky, who helped several of my books to take shape. I also want to acknowledge Susan Fletcher, Director of History and Achieves, History Department, Navigators; Michelle Rozell and the talented staff at the Cripple Creek Heritage Center and Linda Wommack, author of *Cripple Creek, Bob Womack, and The Greatest Gold Camp on Earth* for their dedication for the preservation of the rich history of the Pikes Peak Region. Lastly, I want to extend a most sincere thank-you to Susie Schorsch and Don Kallaus of Rhyolite Press LLC, for their continued support of me as an author.

Thank you,
John

About the Author

Growing up on a small ranch in Colorado, John Wesley Anderson spent endless hours riding horses, collecting coins and reading. One of the first books he remembers reading cover to cover was *The Adventure of Silver Blaze* by Sir Arthur Conan Doyle. After graduating high school in 1972, John joined the Colorado Springs Police Department where he enjoyed a 22-year career. John served six years as a homicide detective and taught criminal investigation courses at the Colorado Springs Police Academy and across Colorado. To teach investigative fundamentals John used quotes from the Canon of Sherlock Holmes, written by Sir Author Conan Doyle.

In 1991 John presented a paper at the 38th Annual Meeting of the Canadian Society of Forensic Science which was held jointly with International Association of Bloodstain Analysts and the Society of Forensic Toxicologists, in Montreal, Canada. His paper, *Sherlockian Theories, Lessons from the Greatest Detective who Never Lived"* was published by the Canadian Society of Forensic Science (June 1992) and reprinted by the internationally acclaimed Sir Arthur Conan Doyle Society of London, England.

In 1995 John was elected to serve as the 26th Sheriff of El Paso County, Colorado. After being term-limited in 2003 he retired from a 30-year law enforcement career and went to work for the Lockheed Martin Corporation, where he focused on homeland security, defense and corporate security. In 2012 John retired from the corporate world to launch a small private consulting business allowing him the freedom to pursue his love of writing, history and the arts. Within two months of John becoming a fulltime author, a judge ruled the first 40 short stories and all four novels in the canon of Sherlock Holmes are now in the public domain.

www.ingramcontent.com/pod-product-compliance
Lightning Source LLC
Chambersburg PA
CBHW010451310726
48979CB00013B/2156/J

* 9 7 8 1 9 4 3 8 2 9 1 7 0 *